STAND BY ME

Sheila O'Flanagan

STAND BY ME

headline
review

First published in 2010
by HEADLINE REVIEW
An imprint of HEADLINE PUBLISHING GROUP

1

Cataloguing in Publication Data is
available from the British Library

ISBN 978 0 7553 4382 9 (Hardback)
ISBN 978 0 7553 4383 6 (Trade paperback)

Typeset in Galliard by Palimpsest Book Production Limited,
Falkirk, Stirlingshire

Printed and bound in Great Britain by
Clays Ltd, St Ives plc

Headline's policy is to use papers that are natural, renewable and
recyclable products and made from wood grown in sustainable
forests. The logging and manufacturing processes are expected
to conform to the environmental regulations of the country of origin.

HEADLINE PUBLISHING GROUP
An Hachette UK Company
338 Euston Road
London NW1 3BH

www.headline.co.uk
www.hachette.co.uk

Acknowledgements

With each book I'm delighted to thank the team that has stood by me so solidly over the years. I am incredibly lucky in having such great support from so many people:

My agent, Carole Blake
My editor, Marion Donaldson
The Headline teams around the world
My overseas publishers and translators

Thanks to my family who've always believed in me
To my friends who are loyal and wonderful
And to Colm who's always there

I'd also like to thank the many, many booksellers who have championed my books and recommended them to readers everywhere. It's always wonderful to meet you on the signing tours even if it means I dismantle your lovely displays!

Most important of all, a massive thank you to my readers, for buying my books, for getting in touch with me and for keeping me inspired. I really appreciate your comments and emails. You can reach me through my website www.sheilaoflanagan.com or my Facebook page. And you can follow me on Twitter too!

Prologue

Dominique was trying to decide the best way to position a dozen coloured Chinese lanterns around the small patio garden when she heard the doorbell ring. Her eyes widened as she glanced at her watch and she hurried through the house, wiping her hands on her black jeans as she walked along the narrow hallway.

'Hi.' A petite redhead with a dark green baseball cap sitting unsteadily on her unruly curls looked at her with a hint of curiosity, and then smiled. 'Mizz Delahaye? I'm Lizzie Horgan. I'm from the caterers.'

'Bang on time,' said Dominique. 'I didn't realise how late it was getting. Everything's through here.' She led the way back along the hallway into the small, square kitchen that she'd tidied that morning. Open French doors led to the enclosed patio where she'd been hanging the lanterns.

'I'm sorry,' she said as Lizzie looked around with unbridled interest. 'It's a bit on the poky side.'

'Don't worry. There's not that much stuff. We've catered for much bigger events than . . .' Lizzie broke off, aware that she could be insulting Dominique by (a) insinuating that her party was too small to worry about; or (b) implying that the client herself was someone who didn't know all about big events. There was a (c) too, of course, and that was that her boss had given her very strict instructions about how she was to treat Dominique Delahaye, and that with her careless remark, she wasn't sticking to Ash's instructions at all.

Those instructions, delivered firmly, were that she was to be as professional as possible. To be ultra-polite. To make the delivery and leave.

She was not, Ash had warned, to engage the woman in casual conversation or make any comments at all that could be construed as interfering or critical or personal in any way whatsoever.

'We're not rubberneckers,' Ash had reminded Lizzie. 'We don't pry into our customers' private lives. No matter what our own opinions on them might be,' she added.

'I'll be discretion itself,' Lizzie assured her. 'But she's having a party, for heaven's sake! She must have something to celebrate. I haven't seen anything on the news, have you? Either about him or about her. I read that she'd gone abroad. That she'd met him somewhere. But that's obviously all wrong. So why d'you think she's doing this? Are they right about her having money? Is she back on the social scene again? Or is it a farewell party because she's leaving the country now?' Lizzie was almost breathless with excitement.

'It's none of our business,' Ash replied. 'It's a private party; she made that perfectly clear. Crystal clear, in fact, so no trying to worm info out of her. We don't know what her situation is now. If she's getting back into the whole party scene, there could be lots of work for us in the future, but not if we upset her over this. So it's simply a question of us doing a good job with the minimum of fuss.'

Lizzie assured Ash that she'd be the soul of discretion, although she couldn't help thinking that her cool, calm and efficient employer would be much better at that. But Ash was working another function that day and couldn't spare the time for what was just a simple delivery job, no matter how famous (or infamous) the client might be.

So Lizzie said nothing further to Dominique Delahaye as she continued to transfer the food from the van to the kitchen as quickly and as unobtrusively as possible. But she couldn't help glancing at the woman from time to time and wondering if any or all of the reports about her were true. Ash frequently said that newspapers and magazines only ever gave one side of a story; the side that they thought was the most interesting, or fitted with their own philosophy.

In the past, stories about Dominique Delahaye were always about her glittering life, her social standing and her charity work. That had all changed abruptly, and the pieces over the last few months had been completely different. But it was a long time now since Lizzie had read anything about their new client in the paper. It was funny, though, she mused, as she plugged in the small wine chiller that the catering company supplied, how *normal* Dominique Delahaye seemed to be. There was, of course, no real reason why the woman shouldn't be normal. But when everything you knew about her was thanks to the news reports in the papers and on the TV, you tended to forget that there was a real person underneath. Lizzie couldn't help wondering what the real Dominique was like. Normal or not, she doubted she'd ever really know.

Dominique hadn't missed the curiosity in Lizzie's eyes. She left the younger girl to finish unloading the van and went upstairs, shutting the bedroom door behind her before sitting down on the edge of the double bed. She released her breath slowly and evenly and then pinched the bridge of her nose with the tips of her finger and thumb. She'd been really looking forward to today, looking forward to doing something fun and frivolous for someone she cared about, looking forward to having some good friends, old and new, to the house; but she was feeling suddenly anxious, and her anxiety had been ratcheted up by the cheerful caterer's obvious attempt at nonchalance.

Would there ever be a time, she asked herself, when people stopped looking at her the way Lizzie Horgan had looked at her? With a mixture of sympathy and disdain and unbridled curiosity? Would there ever be a day when someone would meet her and not make snap judgements based on things they had read or heard?

Probably not, she conceded, as she released another slow breath. Probably not, and that's something I have to live with. Something I have to accept. Something, she reminded herself, I've already accepted, because I'm here today holding a party. There was a time when I thought I'd never even be at a party again. She got up from the bed and stretched her arms over her head. She was doing the right thing. And the party was going to be great. It would be an occasion to look forward, not to look back. For everyone concerned.

'Um, excuse me, Mizz Delahaye. Everything's done now.' Lizzie's voice wafted up the stairs. 'The food's in the fridge, the ice is in

3

the freezer and the wine is in the chiller. I've taken the glasses from the boxes and left them on the table. They're already washed and I've given them a quick wipe too.'

Dominique took another deep breath and ran lightly down the stairs. The caterer was standing in the hallway.

'Thanks,' Dominique said. 'You've done a great job. I appreciate it.'

Lizzie beamed at her. She'd thought she'd done a pretty good job too, unloading and storing everything in record time. Nevertheless, it was nice to get praise from Dominique Delahaye, who had, she knew, once been voted Ireland's Most Celebrated Hostess. Dazzling Domino, they'd called her at the time. Of course, that was before everything had gone totally pear-shaped for her and she'd ended up being called a lot of other things instead. She was hardly dazzling now, was she, in her black T-shirt and black jeans, her hair held back untidily from her face and a streak of dust across her cheek. Although there was still something about her that held your attention, there was no doubt about that.

'I hope you have a fantastic evening,' said Lizzie. 'Housewarming, is it?' As soon as the words were out of her mouth, she wished she hadn't said anything. Ash would freak if she knew she'd asked a question. But she hadn't been able to help herself.

'No.' Dominique hesitated, and then gave Lizzie the ghost of a smile. 'It's a divorce party, actually.'

'Oh.' Lizzie looked surprised. 'I didn't realise . . . well, um, I suppose I should probably say congratulations – would that be the right thing under the circumstances?'

'It's not my divorce.' This time Dominique's smile was wider and there was an undercurrent of laughter in her voice.

'My mistake,' said Lizzie, thinking that the older woman looked a lot less fierce when she smiled. Almost beautiful, actually, with those dark brown eyes softening and two tiny dimples appearing in her cheeks. More like her photographs, in fact. Nearly dazzling after all.

'That's OK. Understandable, even.' Dominique still sounded amused.

'I didn't know that you'd moved to Dublin.' Lizzie felt that

4

Dominique's smile allowed for a certain level of conversation between them, despite Ash's warnings. 'I didn't even think you were in Ireland, to be honest.'

'I never left Ireland,' Dominique told her gently. 'No matter what you might have heard. And I'm from Dublin, so perhaps it was inevitable that I'd end up back here again.'

'The house in Cork was magnificent, though.' Lizzie filed away the information about Dominique's residency. 'And the views were spectacular. I remember the pictures of it in the *Hello!* magazine spread.'

'The Curse of *Hello!*,' said Dominique ruefully, and then smiled her wide smile again.

It was nice to see that she could still smile, thought Lizzie. Obviously, in recent times, there hadn't been much for her to smile about. And then she wondered if the stories that talked about secret trysts and hideaways in the Maldives were true after all and if that was why her client could afford to throw parties and smile so brightly. Keep your head, she told herself. It's none of your business. Remember what Ash said. Don't ask unwanted questions.

'Well, look, have a great divorce party for whoever it is.' Despite the ban on asking questions, she did desperately want to know if Dominique had already got a divorce herself.

'Thank you,' said Dominique. 'We'll do our best. And thank you for the food and the wine and the ice and everything else. If I ever get around to a divorce party for myself, I'm sure I'll be in touch.'

Lizzie blushed. Dominique had known what she wanted to find out and had told her. There was something very controlled about her, Lizzie thought. A wariness, too. But she'd probably had to learn that. She remembered a photograph of Dominique in the grounds of her house in Cork, taken with a telephoto lens, in which she hadn't looked controlled at all. In which she'd clearly been crying. The caption hadn't been sympathetic. It had said something about Crocodile Tears.

If it was me, I don't think I'd ever be able to face anyone again after all that, Lizzie reckoned. I'd just be too embarrassed.

Dominique didn't seem to be embarrassed, though. She was looking straight at Lizzie, her brown eyes steady in a face that was slightly drawn but still attractive, despite the fine lines around the edges of her eyes and a definite crease on her brow. Lizzie wondered whether they'd all appeared in the last few months.

In earlier photographs, the ones in the magazines and the social diaries of the newspapers, before the ones that were taken with telephoto lenses, Dominique had never looked anything other than radiant. But those sort of pictures were always retouched, everyone knew that. Nevertheless, Lizzie was certain that a couple of years ago Dominique wouldn't have been seen dead like she was now, even if she was just meeting the caterers. Especially if she was just meeting the caterers! It would've been unthinkable. All the same, there was something captivating about her. An attraction that wasn't all to do with her slightly angular face and those huge brown eyes.

The Domino Effect. That had been the headline on one of the newspaper articles. But of course they'd only written it then because she was the wife of an influential businessman who'd given her the nickname. Nobody realised the impact that the piece, and its accompanying photograph of Dominique sipping champagne whilst sitting on a marble worktop, would have.

Even people who hadn't read the original article had heard of her afterwards. She'd become a celebrity in her own right, a must-have person at any glittering event and an inspiration to lots of women.

What would it be like, Lizzie wondered, to have it all and to lose it? To have made your way to the top only to have it taken away so abruptly? What would it be like, she asked herself, to know that people were talking about you and wondering whether every word from your lips was a tissue of lies, whether you knew the truth behind everything that had happened and had been part of it all yourself?

She shivered slightly. During the years when she'd read about Dominique Delahaye, she'd envied her. Envied her looks and her lifestyle and especially her attractive, successful husband. Everyone had loved her. Everyone had loved him. Everyone had called them the perfect couple.

That was then, of course. They weren't saying that now. Even though, over the last year there'd been more newsprint than ever devoted to them. Lizzie had read most of it and joined in the gossip.

They'd been a couple well worth gossiping about.

Chapter 1

He was the first person ever to call her Domino.

Until then, she'd always been Dominique. At home, her mother resolutely refused ever to shorten it or to use a pet name for her. Evelyn simply couldn't understand why people would give their children one name only to call them something else entirely. She herself never responded to Eve or Evie but only to Evelyn. Or, naturally, to Mrs Brady. She preferred being called Mrs Brady by people she didn't know very well. She didn't like strangers to be too familiar. She hated the way that chit of a girl in the bank called her Evelyn, as though they were the best of friends, when the relationship between them was that of customer and teller. The world, she thought, was becoming far too disrespectful and everyone was a good deal less deferential than they'd been when she'd been growing up. As far as Evelyn was concerned, that wasn't a good thing, and it wasn't helped by giving children pet names.

So Dominique it was, even though Evelyn's own pronunciation made it sound like the male version, Dominic. During her pregnancy, Evelyn had been certain that she was expecting a second boy, and had already chosen his name. The arrival of a girl had surprised her, but she'd promised St Dominic that she'd name the baby after him and she was a woman who kept her promises.

She prayed that her daughter would be blessed with her namesake's reputed integrity and honour as well as his charitable disposition. Evelyn was heavily involved in charity work herself and was one of an army of women who cleaned and polished the parish church so that the scent of beeswax mingled with the floral arrangements that were renewed every week, while the pews glowed in the light that slanted through the stained-glass windows. On the day she brought Dominique home from the hospital, Evelyn hung a picture of the saint holding a bible and a lily over the baby's cot and asked him to bless her baby and keep her on the straight and narrow. When she was a little older and was sleeping in a bed instead of a cot, Dominique begged her mother to take the picture down, insisting that it scared her; but Evelyn told her not to be silly, that St Dominic was there to look after her and he always would. It wasn't until her teens that Dominique finally replaced the saint's picture with a large glossy poster of Sting, whom she adored and whose lyrics she once told her brother Gabriel were far more meaningful to her than prayers. She also stuck up posters of Simon Le Bon and Annie Lennox in her room. Evelyn pursed her lips at the sight of them, but realised that as far as Dominique was concerned, there was no point in saying anything at all.

At school, Dominique tried to shorten her name to Nikki, but somehow it never quite worked. There were two other Nikkis at the Holy Trinity School for Girls and both of them were adorable and gorgeous, which meant that to be a Nikki she would have had to be adorable and gorgeous too. Unfortunately, she didn't have Nikki McAteer's shiny blond hair and baby-blue eyes, or Nikki Dunne's bouncing auburn curls and perfect skin, and so she stayed Dominique, or sometimes Dommy, which she hated because it didn't conjure up the type of person she would have liked to be. Not perhaps as flighty as the most popular girls in the school (whose only interest was in make-up and boyfriends), but someone who was pretty and fun to be with and who was invited to parties and other social events as a matter of course.

But it was hard to be fun, she thought, when she was stuck with parents like Seamus and Evelyn; and hard to make the most of her decent bone structure and slender figure when her porcelain-pale skin was prone to spots and her almost black shoulder-length hair was boringly straight and curl-free. Tragically, from her point of view, her short sight meant having to wear glasses; and despite the optician telling her that the square tortoiseshell frames (which were all she could afford) were grand on her, she knew that they didn't really flatter her face.

Dominique longed for the kind of sleek looks and outgoing personality that would have allowed her to be part of the group of girls who were acknowledged to be the leaders of their years. But only a favoured few were like the two Nikkis, or Cara Bond, or – the queen bee herself – Emma Walsh, who would regularly flick her chestnut curls from her face with a careless gesture that managed to convey her superiority over everyone else in the class without really trying.

It was in her fifth year of secondary school that things began to change for Dominique. The change wasn't brought about by the sudden disappearance of her spots (unfortunately they were as persistent as ever) or by a new hair product that gave her bouncing curls (nothing worked on her poker-straight mane), but by the fact that she was thrust unexpectedly into the limelight as Judas in the school production of *Jesus Christ Superstar*. This was only because Nikki Dunne was hauled into hospital with appendicitis the morning of the production and Dominique, as her understudy, was told that she'd have to take her place. Dominique had nearly thrown up at the thought. It was one thing singing the part at rehearsals; it was quite another to actually have to perform in front of people. Her original role in the production had had nothing to do with singing at all. She'd been down to sell raffle tickets.

'Ah, don't worry about it,' said Maeve Mulligan, her best friend, as they sat backstage together. 'You're Judas, for heaven's sake. You're the villain of the piece. If you hit a wrong note, people will almost expect it of you.'

'Yeah, but they'll also know I'm not meant to.' Dominique's teeth were chattering with nerves. 'And Cara and Emma will be creased up with laughing at me.'

'They won't,' said Maeve. 'They're not that evil. Besides, they want the show to go well. They'll help you out.'

'Someone else should've been the understudy.' Dominique picked at a spot on her chin. 'You know they only chose me for it because they try to make girls like us part of everything.'

Maeve nodded. She knew what her friend meant. The girls with the smooth skin and glossy hair were the ones who always got picked for the school plays. Everyone knew that. The others, still gawky or spotty or awkward, ended up making scenery and selling tickets, although they were trained as understudies. Most of them accepted that this was merely to make them feel good about themselves. They were never expected to have to actually perform.

'You'll be fine,' she said. 'Your voice isn't that bad anyway.'

'Nothing like Nikki's, though.'

'We'll all be rooting for you,' Maeve assured her. 'My mother has promised to clap like mad every time you open your mouth.'

Dominique smiled faintly. 'Well mine certainly won't. I'm not sure how she feels about me in this role. Judas Iscariot was hardly her favourite person.' She picked at the spot again and this time it started to bleed. 'Damn it,' she said. 'I don't want to be dripping blood all over the stage.'

'If you left them alone, they'd go,' observed Maeve.

'If I leave them alone, they multiply,' Dominique told her. 'I'll have to load on the foundation to hide them.'

Maeve grinned. 'Maybe it's because you're so spotty that they got you to understudy. You know, Judas looking a bit mean and pustular while Jesus Christ is kind of cute.'

'I'm glad you're my friend,' said Dominique grimly. 'Otherwise I'd hit you for saying that. Even if it's probably true.'

Dominique thought she was going to faint as the curtain slowly parted, but although she knew that her voice was very shaky at the start, she grew in confidence as she realised that she was managing to keep it all together, so that by the time the performance ended she was actually enjoying herself and was sorry when the curtain finally closed.

As the applause rang around the hall, she felt both pleased and proud. It was good to be the centre of attention for once and have people notice her. She stood between Emma and Cara and the three of them held hands and bowed while the audience clapped enthusiastically. She felt even prouder when Miss Prescott singled her out for a special mention for having stood in so well for Nikki Dunne at such short notice.

'She's right,' murmured Emma Walsh as they took a final bow. 'You were great, Dominique.'

'Thanks.' Dominique glowed. Emma had been very supportive throughout the performance and Dominique was beginning to think that the other girl wasn't as snooty as she'd originally thought.

'Who's that guy beside your mother?' Emma asked.

'My dad, of course,' she replied, unable to actually see him because without her specs she was far too short-sighted to identify anyone.

'It can't be your dad,' said Emma. 'He's too young.'

'Oh, him.' Dominique squinted. 'That's Gabriel. My older brother.'

'No way,' said Emma. 'Really?'

'Yes.'

Dominique knew why Emma sounded so surprised. While she'd been stuck with the plain gene in the family, Gabriel was almost heart-stoppingly handsome. Three years older than her, he was much taller. His face was chiselled and thoughtful, with a permanent shadow of stubble around his chin. He'd never had a spot in his life. His eyes were brown like hers but not hidden by glasses and a fringe. If she'd looked like Gabriel, Dominique thought, she could definitely have been a Nikki. No question.

After she'd changed out of her costume and into jeans and a jumper, she went to find her family. As she approached them, Emma joined her.

'Introduce me,' she said to Dominique.

'Pleased to meet you.' Dominique's father, Seamus, shook Emma's hand. 'You were very good as Mary Magdalene.'

'Thanks,' said Emma. 'I think she's a tragic figure really.'

'I never approved of her,' sniffed Evelyn. 'But we're all God's children.'

'Even Judas Iscariot,' said Gabriel warmly. 'You were very good too, Dominique.'

'Thank you,' she said.

Emma turned to look at him. 'You would've made a great Judas yourself,' she said. 'All dark and brooding.'

Gabriel smiled and Dominique laughed. 'He wouldn't have had the right attitude towards it,' she told Emma, who, she realised with a sudden spurt of amusement, fancied him. She looked wickedly at her, tickled by the idea that the most popular girl in the class was interested in her gorgeous, unavailable brother. 'He's going to be a priest, you see.'

'No!' Emma's eyes opened wide. 'Not really?'

'It's true,' admitted Gabriel. 'It's my vocation.'

'You're kidding me?' Emma still couldn't quite believe it.

'He's going to make a wonderful priest,' said Evelyn. 'We're so proud of him, aren't we, Dominique?'

'Absolutely,' said his sister, although her tone belied her words. 'He's our very own Superstar.'

'God, what a waste!' Emma said the following week in class. 'I mean, I can't believe that you have such a hunk of a brother, Dominique Brady. Or that I never met him before. Or that he's going to be a priest! Will he go through with it, d'you think? It would be such a loss to women everywhere.'

Dominique shrugged. 'He's always wanted to join the priesthood,' she told Emma and the others who had clustered round. 'Ever since he was small. Other kids played cowboys and Indians and stuff. He said pretend Masses. He said he had a vision.'

'What sort of vision?' breathed Tanya Johnson.

'Oh, of God,' said Dominique dismissively. 'He said that God came into his room one night and told him that he had a mission for him and that it was to do his work or something like that.'

'Don't you believe him?' asked Natasha Howard.

'C'mon!' Dominique looked at her scathingly. 'God doesn't come into people's bedrooms. That's all church stuff. Gabriel wants to be a priest because my mother brainwashed him when he was a kid by making him be an altar boy and telling him he was special and everything. He's not.'

'He's utterly gorgeous,' sighed Emma dreamily. 'I wonder if I could persuade him that his talents lie in other directions.'

'You wouldn't be the first to try,' Dominique told her. 'But you'd certainly be the first to succeed.'

Dominique had hoped that successfully carrying off the role as Judas would make her more popular with her classmates, but it was actually because of Gabriel that she was suddenly in demand. Girls who'd hardly ever spoken to her before asked her about him, wanted to know when he was at home, and took to calling around to her house on the off chance that he'd be in. Evelyn was surprised and not always pleased by her daughter's new friends. She was especially wary of Emma Walsh, who always turned up wearing lashings of mascara, shiny pink lip gloss and low-cut tops. Evelyn considered Emma to be a bad influence on Dominique who was spending more and more time looking critically at her own reflection in the mirror and beginning to use mascara and lip gloss herself. She didn't want Dominique giving in to vanity like so many girls her age. She wasn't worried about Emma's influence on Gabriel. She knew that no girl would divert him from his chosen path.

Despite Evelyn's certainties, saving Gabriel from the priesthood became a mission for the girls in Dominique's class, and they embraced it enthusiastically. They wanted to change his mind before he joined the seminary, because he'd chosen to go to college before devoting himself solely to his vocation. The way they looked at it, they had a year to turn his life around and they were all going to do their best to be the one to achieve it. Dominique wondered what would happen to her new-found popularity at the end of the year when Gabriel departed, as she knew he would, for his training. She wondered if Emma, in particular, would continue to call around to the house. Much to her surprise, she was beginning to like Emma, even if she couldn't help thinking that she was really silly over Gabriel. She was surprisingly generous with make-up tips and suggestions for, as she put it, enhancing Dominique's appearance, although Dominique herself had to admit that she wasn't brave enough to go for bright blue mascara and gold glitter on her cheeks. Not that Emma's flirtation with coloured mascara and glitter was having any effect on her brother either.

'It's like *The Thorn Birds*,' said Cara Bond in school one day. 'He should follow his heart and not his head.'

'Ooh, yes,' agreed Lisa-Anne Downey. 'He has to do what's right for him.'

'His heart is in the priesthood,' said Dominique. 'God knows where his head is. Up his arse most of the time.'

15

'Oh, Dominique, you know that's not true!' cried Emma, who'd been around at the house the previous night, ostensibly to work on a geography project with Dominique and Maeve. As it turned out, Dominique was the one who researched the project, while Maeve drew up a chart of how it would look and Emma spent much of the time batting her (purple) eyelashes at Gabriel, who pretty much ignored her and continued reading his book on philosophy. 'He can't help being perfect.'

Dominique snorted. She was perfectly prepared to admit that Gabriel was a hunk, but as far as she was concerned, his perceived perfection was bloody irritating; Evelyn and Seamus were forever telling her that she should try to live up to his example, which drove her nuts. Deep down, she couldn't wait until he joined the seminary and was out of her life, lifting the pressure to be as wonderful as him off her shoulders.

Emma Walsh definitely didn't want Gabriel to leave. Whenever possible, she would start a discussion with him about God and the Church, which he always took seriously but which left Dominique shaking with suppressed laughter. Maeve, the only one of her friends who didn't fancy Gabriel (she'd known him all her life and, like Dominique, thought he was too good to be true), sometimes got annoyed with seeing Emma at the house so much. But both Maeve and Dominique agreed that the other girl was actually quite good fun when she wasn't flicking her hair from her face and mooning over Gabriel. It would do her good, Maeve added, to realise that not every male in the universe could be charmed by her ever-changing lash colour and glossy lippy (although both of them wished that mascara and lippy would work the same wonders on them as they so clearly did on Emma, who, despite her failure with Gabriel, continued to be the girl most of the boys in their year wanted to date).

Gabriel left for the seminary at the Royal English College at Valladolid, in Spain, just after Dominique left school. By then Emma Walsh was the only one of the gang who still fancied him – all of the others had given him up as a lost cause, and Dominique couldn't help feeling that she'd never again be as popular as she was for the few months when her brother had been the hottest item in town.

Emma continued to drop around to the Brady house until Gabriel left. She was thrilled when Evelyn (despite some reservations, and still thinking that the Walsh girl wore too much make-up and too few clothes) invited her to the family celebration to mark Gabriel's departure for the seminary. It was at the house, and low-key, just family, neighbours and the local parish priest. Evelyn fussed around making sure that they all had plenty of tea and sandwiches, while Gabriel appeared both pleased and slightly embarrassed at the attention.

'I can't believe he's really going,' said Emma mournfully. 'I mean, who becomes a priest these days? Who'd want to?'

Dominique glanced at her brother, who was in the corner of the room talking to their parish priest. 'He was always a bit spiritual,' she conceded. 'I know my mother influenced him too, but he truly seems to believe he has a vocation and will help people.'

'Doesn't help me,' said Emma glumly, and Dominique laughed.

Evelyn made a short speech saying how proud she was of Gabriel, and then Gabriel himself said some words about the great gift that God had bestowed upon him and how he hoped to be found worthy of it. Meanwhile, Dominique wondered if there was anything she could ever do in her life to make Evelyn and Seamus half as proud of her as they were of her older brother.

She did rather better than she'd expected in her leaving exams. Both of her parents had congratulated her on her results, but since the posting of them had coincided with Gabriel's departure to Valladolid, they hadn't given them that much attention. The good results didn't make a lot of difference to her anyhow, because there weren't any jobs to be found. Not even in the local shops or businesses, most of which were struggling in an economy that was going nowhere. The only place hiring temporary staff was the local pub, and both Evelyn and Seamus made it quite clear that Dominique wasn't working in a bar.

'Dirty, smelly places,' Evelyn said, even though she'd never set foot inside the door of their local lounge, which was famous for the quality of its Sunday carvery lunches. 'And not the sort of job you want.'

'I want anything that can help me earn some money of my own,' said Dominique.

'But not a bar,' said Seamus, who, like Evelyn, was a teetotaller and wore a Pioneer Total Abstinence pin on the lapel of his suit. 'There's no way I want you working in a pub. I'll continue to give you an allowance until you get something suitable.'

'It's not the same,' replied Dominique. 'And besides, you don't give me very much.'

'It's all your father can afford,' Evelyn told her. 'I think he's more than generous.'

'Can we go on holidays this year?' asked Dominique, changing the subject. 'Can we go to Majorca like Maeve's family?'

The Mulligans had headed off on holiday after the results of the exams had come out. Like Dominique, Maeve had done better than she'd hoped. Unlike the Bradys, the Mulligans were using it as an excuse to get away for a fortnight.

Evelyn sniffed. 'I can't believe they're wasting all that money on two weeks of lying about,' she said, 'when they could put it to so much better use.'

'I think two weeks lying in the sun sounds fabulous.' Dominique sounded wistful.

'Well I can't think of anything worse,' said Evelyn. 'Now why don't you go down to the parish office and see if you can help with the meals on wheels?'

'It's very unfair to be part of a family that considers Lourdes to be a potential holiday destination,' Dominique told Maeve the following week when she'd arrived back home and shown off her photographs of hunky guys on the beach at Palma Nova. 'We're living in the nineteen eighties, not the fifties! I want to go to Fuengirola, not Fatima.'

Maeve sympathised. She'd had a great time in Majorca and enjoyed her first real romance, with an English guy she'd met at the apartment block where they were staying. She'd sent him three letters since she'd come home, although he hadn't yet replied to any of them.

18

Maeve always felt sorry for Dominique, who had to live in that dreary house with its pictures of the Sacred Heart and the Virgin Mary on the walls and with both Evelyn and Seamus liable to whip out their rosary beads at any moment. It didn't help, either, that Gorgeous Gabe (as the girls at school had christened him) had embraced the whole religion thing too. And it didn't matter how much Dominique might want to live a different sort of life, or even just experience it for a time; it was very difficult to be different in the Brady household.

'You need to get a job,' Maeve told her. 'Any job. Then you'll have some money of your own and you'll be able to go on holidays yourself.'

Dominique nodded. 'I've applied to loads of places,' she said. 'Banks, insurance companies, the corporation . . . but that all takes for ever and there are so many people looking for work. I'm going into town next week to see if the shops are hiring.'

'I heard that Cara Bond is off to the States,' said Maeve. 'She's got a Donnelly visa and she's going to Boston. And my sister is thinking of heading to London.'

'No!' Dominique looked at her friend in surprise.

'There are jobs in the City there,' Maeve told her. 'And of course Lorna is good at all that stuff, what with her degree and everything. So she's giving it a try.'

'I suppose that's where having a decent qualification helps,' said Dominique.

'Your leaving results were very decent,' said Maeve.

'Yeah, but I'm not going to college, am I?' said Dominique. 'I didn't really think hard enough about it, I suppose. Anyhow, my parents couldn't have afforded it so there wasn't any point.' She sighed. 'My mother has the incredibly dated view that some guy will marry me and look after me for the rest of my life!' She made a face. 'How likely is that? It'd be great to go to England and get a job. Then I wouldn't have to live in Shrine Central any more.'

Maeve laughed. 'When we both get jobs, we'll get a flat,' she said. 'Then we can do our own thing.'

'My father would never let me live in a flat,' said Dominique. 'Not in Dublin. Not while I could still be at home.'

'Hey, you're an adult now,' Maeve reminded her. 'You were eighteen last month. You can do what you like.'

'I wish it felt that way,' said Dominique gloomily.

'I promise you,' said Maeve. 'We'll get jobs, we'll get a flat and we'll have a great time.'

But it didn't work out like that. Despite their best efforts, there were no jobs to be found. Dominique eventually enrolled in a secretarial school (Evelyn agreed that it would help her employment prospects if she could type, although she complained that after thirteen years in the education system, it was a bit much to be forced into forking out more money for her daughter to learn a useful skill), while Maeve joined her sister, Lorna, in London. Lorna had landed a good job at Lloyds Bank and was sharing a house with two other girls. There was room for a fourth and, she told Maeve, as there were some vacancies for juniors going in the bank, she should come over and take her chances. Maeve had gone, been offered a position, and happily accepted.

Dominique couldn't blame her friend for going but she missed her when she'd left. Emma was still around but Dominique didn't have the same easy friendship with the prettiest girl in the school as she'd had with Maeve. It seemed to her that everybody was either getting jobs (Emma was working on the beauty counter in Arnotts department store) or leaving the country, and she was doing neither. The trouble was, she wasn't sure exactly what she wanted to do and had no idea what she'd be good at. It wasn't that she was stupid – her exam results proved that – but she didn't have a burning ambition. Or a dream about the sort of life she wanted to lead.

Sometimes she wished she'd been born with Gabriel's certainty. But on the nights she went out with Emma and her other friends – occasionally drinking a little too much and hoping that her parents wouldn't notice the next day – she knew that she did have a certainty about one thing: she sure as hell didn't want a life of penance, poverty and celibacy like him!

*   *   *

The first job offer she got was as a waitress in a hamburger restaurant on George's Street. Evelyn was both pleased that she'd got a job and annoyed that her newly acquired shorthand and typing skills were going to waste. It was the first time Dominique had ever had a wage of her own and, even though the money wasn't great, she felt a rush of independence when she opened her pay packet.

The following morning she went into Peter Mark in Grafton Street and asked for a new hairstyle with a bit more life in it.

'You need to lose the fringe for starters,' the stylist told her bluntly. 'You can carry off something more fashionable. Anything like these.' She handed Dominique a magazine with pictures of Kylie Minogue, Bananarama and the Bangles. Dominique looked doubtful.

'Maybe not quite so . . . so big,' she said finally as she looked at the styles. 'And not too tarty.'

The stylist sighed deeply. She liked giving people up-to-the-minute cuts but she could tell that the girl in front of her was a bit conservative for some of her favourites. She told Dominique that she'd give her something less radical than Cyndi Lauper but she'd try to make her look good all the same.

'You should get contact lenses too,' she advised. 'That way people would be able to see your eyes. You've got lovely eyes.'

Nobody had ever told her that she had lovely eyes before. Dominique felt unexpectedly pleased to think she had a feature that anyone could consider lovely. She couldn't afford lenses, but she did buy herself some new frames for her glasses – big, white and square. They didn't show off her eyes but they were very fashionable. She also invested in some bright blue eye shadow, dark red lipstick and high-heeled shoes. (Years later, when she'd learned what suited her and what didn't, she shuddered to think that she'd been so proud of her primary colour make-up, oversized glasses and ridiculous hairdo.)

She enjoyed her job at the restaurant. She had a good memory for faces and always recognised regular customers. She remembered their favourite meals and would ask if they wanted 'the usual', which made them feel welcome and a little bit special. And she never got an order wrong.

So when the letters started to come back from the banks and the building societies and the insurance companies and everyone else she'd applied to for a job, saying that the positions had been filled by someone 'more suitable' or that she was on a long panel from which vacancies throughout the year might be filled, she didn't feel despairing or rejected. She liked what she did, and even though Evelyn felt she should be chasing up office jobs, she was happy.

Her social life began to improve because she started meeting some of the other waiters and waitresses after work and they'd go for a drink in the Old Stand or Bruxelles, which were always noisy and crowded and fun. Dominique enjoyed being with people who didn't know everything about her and who hadn't known her when she was spotty and unattractive. (Much to her joy, the spots had disappeared almost as soon as she'd left school and even though she still hadn't quite cracked make-up, she realised that she seemed to be growing into her looks a little.) She saw her new friends more and Emma and her gang less. She felt as though she was breaking away from her past and setting out on the road to her future.

Neither Evelyn nor Seamus was entirely happy with the lifestyle Dominique was beginning to lead. They wanted to know what the point of all this partying was. They believed that life was a journey towards something better and they wanted her to be a spiritual person, like Gabriel, and to spend her spare time doing good works, not just having fun. Dominique knew that she wasn't a spiritual person. Especially not now that she was earning her own money and staying out until the early hours of the morning, something that caused intense rows between herself and her mother.

The number of novenas that Evelyn left on her bedside table increased almost daily, especially whenever Dominique stayed out until dawn and threw clothes into the laundry basket that reeked of smoke and alcohol.

'It's not from me,' she told her mother one day. 'I only have one or two drinks at the most and I don't smoke at all. I don't know what you're worrying about.'

Evelyn reminded her that it was easy to acquire loose morals and dangerous to drink too much because you never knew what it could lead to. It was, of course, she told Dominique, a sin to have sex before marriage, and no man would want her if she had a chequered past. Dominique looked at her mother in irritation and said that she didn't think God spent his time keeping tabs on her sex life, but if He did there was something decidedly weird about Him, and besides, her past certainly wasn't chequered. There were times when she wished it was, but so far, despite having snogged a number of men after nights in the pub, she hadn't slept with any of them. No matter how irrational she told herself she was being, she still harboured images of a bolt of lightning striking her down if she lost her virginity to a man she hardly knew.

She served Brendan Delahaye on the third Friday he came in to American Burger for lunch. She knew that he was a regular customer even though he hadn't sat at one of her tables before, and so she smiled the smile that caused two dimples to appear in her cheeks and that did more for her looks than the new haircut and dramatic eye shadow ever could.

'Mushroom burger, well done,' he said in a soft Cork accent. 'And I mean well done. Not just scorched. Cremated.'

'Mushroom burger, cremated,' she repeated.

'An extra portion of chips and a glass of milk.'

She stopped, her pencil poised above her notebook. 'Milk?'

'Yes, milk. Comes from a cow?'

'Gosh, thanks for that information. Otherwise I mightn't have known what you were talking about.' She smiled at him, not intimidated by him as she sometimes was by her customers, because his expression was open and friendly, and because he was from the country after all, and everyone knew that people from Dublin were far superior to their culchie cousins. 'You didn't strike me as the milk type, that's all.'

'Oh.' He sat back in the booth and looked up at her. 'And what type do I strike you as?'

She studied him thoughtfully. Even though he was sitting down, she could see that he was a big man. Older than her by a good few years, she reckoned; must be in his late twenties. Tall and broad. His face strong-featured and slightly weather-beaten. Light brown

23

hair, gelled but curly. Deep blue eyes. Which were now regarding her equally thoughtfully.

'A rugby player,' she said eventually. 'A pint drinker.'

'Rugby!' he snorted. 'That sissy ol' game! Gaelic football is the only game in the world for a man to play.'

His accent had become a little stronger and Dominique stifled a giggle.

'And milk is the only drink worth drinking?' she suggested. 'Preferably from your own cow?'

He stared at her and then laughed, loud enough so that the people nearby turned to look at them.

'When I'm working, yes,' he said. 'I like milk. But I don't have a cow of my own. Not in Dublin, anyway.'

'Where d'you work?' She knew that she should be getting on with taking his order – the restaurant was busy and all her tables were full – but she was enjoying the banter with him.

'On the building site the other side of St Stephen's Green,' he told her.

She nodded. There was an office development being built on the site. She'd read in the papers that the economy was finally beginning to pick up and that there was a real need for office space in the city. She couldn't quite believe it herself, because she still hadn't got a better job offer, but she hoped it was right.

'So you're a brickie, are you?' she asked.

'Jeez, girl, you do know how to put a man down. You don't have to use the term "brickie" as though I'm a no-hoper. I'm working on the site, yes. But when this job is over I'm setting up my own company.'

'Really?' She looked at him in astonishment.

'Absolutely,' he told her. 'That's the only way forward. Things will pick up in this country, and having your own company is what'll make you money.'

'What'll you build?' she asked.

'Houses,' he told her. 'Lots of them. And I'll make a big profit from it.'

She laughed. 'I hope someone buys them from you, so.'

'They will,' he said confidently.

'Everything all right?' Kirsten Jacobs, the supervisor, came over to the booth and looked at Dominique with a degree of irritation.

'Absolutely,' said the customer. 'My fault for delaying your waitress. I was debating what to drink. You know what? I'll have two of those milks.'

Kirsten looked from one to the other and frowned.

'You sure?' asked Dominique.

He nodded.

'Well get to it,' said Kirsten as Dominique hesitated.

When she returned with the two glasses of milk, he apologised for getting her into trouble.

'Sorry, Domino,' he said.

'What?' She was startled.

'Domino.' He grinned at her. 'That's what you reminded me of as you walked back to me, all dressed in black with your white specs and the two white glasses of milk in front of you. A little domino. It's a good game, dominoes. You need luck and strategy and a willingness to take a chance to play it well.'

'That's so weird,' she said slowly as she put the milk down on the table in front of him.

'It's not. It's a very old game,' he told her.

'No. I don't mean that. I mean – what you called me. It's . . . it's almost my name.'

'Really?'

She nodded. 'I'm Dominique,' she said.

'I prefer Domino,' he said. 'It suits you better.'

'Why?' she asked.

'Oh, because I think you're someone who would be willing to take a chance,' he said.

'Depends on what I'm chancing,' she said.

He laughed.

'What's your name?' she asked.

'Brendan,' he said.

'Not a very chance-taking name,' she chided and went off to get his burger and chips.

She was prepared to chat with him again, but he'd opened his newspaper and was engrossed in the sports pages when she came back.

He looked up briefly and thanked her but he didn't engage her in conversation. She was vaguely disappointed. But later, when he was leaving, he waved goodbye to her and called, 'See you, Domino,' even though she was taking another order at the time and so couldn't reply.

Chapter 2

Brendan sat at one of her tables every Friday. He always ordered the mushroom burger, cremated, even during December, when she tried to persuade him to have the turkey and cranberry special. He'd looked at her in horror when she'd suggested it and told her that there was no need to run that by him again, the mushroom burger suited him just fine. Although, he added that day, he did rather like the fact that all of the waitresses in American Burger were wearing Santa Claus hats. Hers, he told her, suited her just fine. She was the prettiest girl in the restaurant, he added, which made her blush to the roots of her newly styled hair.

'I have something for you,' said Brendan on the Friday before Christmas when she brought him his bill.

She looked at him in surprise as he put a small, gift-wrapped box on the table.

'Go ahead,' he said. 'Open it.'

'Really?'

'Of course.'

She glanced around the restaurant. But Kirsten Jacobs was busy and nobody was watching them. So she picked up the box, tore off the gold foil paper and lifted the lid. Inside was a delicate coral necklace. Her eyes widened as she looked at it.

'Happy Christmas, Domino,' he said.

'I can't take this.' She looked at him in dismay. 'It's . . . well . . . they wouldn't let me.'

'And why not?'

She looked confused.

'I bought it for you,' he said. 'So there's no point in not accepting it.'

'It's really lovely,' she told him. 'But I don't think I'm allowed to accept gifts from our customers.'

'I don't see the problem,' he said. 'D'you think it would be easier if you were accepting a gift from someone you were going out with?'

'That's a completely different – oh!' She stared at him, and he laughed.

'What time d'you finish?' he asked.

'Not till ten tonight,' she told him.

'Meet me for a drink when you're done?'

She looked at him in astonishment. She liked Brendan Delahaye. He was the first man she'd never tried to impress, because he was a customer and she was a waitress and she didn't think of him in the same way as she thought of other men; slightly mysterious people she didn't really understand and for whom she had to be someone other than herself. Besides, Brendan was a grown-up, older and (despite not being a Dubliner) wiser than her.

'Are you going to turn me down?' He looked at her enquiringly. 'I hope not. I had to pluck up my courage to ask you.'

'You didn't.' She giggled self-consciously.

'Of course I did. A lovely girl like you. I told myself I'd be devastated if you said no.'

'Would you really?'

'Yes.' His voice softened. 'Yes, I would.'

'In that case I'd better say yes.' She smiled.

'The Dame Tavern,' he said. 'I'll see you there.'

'OK,' she told him. 'I'm looking forward to it.'

'Me too,' he said.

The pub was crowded. Dominique stood on tiptoe, trying to peer over the heads of the other, taller people who were clustered around the bar. This hadn't been a good choice, she thought. Brendan might be here but she'd never see him in the Friday-night crush. Her fingers unconsciously played with the coral necklace around her throat as she looked anxiously for him.

'There you are.'

She turned at the touch of his hand on her shoulder. He'd never touched her before. And although since she'd started going out with the gang from work at the weekend there were other men who'd put their arms around her and held her tight, she'd never got the sudden hot quiver of excitement she had at that first, casual touch from Brendan Delahaye. She was utterly astounded at how she felt. She wanted to pull him to her and kiss him straight away. She wanted to hold him and never let him go.

But she didn't. She just smiled in relief and said that she was glad to see him. He smiled at her too and kissed her quickly on the cheek. And once again Dominique was overwhelmed by feelings she'd never had before.

'What would you like to drink?' he asked.

She asked for a West Coast Cooler, which made him smile, but he ordered it for her and a pint of Guinness for himself, then manoeuvred her to an alcove, where she sat on a high bar stool and he stood behind her.

'A bit crazy to meet up late on the Friday before Christmas,' he said, and she nodded as she took a sip of her drink. 'Don't tell me you like that stuff?'

'Why?' She looked apprehensive.

'A spritzer,' he said. 'What sort of drink is that!'

'White wine and—'

'Oh, I know what it actually is,' he assured her. 'It's just – I'm an ordinary sort of man myself. I don't do fancy drinks.'

She smiled at him. 'I don't think it's that fancy really. It's the only one I like. I can't drink beer and I don't like spirits. In fact,' she shrugged slightly, 'I'm not into alcohol that much, to be honest.'

'Ah well,' he teased. 'Maybe that's a good thing, Domino. There's a lot of people in this bar tonight who're going to wish in the morning that they weren't into alcohol.'

'Are you always going to call me that?' she demanded as she touched the necklace again.

'Always,' he told her. 'Absolutely always.'

She loved having a proper boyfriend. And more than that, because Brendan was nine years older than her, it made her feel superior to other girls her age. She didn't see many of her school crowd these days, but she felt that she'd overtaken Cara and the Nikkis, who'd only gone out with boys really. Whereas she was going out with a man. She'd even overtaken Emma Walsh, who was dating Pete Ferriter from down the road. She was Brendan's girlfriend, Domino, who was far more sophisticated than any of them.

Every time they went out together she fell in love with him a little bit more. He was gentle and kind and he didn't try to get her into bed or do any of the things her mother believed were on the high road to hell. But Dominique knew that the way she felt about him was sinful. She knew she wanted to go to bed with him. She just wasn't sure how many dates it took before it was appropriate.

'When are we going to see this boyfriend of yours?' Evelyn asked as Dominique went out one night, her straight hair agonisingly teased into curls and held in place with industrial amounts of hair-spray (Emma had shown her how to do this, and Dominique wouldn't have spent the time or the effort on anyone but Brendan).

'Sometime,' she replied carelessly.

'I want to know what he's like.'

'He's lovely,' said Dominique, 'and that's all you need to know.'

Evelyn pursed her lips. But she didn't get the opportunity to say anything else. Dominique had gone out, slamming the front door behind her.

The thought of her gorgeous boyfriend meeting her over-strict parents filled Dominique with dread. When she was with Brendan she felt positively grown up, but she knew that her parents would treat her exactly the same in front of him as they always did – as though she was still a child who didn't know her own mind. Brendan frequently offered to pick her up when they were going out together, but she always said that it was too much trouble and that she'd meet him in the city centre. He lived near Portobello and there wasn't a convenient bus that could leave him in Drimnagh. Whenever he pointed out that he could always get a taxi, she'd look at him in horror and said that that was far too expensive. He would smile and say that he could afford it – he was earning decent money on the building site – but she'd shake her head and tell him to save what he had for the company he planned to set up. The office block would be finished soon, she reminded him, and then he'd need every spare penny.

'You're a great girl,' he'd say each time she insisted on it. 'You really are.' But she knew she wasn't. She knew that her main motivation was simply keeping him away from her parents, because she was terrified that the day he met them would be the day he decided that if all girls ended up like their mothers, he should cut his losses with Dominique Brady pretty damn quick, and she was so completely and utterly in love with him that the idea of losing him filled her with horror.

But the night they were invited to a twenty-first birthday party (which was their sixth date), Brendan insisted on picking her up. The party was in Clondalkin after all, he told her, and so calling to the Brady home was more or less on the way. Dominique reluctantly agreed and was ready half an hour before he was due to arrive, so that she could answer the door and be out of the house before her parents even knew he was there. Evelyn, however, was as determined to meet Dominique's boyfriend as Dominique was to stop her. And so as soon as the doorbell had rung, and even as Dominique – who had been waiting in the hallway – opened the door, she was fussing around behind her telling Brendan to come inside, that it was lovely to finally meet him.

'We don't have time,' said Dominique tightly, but Brendan smiled at her and said it was no problem, it would be nice to say hello.

She gritted her teeth as Evelyn ushered him into the front room – the room that was only used on special occasions and which was decked with photographs of Gabriel looking pensive and priestly among the glass and porcelain ornaments that Evelyn liked to collect.

'Our son,' Evelyn explained as Brendan perched on the edge of the sofa next to the sideboard with the biggest picture of Gabriel. 'He's a wonderful lad. He's studying in Valladolid at the moment.' She said the name 'Valladolid' as though she was actually saying 'Heaven'.

'I'm sure you're very proud of him,' said Brendan politely.

'Of course we are,' said Evelyn. 'Now, can I get you a cup of tea?'

'We don't have time, Mam.' Dominique spoke quickly. 'We're supposed to be at the party by eight.'

'Of course you have time for tea,' she said. 'Come along, Dominique, you can help me.'

Dominique shot a helpless look at Brendan, who winked at her. She followed Evelyn into the kitchen. Seamus was sitting at the table, reading the *Evening Herald* but he got up when his wife and daughter entered.

'He's a bit old,' said Evelyn to her husband. 'But you'd better see for yourself.'

'Mam, Dad. For heaven's sake!' hissed Dominique. 'He's not here to be checked out. And he's not old. He's only twenty-eight.'

'He's your boyfriend,' said Evelyn. 'And twenty-eight is much more mature than you.'

'It doesn't matter how old he is,' Dominique retorted. 'We're going out together. There's no need to make a big production of it. Please,' she added, looking at her father. 'You'll make him think he's being investigated or something.'

'I'll just say hello,' said Seamus. 'Man to man.'

Dominique sighed. Her relationship with Brendan was the best relationship she'd ever had in her life. (Well, she corrected herself, the only relationship she'd ever had in her life. She couldn't count two trips to the Carlton cinema with John McNulty, who'd worked behind the bar at American Burger but who'd headed off to New Zealand shortly afterwards; or a boring theatre visit with Tom Fitzpatrick, who wanted to be an actor and who was only working in the restaurant until his big break came along.) Now her parents were about to destroy her chance of happiness. Brendan would see that she came from a house full of religious nutters and he'd think that she was a nutter herself.

'We really don't want tea,' she said as Evelyn filled the kettle.

'Nonsense.' Evelyn shook some custard creams on to a plate. 'He's a guest.'

'He's only here to take me out,' said Dominique desperately. 'Mam . . .'

'We're being polite,' Evelyn said firmly. She put the plate on to her large, gold-rimmed tray along with four cups and saucers, a jug of milk and a bowl of sugar, and carried it into the front room. Dominique stayed in the kitchen, contemplating her ruined relationship.

The kettle boiled and Dominique made the tea. There was no point in trying to outmanoeuvre her parents. They did what they wanted to do. They never listened to her.

There was no sign of Evelyn returning, so she carried the blue ceramic teapot (it matched the cups and saucers; Evelyn had used their good crockery) into the front room.

She thought she saw relief in Brendan's eyes as she walked in. No doubt he was getting the rundown on Gabriel's priestly vocation. Everyone who visited the house got that.

'We only have time for a very quick drop, Mrs Brady,' he said as Dominique put the teapot down on the coffee table. 'You know what it's like trying to get a taxi.'

'You're getting a taxi?' Evelyn looked at Dominique.

'Easier than trying to catch buses,' she said. She had no problem about getting a taxi tonight. She was wearing a lightweight pale pink sleeveless dress with a narrow silver belt, as well as high-heeled pink shoes that she'd bought only that day and which were already pinching her toes because they were a half-size too small. Evelyn had told her before Brendan arrived that the shoes were too high and the dress was too flimsy – and that the neckline was far too low – but Dominique had ignored her. She'd also ignored her mother's complaint that the white jacket she was wearing with it was totally unsuitable for the weather and wouldn't keep out the cold and that her chunky white earrings and necklace were tarty.

'In fact, we'd better go now,' said Brendan. He drained his cup in one large gulp. 'Lovely to meet you, Mr and Mrs Brady.'

'Aren't you going to have a custard cream?' Evelyn picked up the plate and offered them to him.

'There's food at the party,' said Brendan. 'We're grand, thanks, Mrs Brady. Come on, Domino, time to go.'

'Domino?' Evelyn frowned.

'My pet name for her,' said Brendan easily, taking Dominique by the hand. 'Thanks again.'

He hustled Dominique out of the room and out of the house.

They were on the pavement outside before she looked at him contritely.

'I'm so sorry,' she said. 'They—'

'Don't you worry,' he told her. 'They're concerned about you. Like all parents. It's fine.' He put his arm around her and drew her closer to him. Dominique released a sigh of relief. He was holding her tightly. Despite having met her parents. He must really and truly love her.

And she really and truly loved him too.

'Well, what did you think?' asked Evelyn Brady as she cleared away the tea and the uneaten custard creams.

'He's harmless enough, I suppose,' said Seamus. 'He's a builder.'

Evelyn sniffed. 'Not much money there,' she said. 'Very precarious kind of living.'

'I think he cares for her, though.'

'Cares for her? Not loves her?'

'I don't suppose he'd tell me that,' said Seamus. 'But they haven't been going out together that long, so . . .'

'I think he's trouble.' Evelyn frowned.

'Why?'

'Twenty-eight, Seamus. He's at a different place in his life to her.'

'Maybe he'll be a steadying sort of fellow,' said Seamus.

'And maybe he'll just use her. He calls her Domino.'

'That's hardly a reason to dislike him.'

Evelyn frowned again. 'It shows a lack of respect. Though how she expects to get respect when she dresses like she's done tonight, I'll never know.'

'Evelyn . . .'

'*And* she loves him too much.' Evelyn picked up the tray and walked into the kitchen, Seamus following her. 'She loves him too much and he doesn't care enough, and that's always a bad thing.'

The party was in a community hall near the Nangor Road. The hall had been decorated with banners and balloons all wishing a Happy 21st to Peadar, who worked with Brendan on the office block site.

'He's a great man, is Peadar,' Brendan said as they went up and wished him all the best. 'The hardest worker of us all.'

'Yeah, right.' Peadar grinned. 'I cover his lazy ass.'

Brendan slapped Peadar on the back and both of them laughed while Dominique looked around her tentatively. She didn't know anyone and was feeling suddenly insecure about being here with Brendan among his friends.

'Come on, pet.' He grabbed her by the hand. 'Let's get some drinks. We're having a double celebration tonight.'

'Oh?' she asked.

'Today I set up Delahaye Construction and I got my first job – a house extension on Donard Road.' Donard Road wasn't all that far from Dominique's house, and she smiled at the idea of being able to see him when he was working.

'That's fantastic,' she said.

'Aye.' He grinned at her. 'They want a new kitchen added on to the side, which is an easy enough job. Things have been on the up and up for me ever since I met you, Domino. You're my lucky charm.'

She blushed. 'You really think so?'

'I absolutely know so,' he said as he waved at the barman and ordered a round of drinks.

By the time they left the party in the early hours of the morning, she was feeling woozy. They hadn't had any West Coast Cooler at the bar, and so she'd drunk Bacardi and Coke instead. She'd grown to like it, but hadn't realised the effect it was having on her until she got up from the table where she'd been sitting and nearly toppled off her high-heeled shoes. She'd had to blink a few times to focus properly and had walked very carefully to the loos.

'I think you've had enough,' Brendan said when she came back. 'And it's getting late. Time for us to go.'

She nodded and waited for him while he said goodbye to Peadar and his other friends (she'd liked them; they were all very easy-going) and then, when he came back, she clung to his arm so that she didn't topple over again.

35

'It's my fault,' he said when they were outside. 'I didn't realise that the drink would hit you like that.'

'I'm fine,' she told him. 'Absolutely fine.'

'You are that.' He looked down at her and she looked up at him, and then he kissed her, and she didn't know whether she was drunk on alcohol or simply intoxicated by him, but she felt as though she was floating on air.

'I love you.' She'd never intended to say that to him. All the advice in the magazines she read warned against girls saying those words first. But she couldn't help herself. 'I love you.'

'I love you too,' he said, and she knew that she was the happiest person in the world.

They still hadn't slept together. There had been kissing, of course, and holding each other close, and Dominique had sometimes felt as though she wanted to rip Brendan's clothes off and make love to him on the spot. But he hadn't made any moves to take things further. He'd stop and say that when the time was right . . . and then his voice would trail off. She thought about it all the time, wondering if, when he decided the time was right, he might bring her to a luxury hotel and woo her with champagne and chocolates. Not that he had the money for champagne and chocolates – he earned more than her and might have been OK with taxis, but luxury nights away were asking a bit much. It was a nice dream, though.

As they walked through a nearby housing estate, she wondered what it would be like. And she thought that she should really go to a family planning clinic if she was thinking those kind of thoughts. Sleeping with Brendan would be a major step. But getting pregnant would be a major disaster.

She fell off her shoes again despite his steadying arm. He lifted her up and looked at her.

'I think I'm going to have to carry you,' he said.

'You can't,' she told him. 'Your arms will be pulled out of their sockets with the weight of me.'

'You're a little feather.' He scooped her up into his arms. 'That's all. A little feather.'

She was light-headed and giggly. He walked about a hundred

yards and then he stopped. They were at the edge of a large field that bordered the estate. Crossing the field, which was dotted with trees and bushes, gave them a short cut to the main road.

'You're right,' he said breathlessly. 'My arms *are* falling out of their sockets. You're the heaviest little feather I ever knew. I can't make it across there with you. I'll end up stuck in the mud!'

'I'm so sorry.' She kissed him as she slid from his arms and stood beside him. 'I'll try to be a good girl and stay on my own two feet.'

'You're always a good girl.' He grinned at her. 'A good Catholic girl.'

'Brendan!' She sounded insulted and he laughed.

'I like it,' he assured her. 'I like the fact that you've obviously been brought up well.'

'Too bloody well,' she said irritably.

'Ah, not really.' He leaned forward and kissed her on the lips.

She pulled him tightly towards her so that she could feel every part of him through the light jacket and the pink dress. She knew she was still a little dizzy from the drink, but she was even dizzier with desire. She wanted to melt into him completely, be part of him. She didn't want to ever let him go.

'I love you,' she whispered again as they came up for air.

His eyes were gazing directly into hers and she wondered if it was her own desire that she could see mirrored in them. She knew that she was trembling, knew that she wanted him more than anything else in the world.

From the corner of her eye she could see a group of large chestnut trees, their bare branches outlined against the dark sky. She tugged at his hand and led him towards the trees. He followed her until they were among the trees and hidden from both the housing estate and the main road. She could hear the hum of cars in the distance, but much, much louder than any other noise was the sound of her own breathing.

'Domino . . .'

'Ssh.' She kissed him.

He kissed her back, and she felt herself leaning against the biggest of the chestnut trees. She pulled him closer and slid her hand beneath his cotton shirt. His body was warm despite the coldness of the night. She pushed her fingers through the knot of hair on his chest and then traced them to the top of his jeans.

'Domino . . .' He was speaking with an effort. 'You must know how much I want to . . . but this isn't how I planned it.'

'Why does everything have to be planned?' she asked, sliding her fingers inside his jeans.

And then she felt his hand on her thigh, easing the fabric of her skimpy pink dress higher.

Her breath was coming in short gasps. The thought careered through her mind that maybe he was right and maybe there would be a better time. But she didn't want to wait. She wanted him here and now. She didn't care if they were in a field. She didn't care that the rain had started to drizzle down on top of them. And she certainly didn't care that Evelyn would be on her knees and praying for her eternal soul if she knew what her daughter was doing.

Chapter 3

Her pink dress was ruined, her shoes were filthy and she'd lost the chunky white necklace.

She didn't really care about the necklace, and the shoes could be cleaned, but as she looked at the dress in her bedroom (Brendan had dropped her off in the taxi they'd finally managed to hail having walked almost two miles towards the city first), she didn't think that she'd ever be able to wear it again. It was stained, wet from the rain, and the hem had also been ripped by a piece of bark from the chestnut tree. She was horrified by the tear but still elated about having made love to Brendan, even though her elation was tempered by a frisson of worry that, having had sex with her, he might not want to see her again. (The magazines that warned you against saying 'I love you' also warned about men who were 'only after one thing'. None of the ones she'd read had ever mentioned that it might be the woman who'd decide that she wanted to have sex with the man. That she might be the one to forgo the luxury sheets for outdoor passion.)

But she didn't need to worry. Because what Brendan had said afterwards as they'd made their way through the by then muddy field was that it had been wonderful and that she was wonderful. She was the loveliest, most fantastic girl in the world and he adored her.

She couldn't believe that he'd actually said 'adore'. She hoped he meant it. Having him make love to her and say things like that to her were surely worth ruining a dress over. All the same . . . she balled it up and shoved it into a plastic bag, which she pushed to the back of her wardrobe . . . it would be an awful waste of money to only get one wear out of it!

She slid between the sheets of her single bed and exhaled slowly. It had been worth it really. She was Brendan's girl. His lucky charm. His lucky Domino. That was what he'd called her just after his muffled cry of pleasure. My lucky, lucky Domino.

It was the sound of Evelyn vacuuming the stairs that woke her the following morning. She groaned softly, because the noise had set off an unwelcome pounding at the back of her head. It was a few minutes before she felt able to open her eyes again, and when she did, she looked at the old-fashioned alarm clock beside her bed, which was showing almost eleven. She blinked a couple of times – eleven was unforgivably late in the Brady household. Evelyn was always up by seven so that she could go to eight o'clock Mass each morning, and Seamus's idea of a lie-in at the weekends was to get up when he heard Evelyn leaving the house.

Dominique pushed the covers from her bed. She was sore, and her legs ached as she walked over to her small dressing table. She took a deep breath and looked at her face in the oval mirror. She didn't look any different. Her eyes weren't brighter, her hair wasn't shinier, her face didn't glow. But inside she felt completely different. She'd made love to her boyfriend. She was a grown-up at last.

As Dominique walked out on to the landing, her dressing gown wrapped around her, Evelyn switched off the vacuum cleaner.

'You came home very late last night,' she said.

'It was a party,' said Dominique. 'It wasn't over till late.'

'I'm sure it was over well before four,' said Evelyn. 'Which was the time you got in at.'

'It took ages to find a taxi,' said Dominique. 'They're not exactly plentiful in the wilds of Clondalkin, you know.'

Evelyn looked at her sceptically. 'You mustn't have been looking very hard.'

'I swear to God,' said Dominique. 'We were standing at the side of the road for hours!'

Which was almost true. She'd had blisters on her feet by the time Brendan had stopped a passing taxi with a piercing whistle. (That ability had impressed Dominique immensely. She'd never known anyone who could actually whistle loud enough to stop a taxi before.)

'You look a wreck,' said Evelyn.

'It was raining,' Dominique reminded her. 'We got soaked.'

'I told you you should have worn a coat.'

Dominique shrugged impatiently.

'I'm doing a wash this afternoon,' said Evelyn. 'If you want your dress and jacket done, put them in the laundry basket.'

Dominique had no intention of doing any such thing. She grunted non-committally at her mother and went downstairs to make toast.

She washed the dress herself the next morning when both Evelyn and Seamus were at ten o'clock Mass. She'd gone into town after breakfast on Saturday, having retrieved the dress from the wardrobe and hidden it under her mattress, just in case her mother found it. She'd left the jacket – which had a long green streak on the shoulder – on a hanger suspended from the handle of her wardrobe. When she'd come home, Evelyn had asked her about the dress and she said that she'd forgotten to put it in the laundry.

'I looked in your room,' said Evelyn. 'It wasn't with the jacket. You didn't put that in either, and I'm not sure that mark is going to come out.'

'Won't it?' Dominique was shaking inside. She'd been hoping that the mark on the jacket would distract Evelyn from asking about the dress. She didn't care that she'd had sex with Brendan but she certainly didn't want her mother to know. Especially that it had been outdoors in the rain. Evelyn would think the wrong things about it. She'd think of it as cheap and nasty, just because it didn't fit in with her picture of what sex should be. (Beneath the sheets with the light out, Dominique was certain of that.) But what had happened between her and Brendan hadn't been cheap and nasty. It had been wonderful. And, she had to admit, there had been a certain excitement in doing something in an empty field with the (admittedly slight) chance of being caught that (a) in her mother's eyes was a sin and (b) was usually done indoors. All of those things, as well as the fact that it had been with Brendan, and she was madly and crazily in love with Brendan, had made it an experience to remember.

Evelyn had looked at her impatiently while all these thoughts had gone through her mind. Dominique had told her that the dress had probably slipped off the hanger or something and she'd wash it herself later, all the time wishing that her domineering mother would butt out of her life. Also, she thought, it wasn't right that Evelyn should just walk into her room whenever she felt like it. It was her room, not Evelyn's. Her private space.

Of course, she admitted to herself as she hung the dress on the line to dry, it wasn't unusual for Evelyn to come into her room to pick up her washing, and normally she didn't mind. It was only guilt that was making her feel that her mother was overstepping the mark. Nevertheless, things had changed. She would have to set boundaries that Evelyn couldn't cross.

She looked at the dress as it flapped on the line. The stains were gone but the rip was very obvious. Her mother was bound to want to know what had caused it.

'So, how did it happen?' Evelyn asked as she examined the rip.

'I'm not sure,' lied Dominique. 'Maybe when we were dancing.'

'It'll be hard to mend.'

'Impossible,' said Dominique.

'Oh, I'll manage it,' said Evelyn. 'You young ones think nothing of throwing clothes out, but it was different in my day.'

Dominique hoped she wasn't going to launch into one of her favourite 'in my day' speeches, in which life had been tough beyond belief and there'd been none of the luxuries of the 1980s. Besides, it was ludicrous to say that Dominique threw out clothes. Maybe she didn't have to darn socks like Evelyn used to, but she couldn't afford to buy new things that often.

'Thanks,' she said, her tone offhand.

'I told you it was unsuitable in the first place,' said Evelyn. 'There's nothing to it. It's no wonder it ripped.'

'But it's lovely,' Dominique told her.

Evelyn looked sceptical. 'Hmm,' she said. 'I can't see why you spend your hard-earned money on something so unsubstantial.'

'Didn't you ever want to?' asked Dominique with genuine curiosity. 'Didn't you ever want to wear a dress that was just a silly bit of fabric simply because it was gorgeous?'

'I never had the opportunity.' Evelyn was looking in her big wicker sewing basket. 'My life wasn't like that.'

'How about now?' suggested Dominique. Critically she appraised her mother's lilac tweed skirt and blue cotton blouse with its ruffled collar. 'You're not that old. You could look more . . . more . . .'

'Appearances mean nothing.' Evelyn took a spool of thread from her basket. 'It's all superficial. You should know that.'

Dominique nodded. But she couldn't help thinking that Evelyn, in her late forties, looked decades older than Maeve Mulligan's mother, who enjoyed Majorcan holidays and going to the pub every Friday night. It didn't matter that there was only a couple of years between them; Evelyn was an entire generation older in attitude than Kay Mulligan.

I don't want to be like her, she thought. I don't want to think like an old person when I'm not. And I want to wear fashionable clothes that make me feel good. All the time.

'Did Brendan ring you today?' asked Evelyn as she threaded a needle.

Dominique shook her head. 'He was meeting a friend who's coming up from Cork for a job interview tomorrow,' she said.

'Don't do anything stupid.' Evelyn's voice was suddenly taut. 'Don't let yourself down with him, Dominique.'

'I don't know what you're talking about,' said Dominique as dismissively as she could, even though she could feel a cold sweat enveloping her.

'Of course you do.' Evelyn slipped a thimble on to her finger. 'You're easily led, Dominique.'

'No I'm not.'

'You are. You do things because you think they'll make people like you. But they have to like you for what's inside.'

'You have such a low opinion of me!' cried Dominique. 'And you don't know me at all.' She clamped down on the guilt that was wrapping itself around her. Her mother couldn't possibly know that she'd had sex with Brendan. She couldn't possibly know that she was feeling elated, excited, in love – and scared too, because even as they'd started walking back to the main road to get a taxi, the awful thought had struck her that she could be pregnant – she hadn't been to the family planning clinic yet; that would have been admitting that she wanted him to sleep with her.

He hadn't had any condoms, and she wouldn't have known what to do with one if he had. After all, chemists didn't regularly stock them. The priests and politicians were still trying to pretend that premarital sex didn't happen in Ireland. They were still in the Dark Ages compared to the rest of Europe.

Brendan had apologised about the condoms, had said that he wasn't prepared because he hadn't imagined that she would want . . . and she'd shut him up with a kiss and then he'd said not to worry, he'd be careful. She'd wondered fleetingly about that, wondered where and how and with whom he'd had the experience to know how to be careful. But she still hadn't stopped, because she'd been totally and utterly overwhelmed by her desire for him.

All the same, she thought now, her heart hammering in her chest, if I *am* pregnant, if Brendan got it wrong, my mother will kill me. She knew that Evelyn's reaction should really be the least of her worries, but it was what concerned her most of all. In her head she composed a quick prayer to St Jude (obviously she wasn't a lost cause yet, so praying to the patron of lost causes might be a bit extreme, but better to be safe than sorry as far as saintly interventions went). Please let me not be up the spout, she asked mentally. I'll go to the family planning clinic next week and go on the pill. It occurred to her, as she finished the prayer, that St Jude might not be in a receptive mood. After all, he was a saint and she was asking him to condone a sin. It was a tricky situation to be in.

'I don't have a low opinion of you. But men aren't like women,' Evelyn was saying now. 'They don't always think with their heads and their hearts, you know.'

Dominique couldn't quite believe that Evelyn was having this conversation with her, however obliquely. Her mother never discussed relationships and sex. When Dominique had turned thirteen, Evelyn had given her a copy of *Sex Education: Training in Chastity*, which hadn't exactly been helpful. She'd learned more from the girls talking in school and from the teen magazines she liked to read than she had from Evelyn's book. Dominique always thought that Evelyn found the whole business distasteful. She knew that children couldn't imagine their parents ever having sex, but the idea of Evelyn and Seamus doing what she and Brendan had done was utterly impossible to comprehend, and the idea of them enjoying it was beyond imagining. Doing it at least twice, too! She shuddered.

'Don't do anything stupid,' repeated her mother. 'Remember everything I've ever told you. Remember the Church's teaching. Remember that one day you'll want to get married and have children and that you'll want to have a good life with the right man.'

'Yeah, right, I'll remember all that,' said Dominique. She got up and went to her bedroom. And remember, she told herself as she lay on her bed and stared at the ceiling, that you've already met the man you want to marry. That you have made love to him and that it was wonderful And that he's already said he loves you too.

He phoned the following evening while she was still at work, and so she didn't get to talk to him till the day after that, when she called him back.

'I forgot you were working late yesterday,' he said.

'It wasn't busy,' she told him. 'I was going to try to ring you from the restaurant, but Melanie Lynch is nearly as bad as Kirsten for throwing her weight around and not letting you grab a minute here or there.'

'I miss you,' he said.

'And I miss you.'

'I had a great time on Friday.'

'Me too.'

'I have to see you again. Really soon.'

Dominique felt a rush of warmth flood the pit of her stomach. 'Why's that?'

'You know why,' he said. 'You were amazing. And for your first time too . . . I didn't think . . . You're astonishing, Domino. You really are.'

She flushed with pleasure. 'Everything about it was astonishing and amazing,' she said. 'And I loved every second.'

'But we should do it properly,' Brendan told her. 'I had a plan, you know.'

'Really?'

'Yes. I thought I'd be taking a shy little maiden somewhere great and initiating her into the secrets of fantastic sex. But you weren't one bit shy, my little Domino. And you were fantastic.'

'Is that all right?' She worried suddenly that he thought she was too forward. Too tarty. Too slutty.

'Oh yes,' he assured her.

'When can we meet?' she asked.

'Tonight? You can come back to my place. The other lads will be out.'

She realised that she was shaking thinking about it. Shaking because she wanted it so much.

'OK.'

'Usual place for a couple of drinks,' said Brendan. 'And afterwards . . .'

'Yeah. Afterwards . . .' She replaced the phone. She couldn't wait.

It was better the second time for a whole heap of reasons, but principally because this time she was lying on a bed, the rain wasn't dripping down her collar and her feet weren't crippled from shoes that were too tight. Brendan took more time, too, to kiss her and stroke her and do things to her that she liked, so that she was quivering with desire. (She'd read the phrase in one of the historical romances she liked to read and she'd often wondered what it really meant, but after that night with Brendan, she knew.) And this time he had asked if she was OK with condoms and she'd said of course because she'd read that they had a nearly ninety per cent success rate, which was pretty good. She wasn't worried about the other ten per cent. Brendan had called her his lucky Domino. Lucky Dominos didn't get caught out.

She was also able to freshen up in the bathroom afterwards, although she wasn't sure how much of a bonus that actually was – she couldn't help thinking that her idea of a clean bathroom clashed fairly fundamentally with how four single men saw it. She'd had to rinse out the sink before she could use it, and she opted not to take advantage of a bar of green Palmolive soap that was caked with stubble.

46

When she returned to the small kitchen, Brendan had made her a cup of tea. She was touched by the gesture, even though the tea was far too strong for her taste. She sipped it cautiously, determined to drink it all. Brendan himself was swigging from a bottle of beer, which he'd taken from the small fridge, and turning over the sports pages of the evening paper. He'd started to tell her about Cork's great win in the all-Ireland hurling final, and she was trying to look interested, when the door opened and another man walked into the room. Brendan introduced him to her as Eamonn, who came from the same area of Cork as he did and who was an electrician.

'You're a fine-looking girl,' Eamonn told her. 'Jeez, Brendan, you get all the good ones, pal.'

Dominique flushed with pleasure. It seemed to her that her life was getting better every single day. She liked her job, she had a great boyfriend, they were having incredible sex and other men thought she was a fine-looking girl. Maybe she was becoming more attractive, she thought. Maybe she was one of those people who were late bloomers. She flicked her hair out of her eyes with the same gesture that Emma Walsh used to use, and laughed.

She fully intended to go to the family planning clinic and fulfil her promise to St Jude, but she was very nervous about it. What if someone she knew saw her? What if she actually met someone she knew? What if her mother got to hear about it? She told herself that she was an adult woman in a serious relationship taking sensible precautions. She knew that in most countries girls were having sex younger and younger these days – being a virgin past your early teens was practically shameful in some of them. So it was utterly ridiculous of her to feel like a naughty schoolgirl about such an important part of her life. But the problem was that thinking about family planning was admitting to herself that she was having sex for fun, and she hadn't been brought up to think of sex as something you did for fun, no matter how the rest of the world viewed it. She hated Evelyn for having made her feel this way. She wished she could feel differently.

But she couldn't. She decided to leave going to the family

planning clinic a little longer. Brendan had the condoms, with their ninety per cent success rate, after all.

Gabriel came back to Ireland for a couple of weeks, much to Evelyn and Seamus's delight. He was attending a conference in Maynooth but returned home each evening. Dominique told him that he was looking well on his time in Valladolid. He'd acquired a tan, which made him look even more handsome, especially when he wore white T-shirts and blue jeans. He didn't, for one second, look like a priest. More than ever she wondered how any sane and rational God could have given Gabriel all the good-looking genes in the family. (Brendan's constant assertion that she was a fine thing didn't delude her into thinking that she actually was.)

Hearing that Gabriel was in the country again, Emma Walsh called around. Dominique, who hadn't seen her for a few weeks, realised that Emma had clearly raided the beauty counter before coming around to the house. She looked like she'd stepped off the cover of a glossy magazine, with her heavily kohled eyes, her dramatic eyelashes and her highly glossed lips. Her chestnut hair had been teased and moussed into studied messiness and was held back on one side by a diamanté clip. She wore two chunky diamanté crucifixes in her ears and a large crucifix with a long string of beads around her neck; she was dressed in a short denim skirt over black lace leggings, a cropped black T-shirt and a faded denim jacket covered in sequins. On her feet were black ankle boots. On her hands, black lace fingerless gloves.

When she opened the door and let Emma in, Dominique couldn't help thinking that the Madonna look was wildly inappropriate for anyone trying to attract her brother, but Gabriel smiled at Emma and said that it was nice to see her again. Emma sat down in the armchair opposite him, crossed her legs, and asked a litany of questions about Valladolid and his life there. Every so often she recrossed her legs and ran her fingers through her hair, which Dominique found extremely funny. But she grew bored listening to Emma's inane questions and Gabriel's polite answers, and eventually left them alone and went up to her room, where she filed her nails and painted them with pearly pink varnish. (She was very proud of her nails. She'd stopped biting them shortly after meeting Brendan, and they were now a neat, even length.) When she came downstairs again, Emma had left. Dominique hadn't heard her go, and she was peeved at her friend for not even bothering to say goodbye.

'When did she leave?' she asked Gabriel, who was still in the living room although now reading the newspaper.

'About ten minutes ago,' he replied.

'And did she swear undying love to you?'

He smiled. 'It's just a crush,' he said. 'She'll find someone else.'

'So you'd think.' Dominique shook her head. 'Honestly, I don't know what she sees in you.'

'Thanks,' said Gabriel.

'Oh, you know what I mean,' Dominique said. 'She's really pretty and everything and at school she had all the guys panting after her, but she's got it into her head that you're her one true love or something.'

'She's lacking in self-confidence,' said Gabriel. 'Telling herself she's in love with me means she doesn't have to risk getting hurt in a real relationship.'

'That's a load of shite,' Dominique told him baldly. 'She's not in the slightest bit lacking in self-confidence. She knows she's gorgeous. She's always had half a dozen different boyfriends on the go at any one time.'

'Quantity and quality aren't the same thing.'

'I know that,' said Dominique. 'But you're wrong about Mizz Walsh. I think she's superconfident.'

'You're very naïve.'

'No I'm not.' Dominique made a face at him. 'She's my friend, not yours. And I know what she's like.'

She went out of the house and pulled the door closed behind her. She was luckier than Emma. She had a real boyfriend who was the love of her life. And later that night she'd be having great sex with him, which at the moment was something Emma Walsh could only dream about.

It was actually easier to find pregnancy tests in the chemist's than condoms, which had only recently become more freely available over the counter in Ireland. There was quite a choice of tests, but she just grabbed the first one off the shelf. She didn't really believe she was pregnant. She reckoned she was just stressed because she'd chickened out of the family planning clinic again. She couldn't understand why she was so nervous about it. It was the sensible thing to do, after all. But she hadn't gone, and now she was late; but being pregnant simply wasn't possible. Brendan had promised her, and he always kept his promises.

They'd made love half a dozen times altogether and only once without a condom. So it must have been that one time, against the tree in the rain, that had been the one to leave her staring at the two pink lines in front of her and realising that she was going to have a baby.

There was a part of her that didn't believe the test, a part of her that said that it was impossible, simply impossible, for her to be pregnant. She wasn't the right sort of person. She didn't go to loads of parties and have flings with different boyfriends. She didn't live the kind of life girls she thought would get pregnant lived. Girls like the Nikkis and Cara and Emma. They were the party girls. They were the ones who gambled with their futures. Not her. There had to be a mistake. She did the test again. And again. And then she did it one more time, just to be sure.

She couldn't breathe. She was getting ready to meet Brendan, coating her eyelashes with Maybelline Great Lash so that they appeared wider and bigger, because she knew that he liked her eyes like that, and then, quite suddenly, as she looked at her reflection, she realised that she wasn't breathing. She opened her mouth and tried to suck in some air, but she couldn't. She could feel herself starting to tremble and she tried to steady herself by resting her hands on her narrow dressing table. But she couldn't feel her hands and she couldn't feel the dressing table and she still couldn't breathe.

It was Evelyn who ran up the stairs to Dominique's room when she heard the loud thud and the clatter of falling objects, so it was Evelyn who Dominique saw when she opened her eyes.

50

'What happened?' she asked.

'You tell me.' Evelyn looked at her with concern. 'Did you fall? Bang your head?'

And then it all came back to Dominique and she remembered that she was pregnant and that she was going to tell Brendan that night but she hadn't been able to breathe and that was why she'd fainted. And she knew that even if she could breathe, she wouldn't have much time for it, because if she told her mother she was pregnant, Evelyn would kill her.

But she didn't need to tell her. Suddenly Evelyn stared at her with knowledge dawning in her eyes.

'Is there something I need to know?' she demanded.

'Like what?' Dominique could only mumble as she struggled to her feet and then sank into the old armchair that had been donated to her room a few years earlier.

'You know what,' said Evelyn.

Dominique said nothing.

'I'll get you some water.' The concern had gone out of Evelyn's voice, replaced by an undercurrent of hardness. She left the bedroom and returned a few seconds later with a glass of water. Dominique sipped it slowly.

'So?' Evelyn stared at her.

'Leave me alone,' said Dominique.

'You collapsed in your bedroom,' said her mother, 'and I want to know why.'

'You've guessed why.'

'Tell me.'

'What do you want me to say?'

'I want you to tell me if there's something wrong with you.'

'Depends on what you mean by wrong,' said Dominique.

She knew she was playing for time. Not wanting to have to say it out loud. The thing was, being pregnant and unmarried wasn't the absolutely major deal it had been ten years earlier, when Dominique remembered Sandra Sheehan, from three doors down, being sent away somewhere to have her baby in secret. She had heard the whispered conversations about Sandra, a pretty teenager who'd babysat her occasionally when she was smaller. All she'd known then was that

Sandra was 'in trouble'. She had assumed that 'in trouble' meant the same to Sandra as it did to her – that she'd broken something or told a lie or been disobedient. It wasn't until a couple of years later that she realised exactly what sort of trouble Sandra Sheehan had been in. She hadn't seen Sandra since. She'd no idea where she was now. But she did know that her baby had been adopted.

Yet only a few years after Sandra's pregnancy, Minnie Carpenter, from the other end of the street, had – as Evelyn once said – flaunted her pregnancy and her single status and nobody had said a word. So it was OK now, wasn't it, to be pregnant and not married? It wasn't such a terrible thing. It wasn't so awful.

She swallowed hard and told Evelyn that she was expecting a baby. And her mother slapped her across the face.

'I warned you!' Evelyn's face was white with fury. 'You stupid, ungrateful, sinful girl. I warned you!'

Dominique opened her mouth but didn't get the chance to say anything.

'You were brought up properly,' Evelyn raged. 'We taught you right from wrong. You were raised in a loving, Christian home with Christian values. And this is how you repay us. By dressing like a tramp and sleeping with the first boy you meet.'

'It's not about repaying you!' Dominique found her voice again. 'It's about me, and how I want to live my life. And it's about Brendan too.'

'Oh, don't be so bloody silly!' cried Evelyn. 'You think he loves you? You think he really wants to marry you?'

'Yes.' The tears were coursing down Dominique's face. 'Yes he loves me and yes he'll marry me.'

'And if you believe that, you're even more stupid than I thought,' said Evelyn.

Her hands were shaking as she picked up the phone and called O'Neill's bar, which was where they'd arranged to meet that night. She was left waiting for five minutes, and she thought that perhaps Brendan wasn't there yet, but then she heard a rustling noise and the receiver was picked up and she heard him say, 'Domino?'

'Hi.' Her voice was shaky.

'Domino. Are you all right?'

'Yes,' she whispered. 'I'm OK.'

'You don't sound it. Why aren't you here?'

'I . . . wasn't well earlier,' she said.

'What was the matter? You sound dreadful now.'

'Oh, Brendan . . .' She sniffed. 'I'm sorry.'

There was a silence at the other end of the phone. And then he replaced the receiver.

She didn't want to admit that Evelyn had been right. That she'd been a naïve, stupid girl who'd got carried away and slept with her boyfriend and made a basic, basic mistake. She was supposed to be more intelligent than that. But clearly she wasn't. She'd managed to ruin her life before it had even started.

She was surprised by the ringing of the doorbell, and even more surprised to hear Brendan's raised voice. Evelyn had answered the door, and she was clearly giving him a piece of her mind.

'I'm here to see Domino,' she heard him say. 'If you don't want to let me in to the house, then tell her to come out here to me.'

She opened her bedroom door and came downstairs.

'Talk then.' Evelyn looked between them. 'Talk for all the good it will do.'

'I'm sorry,' said Dominique again as she led him into the unwelcoming front room. 'She's furious with me. I've let her down, you see. All of her parish friends . . .' She shrugged.

'First of all, let's get things straight,' said Brendan. 'Have I guessed correctly? Are you pregnant?'

'Oh God, I'm so sorry about that too.' She rubbed at her eyes. 'It's my problem.'

'Do you have such a low opinion of me?' Brendan looked at her intently. 'Do you think I'm just going to walk away?'

'I'll understand,' she said. 'It wasn't as though we were . . . well, you know.'

'Hey, Domino, I told you I loved you. I meant it.'

'Brendan, I'm pregnant. It's a whole new ball game.'

'True. But if we'd got married the day I met you, people would be asking us now if there was "any news".'

Her smile was watery.

'This isn't the way I wanted it to be,' he admitted. 'But I love you, Dominique Brady. You're the girl for me. And I want kids. Lots of 'em. If we've had an early start, so what?'

She stared at him.

'You said you loved me too.' He looked at her with the same slightly anxious look he'd worn when he'd first asked her out. 'Did you mean it?'

'Of course I meant it,' she said. 'It's just that . . . I thought that guys didn't want to settle down. That you wanted to kind of play the field and stuff.'

'I'm twenty-eight,' he said. 'I've given the field a bit of a going-over already.'

She laughed shakily.

'So how about it?' he said. 'How about cheering up your ma and da and telling them that we're engaged and that they don't have to worry about their future grandchild? Though I have to say, Domino, they're the most old-fashioned people I've ever met in my entire life. They haven't moved out of the fifties, you know.'

'I know.'

'Well?'

She'd always imagined that a marriage proposal would be more romantic than this. But, she told herself, it was being proposed to by the right man that was the important thing. And so she smiled at him and told him that he was the only man in the world for her and that she loved him with all her heart. And then he kissed her in the drab front room, while two generations of Bradys stared unblinkingly at them from the frames of their black and white photos.

Chapter 4

The wedding was arranged for the following month. Dominique rang Maeve and asked her to be her bridesmaid, and Maeve shrieked with an excitement that was a little more muted when Dominique told her about her pregnancy, although she didn't tell her about the horrible, horrible night when her mother had found out and when she'd feared that Brendan had hung up on her for ever.

'Of course it was a shock,' she admitted to Maeve now. 'And I know I should've been more careful. Even when we were . . . you know . . . there was something in the back of my mind telling me that I might regret it. But I don't, Maeve. I really don't.'

'I realise you're madly in love with him,' said Maeve. 'All the same, Dominique – a baby!'

'It's not ideal,' agreed Dominique. 'But the thing is, I love him and I want to get married to him and he loves me too. He really does. So what's the point in waiting?'

'He's a bogger, though.'

'He's the sweetest, nicest person you ever met,' Dominique told her. 'I want to marry him, Maeve. I really do. It's nothing to do with being pregnant.'

'Fair enough, so,' said Maeve. 'I bet everyone in our class in school would be shocked if they heard you were getting married.'

'I bet they would too.'

'So where are you going to live?'

'We've bought a house.' Dominique couldn't keep the excitement out of her voice. 'It's in Firhouse, near Templeogue. Brendan knows the builder and we're getting a really good deal on it. Although he says that when he makes lots of money from his own construction company, we'll move somewhere bigger and even better.'

'You have it all worked out.'

'Yes,' said Dominique. 'We have.'

Gabriel wrote to say that he would come back from Valladolid for the wedding. His letter to Dominique told her that all of God's children were loved, even those who had slipped off the path. She gritted her teeth as she read it and then screwed it into a tight ball before throwing it in the bin. She didn't want to hear Gabriel's pious thoughts. At least she was living her life, not locking herself away in a monastery or whatever, doing nothing but praying. Anyway, she thought with a sudden flash of amusement, between the prayers of her parents and those of Gabriel, her immortal soul was probably just fine. If she believed in all that claptrap. Which she didn't.

Brendan brought Dominique to Cork to meet his family the day after he'd given her a simple gold engagement ring with a small solitaire diamond.

Dominique, stressed by her mother's disapproval and her father's grim looks, was delighted to escape from Dublin for a weekend, although she was nervous about meeting the Delahaye family for the first time.

'Your parents might hate me,' she said.

'They won't hate you,' Brendan assured her. 'They'll be delighted to meet you.'

Dominique wasn't so sure about that. No Irish mother liked to think that her son was marrying a woman because she was pregnant, even if he insisted that they were going to get married anyway. Dominique feared that Lily Delahaye would think that she'd trapped her son and that she'd despise her for it. It was bad enough that her own mother thought of her as some kind of immoral trollop, without her future mother-in-law harbouring the same notions. But she didn't say this to Brendan.

The day they travelled down to Cork was warm and sunny, and Dominique felt unexpectedly light-hearted as the train wound its way through the unfolding countryside with its patchwork of green fields. She'd been to Cork a number of times on holiday with her parents, and she liked it (although, as a Dubliner, she could never admit to that). She noticed, though, that Brendan's accent grew broader with every passing mile, so that by the time they arrived at Kent station, to be greeted by his younger brother, Greg, who was picking them up, she could hardly understand a word he was saying.

'Ah, don't be worrying about it,' he joked when she told him he was morphing into a true culchie before her very eyes. 'You'll soon pick it up, my little Dublin jackeen.'

Greg Delahaye was six years younger than his brother. He was more reserved than Brendan, but nevertheless he gave Dominique a welcoming hug and told her that they'd heard a lot about her and he was delighted to finally meet her. Dominique felt herself really relax for the first time since she'd discovered she was pregnant, as the two brothers chatted on the drive to the bungalow in the small coastal town of Castlecannon where the family had lived for generations. Greg reminded her of Gabriel, but without her brother's quiet assurance. He was a gentle sort of man, who tried to draw her into their conversation, although since much of it revolved around the fate of the Cork County Gaelic football and hurling teams, she wasn't able to add any words of wisdom. Nevertheless, she made a few jokes about culchie games, which made Greg laugh and Brendan say that he'd eventually convert her. Despite the light-hearted chat in the car, though, she tensed up again when they arrived at the house and clutched her overnight bag tentatively while she waited for Brendan to open the front door.

She followed Brendan and Greg into a wide hallway, which led into a large, bright living room bathed in sunlight that poured through a long picture window with a view towards the sea. The upper halves of the walls were rag-rolled in a pale orange paint, which reflected the light, while the lower halves were covered in mauve wallpaper. A wide border ran around the middle of the walls, dividing the two colour schemes. The carpet was orange with swirls of mauve and the curtains were mauve with orange flecks. There was a large painting of a sailing boat over the mantelpiece, while the other walls were hung with family photographs. It was very, very different to the pale floral wallpaper and grey twist carpet of the house in Drimnagh.

'You must be Domino, lovely to see you.' The woman who'd been sitting on the mauve sofa, a magazine in her hand, stood up. She was tall, and was wearing a red and white shell suit and white trainers. Her fair hair was cut in a bubble perm and her glasses, although the frames were blue, were similar to Dominique's own.

'Mrs Delahaye?' she said doubtfully.

'Lily,' said the other woman. 'Mrs Delahaye makes me feel ancient.'

Dominique knew that Brendan's mother was a few years older than her own, but she never would have guessed it. Although Lily Delahaye's face had more lines than Evelyn's, her easy smile and made-up face made her seem younger.

'And this is Maurice,' she said, indicating the man who had just walked into the room through another door. 'Brendan's dad.'

Maurice Delahaye was an older version of his son. He had the same strong build, the same curly hair and the same blue eyes. His face was more weathered than Brendan's and his hair was streaked with grey, but they were very clearly father and son. Looking at them side by side as Brendan hugged his father, Dominique suddenly felt connected to both of them through the baby she was carrying. She imagined her child running along the beach with them; pictured them sitting on the rocks together or walking along the road side by side.

'Pleased to meet you.' Maurice held his hand out to her and she grasped it.

'June and Barry will be coming for dinner later,' said Lily. 'Roy's out on the boat but he'll be back soon.'

Dominique knew that June was Brendan's sister, younger than him by a couple of years, and that Barry was her husband. Roy, the youngest in the family, was, at eighteen, just a few months younger than Dominique herself.

'You'll probably want to put your things away and freshen up,' said Lily. 'Brendan, we've put the two of you in the guest room. Your old one is too small and it's a bit late for you to be in separate rooms, isn't it?'

Dominique felt herself blush, but Brendan laughed and his mother winked.

'A bit of a wash-up would be good,' said Brendan. 'And I'm looking forward to some home cooking.'

'Get away with you.' Lily grinned at him. 'That's all I'm good for as far as you're concerned. Filling you with food.'

'The way to a man's heart,' said Brendan.

'Something you'll need to remember, pet,' Lily told Dominique. 'He's a ferocious eater. Loves his spuds. Likes them well mashed with a knob of butter and a decent sprinkling of salt and pepper.'

'Right.' Dominique was a little overwhelmed by the information. She didn't cook very much at home, and Evelyn never encouraged her. Evelyn herself – although she wouldn't admit it – wasn't great in the kitchen. Her mashed potatoes were always lumpy.

'Come on then.' Brendan put his arm around Dominique and steered her out of the living room. 'Let's go upstairs.'

They made love before dinner, even though Dominique was terrified that someone would hear them.

'But that's half the excitement,' said Brendan as he propped himself up on his elbows above her. 'And the other half is knowing that you're the loveliest girl in the whole world.'

It was the only time she'd ever felt uncomfortable making love to him, although hearing him say that she was the loveliest girl in the world made her melt inside. Afterwards she changed into a prim navy-blue dress with white piping on the collar and high-heeled shoes, while Brendan watched her in amusement.

'Where on earth did you get that outfit?' he asked.

'Don't you like it?' She looked anxious.

'It's very nice,' he said. 'So not you, though.'

'I can't wear miniskirts and stuff for dinner with your mother,' said Dominique.

Brendan guffawed. 'She wouldn't mind. Really. She's not into fashion. She's a sporty kind of woman herself, as you probably noticed. She's the manager of the under-sevens football team.'

'All the same,' Dominique smoothed the bodice of the dress, 'I want her to know that I'm a respectable girl and that I can look nice.'

Brendan guffawed again and Dominique blushed.

He hugged her. 'You look absolutely lovely,' he assured her. 'No matter what you wear.'

'Thanks,' she said, and he kissed her on the nape of her neck.

She'd heard people arriving as she'd been brushing the blue eye shadow on to her lids, and so she wasn't surprised to see June and her husband in the living room when they came down. She was surprised, however, to see that June was also pregnant, although given the size of her bump, she was a lot closer to having her baby.

'It's due next month,' said June after she'd said hello. 'And the sooner the bloody better. I hate being pregnant. It's terrible.'

'I don't mind it,' confessed Dominique. 'I feel fine and my skin has improved no end.'

'Lucky you.' June eased herself on to a chair. 'But don't count your chickens yet. Wait until you're my size. It's the piles that get you.'

'June!' Brendan, Barry and Lily all spoke at the same time. 'Spare us the disgusting details,' added Barry. 'I know I get to hear them – to live them, even – but nobody else should have to suffer.'

'Domino needs to know,' said June. 'No point in her thinking it's all a bed of roses.'

'I don't think that,' said Dominique.

'I did.' June's voice was grim. 'Not a bloody bother on me for the first three months, even though everyone says that's when you're sickest. But since then – nothing but trouble.'

'It's nearly over now, darling,' Lily told her comfortingly. 'And you'll have a lovely baby at the end of it.'

'Huh.' June didn't look mollified. 'I hope he or she is suitably grateful.'

'None of your children are ever grateful,' said Lily. 'Now come on, let's go into the dining room. Roy!' She raised her voice. 'Get yourself down here now.'

There couldn't have been a bigger contrast than that between the Bradys and the Delahayes, thought Dominique. Maurice, Lily and their children talked incessantly, arguing and interrupting each other constantly throughout the meal. They'd tucked in without saying grace, too, which rather shocked her even though she knew it shouldn't. After all, nobody in American Burger ever said grace before attacking their hundred per cent pure beef meal. But at home, around the dinner table, Dominique was accustomed to saying grace. And it felt wrong to start eating without it. So she'd hesitated for a split second while everyone else started, muttering it quickly and silently to herself, and only then helping herself to vegetables from the big tureen in the centre of the table.

The food was great, and Dominique couldn't understand why the Delahayes talked instead of eating. She concentrated on her plate and on listening to the conversation rather than getting too involved herself, while Brendan and Maurice discussed how busy the nearby port town of Ringaskiddy was becoming (Maurice had worked at the ferry terminal since the 1970s), and Lily and June talked about June's recent decoration of the nursery at her house near Cork city. Later, Roy, Brendan, Maurice and Barry argued over Cork's chances of winning another all-Ireland hurling medal, with Greg interjecting from time to time to keep the peace.

'You're very quiet, pet,' said Lily to Dominique when there was a brief lull in the conversation. 'Are you all right? Would you like some more food?'

'Oh, gosh, no thanks, Mrs Delahaye,' said Dominique. 'I'll explode if I eat any more.'

'I hope not. There's still apple pie. And you've got to call me Lily.'

'Of course. Lily.' Dominique felt shy about using the other woman's name. 'And just a sliver of apple pie for me. I'm sure it's gorgeous but I really am stuffed.'

Lily nodded, although her idea of a sliver and Dominique's differed greatly. But the apple pie was as delicious as the roast beef had been earlier.

After dinner they sat around and chatted with the TV on in the background. Lily said that they were looking forward to the wedding and to meeting Seamus and Evelyn, and Dominique smiled tightly and replied that she was sure her parents couldn't wait to meet them either. 'Although,' she added, feeling that she owed it to the

Delahayes to be perfectly honest with them, 'my parents aren't at all happy about me and Brendan.'

Beside her, Brendan frowned. 'I thought they were fine about it,' he said. 'I thought that us getting married meant everything was OK.'

'To a point,' agreed Dominique. 'But my mam thinks we were wrong to . . . well, you know. And she finds it hard to forgive me.'

'She'll be grand after the baby is born,' Lily assured her. 'And lookit, child, we weren't exactly delighted ourselves. But the truth is that our lump of a son should be married by now and so we're glad you're going to take him on.' She grinned widely and winked at Dominique. 'And if you need any advice, or if he annoys you in any way, you only have to give me a shout and I'll knock some manners into him.'

Dominique laughed. She loved the Delahayes. She loved Brendan. She loved her life.

Chapter 5

It was a small wedding.

As Dominique walked up the aisle of the church on her father's arm and saw Brendan at the altar waiting for her, she was filled with a sense of purpose. This was her dream and her ambition, after all. This was what she'd always wanted. To be with someone who loved her and thought she was the most important person in the world. She felt lucky to have found him.

The reception was being held in the Green Isle Hotel on the Naas Road, which was also where the Delahaye family were staying. Dominique had been a little concerned about all of them being in the same hotel, but Brendan had laughed and told her not to worry; his family would be up all night partying, he assured her, whereas they would be leaving them to it and continuing their own party action in their room.

He was right, of course. The Delahayes had a great time at the reception. Greg, as the best man, was heckled occasionally during his speech, and they all whooped and cheered when Brendan got up and uttered the words 'my wife and I', which made Dominique flush with pride and pleasure.

'Honestly,' muttered Evelyn under her breath to Seamus, 'you'd think this was all a great laugh instead of a shotgun wedding because our daughter, who should have known better, shamed herself and us in front of everyone.'

'Times have changed,' Seamus told her. 'People don't care any more.'

'I know,' said Evelyn grimly. 'That's half the problem. If girls were a bit more concerned about the shame, then they wouldn't get themselves into this sort of trouble.'

The Bradys had had the same conversation a hundred times since Dominique had broken the news.

'I wish it had been different,' agreed Seamus. 'But what can we do? She's our daughter and we have to support her.'

'I'd've liked to have given her a good hiding,' said Evelyn.

'It wouldn't have changed anything.'

'It would've made me feel a lot better,' Evelyn told him. 'And what she's marrying into – this crowd. They're so disrespectful too. All this laughing and joking and shouting and stuff.'

'I suppose they want to have a good time,' said Seamus.

'At our expense.'

'They're not my sort of people,' agreed Seamus. 'But we're related now so we'll have to put up with them.'

'That woman is a fright.' Evelyn folded her napkin and dropped it on the table as she glanced down towards Lily Delahaye. 'What does she look like?'

Lily was wearing a canary-yellow chiffon dress with matching yellow shoes and a white hat with yellow and blue feathers in the crown.

'It's an in-your-face outfit all right,' agreed Seamus.

'Restraint is what's needed today,' said Evelyn. 'A bit of humility. Am I the only person to see that?' She frowned as an explosion of laughter erupted from the Delahaye table. 'It's not a joyous occasion.'

'Maybe it is,' suggested Seamus. 'She is married, after all. She's having a baby.'

Evelyn sighed. 'She's taken the joy out of it for me. I had it planned very differently.'

'Will you be happy?'

Gabriel and Dominique were sitting together in a corner of the room while the guests talked among themselves and some of them danced to the music of the DJ that Brendan had organised. It was the first opportunity they'd had to speak together since the wedding ceremony. Gabriel had assisted Father John, which, Dominique had to admit despite herself, had made it all the more special and memorable. She'd struggled to stop an emotional tear from sliding down her cheek when Brendan placed the ring on her finger, and she'd felt, profoundly, a sense of warmth and peace descend on her when Father John had pronounced them man and wife.

'Of course,' she assured him.

'It's a pity it happened like this.'

'Oh, please, give me a break.' She sighed deeply. 'I've heard nothing but that from Mam since I told her. It's a matter of timing, that's all. So what's the big deal?'

'Dominique.' Gabriel's voice was gentle.

'I know I'm a terrible sinful girl in the eyes of the Church, but I am very, very happy,' she said.

'You take it all so lightly,' Gabriel told her. 'It's not just the getting pregnant. I'm not a fool, Dominique. I know these things happen. But getting married and having a baby when you're so young is a very big step. Life is more complicated than you think.'

'I want to get married and I want to have a baby and I know life isn't always easy,' she said. 'I love Brendan and that's what matters.'

'But do you know him?' asked Gabriel.

'Yes,' retorted Dominique. 'I do. And I'll tell you something else, Mr Smarty-Pants-Holier-than-Thou Brady, you shouldn't be trying to put doubts into my mind. Not now. I'm married, and as far as you're concerned it's for life, so what you should actually be doing is giving me hints on how to make my marriage work. Not that I need them, because it will work. Just so's you know!'

Gabriel smiled at her. 'I'm glad you love him,' he said. 'I am, truly. And I know that things aren't the same as they were when Mam and Dad were growing up. I know the world is changing. I just want to be sure that you're happy, Dominique, that's all.'

'I am,' she assured him.

'Hi, Gabriel!' Emma Walsh, looking stunning in a skin-tight red dress with a sequinned bodice and wide shoulders, sat down beside him and prevented Dominique from giving her brother the hug she'd intended. 'How's it going?'

'Great,' said Gabriel. 'And you?'

'Oh, I'm good,' Emma told him. 'Working hard. I was promoted last week.'

'Excellent news,' he said. 'I'm sure you deserved it.'

'Absolutely,' said Emma. 'How are you? How're things in the seminary?'

'No different from when we last spoke,' said Gabriel. 'Still lots to study.'

'Haven't you decided it's all a bit of a waste of time yet?' asked Emma.

'In what way?'

'Well, when you're ordained, you're going to work in a parish, aren't you?'

'I hope so.'

'In which case, most of your time will be spent dealing with crazy old bats arguing over whose turn it is to do a reading at Mass or arrange the flowers for the altar or stuff like that. Or you'll be visiting the sick – that's a big thing in parish work, isn't it? But you know, Gabriel, I visit my gran every week and do her shopping for her and make sure she's taking her medicine and stuff, and I can manage it. You hardly need to do much studying for that.'

'You have a point,' Gabriel agreed. 'But we do need to know and understand scripture. And there's a whole spiritual side to the journey—'

'Oh, bollocks,' said Emma, which made both Gabriel and Dominique open their eyes wide in astonishment. 'Well, honestly,' she continued. 'Spiritual journey my arse. What you need, Gabriel Brady, is someone to put their arms around you and say that they love you.'

Gabriel smiled at her. 'I have what I need, Emma. I really do.'

'You're such a fool,' retorted Emma.

'Emma!' Dominique looked at the other girl, who'd clearly had a couple of drinks too many. 'You can't say things like that to Gabriel. He's a genuine believer.'

'It's sad,' said Emma. 'It really is. That he thinks that way and that you believe him.'

Dominique shot a sympathetic look at her brother, then stood up and smoothed down the ivory dress Evelyn had made for her.

'Come on, Emma,' she said. 'Let's go and find Maeve. Have a talk about the old times in school.'

'They weren't that long ago,' said Emma, who didn't want to move.

'You should go with Dominique,' said Gabriel. 'I need to talk to her parents-in-law.'

'You'll make a lousy priest,' said Emma.

'He won't,' said Dominique. 'You know he won't.'

'I'll circulate.' Gabriel smiled at both of them. 'Talk to you later.'

He walked across the room and began talking to Maurice Delahaye. Dominique hauled Emma to her feet.

'You're being really silly,' she said. 'There's no point in saying that sort of stuff to him.'

'I need to save him,' said Emma.

'From what?'

'From himself.'

'Gabriel's fine,' said Dominique.

'You're wrong. You think you know him, but you don't. He's not a man for celibacy and loneliness.'

'He's my brother,' Dominique told her, 'and I know him. He truly does have a vocation. He's not interested in women or sex. He lives his life on a higher plane. You have it all wrong, Emma. And I didn't realise that you still felt . . . I'm sorry. I shouldn't have asked you here today. It wasn't fair.'

'I wanted to come. I still can't stop thinking about him.'

'You need displacement activity.' Dominique took her by the hand. 'Come on, I'm going to introduce you to my brother-in-law, Greg. He's Gabriel-lite.'

'Huh?'

'He's a bit soulful but at least he's not a priest.'

Emma smiled faintly. 'OK.'

'Great,' said Dominique. 'Let's go.'

Dominique had been right about Greg, thought Emma, as she rested her head on his chest while the band played some slow, smoochy numbers. He was a quiet man who let her talk about herself. Gabriel had also encouraged her to talk about herself, but the difference between the two of them, she realised now, was that Gabriel seemed to think of her as some kind of case study, while Greg treated her like a person.

She lifted her head and smiled at him. He smiled back. Out of the corner of her eye she saw Gabriel Brady glance in her direction. So she kissed Greg quickly on the lips, and then rested her head on his chest again.

Dominique hadn't expected to spend her wedding reception dishing out advice to Emma, nor to Maeve, who suddenly cornered her and asked her if she thought that sleeping with a guy on the first date was a bad idea (Dominique thought it probably was, but she told Maeve she hadn't a clue), nor to Suzy McIntyre from two doors down, who asked her how she knew that Brendan was the one. Dominique realised that they respected her more because she was married, even if it had only been for a few hours. But she felt different inside. More mature, perhaps. Wiser. More grown up.

And then Brendan came up to her and said it was time to dance again, and they did the birdie song and she didn't feel grown up at all.

Everybody knew that they were staying in the hotel and not going anywhere that night, but when the DJ finished for the evening, he still made all the guests form a tunnel of love for the happy couple, and so Dominique and Brendan ran beneath an arch of outstretched hands to the door of the small function room, where Dominique threw her bouquet into the crowd and Maeve, squealing with excitement, caught it.

Then they went upstairs to their room, where they opened a bottle of champagne (she thought she could get to like champagne; her first taste of it had been at the reception itself), and after that they made love and Brendan fell asleep.

Dominique was too excited to sleep. The wedding itself had been great fun, but there was still the honeymoon to look forward to. They were going to Majorca for a week, despite the fact that Brendan had told her that he was terrible in the sun and that he went a glorious tomato red. But ever since Maeve had been to Majorca,

Dominique had wanted to go too. Brendan had given in on the honeymoon and Dominique had kissed him over and over again and told him that he was the best fiancé in the whole world and he was going to be the best husband in the world too. The flight wasn't until later the following day, but now that the wedding was over, the thought of it was keeping her awake. She sat on the bed while Brendan snored gently and told herself over and over again that she had hit the jackpot the day Brendan Delahaye had sat at her table in American Burger. She told her baby that he (she'd decided that it was definitely a he) was a lucky boy because he had a mother and father who were crazy about each other and who'd be crazy about him too.

She pulled the covers around her and tried to sleep, but she failed miserably. An hour later, with Brendan still out for the count, she got up, put on her loose jeans and a jumper and went downstairs. She expected the public areas to be deserted, and they almost were. But there was a man sitting in one of the big armchairs, holding a glass of whiskey in his hand and staring into space.

'Greg?' She walked over to her brother-in-law. 'Are you OK?'

'Domino.' He looked at her in surprise, and she grinned at him. 'I love the way you all call me that,' she said.

'It's what Brendan calls you,' said Greg. 'We thought it was your real name. My mother wondered what sort of person would call her daughter after a game. That sort of game, anyway. If you'd been called Camogie, or even Hockey, she'd have understood.'

Dominique laughed, and told him that she was named after a saint.

'Having met your parents, that makes more sense,' agreed Greg. 'So why are you out of bed? Something the matter?'

'No,' she told him. 'Just too excited to sleep, although Brendan is dead to the world.'

'He's a good sleeper, is Bren,' said Greg. 'Likes his eight hours. Gets up early, though.'

Dominique scrunched up her nose. 'Not good,' she said. 'I hate the morning.'

'Night owl?' asked Greg.

'Only since I met Brendan,' she told him. 'Which kind of contradicts what you've said, because we usually stay out really late.'

'Maybe you've changed him,' Greg told her.

'Maybe.' Dominique smiled. 'Though I'm not sure that people can change other people.'

'You're probably right about that.' Greg took a sip of his whiskey.

'Are you OK?' asked Dominique again. 'You seem a bit down.'

'Me? Down?' Greg shook his head. 'No.'

'You're not thinking of becoming a priest, are you?'

'What!' There was complete astonishment in Greg's voice.

'It's just that Gabriel goes all kind of thoughtful like you,' Dominique told him. 'You remind me of him sometimes.' She grinned. 'I told Emma that you were Gabriel-lite.'

'Ah, Emma,' said Greg.

Dominique nodded. 'She sort of has this unrequited love thing going on with Gabriel,' she told him.

'Oh.'

'It's just because she can't have him,' said Dominique. 'Emma usually gets whoever she wants.'

'So you introduced her to me even though you knew she was pining after the priest?'

Dominique grinned. 'I thought you'd take her mind off him. She only *thinks* she's pining.'

'I asked her out.'

'Did you?'

'She seemed . . . sympathetic.'

'Not a quality I'd generally have attributed to Emma Walsh,' said Dominique. 'But maybe you're good for her.'

'You think?'

'Possibly. Is she going to go out with you?'

Greg nodded. 'I'm meeting her tomorrow.'

'I know I kind of threw her at you.' Dominique frowned. 'And I'm glad you asked her out, but it will be a bit awkward if you hit it off, what with you living in Cork and her in Dublin.'

'Yes.' Greg laughed suddenly. 'Maybe that's why I asked her. No chance of being trapped.'

'Like Brendan?' Dominique's voice was edgy.

'Of course not, Domino. None of us think you trapped Brendan. We all think you'll be good for him.'

'You do?'

He nodded. 'Mam thinks you're lovely. So does Dad.' He smiled slightly. 'So do I. You looked really beautiful today too.'

'Thank you.'

He was sweet, she thought, always trying to make her feel welcome. 'What about June? And Roy?' she asked suddenly. 'What do they think?'

'Roy's only a kid,' said Greg dismissively. 'He knows nothing. And June . . .'

Dominique didn't remind Greg that Roy was only a few months younger than her. She was more interested in his thoughts about his sister, who, she'd thought, had been very dismissive of her.

'June's always felt a bit special, being the only girl. I think she's a tiny bit jealous.'

'She needn't be,' Dominique said. 'I'm only a blow-in.'

'That's true,' Greg teased her. 'The Dublin jackeen.'

'Sod off, you Cork culchie.'

They both laughed, and then Dominique yawned.

'I'm suddenly tired,' she said. 'Which is a good thing. I'd better get back to bed.'

Greg nodded.

'How about you?' she said. 'Not tired at all yet?'

'No.'

'And you're sure you're OK?'

'Absolutely.'

'Right then.' She got up. 'I'll say good night.'

'Sleep well, Domino,' he said.

'You too.'

He got up when she did. He smiled at her, then hugged her awkwardly and kissed her on the cheek.

Dominique walked over to the lifts and pressed the call button. She glanced back at Greg before she stepped in to the lift, but he was sitting down staring into space again, not looking in her direction. Then the doors slid closed and she was whisked upstairs to her sleeping husband.

71

Chapter 6

Dominique loved Majorca.

She loved the bright sun and the endlessly blue skies. She loved having breakfast overlooking the sea and dinner in the open air. She loved watching her skin gradually change from porcelain to light gold, and she loved the smell of heat on her body as she lay beneath the colourful parasols.

Brendan was surprised that she didn't burn because she was so naturally pale. But she was slavish about covering herself in protection cream, only venturing out from beneath the parasol when the shadows started to lengthen along the beach. Brendan himself spent most of his time beneath the parasol too, or at the shaded beachside bar, drinking beer and water in equal measure. He couldn't sit out in the sun at all, not even later in the afternoons, when the searing heat had gone out of it. No matter how much cream he put on himself, he still turned lobster red and his skin peeled off in handfuls.

He was looking forward to getting back to the cooler air of Dublin and starting on his next building project. The extension on Donard Road would be finished by the time he got back, and they were going to do a similar job on another house nearby. He'd also been asked to quote for a much bigger extension to a house in Tallaght, and he hoped that he'd be able to close a deal on buying some land to build on. He knew that it would work out for him, because the land was the field in which he'd made love to Domino for the first time which, as far as he was concerned, showed it was meant to be.

Brendan believed in fate and chance and he was convinced that his luck had begun to improve ever since the day he'd first sat at Domino's table in American Burger. He didn't really know why he felt luckier with her in his life but he knew that he did. Besides, she was the loveliest girl he'd ever gone out with. She didn't seem to see it herself because she was always faffing around with mascara and blusher and being supercritical of how she looked, but the truth was that her combination of dark hair and ivory skin was stunning. (Despite her affection for her new golden colour, he was looking forward to her tan fading again.)

He'd been thinking about marriage to her before she dropped the pregnancy bombshell, but he hadn't been ready to ask. However, there wasn't a rat's chance in hell that he'd leave her and his future son living in that creepy house with her crabby mother and henpecked father. They both deserved better than that, and he'd give it to them.

He thought about the site again and the serendipity that had brought them to it. After they'd made love beneath the chestnut tree and were walking towards the road (squelching, really; it had become very muddy and Domino had been yelping that her shoes would be wrecked), he'd spotted the estate agent's sign in the corner. He'd phoned them the following Monday, seen the bank manager and now the deal was under way. He was looking forward to starting the houses when the deal was eventually completed, and in the meantime there was plenty of work on the house extensions. He'd keep the same crew for the building work. Peader, of course. Then Miley, Micko, Christy and George. Between them they'd get the houses built quickly and they'd make a good profit. Brendan knew that the best money to be made was in working for yourself. He wanted to make money. Lots of it. He didn't want to be like so many Irish people he knew, who'd had to go abroad to make a living. He'd done it for a while, of course. Almost everyone he knew had. He'd worked on sites in Birmingham and Liverpool and had learned a lot about how to run a crew. Now he was ready to do it for himself, and do it at home.

He gazed towards the sea and saw Domino paddling at the water's edge. He needed to make money now to support his wife and child. Getting married and having children had always been on his agenda.

Brendan liked family life and he missed it sharing the house in Dublin. Until he met Domino he used to go home three weekends out of four to get his fix of the relaxed atmosphere of his parents' house. He wanted to recreate that with Domino and their children. He hoped they'd have a large family. Though not yet. He didn't want her to spend most of her youth being pregnant. He wanted to have a lot of that hot lovemaking again first.

Brendan smiled as he thought of Domino in bed, where all of her usual inhibitions seemed to simply disappear. Her acid-faced, sanctimonious mother would be astonished, Brendan told himself, if she realised just how passionate her daughter was between the sheets. How willing she was to try new things and how much energy she put into their lovemaking. Brendan had been pleasantly astonished himself. And it was Domino's ability to seem prim on the outside while being anything but in private that made him certain that she was the girl for him.

He was looking forward to being a father, too. He liked the idea of taking his son to hurling matches and maybe even the occasional soccer match; even though he regarded soccer as a lightweight game in comparison to traditional Irish sports, he did follow, in a casual way, the fortunes of Liverpool Football Club. He'd gone to a few of their matches when he was working there and felt an affinity towards them. So if his son got involved in football at all, it would be Liverpool he'd learn to support. But Cork for the hurling. Obviously.

He watched as Domino walked into the sparkling sea and began swimming away from him. She was an unorthodox swimmer, thrashing through the water and churning it up, but she could keep going for much longer than him. Now, a good distance from the shore, she faced the beach and trod water. He knew that she couldn't see him. She was utterly blind without her glasses. She hadn't worn them on their wedding day, and she'd told him that she'd had to trust that it was him standing at the altar waiting for her, because all she could see as she walked up the aisle were blobs in suits. He'd laughed at that. She was great at making him laugh. She loved teasing him and joking with him. She loved – so she told him – having fun.

He could understand that. He knew that her life at home hadn't been much fun. And how could it have been, he asked himself, when it was lived with those two aul' cranks? Brendan had little time for Seamus and Evelyn's brand of religion, which was critical and unforgiving and concentrated far too much (in his view) on feeling guilty. Once, after a particularly inventive bout of lovemaking, Domino had disappeared into the small shower in his house and had spent ages there, using up all of the hot water. When he'd asked what on earth had kept her so long, she'd blushed and told him that she'd needed to wash away her sin. And then she'd blurted out that it couldn't have been a sin because she loved him so much and it had been so great, but she couldn't help feeling that something that good just had to be bad too.

Those people had messed with her head, Brendan thought grimly. And the priest-in-training brother hadn't helped either. However, it would be totally different from now on. She was married to him and they were going to have a baby and he was going to make loads of money so that their future would be secure. Domino didn't yet know just how rich he was going to make them.

She walked out of the sea, water dripping from her body.

'Hey, Domino!' he called. 'Over here.'

He saw her squint and waved vigorously until she spotted him. She trudged her way through the sand and sat down beside him.

'Enjoy?' he asked as he ordered a lemon juice for her. (Except for the champagne at their wedding reception, she'd given up alcohol when she'd discovered she was pregnant.)

'The best week of my life,' she told him simply. 'Without question.'

'Mine too.' He kissed her on the lips. 'Even though my poor burnt shoulders will never be the same again.'

His shoulders were still a bit raw when they got back to Ireland, and he winced every so often as the rough fabric of his polo shirt scratched against the sensitive patches. Domino teased him unmercifully about it, revelling in her own unaccustomed tan and her now completely clear skin.

'You'll peel eventually,' he told her as they waited for a bus to bring them into town from the airport. 'And it'll be disgusting.'

76

'Won't.' She stuck out her tongue at him.

'Shove that in before you're left that way.'

He grinned at her and she grinned back, then hopped on the bus, which had just pulled up in front of them, leaving him to wrestle with their suitcase.

The bus dropped them in the city centre, where Brendan insisted on them getting a taxi to their new house in Firhouse. Dominique was very excited about the house. She hadn't been inside it since two weeks before the wedding because Brendan was getting the kitchen appliances fitted and furniture delivered and he told her he wanted it perfect before she saw it.

She was almost dizzy with anticipation by the time the car pulled up in front of the house and waited impatiently at the kerbside while Brendan paid the driver.

'Right,' he said as he took the key from his pocket. 'This is it. Welcome to your new home, Mrs Delahaye.' And he picked her up and staggered into the hallway with her in his arms.

'You're far too keen on trying to carry me places. For God's sake put me down before you do yourself an injury!' She was laughing, but serious too. She'd put on a lot of weight in Majorca and her bump seemed to have suddenly doubled in size.

'Too late,' he said mournfully. 'I'm wrecked already.' And then he led her through to the kitchen diner, where the new cooker, fridge and washing machine had all been installed. Exclaiming with delight, she then followed him into the living room (now carpeted in a pale beige), then upstairs to the bedrooms. The two guest bedrooms were empty of furniture, but the main one contained a divan bed with a pine headboard, a matching pine chest of drawers as well as two bedside lockers and a small dressing table. There were yellow curtains at the windows, held back by tasselled ties.

'It's fabulous!' she cried. 'Utterly, utterly fabulous!'

She threw her arms around him and held him close to her. 'I love you so much.'

'You love my skills as a DIY man,' he said.

She giggled. 'And your other skills.'

'Domino Delahaye!' He tried to sound scandalised but he was laughing.

'So come on!' she cried as she bounced on the double bed. 'Let's see how it all holds up.'

The house couldn't have been more perfect. It was bright and airy and always seemed to be inviting, in complete contrast to the family home in Drimnagh, which had always seemed so dark and unforgiving. Dominique had bought lots of floral prints for the walls, too – sunflowers, tulips and daffodils – to emphasise the light, cheerful mood.

When Evelyn and Seamus called by for tea at the end of the first week, Evelyn commented on the prints, saying that they were very pretty, and then asked her daughter why there were no pictures of the Sacred Heart or St Dominic.

'I'm not getting any,' said Dominique forcefully. 'I never liked them and I don't want them.'

'You need to have at least one holy picture,' said Evelyn.

'They always scared the shit out of me at home,' said Dominique. 'And I'm not letting that happen here.'

'Dominique Brady!' exclaimed her mother. 'Please don't use that sort of language in front of me again. You may think you can do what you like now that you're married, but I do assure you, young lady, that I will not permit swearing in front of me.'

'Dominique Delahaye,' she corrected her mother. 'And this is my house. So I'll swear if I want to.'

'But you wouldn't want to,' Brendan intervened as Domino's face flushed red with annoyance. He turned to his mother-in-law. 'Evelyn, we don't normally swear.'

'I'll bring you round a picture tomorrow,' said Evelyn.

'I'm working tomorrow night,' Dominique said. 'So don't waste your time.'

Evelyn turned up at half nine the following morning with a large oblong parcel under her arm. Dominique, who'd stayed late in bed, groaned as she heard the doorbell ring and groaned even more when she saw her mother on the front step.

'Are you only getting up now?' demanded Evelyn as she walked past her daughter into the kitchen. 'What sort of life are you leading?'

78

'I'll be working until midnight tonight,' Dominique told her. 'I need my sleep.'

'You shouldn't be working at all in your condition,' Evelyn said.

'I need to work.' Dominique filled the kettle. 'We have a lot of expenses, you know.'

'You'll have more after the baby is born.'

'Of course we will. But Brendan is very confident about his business.'

'Far too confident.' Evelyn sniffed.

'You don't know him,' said Dominique.

'Indeed. Well, we didn't get much of a chance.'

'Don't go there.' Dominique was surprised at the force in her own voice, and she could see surprise on Evelyn's face too. 'You can't come here and criticise me and my choices,' she continued. 'I've my own life to lead.'

Evelyn opened her mouth but then closed it without speaking. She stayed silent while Dominique made the tea and then opened a blue Tupperware box containing a packet of McVitie's Goldgrain. The Goldgrain were a favourite of her father, but she knew Evelyn wasn't a fan.

Nevertheless, her mother took a biscuit and dunked it into her tea so that the edge became sodden and a small portion of it broke off and fell into the cup.

'What time does he get home in the evenings?' asked Evelyn, dunking the biscuit again and losing more of it in the process.

'It depends,' Dominique replied. 'He's just started work on a complete house renovation and so they'll keep working as long as they can. But it doesn't matter to me, because I'll be working too.'

'And what happens when the baby comes along?'

'We'll see,' said Dominique. 'Maybe I'll get something closer to home. There's a new restaurant opened in Templeogue village.'

'You should be working in an office,' said Evelyn. 'It cost enough to put you through that secretarial course.'

'If an office job comes up, I'll take it,' Dominique assured her. 'It'd be a lot nicer to sit on my backside instead of being run off my feet all day. But so far nothing has.'

'You need to send your CV out,' Evelyn said.

'I applied to millions of places last year,' Dominique reminded her. 'I'm not sure there's any point in doing it again.'

'You've got to keep trying,' said Evelyn.

'But no real point until after I have the baby,' said Dominique. 'After all, if I go to an interview now looking like a giant pumpkin, I'm not going to get the job.'

Evelyn finished the biscuit and drained her tea.

'You're right about that,' she agreed. 'And you need to be at home to bond with your baby.'

Or not, Dominique thought darkly as she cleared away the cups and put them in the sink. Evelyn had been a stay-at-home mother, but they hadn't bonded, had they? She wondered how it worked, the connection between a mother and her baby. Should it automatically kick in? Would it, for her and Junior? Why hadn't it between her and Evelyn?

She sat back down at the table and Evelyn picked up the parcel. Dominique knew what it was and didn't want to unwrap it. But she didn't feel as though she had a choice, and so she peeled back the brown paper to be confronted with the image of St Dominic that had been in her bedroom for so many years.

'I know you think you're fine with your fancy flowery pictures and your modern house, but you need him to guide you,' Evelyn told her.

'I don't, you know.'

'I thought you could put it in the hallway.'

Dominique said nothing.

'He'll remind you,' Evelyn said, 'of where you come from and where you're going to.'

'We'll see,' said Dominique non-committally.

After her mother had gone, she stashed the print in the cupboard under the stairs. Then she washed the cups, wrinkling her nose at the sodden biscuit pieces at the bottom of Evelyn's. When she'd dried them, she put them back in the cupboard. The tea set, courtesy of Brendan's mother, had been a much more welcome gift, she thought. And useful into the bargain.

It was the following evening when the decision about her future job was taken. Brendan had come home late and tired after his long day on the site. He'd decided to take a bath, and while he was relaxing in the warm water, Dominique began to tidy away the bundles of invoices he'd left on the table. They were crumpled and encrusted with dried cement. She could see that some of them were overdue bills, and she frowned. She knew that businesses had to be run on credit, but the words of her father 'neither a borrower nor a lender be' were etched into her mind. Dominique didn't have a credit card and never bought clothes that she couldn't actually afford. Seamus had told her that clothes and holidays were current expenditure and that she should never borrow for current expenditure. The only things worth borrowing for, he would insist, were your house and possibly a car. Now she divided Brendan's bills into ones that were overdue and ones that still had a credit period to expire. There were also a few invoices that Brendan had sent to people who owed him money for small jobs he'd done in the few weeks after he'd left the building site and before he'd started the bigger work.

She totted them all up and realised that he owed more than he was getting in. She nibbled at her fingernail, suddenly worried. They couldn't live owing more than they earned. Maybe Brendan setting up his own business wasn't such a good idea after all.

'Of course it's a good idea,' he told her after he'd come downstairs from his bath. 'I'm going to make a nice sum out of all the stuff we have on at the moment, especially the renovation. Plus I have more jobs lined up. But I didn't realise so many other people still owed me money. I should chase them up. That would help the cash flow a lot.'

'You don't have time,' said Dominique. 'You're out on the site all day.'

'I really need to set up an office,' said Brendan thoughtfully. 'I know the company is small now, but when we start to grow it'll be important.'

'Have we no money right now?' asked Dominique. 'After all, you owe so much . . .'

'We've plenty,' Brendan assured her. 'I have a line of credit with the bank.'

'But that's for the construction company.'

'I also have one for my other expenses.'

'That means we're totally living on borrowed money.' She looked horrified, and he laughed at her.

'Only until I get paid.'

'But what if they don't pay you?'

'Domino, Domino, of course they will. But in the meantime, if I get someone to look after the invoices, I can certainly cut back on the size of the overdraft.'

'Why don't I?' She spoke almost without thinking, but then, more confidently, 'I could do this, Brendan. I learned some book-keeping at my secretarial course and I know how to type. It would look a lot better if you sent out typed invoices.'

He studied her thoughtfully for a few minutes, and then he nodded.

'You'll be off work anyway when the baby is born. It'll give you something else to do.'

'I'm sure I'll be plenty busy with your son,' she chided him. 'But I want to help too. I want to be part of your business.'

'OK,' he said. 'Tell them that you're leaving the restaurant and come and work for me.'

'Will you pay me?' she asked.

He laughed. 'Of course I will.'

'A decent wage.'

He mentioned a figure and she made a face. 'That's not as much as I earn now.'

'With or without tips?'

'With,' she admitted.

'And you won't have the expense of getting in and out of town . . .'

'Give me an extra fiver a week and I'll do it,' she suggested.

'You drive a hard bargain, Mrs Delahaye,' said Brendan. 'But you're on.'

She liked working for him. It wasn't difficult work and it didn't take up too much of her time, which was good because now, nearing the end of her pregnancy, she felt big, ungainly and tired very easily. She was astonished at how tired she felt. Astonished at how ugly she felt too. She was beginning to hate being pregnant, and she wished it was all over and they had their lovely baby sleeping peacefully in his cot instead of apparently doing cartwheels in her stomach. Working distracted her, and so every day she checked the invoices and balanced the bank account, a task that Brendan had added to her responsibilities. She'd felt honoured when he'd let her do this.

'There are no secrets between us,' he told her. 'You should know what's going in and out of the account. That way you also know how well we're doing and whether you need to be buying the Yellow Pack stuff in the supermarket or whether you can go for the quality items.'

'I'm more concerned with making sure that your work stays within budget,' she said.

'Quite the little Scrooge, aren't you?'

'Just being cautious.'

'Pretty little Domino. That surely goes against your inner instincts.'

'Partly,' she admitted. 'But I think I can be a very sensible person when I have to be.'

Brendan laughed. 'I didn't marry you for your good sense,' he said, and kissed her on the back of the neck. 'Now let's go and do something very *un*-sensible.'

'OK, Mrs Delahaye.' The obstetrician looked at her over the green file he was holding. 'Your baby is breech at the moment, but there is a good chance he'll turn around in his own good time, so there's no need for you to worry.'

Dominique looked at him wordlessly. She'd discovered that the baby was lying sideways at her previous visit and she hoped that he'd do as the doctors expected and turn around. They'd talked about the possibility of a Caesarean if he didn't, but she hadn't really been listening to them. She knew that she should listen and that she should know everything there was to know about her baby's imminent arrival, but the truth was that she didn't want to know. She wanted to imagine that one day she'd be sitting at home pregnant and the next she'd somehow have the baby in her arms and there wouldn't be too much of the pulling and pushing and frankly quite awful stuff that seemed to go on at childbirth. Dominique

83

had realised halfway through her pregnancy that she wasn't really the earth-mother type. That she wanted it all over and done with as easily and painlessly as possible. She felt slightly guilty about this, as though she was in some way letting the whole cause of motherhood down, but she couldn't help it. As far as she was concerned, she was leaving it all in the hands of the doctors and she'd do whatever they said.

Although she didn't know how to feel about the possibility of a Caesarean. The obstetrician was pretty relaxed about it, but most of the books she read championed the whole natural childbirth thing. She'd nodded at the obstetrician's various scenarios but had mentally tuned out when the words episiotomy and forceps were used. She simply couldn't imagine how horrible that might be. He'd also spoken about epidurals and anaesthetics, but Dominique wasn't able to get her head around those. She wondered whether she was particularly stupid, because the other mothers she'd spoken to in the prenatal clinic seemed to be remarkably well informed. They kept talking about what they wanted from the birth experience and how to enhance their baby's journey into the world. All she wanted was to give birth as soon as possible and exchange her massive bump for a cute little baby.

She couldn't believe how much she'd ballooned in the last few weeks. She hated not being able to see her feet. She hated the constant heartburn. She hated that her ankles hurt and that her back was perpetually sore. And she hated – as her sister-in-law June had predicted – that she was now suffering terribly with piles, which meant that she found it difficult to walk, sit or sleep. She felt big and bloated and ugly and horrible and it made her laugh (although not with any humour) to think that she'd thought of herself as unattractive as a teenager. By comparison to how she was now, she'd been an absolute babe! She couldn't even look at Brendan without thinking back to the rainy field in Clondalkin and wondering what on earth had come over her to make her jump on him in the way she had. Right now she couldn't imagine wanting to jump on him ever again. She wondered if anyone else in the world had ever felt like this. All the magazine articles she read seemed to focus on how lovely being pregnant was and how she'd forget all about the discomfort when she had her baby in her arms. (If the piles didn't go, Dominique thought grimly, she wouldn't be holding anyone!) She was struggling with the guilt such feelings were causing her too, as well as the guilt of knowing that she was hell to live with right now. During the last couple of weeks she'd probably been driving Brendan crazy, and she certainly wasn't anything like the girl he'd once called attractive and gorgeous. So she didn't care what way her baby was born, as long as it happened soon.

She was at home alone when she felt the first proper contraction. She sat on the edge of a chair thinking that maybe she'd been mistaken, because she'd previously panicked about contractions that had turned out to be routine. (Braxton Hicks, the nurse had told her, as if she should have known what that meant.) And then another contraction came and she knew that this was different. She wished Brendan was home, but he never left the site until it was dark. She didn't know whether the contractions meant that the baby had turned or not. It had been doing so much moving around in the last few days that Dominique felt as though she was a character in the *Alien* movie. It wouldn't have surprised her one little bit if her baby had simply punched his way out of her stomach and run laughing across the room. She'd actually dreamed about it one night and had woken up in a lather of sweat and fear.

The next contraction was so painful that she cried out loud. She really, really wanted Brendan to come home, even though she could hardly blame him for the fact that he'd been working late so often lately. She'd been a bear to be around. Dominique whimpered. She knew that labour could last for hours. But what if she was one of those people who had really quick labours, and what if her baby hadn't turned around, and what if she was going to give birth here and now on the kitchen floor? She needed to get someone to help her. She thought about calling her mother, but the idea of Evelyn being beside her when she gave birth was almost worse than the idea of being alone. Her mother wouldn't be calm and reassuring, thought Dominique. She'd simply tell her that she was getting her just deserts.

She could ring for an ambulance. But would they come out on

85

her say-so? Or would they tell her that she was a pregnant woman, that was all, and that she should get to the hospital herself? Ambulances were for emergencies and she wasn't an emergency. Even though she felt like one.

She gasped again as another wave of pain passed through her, and then jumped, because the doorbell had rung. Maybe Brendan had come home early after all, she thought, as she shuffled along the hallway to answer it. Which would mean they'd go to the hospital together and she'd have her baby and everything would be just fine.

Her next-door neighbour, Fionnuala, was standing on the doorstep, a form in her hands.

'I'm just collecting signatures for the residents' association,' she said brightly. 'Can you—' and then she broke off, because Dominique burst into tears and told her that she might be going to have her baby.

Fionnuala was everything that Dominique wasn't when it came to calmness and efficiency. She told her to get her bag, write a note for Brendan to tell him they'd gone to the hospital and get into her car right away. Dominique, still struggling with contractions and furious with herself for not having paid more attention in the prenatal classes, was only too happy to do what Fionnuala told her.

The hospital was confusing. Dominique had expected to have Brendan beside her, and she fumbled her way through the questions that the admitting nurse asked her. They'll think I'm incredibly stupid, she thought, but they might be right. Her brain seemed to be operating in some kind of separate world to her body. She really, really wanted all this over very soon.

And then she was in a bed and attached to a monitor and feeling slightly less stressed as her quiet, confident obstetrician arrived. He was getting ready to examine her when Dominique gave a cry and her waters broke. And then abruptly everything changed. The flurry of activity was sudden and frantic, and Dominique was completely taken aback by the urgency that had come into her doctor's voice as he called for a medical team. The cord had prolapsed, he told her. She needed a Caesarean. And she needed it right now.

Dominique couldn't remember anything in the prenatal classes about prolapsed cords, but she knew that it didn't sound good.

And from the speed that everything was happening, she knew that nobody else thought it was good either. She could feel her heart racing so fast it was making her tremble. She wanted Brendan. She was scared of being on her own. Fionnuala had left her in the care of the doctors, assuming that everything was now fine.

Dominique knew that it wasn't fine. She was afraid that she was going to die. Or that her baby was going to die. She knew that she was crying. She felt weak and stupid. This wasn't the way it was supposed to be.

They clamped an oxygen mask on her face and she struggled at first, not realising what was happening.

'You need oxygen for the baby,' said one of the nurses. 'Come on, Dominique. You've got to do what we tell you.'

She tried to breathe deeply, even though she felt totally claustrophobic with the mask over her face. And then she heard a doctor tell the anaesthetist to put her out.

She knew that she was somewhere else. She just didn't know where. She could feel her stomach pulsating and she was in the *Alien* movie again and the baby, the creature, was tearing her apart. She wanted to scream. But she couldn't.

She felt sick. She didn't know whether it was from the anaesthetic or from terror, and she was afraid that if she actually was sick the retching would split her stomach open. But hadn't the alien creature done that already?

'Relax, Domino,' said Brendan. 'You're fine, don't worry.'

Her eyes fluttered open. She didn't know how Brendan had suddenly appeared in the delivery room. She hadn't heard him come in.

'Everyone's fine,' he repeated. 'You and the baby.'

She looked at him with a total lack of comprehension. And then she realised that she wasn't in the theatre any more; she was in a room in the hospital and she was still alive.

'Baby?' Her throat was dry, and she realised that every muscle in her body ached.

He grinned at her. 'A girl,' he said. 'A real little fighter.'

'Oh.'

'She's OK,' said Brendan, misinterpreting the croak in her voice.

'You were great. She was great. And the surgical team was great too. The whole thing only took five minutes.'

Dominique blinked slowly.

'She's in the neonatal care unit at the moment,' said Brendan. 'But she's doing fine.'

'I'm sorry,' she whispered to Brendan, who was still holding her hand. 'You wanted a boy.'

'We have a beautiful baby,' said Brendan. 'And that's all I wanted. Sure, you can go for a boy the next time!'

Chapter 7

It was all wrong.

Dominique shuddered as she listened to the baby screaming. The baby was always screaming, her little monkey face screwed up into a red ball of fury as the sounds of her impotent rage filled the air. Dominique never knew what she wanted when she screamed like that. And even if she had known, she wouldn't have been able to give it to her.

She sat on the sofa, her legs curled under her, and blocked out the sound of the furious cries. She'd never been able to do that before. When she was younger she'd always wanted to pick up crying babies. Other people's crying babies. She couldn't imagine anyone being able to ignore them.

But it was easy, she knew now. You just put the noise somewhere else. You tried not to hear it. You tried not to let the crushing weight of responsibility press down upon you. You tried not to wonder what the neighbours thought of the constant screaming or if they wondered why it was so quiet in the evening, when there was someone else there. You sat and stared at the wall. That was what you did. And you blanked everything else from your mind, because otherwise you'd be overwhelmed by the panic and the devastation and the sadness that threatened to engulf you.

Brendan was caught between sympathy and impatience and he didn't know what to do. Before the birth, he and Dominique had sat on the sofa and thought about baby names and joked about how their lives would be changed for ever when he (they'd always thought of the baby as a he and hadn't asked to be told otherwise) arrived home.

They talked about having him in the carrycot in the room all the time, not leaving him alone ever. They'd put the pine crib in the bedroom and hung a brightly coloured mobile above it. They'd talked about playing with the baby, laughing with him, enjoying having him as part of the family. Brendan had dreamed about coming home to his wife and child and feeling as though he was master of the house. An old-fashioned dream, he knew. But one he liked. He wanted the security of a family. He wanted them to be happy together.

'Why?' he asked her every single day. 'Why are you crying?'

And she would shake her head and say that she didn't know.

Evelyn told her, although with an unaccustomed note of concern in her voice, that she had to pull herself together.

'Your baby needs you,' she said. 'Brendan needs you. You can't sit around in your pyjamas all day.'

'I don't want to get dressed.' Dominique found it hard to talk. It was as though the words were stuck somewhere in her head and she had to struggle to speak.

'You have to make an effort,' said Evelyn. 'I know it's hard. I was exhausted after you were born, but I still did my best.'

Dominique shrugged helplessly.

'Every mother gets the baby blues,' Evelyn told her. 'It'll pass. It always does. But you have to snap out of it.'

She picked up the baby from the pine crib, which Brendan and Dominique had chosen with such love and care.

'Hold her,' she said.

Dominique flinched.

'She's your daughter,' Evelyn said. 'She needs you.'

'I know that.' Dominique raised her big dark eyes to her mother. 'I know she's my daughter. I'm responsible for her. I know that too. I have to feed her and clothe her and look after her because it's my fault that she's here. I know. I do feed her. She's clamped to me half the day.'

They'd encouraged breastfeeding at the hospital. They'd told her it would be best for her baby and it would be good for her too. Much better chance of losing that bulge, they said cheerfully, if you feed her yourself.

Dominique had looked down at her stomach then. It was a war zone. Scarred and bruised from the Caesarean, of course. And still podgy and wobbly and patterned with stretch marks. She knew that she'd been incredibly naïve to think that everything would simply spring back into place after the baby had been born, but she'd expected some change. As it was, she still looked pregnant. Which was horrifying, because every time she looked at herself she remembered the terror she'd felt when the doctors had rushed her to theatre and she'd been sure that she was going to die.

And more than that terror was the guilt that her first thought had been for herself and not for her baby. Everyone knew that mothers thought of their children before themselves. It was an instinct. Only Dominique's instinct had been to be afraid for herself. And to want to get rid of the baby because it was killing her. She was, she knew, the worst mother in the whole world. A disgrace to the name. She didn't deserve a baby. And it was no wonder that both of them cried morning, noon and night.

The thoughts came to her when she least expected them. Thoughts of picking the baby up and throwing her against the wall. Of putting her in the car and driving off a cliff. Of bringing her to the supermarket and just leaving her there. She tried to push them away but she couldn't. Sometimes she even felt comforted by them; sometimes it was nice to allow them to take over her mind.

It wasn't all in her mind, said Lily Delahaye. It was post-natal depression and she needed to see a doctor. Dominique replied that the doctors wouldn't understand. They had been so great at the hospital, saving her and saving the baby. They'd worked miracles to keep them both alive. How could she possibly admit that now she wished they'd both died? They'd be angry with her and she couldn't blame them, because everyone was supposed to be happy.

'They won't be angry with you,' said Lily. 'You're not well, Domino. You need to get better.'

Lily had come to Dublin immediately after the baby was born, and although Dominique had been quiet and a little weepy in the hospital, Lily had put it down to the drama of the birth. She'd gone home with pictures of both of them, thinking that the baby was definitely a Delahaye and hoping that her daughter-in-law would pick up when she got home. But then Brendan had phoned and told her that things were actually worse and that Dominique was spending the entire day sitting on the sofa chewing on strands of her hair. That the only time she touched the baby was when she was feeding her, and when she changed her daughter's nappy she did it in a way that made it perfectly clear that she didn't want to be doing it at all.

Brendan was worried about Dominique, but even more worried about the effect her behaviour was having on their daughter. He didn't know what to do. Dominique refused to talk to Evelyn. She refused to go to the doctor. She refused to have anything to do with anybody. That was why he'd asked his mother to come and see her. He knew that Domino liked Lily. He knew that she got on well with his mother. If anyone could help, Lily could.

But Lily hadn't been able to get through to her either.

The dreams had started after they'd left the hospital. They were always the same. In them, the baby had been taken away from her and they were telling her that she wasn't her real mum. That she couldn't be. And she was saying that she was, she knew she was. But they replied that there was no proof. She hadn't given birth to her, had she? She could be anybody's baby. Besides, they said, she wanted someone to take her away. Didn't she think that every single day?

She would wake up from the dream frightened and sweating. She would get out of bed and look into the cot and tell herself that this was her baby, that she'd loved her when she was pregnant with her and that she loved her now. But no matter how often she said the words, how many times she tried to force a connection, she simply couldn't make it happen.

Emma had called to the hospital but Dominique hadn't wanted to see her. She phoned when Dominique was home and Brendan told her that she wasn't ready to see people yet but to call back in a week or so. Maeve called too and he said the same thing. But Dominique never wanted to talk to them or see them and eventually both of them stopped trying.

June turned up with her own baby, the angelic Alicia, who chuckled and gurgled her way through the visit. June said that she knew how Domino felt, that childbirth was scary and painful and not at all an empowering experience. Not until afterwards, she said, when you realised that you'd actually done it and they put the baby in your arms. Then, June told her, you felt it, the rush of love so primeval and overwhelming that you knew you'd walk over broken glass and hot coals for your baby. It was like nothing she'd ever experienced before.

Dominique stared at her. She'd thought June might be different, might say different stuff. After all, she hadn't really enjoyed being pregnant. She'd said that it was boring and uncomfortable. So she'd thought that maybe June understood what she was going through now. But she didn't. Her sister-in-law was in love with her baby. Dominique could see that in her eyes. She wondered what June saw in her eyes. She hoped she didn't see how she really felt.

She heard the front door opening and she pulled her dressing gown around her shoulders. Brendan came home at all hours during the day to make sure she was OK. At least that was what he told her. Dominique was certain he was coming home to make sure she hadn't done something terrible to the baby. She understood why he'd be worried. She'd be worried about what she might do if she didn't already know that she hadn't the energy to do anything at all.

'Domino?'

It wasn't Brendan, she realised. It was Greg. Even worse. What was he doing here? Why had Brendan given his brother the key to their house? She pulled the dressing gown even more tightly around her shoulders. If Greg had come up to Dublin, Brendan had probably asked him to check on her. She kept her eyes tightly closed. She didn't want to see Greg. She didn't want him to see her. Not like this.

'Hey, Domino.' He walked into the kitchen and put some bread and milk as well as a bouquet of flowers on the table. 'How are you?'

She knew that he was doing his best to hide his revulsion. She

93

knew that she looked truly dreadful. She hadn't got out of her pyjamas in a week. She hadn't washed her hair in more than that. She smelled of baby milk and baby sick. She was disgusting.

'I'll put the flowers in water,' he said.

She was going to cry. She'd only just stopped but she was going to start again. Her cheeks were raw from her tears.

'I like flowers,' said Greg as he arranged them carefully in the Waterford crystal vase that had been a wedding present from one of Brendan's friends. 'I like the colours.'

He was trying to lift her mood. But it wasn't a mood. It was the way she was now. She was a mother who wasn't in the slightest bit interested in her baby. She hated herself for that. She hated herself for being such an awful person. For not appreciating the miracle of life. For not being grateful to the doctors and nurses at the hospital. She hated herself for not loving Brendan any more because it was Brendan who'd got her pregnant and Brendan who'd married her and Brendan who'd gone on and on about how fantastic their life would be with a baby in it but who'd been utterly, utterly wrong about it.

'So.' Greg sat down beside her. 'It's all been a bit of a shock, hasn't it?'

She opened her eyes slowly. She did everything slowly these days.

'The way you were brought into hospital. The whole emergency thing. Not at all what you expected, I suppose.'

She stared blankly at him.

'It must have been terrifying,' said Greg. 'It's not surprising you're reacting like this. Men are so lucky not to have to go through it.'

She closed her eyes again. She wasn't going to listen to him. She was going to stay in the space that she'd found. The quiet room inside her head where nobody, not Brendan, not Evelyn, not Lily and most of all not the baby, could get to her. She was going to be by herself.

She didn't deserve anything else.

'I feel like you do sometimes.' Greg's voice drifted into her head. 'Sometimes I want to lock myself away and sit on the sofa and cry.'

Her eyes flickered open again.

'I guess it happens to everyone at some point in their lives,' he told her. 'We think we're able to cope with everything, that we're ready for the challenge, and then things don't turn out the way we expect and we don't know how to deal with them at all.'

She couldn't help listening, wondering what had happened in Greg's life that he hadn't been able to cope with, that had left him sounding so sad.

'But the truth is that in the end we have to move forward with our lives, don't we?' He was watching her closely. 'We can't just give in.'

'Give in?' Her voice came from miles away.

'To the darkness,' he said carefully.

'It's not dark.' A tear trickled down her face. 'It's not dark, it's just . . . wrong.'

'What?' he asked. 'What's wrong, Domino?'

She covered her face with her hands. 'Everything.'

'Tell me.'

Why would she tell him when she couldn't even tell Brendan? Brendan was her husband. She should be able to tell him. No secrets, he often said. But sometimes the secret was so terrible that you couldn't share it. Especially not with the man you were supposed to love.

'I hate myself.' The words were out, and suddenly she couldn't stop. 'I hate myself because I don't love my baby. She nearly killed me. Everyone was shouting and yelling and they were talking about blood and haemorrhaging, and I knew it was me. They were all afraid and so was I, and it was her fault, only of course it wasn't her fault. She didn't ask to be born, did she? But she was killing me, and I hate myself for being afraid of her and afraid of dying and for not being happy because both of us are absolutely fine. I hate not wanting to hold her and I hate that every time I do she reminds me of being in the hospital. I hate that she's a girl, because we picked names for a boy and Brendan wanted a boy so's they could share things. I hate that I don't want Brendan near me. I hate that I think about killing myself. I hate the blackness and the numbness and that everyone is looking at me and talking about me . . .' The tears were streaming down her face and hands. 'I hate that I was so stupid as to get pregnant in the first place. To think that just because Brendan married me everything would be perfect. I hate that my mother was right and that I'm being punished for being a wilful, selfish person who wore dresses that were too short and heels that were too high . . .'

'Oh, Domino.' Greg put his arm around her and pulled her tightly to him. And although she hadn't been able to let Brendan or Evelyn or Lily touch her since the baby's birth, she was suddenly comforted by him. She didn't know why she had poured out her darkest thoughts to Greg. She only knew that as he rocked her gently in his arms, she suddenly felt safer than she ever had before.

She went to see the doctor the following day. Brendan was with her in the surgery as Dr Stevenson examined her and listened to her. He told her that she was certainly depressed and that this happened with one in ten new mothers and she didn't have to suffer on her own. He told her that he would arrange counselling for her, which would help her enormously because she'd see then that she wasn't alone in the feelings that she was having. Additionally, he said, he was going to prescribe a course of antidepressants. It would take a few weeks for them to kick in, he told her, but they would make a big difference. He promised her that. She took the prescription and tucked it into her purse.

'Things will get better, Dominique,' said Dr Stevenson. 'They really and truly will.'

She didn't believe him. She didn't believe anything anybody told her any more. But because Greg had begged her to do this, and because she trusted Greg, she would do whatever they wanted.

Chapter 8

The decibel level was off the scale. Even from the front bedroom upstairs, Dominique could hear the yells and shrieks as Kelly and her friends ran riot in the garden. It was impossible to believe, thought Dominique, that ten-year-old girls could make such noise. But they were like chattering magpies as they communicated at top speed and at the tops of their voices with each other.

They'd been at it for two hours already, and Dominique had come upstairs to give herself a momentary break from the bedlam. Linda and Cherise, two of her neighbours, whose daughters were also Kelly's best friends, were still outside, supervising the bouncy castle and the face-painting for the younger children and trying to keep a modicum of control over the birthday group. It was a good thing, Dominique thought, that their new house in Terenure had such a big garden. At least it meant that there was plenty of room for the energetic children to work off their high spirits.

Dominique always thought of the house as new, even though they'd been in it for a number of years now. She'd been surprised the day Brendan had come home and told her that this was an opportunity they couldn't turn down.

'But I thought you liked it where we are,' she said slowly. 'We've got the place exactly how we want it.' She'd looked around the kitchen – much bigger than it had been when they'd first moved in, because Brendan had built an extension that stretched the entire width of the back of the house. 'It seems daft to move on now.'

'I'm picking up this place at a great price because it needs a bit of work,' Brendan had said. 'And there's demand for houses in this neck of the woods right now.'

'How much work?' Dominique knew that Brendan's idea of 'a bit of work' and hers differed substantially. As far as Brendan was concerned, the extension had been a minor job. It had taken two months, during which Dominique had fought a losing battle with dust, grime and jackhammers (and, occasionally, her sanity).

'A fair bit,' he'd conceded, and then, seeing the expression on her face, added quickly, 'But it's priced cheaply because of it. It's a great chance to pick up a fantastic property in a really good location and we'd be crazy to pass it up.'

He'd brought her to see the house, a red-brick Victorian building with a long, narrow south-facing back garden where overgrown bushes and grasses hid the path to a dilapidated shed. Her heart had sunk at the state of the garden, and at the peeling wallpaper and flaking paint in the high-ceilinged rooms of the house itself, but Brendan had insisted that she needed to look past the long grass and the cracked windows and imagine how it could look.

'I wish I had that kind of imagination.' All Dominique could see was months of work ahead of them.

'I have,' said Brendan.

She knew he had. He was a visionary when it came to buildings; an artist, she sometimes told him. She knew that when his heart was set on a property and he could see its potential, nothing could stop him. Brendan gutted the house in Terenure, rewired it, replastered the walls, sanded the beautiful wooden floorboards, which had been hidden beneath musty brown carpet, and replaced the cracked windows with double glazing. He bought a new shed and got the garden landscaped. By the time he'd finished, the place was unrecognisable. When it came to building and renovation, Brendan Delahaye knew what he was doing.

Over the last ten years, Brendan's company had gone from strength to strength, building extensions for half of the housing estate in Firhouse (although none as lovely as their kitchen, Dominique thought complacently) as well as finishing and selling the development of six houses in Clondalkin. Even when times were quiet, Brendan was never out of work, and the money flowing through the books increased every month.

Dominique no longer did the accounting work for Brendan and

the company. During her months of post-natal depression, when she was unable to do anything at all, he had brought in an accountant to look after things. Matthew Donnelly was the brother of Miley, who worked for Brendan on the sites. He was quite unlike Brendan and Miley, who would often sit in the kitchen in their cement-caked overalls and sweaty T-shirts, drinking cups of strong tea and talking about the next job. Matthew always wore three-piece suits and pastel-coloured shirts with white collars and cuffs. He changed the way the books were kept and spoke confidently about accurals and cashflow. His advice had left them with enough money to turn the Terenure house into something really special.

Dominique had known she couldn't say no to the move, even though she really would have preferred to stay where she was, no matter how great the potential of the new house. She knew that she would do whatever Brendan wanted, because despite everything, he was still with her. She had been certain, ten years ago, that he would leave, and the idea had utterly terrified her. She wouldn't have blamed him, of course. Who would? Why would anyone want to come home to a wife who didn't care about anything? Who'd lost interest in everything, particularly in herself, so that she didn't bother going to the hairdresser or going shopping any more, and sloped around the house in shapeless tracksuit bottoms, her hair long and unkempt, her face paler than ever and her expression mournful? She'd imagined him leaving her and taking Kelly with him, and even though she told herself that that would surely be a good thing, because she didn't love the baby and he did, the idea filled her with dread. There were times when she couldn't quite believe that he'd stuck it out until her depression had lifted, and times when she wondered why he had. But she wasn't going to question him. She never questioned him. She never argued with him. And she allowed him to make all the important decisions about their lives.

Kelly's well-being was her number-one priority now. During the weeks of counselling after her post-natal depression had been diagnosed, Dominique had learned that children who remembered having low levels of maternal care had a high risk of suffering post-natal depression themselves. She had learned, too, that Evelyn had suffered from what she still insisted on calling 'the baby blues' for a long time after her own birth. It explained a lot, Dominique thought, that Evelyn had been perfectly fine after she'd had Gabriel but not after her. She'd tried to talk to her mother about her experiences, but Evelyn had been withdrawn and uncommunicative. Dominique now understood better the distance she felt between herself and Evelyn, and understood, too, the closer bond Evelyn had with her brother. Understanding it didn't make her feel any better about it, but it did help her to put it into context. Given that she had neglected Kelly for the first months of her life, Dominique was now very careful to make her daughter feel loved and wanted at every available opportunity. And since Kelly was the most important person in her life and she loved her totally and unconditionally, that wasn't hard.

It had taken four months from the date of her visit to Dr Stevenson until the day she'd woken up without her first thought being about the heaviness of her body and the difficulty of getting out of bed. That day was the first when she hadn't dreaded the empty hours stretching ahead of her. She realised that she had actually slept through the entire night and that, unexpectedly, she was cheered by the sunlight filtering through the slats in the window blinds and the sounds of the blackbirds on the roof of the house.

She'd pushed back the covers and opened the blinds and she'd seen the colours of the street for the first time in a long time. She'd seen Linda's bright red car in the driveway next door. She'd seen the yellow and orange marigolds swaying in the pots outside Cherise's front window. She'd noticed that Tess McDonagh had added a porch to the front of her house. (Had Brendan done it? she wondered. It was a design he favoured, but she couldn't remember him ever talking about it as a job. But there was so much, she knew, that had passed her by over the last few months.) As her gaze moved along the road, she could see the blue sky and the white clouds and the green leaves on the trees. And all of these things made her smile.

She'd gone to the cot then, and looked inside. Her baby was staring up at her, her hazel eyes wide open, a puzzled expression on her face. And she'd leaned over the rail of the cot and picked her up and inhaled her sweet baby smell, and suddenly it didn't remind her of being in the hospital at all. The scent of her baby was very, very different. She didn't know how she could ever have thought otherwise.

I love you, she thought as she held her daughter close to her and kissed her soft face. I really and truly love you.

She'd taken time getting ready before going to her post-natal depression group meeting. She'd washed her hair and dried it with a hairdryer, instead of simply letting it dry by itself as she'd been doing for so long. She'd thought about what top to wear with the jeans that had once been a bit tight for her but now felt loose around her waist. She'd even pulled a pair of boots with heels from the back of the wardrobe.

She realised that she was looking forward to going out, even if it was only to the meeting. She'd never really seen the point of talking to a bunch of equally depressed women before. But that day it had been different. For the first time, she'd truly related to what the other women were saying. And she realised that her life wasn't as bleak as she'd thought. She'd been excited afterwards, had actually hummed to herself as she tidied the house and roasted a chicken for dinner that evening. She'd phoned Greg too and told him how well she was feeling, and he'd been pleased and delighted for her and reminded her that she could, of course, call him any time. She said that she was sure he had better things to do in his life than worry about her, and he said that he wasn't in the slightest bit worried about her but that he wanted her to know that she could always count on him.

Brendan had been overjoyed when he came home that night and found her sitting on the sofa with the baby in her arms, her hair smelling of apple shampoo as it gleamed under the glow of the recessed lights. He'd looked around the living room, which was clean and tidy even though there were stuffed toys on all the chairs. He'd smiled at her and she'd smiled back and then laughed. Which made the baby gurgle with laughter too.

But then, the next morning, the black clouds had rolled in again and the thoughts of getting up were too much to bear and she cried to herself because she hadn't turned into the perfect wife and mother after all; she was still hopeless, useless Domino. And when Brendan came home, she simply fried a couple of eggs and shoved some frozen chips in the oven for his dinner and ignored the look of disappointment on his face. The house was a mess again too.

Later, when the good days began outweighing the bad ones, when the black clouds changed to lighter shades of grey and started to disappear altogether, Brendan told her that he could tell the state of her mind from the state of the kitchen. She apologised to him then, told him she was sorry to have caused so much trouble, to have messed up his life. A dark expression passed across his face but he told her not to worry about it. She'd been sick, he said. Not her fault. And so she ignored the ripples of fear that his expression had evoked in her and reminded herself that things were now on the up. Kelly was the best daughter in the world and she loved her and she loved Brendan. She couldn't fix everything that had happened in the past but she could look forward to the future.

Nevertheless the fear stayed there, beneath the surface, because she always remembered the telephone conversation she'd overheard during her grey period. (Dominique had divided her depression months into three distinct periods: her black period, when everything had been so awful that she hadn't even been able to function like a normal person; her grey period, when the clouds lifted but not completely, when she could go for hours without feeling the crushing weight of despair engulf her again but she knew that it might; and her blue period, when she was fine for weeks but, unexpectedly, would start crying for no apparent reason.)

She'd been sitting in the living room, staring blankly at the TV, when the phone had rung and Brendan had answered it, even though the handset was right beside her. He'd gone into the kitchen with it but she'd heard him talking anyway.

'It's not what I signed up for,' he said, and she could sense the anger in his voice. 'I married her because I loved her, she was pregnant and I thought we could make a go of it. But even if she was the only woman on earth for me, this would be too much. I never know when I'm going to come home and find the place in a mess and her with her head down bawling her eyes out.' There had been a silence

102

while whoever was at the other end spoke, and then Brendan continued: 'It's not what anyone wants or expects. I'm out all day working my butt off. Well, that's one good thing to come out of it – it's too much of a knife-edge to be home, so the business is expanding at a rate of knots! I'm so knackered every night that the fact that she won't let me near her isn't as much of a big deal as it should be. But I want someone to love me. Not someone I have to treat like a piece of effing china. No, thing is, if it doesn't improve, I have to . . . well, nobody can live like this for ever.'

At the time, the tone of his conversation and the meaning hadn't registered with her. It was only later that she recalled it (word for word) and was shocked by it. Shocked and scared at the thought that he might one day leave her. She didn't want to be alone. Even worse, she didn't want to be alone with the baby. The thought made her shake with fear.

Dominique knew that she was the only person who could make herself better. She wanted to do everything she could to keep Brendan happy and their marriage steady. She loved him. She would always love him. He needed to know that. And she needed to show him. So as she began to get better, she tried to be as perfect a wife for him as she possibly could be. By always agreeing with him, always being there for him, always supporting him in everything he did. And it had worked.

He'd stayed.

The doorbell rang and she went to answer it. Evelyn and Seamus were standing on the step, looking upwards at the leaded porch windows and the elegant lamp in its ceramic shade, which swung gently in the breeze.

'Hello, Mam, Dad.'

It was the first time in nearly two months she'd seen her parents.

'You're looking well,' said Evelyn as she stepped inside.

Her tone wasn't entirely approving, but Dominique knew that it was because she was wearing a low-cut top and a short skirt and Evelyn didn't think they were suitable clothes for a married woman with a ten-year-old daughter. Dominique didn't care what Evelyn thought. It was a warm day and the skirt and top suited her figure, which had stayed slim thanks to healthy eating and occasional visits to the gym with Linda and Cherise.

'Have you changed things in here again?' Evelyn looked around her.

'We repainted, but that was months ago,' replied Dominique.

'You're never content to leave things well enough alone.' Evelyn followed her through to the kitchen, where party food was piled on the huge pine table.

'I can't stop Brendan,' Dominique said. 'It's in his blood.'

'Where is he today?' asked Seamus.

'Working.'

'On a Saturday? When Kelly has a party?'

'He went out ten minutes ago and he'll be back a bit later,' said Dominique. 'He needed to meet one of his foremen or something.'

'Gran! Gramps!' Kelly saw them immediately and ran the length of the garden, her long red-gold hair glinting in the sunlight.

'Happy birthday, sweetheart,' said Seamus, who had been entrusted with the task of giving their granddaughter her present. 'You look lovely.'

Kelly was wearing a lime-green dress with a wide skirt that flared out whenever she twirled, which she did now in front of them. It was a big change from the shorts and jeans she normally preferred. Kelly, Dominique knew, took after Brendan with her love of sports and the outdoor life and her lack of interest in pink sparkly dresses. But today she'd given in to her inner girl and was flouncing at every opportunity.

'No need to show off,' said Evelyn.

'But it's very pretty,' added Seamus.

'Mammy bought it for me specially,' Kelly said.

Seamus handed over the present – a pair of pink Barbie roller skates.

'Great, thanks.' She kissed both her grandparents and ran back to her friends again.

'You spoil that child,' said Evelyn. 'She barely gave those skates a glance.'

'She's excited, that's all,' said Dominique. 'It's the first birthday party like this she's ever had.'

'Indeed.' Evelyn looked at the gaggle of children laughing and shrieking as they jumped on the bouncy castle.

'She deserves it.'

'I'm not saying—'

'Evelyn.' Seamus put his hand on his wife's arm. 'It's fine.'

Evelyn hesitated and then nodded.

'Would you like a drink?' asked Dominique. 'There's beer, Dad. And a variety of lemonades.'

'I'll have a beer,' said Seamus.

'Orange juice for me.'

Dominique handed a bottle of Harp to her father and poured a Britvic for Evelyn. Her mother's hand touched hers fleetingly as she passed her the glass. Dominique felt herself tense and then relax again. She was trying really hard to get on better with Evelyn. It was important both for her and for Kelly.

'How's Gabriel?' she asked.

Evelyn's eyes lit up. 'He's coming to stay with us for a few days next month,' she said. 'It'll be a nice break for him and lovely for us to see him again.'

After his ordination, Gabriel had worked for a time in Dublin, but five years ago he had been sent to a remote parish in the north of Donegal. Dominique had spoken to him a few times on the phone, but not recently.

Gabriel had tried to help her during her depression too. He'd come to the house to see her, but she'd said over and over again that he couldn't possibly know what she was feeling and he couldn't possibly help her and that he was totally out of touch with reality. Gabriel had told her he'd pray for her, which made her laugh, although not with humour. If there was a God, she'd asked him, what good reason could He have for letting her feel like this? And Gabriel hadn't been able to give her any answer she'd wanted to hear.

He'd assisted at Kelly's christening, though, an event that Dominique remembered only vaguely. She'd been on the anti-depressants at that time and everyone had said that she was looking great, but she'd still felt as though she was an observer in her own life.

105

Dominique hadn't chosen her daughter's name. It had been Brendan's decision, because at that time she hadn't called her anything but the 'baby'. Brendan had suggested lots of different names to her, but she'd shrugged at all of them and said that he could call her whatever he liked. He'd chosen Kelly because it was his mother's maiden name. By the time they got round to baptising her, neither Brendan nor Dominique could ever think of her as anything else, even though Dominique had overheard Evelyn whispering to Gabriel that she'd hoped they'd put something a little more traditional on her birth certificate. A nice saint's name, she said, would be much more appropriate.

'You should come and see him.' Evelyn's words broke into Dominique's memories of Kelly's christening.

She nodded slowly.

'I'll phone you when he gets here.'

Dominique nodded again at her mother's words. Her attention had been drawn back to the garden where Kelly and three other children were balancing precariously at the top of the climbing frame. Kelly was laughing happily, her hair tousled by the breeze as she stretched her arms over her head.

She was a breathtakingly beautiful child. Dominique could never look at her without being astonished at how her strawberry-blond hair, hazel eyes and heart-shaped face all came together in perfect proportions so that nobody who met her was able to help themselves exclaiming at how lovely she was. As she watched her now, Dominique couldn't quite understand how it was that she had been so unable to bear the sight of her ten years earlier.

'What's Brendan working on now?' asked Seamus. 'I saw his scaffolding around a site in Harold's Cross as well as near The Square in Tallaght.'

'He's looking at apartments for the Harold's Cross site and a hotel in Tallaght.'

'A hotel!' exclaimed Evelyn. 'What's he doing building hotels?'

'It's a consortium,' said Dominique. 'There are three builders involved. He says it'll be very profitable.'

'I hope he's not getting out of his depth,' said Seamus.

'Oh, I think Brendan knows what he's doing,' Dominique said.

'He certainly seems to have a business brain,' said Evelyn. 'Not that I would have credited him with it at first.'

Dominique said nothing.

'You were lucky,' Evelyn told her. 'He stood by you twice.'

This time Dominique could feel herself grinding her teeth.

'I'm his wife,' she said tightly. 'He's supposed to stand by me.'

'Your mother doesn't mean—'

'Yes she does.' Dominique cut her father off as her good intentions about getting on with Evelyn swiftly evaporated. 'She'll always think of me as someone who was up the pole when she got married and so should be living in penance for the rest of her life. And she secretly thinks that what happened to me after Kelly was born was a judgement for me being flighty and irresponsible and for throwing out her stupid picture of St Dominic.'

'Dominique! That's not what—'

'It bloody is,' said Dominique. 'It bloody always was. Now unless you want to mix with people and be nice, you might as well just go home.'

'And they did,' she told Brendan later that evening when they were sitting in front of the TV. She was sipping a glass of wine and he had a drink in front of him as she filled him in on the party. 'Though Dad at least finished off his beer first.'

'I know she's a pain in the arse, but you shouldn't allow her to rile you.' Brendan yawned.

Dominique put her half-full glass on the coffee table. 'I know that too,' she said. 'I do try, but we totally rub each other up the wrong way.'

'They do their best,' said Brendan. 'Of course they're a pair of miserable gits, but that's the way they were brought up.'

'You're very tolerant,' she said.

'No point in me wasting my time worrying over them,' he told her. 'I've much more important things to concern me.'

'Like what?'

'Things are progressing fast on the hotel,' he told her. 'I had a meeting with the solicitor this afternoon.'

'On a Saturday?'

107

'Business doesn't stop on Saturdays any more. We have a meeting with the banks on Monday and we wanted to make sure that everything was on track.'

He yawned again and she didn't ask any more questions. Things had changed from the early days of their marriage, when he'd shared everything about the business with her. She knew that he tried to hide problems from her now, because he was afraid that telling her about potential worries would set her on the road to depression again. She tried to explain that she was fine, but she knew he dreaded a return to the past. And so that was why their mantra of 'no secrets' didn't count any more.

'Don't forget to wear your good suit to the meeting,' she said as she glanced at his ancient T-shirt with its streak of paint across the shoulders.

'I won't.' Brendan cracked open another beer. 'Don't you worry. I scrub up well.'

He came home on Monday with a smile on his face and a bottle of very expensive champagne in his hands.

'I thought we should celebrate,' he said as he eased the cork out of the bottle. It didn't come out as smoothly as he'd expected, and they had to rush to fill their glasses before the golden liquid fizzed on to the kitchen floor.

'Oh, wow, this is great.' She laughed as she sipped the drink, suddenly feeling as she had when she'd first met Brendan and she was permanently bubbling with excitement. 'I do so love champagne.'

'This is just the start,' he told her. 'Delahaye Developments will be tendering for a lot of business in the months to come. There are opportunities out there and I plan to grab them with both hands.'

'I'd much prefer if you just grabbed me with both hands,' she said.

His eyes lit up. 'Where's Kelly?'

'Sleepover with Anastasia and Mel. No school tomorrow, it's an in-service training day.'

'Well, well, Mrs Delahaye. What perfect timing.'

'I do my best,' she teased as she wrapped her arms around his neck and pulled him towards her.

'I'm glad to hear that it's all going well for you.' Gabriel was sitting opposite her at the kitchen table in the family home. He was, thought Dominique, still astoundingly handsome. His hair was slightly too long, but it gave his dark eyes, visible beneath his sweeping fringe, an extra-soulful look. (Emphasised, she acknowledged, by his black suit and dog collar.)

'The company will make a lot of money in the next few years,' she said. 'I'm very, very lucky.'

'Yes.' His tone was measured and she looked at him in irritation.

'There's nothing wrong with making money,' she said.

'I never said there was,' he protested.

'I know you,' she told him. 'You think that we'd all be better on our knees in poverty.'

Gabriel laughed. 'I don't. Really. I truly am glad that things have worked out so well for you, Dominique.'

'So am I,' she said. 'How about you? How's the parish?'

'I like it,' he told her. 'It's a great community. A dwindling congregation, unfortunately. So many young people have left over the last ten years. But we do our best. So I'm happy there.'

'You don't regret it?' she asked suddenly.

'Regret it?' He spoke quickly. 'Regret my vocation? How could I?'

'I knew you wouldn't,' she admitted. 'I told Emma Walsh that thousands of times. I just wondered if sometimes you didn't think that you were stuck in the arsehole of nowhere ministering to the elderly.'

'Rossanagh isn't the arsehole of nowhere,' he told her.

'That's your opinion.'

He laughed. 'You're such a Dub. How's Emma keeping?'

'Fine,' said Dominique. 'She's happy.'

Gabriel nodded. 'I always knew she would be.'

'D'you know everything?' Dominique teased.

'I'm a man of the cloth,' he told her. 'So . . . yeah!'

This time they both laughed.

'Would you ever like to come back to Dublin?' asked Dominique.

He shook his head. 'I like being away,' he said.

'Away from the clutches of the parental home.'

He smiled slightly and she shrugged.

'I suppose it wasn't the same for you. They loved you.' She sighed.

'Dominique, they loved both of us. They still do.'

'But not equally.'

'You're wrong about that.'

She shook her head. 'I don't have a connection with Mam,' she said. 'I never had and I never will have. It messed me up a bit, and although I understand it now, I can never quite get over you being the favourite.'

'Ah, Domino. Don't be so silly.'

'I can't help it,' she said and then smiled at him. 'But I forgive you.'

'How's your own connection with Kelly?' he asked.

He'd continued to offer to talk to her during her depression. She'd told Brendan that she didn't want to see him. Didn't want him preaching at her. It was much easier to talk to her counsellor, Sarah. And to Greg. She didn't see Greg much after the day when she'd cried on his shoulder. But for a full year after that they talked once a week on the phone, when she shared with him the fears that she simply couldn't share with Brendan. Over time their phone calls had dwindled. And after Greg got married they stopped altogether, because Dominique knew that it would be impossible for anyone else to understand the bond they shared.

'We're great,' she said warmly. 'We have fun together and I enjoy being her mother. I can't honestly say that I'll ever feel close to Mam and Dad, but I am very, very close to Kelly.'

'I'm glad,' said Gabriel. 'Obviously my prayers for your happiness were answered.'

'I think in the end happiness has more to do with getting on with it yourself than with prayer,' she said.

'But it can't hurt.' Gabriel smiled at her.

'So do you pray for me every day?' she asked.

'Of course.'

'Really?'

'Yes.'

She chuckled. 'You think it's your prayer that's made the business go so well and got us our lovely house?'

'I don't pray for material things,' said Gabriel. 'There are other things in life too, you know. Everyone needs another side to their existence.'

'Of course it's not all about material things,' she agreed. 'With Brendan, it's about being secure, that's all. And I do have another side. It just doesn't involve spending time on my knees, that's all. At least . . .' there was a sudden wicked gleam in her eye, 'not in prayer, at any rate.'

Which made Gabriel splutter over his cup of tea and reduced Dominique to fits of uncontrollable laughter.

Chapter 9

The following Friday, as she was loading up the washing machine with laundry, she got a phone call from Emma saying that she was at Heuston station and asking if Dominique would like to meet her for lunch.

'Love to,' said Dominique. 'Kelly's going to drama class after school so I've got the time.'

'I'll be in Blooms from twelve,' Emma told her. 'I'll see you there.'

Dominique glanced at her watch. 'It'll probably be closer to one, to be honest.'

'No problem,' said Emma. 'I'll wait for you.'

Dominique hung up, added powder to the washing machine and started the cycle. Then she hurried up the stairs and opened her wardrobe doors. She knew that she could never compete with Emma in the up-to-the-minute style stakes, but it was important not to look like a suburban slob, so she did a quick change from her comfortable baggy M&S jeans and fleece into a less forgiving pair of Calvin Kleins and a plain white T-shirt. Despite her slimmed-down silhouette, it was always a struggle to get into the jeans, but Dominique felt it was worth it so that she didn't appear totally inadequate next to Emma. She told herself, as she always did when she had feelings of inferiority, that she was a perfectly capable woman who always did the best she could. Sarah had taught her that it was OK to feel inadequate sometimes. Greg had taught her that too. But she didn't want to feel as though she hadn't tried.

She swirled bronzer across her face, dabbed gloss on her lips and ran a brush through her hair. Then she decanted her bits and pieces from her ancient black handbag to a smaller, neater version.

She looked at her reflection in the mirror, awarded herself six out of ten and hurried off to catch the bus.

Emma was sitting in the hotel bar, flicking through a magazine. Her chestnut hair was pulled back into a casual ponytail. She was wearing a light dress and matching jacket in palest lilac, and Dominique could see, as she turned the pages of the magazine, that her nails were perfectly manicured and painted a vibrant red to match the colour of her lipstick. She sighed involuntarily. She would never, ever look as casually sophisticated as Emma, no matter how hard she tried. Emma would always be ten out of ten.

'Hi!' Emma smiled. 'How're you doing, Domino?'

Dominique grinned in return. Emma used the Delahaye nickname for her all the time now. Naturally. She was part of the family too. Emma Walsh had married Greg Delahaye in a very glitzy wedding ceremony in County Cork a few years earlier. The reception had been a million times bigger and brasher than Dominique and Brendan's. This was due to the fact that Maura and Norman Walsh were delighted that their daughter was marrying Greg, and were happy to pay for an over-the-top do for her. In fact they'd encouraged her to invite as many people as she wanted. Emma had taken them at their word and pulled out all the stops.

Dominique hadn't exactly been envious of the glamour that had been on show that day, but she hadn't been able to help comparing the extravagant floral arrangements, the apparently unending bottles of champagne and the excited, happy speeches with the far simpler event and briefest of speeches that had been her own wedding, and she couldn't help feeling that the Delahayes were making comparisons too. Emma had looked like a princess in her Pronuptia fitted dress with its long sequinned train and with her hair sculpted around a dazzling tiara that secured an intricate lace veil. Dominique's dress had been designed to hide her bump and not bestow a princess look.

Dominique had been surprised at first when Greg and Emma announced their engagement. Even though she'd been the one to bring them together, she sometimes thought that Greg was a bit too quiet and home-loving for Emma. And she couldn't help wondering if her friend was just a bit high-maintenance and party-loving for Greg. But the truth was that she was delighted that her friend and her brother-in-law (who she also considered to be a good friend) had decided to get married, even though it meant that Emma would be moving to Cork.

She said as much to Greg at a family dinner after they'd announced their engagement, and he grinned at her.

'I never would've guessed that I'd meet my future wife at your wedding, Domino. So thank you.' His voice softened. 'I know we're two quite different people. But I also know Emma is the right girl for me. She's upbeat and chirpy and she doesn't let me obsess about things. She's optimistic whenever I'm pessimistic. And I love her.'

'I'm very glad,' Dominique said. 'And I'm even more glad that I brought the two of you together.'

She would have to find another confidante now, she told herself on the day of the wedding, as she watched the bride and groom take to the dance floor. Over the years since Kelly's birth, Greg had been the one she turned to when she was feeling down. She could never feel anything but gratitude towards him for his role in helping her to get treatment for her post-natal depression and his support for her afterwards. He was still a source of support. She never had to pretend with Greg, as she sometimes did with Brendan, that everything was absolutely fine. There were days when she still struggled, but she didn't want Brendan to know. She didn't want him to feel that he had made a mistake in staying with her. She didn't want to be a moaning, complaining, depressing wife.

'We all struggle sometimes, Domino,' Greg told her one day when they were sitting in the living room. He'd come to town to take Emma to a concert and had called in to see her while she waited for his girlfriend to finish work. As always Dominique was pleased to see him, even though his visit was unexpected. It had been a tough day, full of small inconveniences (like the dishwasher overflowing and the kettle boiling dry) that had mushroomed in imagined importance as the hours passed, making her feel stupid and useless. She'd vented her annoyance at him and he'd laughed at her so that suddenly she found herself laughing too.

'How are you so good at this?' she demanded. 'Where did you learn?'

She knew from the expression on his face that however he'd learned, he'd learned it the hard way, and she suddenly felt that she'd trespassed into a secret corner of his life. 'It's OK,' she said hastily. 'No need to tell me. I'm being nosy.'

'You should be,' said Greg. 'And . . . well, Domino, I'd like to tell you.'

'I know.'

'It was a girl,' he said.

She was surprised. There had been a time when she'd wondered if Greg was gay, although his engagement to Emma had put paid to that idea (Emma had confided in her that Greg was way hotter in bed than she'd ever expected. Too much information, Dominique had told her, and then added that it must be a Delahaye trait, because Brendan was no mean performer himself.) Nevertheless, Dominique sometimes thought that Greg was far too sensitive for a man. Even so, she hadn't imagined that he was the sort of person who'd let his heart be broken by a girl.

He had met her when he was nineteen and she was seventeen. Maria and her family were in Cork on holiday, he explained, three weeks in a caravan near the seashore. They'd met on the beach and he'd fallen instantly in love with her.

'I say that now,' he told Dominique, 'but we were only kids. I couldn't have been in love with her. I just thought I was.'

Dominique didn't say that she hadn't been much older than him when she'd married his brother, and that nobody had considered her to be a kid.

Greg and Maria had made vows to write to each other every day and phone whenever possible. He'd written five letters before he realised that she wasn't replying, and when he'd called the house he was told that she was busy and didn't want to talk to him. So he went to find her.

She lived in the Midlands, in an even smaller town than Castlecannon. He arrived at the house late one afternoon and demanded to see her. Her father came out and told him that if he ever showed his face in the town again, he'd kill him. Greg had been mystified by the older man's anger.

And then he'd learned the truth from Maria's older sister. Maria had been pregnant. She'd tried to kill herself.

'God Almighty.' Dominique was shocked.

'Think about it, Domino,' said Greg. 'It was Ireland in the eighties. No contraception. Abortion totally out of the question. She was from a tiny village. She couldn't handle the shame.'

Dominique understood. A few years earlier and it could have happened to her too. It had been a different time. A different country.

'She'd taken sleeping tablets. They got her to hospital, but she lost the baby.' He cleared his throat. 'My baby.'

'Oh, Greg.'

'Everyone thinks it's only women who are traumatised by unplanned pregnancies or miscarriages or anything to do with child-birth, but I . . . I couldn't stop thinking about everything. About her. About her taking the tablets. About the baby. Whether it felt anything. I obsessed about it, Domino, until I simply couldn't get up in the mornings. And so my parents – Irish parents of a gener-ation who didn't believe in therapy or anything like that – finally realised that I had to see someone. They arranged for me to go to a therapist and ultimately I got through it, but it was the hardest thing ever for me.'

'Did they know?' asked Dominique. 'About the girl and the baby?'

'Eventually,' he said. He looked rueful. 'I think they thought it had all been for the best. That it would have been a disaster if she'd had the baby.'

'Yes,' said Dominique. 'I can see how they might think that way. I can also see why you wouldn't. Does Emma know?'

He shook his head again. 'It was a long time ago,' he said. 'I put it into my past. It's not something I want to talk to her about. It's not the same with you. I was reminded of what it was like . . .'

'When I had my depression after Kelly?'

'I know it was a very different situation, but I understood what you were going through. And I desperately wanted you to connect with Kelly. I couldn't bear to think that you couldn't love her.'

'I love her more than anything,' said Dominique simply. 'And you've been a total tower of strength for me, Greg.'

'I'm glad,' he said. 'I care about you, Domino. I want things to work out for you and Brendan and Kelly. It makes me think that life can be OK when I see you all together.'

Dominique liked having someone who understood how she'd once felt, and who understood, too, that if she ever felt down now, it didn't mean that she was about to lose herself in a full-blown depression. With Brendan she always tried to appear upbeat, no matter how she was feeling inside. With Greg, she didn't have to. And that was why she and Greg had a connection that she knew she could never have with anyone else.

She was feeling upbeat now, as she sat down beside Emma, welcoming the time out with her friend.

'All's good with me,' she said. 'What has you in town? Shopping spree?'

'Mam isn't too well at the moment,' Emma told her. 'I've come up for a few days to keep an eye on her.'

'Oh, gosh, sorry to hear that. What's the matter with her?'

'Stomach trouble. She feels sick all the time and isn't eating.'

'Has she seen a doctor?'

Emma nodded. 'He's sending her for tests. Dad says she seems to be getting a bit better, but I thought I should come up.'

'Greg didn't come with you?'

Emma shook her head. 'He's busy at work and he's got stuff to do at home too.'

A waiter asked them if they'd like something to eat, and both of them ordered sandwiches and coffee.

'I'm sure everything will be fine,' said Dominique.

'Thanks.' Emma smiled at her. 'I'll let you know, of course.'

'I haven't spoken to Greg in ages,' said Dominique idly, after a lull in their conversation. 'He's well?'

'Sure.'

'Is work going OK for him? He seems to be busy all the time. I remember the last time we talked he said he was under a heap of stress. I didn't realise IT was so demanding.'

'You're always far too worried about Greg.' Emma said. 'He's fine.'

'I'm not at all worried about Greg,' Dominique told her. 'I'm just hoping that everything's all right for him, that's all.'

'You should be more concerned about me,' said Emma.

'Why?' Dominique looked anxious. 'Is there something wrong with you?'

'No, no,' said Emma. 'I'm pregnant, that's all.'

'Hey, Em! That's great news!' Dominique's face lit up.

'We were trying for a while and it was taking longer than either of us expected, but now that it's happened I'm a bit scared,' confessed Emma.

'Oh, listen, I'm sure you'll be fine and not a basket case like me,' said Dominique cheerfully. 'And I bet you and Greg will be great parents.'

'We'll do our best.'

'If you're worried about anything yourself, just give me a call. When are you due?'

'I'm just three months gone.' Emma couldn't keep the excitement from her voice.

'And how are you feeling?'

'OK so far,' said her sister-in-law.

'Stand up and let me see you.'

'Don't be stupid.'

'Oh, go on! You don't look like you have a pick on you.'

Emma grinned but stood up and turned around.

'You still don't look like you have a pick on you,' said Dominique as she sat down again.

'I feel really fat, and sooner or later I'll balloon out,' said Emma. 'But I'm hoping to keep wearing my proper clothes for as long as I can.'

'You make me laugh, Emma Walsh,' said Dominique in amusement. 'You know that you're absolutely gorgeous and you'll probably be the most stunning pregnant woman in the history of the world.'

'Get lost.' Emma laughed but looked pleased all the same.

'And is Greg delighted?'

'Absolutely thrilled,' confirmed Emma. 'He's definitely going to

119

be a great dad. To be honest, he drives me demented. He never stops giving me advice and telling me to take it easy and . . . Well, at this stage he's read more books than me about it!'

'That's Greg for you,' agreed Dominique. 'Takes it all so seriously.'

'Yes, well, if I've to go through nine months of being wrapped in cotton wool . . .' Emma shook her head. 'However, I'll do my best.'

She reached into her bag and took out a small parcel wrapped in glossy pink paper. 'Oh, and before I forget, I have a present for Kelly. It's a pretend make-up set. I hope it's not too girlie for her.'

'She'll love it,' Dominique told her. 'She's turning from a happy scruff into the vainest child you could possibly imagine. It's because everyone keeps telling her how pretty she is.'

Emma smiled. 'She's a dote.'

The waiter returned with their sandwiches and coffee.

'Is that OK?' said Dominique as she watched Emma scrape coleslaw from between the bread.

'Should have asked for it without, can't bear the taste right now.'

After a couple of minutes, Emma shoved her half-eaten sandwich to one side.

'Not hungry,' she told Dominique. 'I think I'm starving and then I feel full after a few mouthfuls.'

Dominique nodded. 'I remember what that was like.'

'Haven't you ever wanted another child?' asked Emma curiously.

'No.' Dominique's face tensed for a moment. 'I just couldn't do it again.'

'Ah, you're right if you don't want to. No bother to June to keep popping them out, though.' Emma knew not to pursue the issue with Dominique. It was one thing she knew she never discussed.

Dominique relaxed and smiled. 'I know. She made such a fuss about Alicia but then kept on going.'

'Alicia is lovely, but that Joanna is a spoiled little madam and Maurice Junior is a lethal force.'

'Agreed.' Dominique glanced at her watch. 'D'you want another coffee?'

Emma hesitated and then nodded. 'And then I'd better get going. I told Dad I'd be there before four.'

'If there's anything I can do to help with your mum, just tell me,' said Dominique after she'd ordered the coffee. 'We're all family now.'

'I know.' Emma began to pick at the crusts of her discarded sandwich. 'Speaking of family . . . how's Gabriel?'

'He's fine,' Dominique replied. 'Ministering away.'

'Still in Donegal? No sign of him moving parish?'

'Not that I know.' Dominique shook her head. 'Though I'm sure he must be getting tired of Rossanagh by now. The population's only a few hundred. I sometimes think of him rattling around like Father Ted in some creaky old parish house with ancient furniture and a mad housekeeper and I feel sorry for him. But he's probably happy as a pig in shit there.'

'Domino!'

Dominique grinned. 'It's true.'

'I heard he was in Dublin. Did you meet him?'

'How on earth did you know that?' Dominique looked at her in astonishment.

'Oh, Greg mentioned it. Brendan told him that your parents had called around for Kelly's birthday and annoyed you. And then he said you were going to see Gabriel.'

Dominique nodded. 'It was only a flying visit,' she said. 'Anyway, there's no sign of him leaving his ancient parishioners and their sheep for the bright city lights.'

'I was wondering . . .'

'What?'

'D'you think he'd mind if I called him?'

'What on earth for?' Dominique replaced her cup on its saucer.

'To see if he'd do a novena for Mam.'

'Oh.'

'And for me too, of course, for the baby. Every little helps, and it's his job to pray, after all,' said Emma.

'Well, yes. But do you believe in all that stuff?'

'Can't hurt,' said Emma. 'Do you have a number for him?'

'Sure. Hold on a second.' Dominique opened her handbag and took out a slimline diary with the interlocking double-D logo of Delahaye Developments on it.

She opened the diary, found the phone number for Gabriel's parish house and gave it to Emma.

'I'm sure your mam will be fine,' she said comfortingly.

'I hope so.' Emma looked worried. 'To be honest, I have a bad feeling about this. But maybe I'm just being hormonal. That's why I wanted to talk to Gabriel about the prayers.'

'D'you want to drop by and visit us later?' asked Dominique. 'You're very welcome, and Kelly will certainly distract you from your hormones.'

Emma smiled. 'No doubt she would. And I'd love to call by, but not this weekend. I have to stay with Mam.'

'Sure, no problem.'

Emma looked at her watch. 'I'd better be going. I don't want Dad fretting.'

'And I guess I'd better be home before my daughter,' said Dominique.

'I find it hard to think of you as a married woman with a ten-year-old,' said Emma.

'Really? Why?'

'Back at school, I never thought of you as the marrying kind.'

'I suppose not,' said Dominique, remembering the time that Emma had called her an ugly cow who'd die an old maid because no guy in his right mind would fancy her.

'And here we are related now. Who would've put money on that?'

'Who indeed?' asked Dominique.

'Life's funny that way.'

Dominique glanced at Emma. 'Remember the ridiculous crush you had on Gabriel?'

'We've all moved on since we were living in Drimnagh,' said Emma impatiently. 'We're totally different people now.'

Dominique nodded. Her life had changed immeasurably since those days. And yet somehow she didn't feel different at all.

'I didn't think Greg had it in him,' remarked Brendan in bed that night when Dominique told him Emma's news. She looked at him in surprise.

'Well, really,' he said. 'They've been married for ages.'

'Yes, but not everyone rushes into having kids,' said Dominique.

'True. Are they planning a big family?'

'I don't know.' She glanced at him. 'That's not the sort of question you ask.'

'I suppose not. And the answer might well depend on how well things go first time.'

She said nothing.

'That wasn't a dig,' he told her. 'Just a statement of fact.'

'I know.'

'So don't go all gloomy on me.'

'I'm not.'

'Good,' he said as he loosened the ribbon on her flimsy nightdress. 'I'm not in the mood for gloomy.'

'Neither am I,' she assured him and slipped the nightdress over her head.

Chapter 10

It had, in fact, been nearly six months after Kelly was born before they'd had sex again. For much of that time Dominique hadn't been interested, although she was acutely aware that this was something that had the power to destroy her marriage. But even though she knew that turning away from Brendan at night wouldn't make things any better, she was utterly unable to make love to him. Sometimes, as the depression lifted, she would turn to him and he would kiss her and hold her and she knew that he wanted to make love to her. And she wanted to make love to him too, but every time she thought about the possibility of getting pregnant again, she would tense up so much that he knew there was no point in coming near her. It wasn't until after she'd mentally replayed over and over again the phone call in which he'd talked about leaving her that she spoke to the doctor about it. He prescribed the pill, telling her to come back to him immediately if it started having side effects, because she was still taking the antidepressants too. She thought that she'd feel even more useless then. But to her surprise she didn't. Being on the pill gave her a sudden sense of release. She could make love to Brendan and she wouldn't get pregnant and everything would be OK.

And it was.

Until he asked if she felt ready to have another baby.

He'd first broached the subject after Kelly's second birthday. By then, Dominique had completely recovered from her post-natal depression. She was no longer taking antidepressants and the feelings of despair that used to overwhelm her had passed. There were no black days or grey days or even blue days. She could even look back and recall her emergency Caesarean without thinking that it had been the worst moment of her life. The dreams in which her motherhood of Kelly had been questioned had stopped too. She felt like a real person again.

She was involved in the residents' association, in charge of producing their quarterly newsletter. She liked feeling part of the community and was comfortable with the other people on the committee. She didn't need to go to her support group any more. Socially, she was having a good time with Brendan. Their increased income meant that they went out more often, and occasionally, too, they held dinner parties at home, which she always enjoyed, because she was good at entertaining, realising she had a knack for sitting the right people beside each other. Secretly, too, she liked the compliments afterwards. Despite everything she'd become involved in, however, she liked being a mother most of all. Now, when she was with Kelly, she felt what she had always thought she should feel, what she had been so guilty about not feeling: a surge of love and a desire to protect her daughter no matter what. When Kelly cried, she hurried to see what was wrong. When Kelly laughed, she laughed too. Suddenly she was all right with being a mother. She knew how to do it. She was, she thought, actually quite good at it.

But when Brendan suggested to her that perhaps it might be time to think about a brother or a sister for Kelly, she felt a sinking feeling in the bottom of her stomach and for a moment she thought that she was going to faint. It wasn't the physical aspect of what might happen that worried her the most, although she knew that she was terrified about the idea of giving birth again.

It was the fact that this time she might fail her baby.

She'd almost failed Kelly. She couldn't take that risk again.

She didn't say this to Brendan. He'd done his best while she'd been unwell but she knew he hadn't really understood it. And she knew that he thought it was a result of Kelly's crisis delivery. They'd both been told that if she was going to have another child, an elective Caesarean would be a good idea, so there was little chance of things developing into a full-blown emergency as they had before.

But she was still afraid. She was disgusted by herself and her fear. She was appalled by her inability to do what Brendan wanted.

What he deserved. Yet she knew that if she stopped taking the pill, she wouldn't be able to make love to him. She knew that without even having to think about it.

She lied to him. She told him that she'd stopped, but actually she moved her supply from the bathroom cabinet to the inside pocket of her kitbag. She went to the gym once a week for the mother-and-baby swim with Kelly. Brendan had no need to go near her bag. And she knew that he would never suspect her of lying.

She knew it was foolish of her to think that he wouldn't wonder about it. After all, she'd got pregnant pretty easily the first time. He couldn't understand why she wasn't pregnant now. He wondered if there was something wrong and whether it would be worth seeing a doctor. She told him that if they went to the doctor he'd tell them to relax and keep trying. Give it a little more time, she suggested. We'll worry about it in a couple of months.

But deceiving him was stressing her out completely. She knew that what she was doing was wrong, and every day she felt worse and worse about it. But it was too late to tell him about the pill. He'd kill her if he found out. Well, leave her at any rate. And she couldn't let him leave now.

Greg came up to Dublin for a technology course. He rarely stayed in the city overnight, but whenever he did, he stayed with Brendan and Dominique. When Dominique made up the guest room, Kelly, who loved Greg passionately, insisted on leaving chocolate buttons on the pillow for him as a present.

He arrived at the house at five o'clock in the evening, while Brendan was still out at work. His eyes were red – from too much peering at the computer screen, he told Dominique, who got him some Optrex from the bathroom cabinet.

'So how are you?' he asked as he swilled the liquid around his eye.

'Grand,' she told him.

'Where's the lovely Kelly?' He refilled the plastic eyebath and washed his other eye.

'Having a nap,' she told him. 'When she wasn't helping me to do up your room, she was playing in the garden with her friends, and she's just flaked out. Well, I say playing, but most of it was fighting with the cute little boy from down the road. She gave him such grief.'

'A lovely little thing like her! I don't believe you.'

Dominique laughed. 'Kelly is a demon. Brendan says that she's as tough as a boy, which always causes a row, because girls are tough anyway. Though not always rough, perhaps.'

'Aha! A closet feminist.'

'Not at all,' she assured him. 'Just stating a fact.'

'Oh well, you know how old-fashioned Bren is about things. He still thinks women are weak and fragile creatures who need to be protected from everything.'

Dominique busied herself filling the kettle.

'And I guess he still dreams of a son, so that he has someone to follow him into the business,' said Greg carefully.

She turned to look at him. 'Has he said anything to you?'

'Only that you're trying again. I'm sure it'll be fine this time, Domino.'

She turned away again. The tears had flooded her eyes and she didn't want him to see them. But he knew anyway. He got up and walked over to her.

'What's the matter?'

This was one thing she just couldn't share with him. He'd be horrified that she was lying to his brother. He'd have to tell Brendan. And then what would happen?

But she couldn't stop herself. It was just like when he'd called to see her during her depression. Suddenly the words spilled out of her mouth and she told him about hiding the pill and that she was the most horrible person in the world and that she didn't know what to do.

'You have to tell him the truth,' said Greg after she'd finished. 'You can't live a lie, Domino.'

'I know, I know. But he'll hate me for ever.' She wiped her eyes with the back of her hand. 'Oh, Greg, he married me out of pity but I couldn't bear to lose him.'

'He married you because he loved you, and he still loves you,' said Greg firmly. 'You have to tell him the truth.'

'I can't.' She was crying again, and he looked at her sympathetically and then folded her into a hug and held her close. 'We used to say that we had no secrets from each other, but that's all changed and it's my fault. Whatever else, I can't tell him about this!'

'You don't have to tell him about the pill,' said Greg. 'Just that you don't want to have another child.'

Dominique looked up at him.

'You owe it to him to say it,' Greg told her 'Otherwise you're living a lie and your marriage will eventually fall apart.'

'Oh, Greg.' She buried her head in his shoulder again. 'Why is it I can spill my guts to you but not to Brendan?'

'I don't know,' said Greg.

'And why are you always right?' She sniffed.

'I don't know that either.' He pushed her away from him and looked at her blotchy face. 'I'm good at knowing what's right for other people. Not always so great at it in my own life, though.' He kissed her on the forehead.

'You won't say anything tonight?'

'Of course not,' he said. 'Now go on, wash your face before he gets home and wants to know why you're sobbing your heart out in front of me.'

It took her a week to pluck up the courage to talk to Brendan. In bed one night, she did as Greg had suggested and simply said that she didn't think she was ready for another baby.

'Why?'

She told him of her fears, although she still couldn't verbalise her anxieties in the same way as she could with Greg.

'So you're saying no more children? Not ever?'

'Not not ever. Just not yet.'

'And when will you feel ready?'

'I don't know, Brendan. Just not yet.'

He said nothing else but rolled over from her and pulled the covers around his shoulders. She lay on her back for a while and then turned towards him. She put her arm tentatively around him. She was afraid that he'd shake it off. But he didn't. He snored gently. She held him close.

* * *

129

He didn't once ask her about birth control. He didn't talk about having more children again. They continued to live their lives as they'd always done, but they never discussed increasing their family. Dominique sometimes thought that she should raise the subject, but she didn't want to start a discussion when she didn't know where it might lead. And so she waited for Brendan to be the one to say something.

Which wasn't until nearly two years later when, as they lay once again side by side in bed, he told her that he was happy with the family the way it was.

'Huh?'

'I don't ever want another baby.'

Dominique felt waves of guilty relief wash over her.

'Are you sure?' she asked. 'I know that we talked about a son . . .'

'That was macho talk. Besides, Kelly could follow me into the business. She's a tough little cookie. Delahaye and Daughter.' He laughed.

She didn't know what to say.

'I know you think about it.' He propped his head up on his hand and looked at her. 'I know you feel guilty about it. But in the end, you're right. There are too many kids in the world already. Besides, I'm out all the hours God sends. I don't have time for more family stuff. And I've got new projects lined up that will take even more time.'

'Are you just saying this to make me feel OK?'

'No,' Brendan said seriously. 'I mean it. I've been doing a lot of thinking about the future, and the truth is that I don't need the distraction of a newborn baby; all those middle-of-the-night feeds and dirty nappies.'

'If you're sure . . .'

'Well, you're pretty sure, aren't you?'

'Yes, but . . .'

'Enough said. I might've thought differently a while ago, but I've changed. It's fine. Kelly is the most important person in the world to me, and what I'm doing now will provide for her well into the future.'

'Which is?'

'Overseas property. That's a real growth area. People wanting a slice of the sun.'

'Are you mad?' she asked. 'Who can afford houses in the sun?'

'Not very many people now,' he admitted. 'But prices there are so low relative to here. People are saying it all the time. And some day they're going to want to buy one for themselves.'

'So you're going to build holiday homes?' She was still astonished.

'Yes,' he said. 'I talked to Ciara, my solicitor. And to Matthew. We're looking at forming a partnership with an overseas company.'

'But . . . but what about here?'

'What about it?' he said.

'How are you going to build here and there?'

'I won't physically build everything,' he told her. 'I'll contract it out.'

She looked thoughtful.

'It's going to make us a fortune,' he said. 'And that's why I don't have time to make babies too.'

She knew that she should have been relieved. She was, of course, very relieved. Yet she knew something had changed between them. And she didn't know exactly what that was. She couldn't help wondering what had made Brendan change his mind. For a long time the issue had been like an unlit fuse between them. Every single day she had expected him to ask her if she was ready. If now would be a good time. But he'd accepted that no time would ever be a good time. And although she felt profoundly grateful that she didn't have to worry about babies any more, she also felt as though a part of her had died. Which, she told herself, was crazy. After all, knowing that she didn't have to worry about babies any more should surely make her feel more alive than ever.

Her old school friend, Maeve Mulligan, came back from London. They'd kept in touch sporadically but had only met about half a dozen times since Maeve had left. She usually came home at Christmas but didn't bother the rest of the time. However, when she'd finally settled back in Dublin, renting an apartment in the newly developing docklands area of the city, she called to see Dominique. She arrived

131

at the house with a bunch of flowers and a bottle of wine and she was suitably impressed by the high ceilings and intricate plasterwork as well as the modern kitchen and carefully landscaped gardens.

'You've *so* landed on your feet,' she told Dominique.

'I know.'

'I see hoardings for Delahaye Developments everywhere. I never realised Brendan was such a major businessman.'

'Not quite everywhere,' Dominique amended. 'But the company seems to be expanding every day. He's got an office now in the docklands.'

'I never would have thought it.' Maeve took one of the oatmeal cookies that Dominique had baked and bit into it. 'Umm, gorgeous. Is that what you are now?' She grinned. 'A cookie-baking yummy mummy?'

Dominique snorted. 'I don't think so. Those cookies are the only thing I'm really any good at. But I'm not bad at the whole entertaining scene, which is kind of weirdly grown-up for me.'

'I envy you.'

'Why?'

'You're twenty-nine and you've got your life sorted. I'm part of the whole singleton generation and I'm utterly hopeless. Have you read *Bridget Jones's Diary* yet? It's so me.'

Dominique shook her head.

'It's about a girl who eats too much, drinks too much, smokes too much, weighs too much and who's looking for a boyfriend.'

Dominique laughed. 'You're her?'

'Totally,' affirmed Maeve. 'London's tough for the single girl who wants to settle down, and I'm sure Dublin's not much better.'

'Why d'you want to settle down? The eating, drinking and smoking life sounds fun.'

'You've got to be kidding me. We're all out there looking for Mr Right. Only there isn't a hope in hell he's anywhere nearby. You've already found him.'

'Had to go about it the wrong way,' said Dominique.

'Doesn't matter once you get a result.'

The kitchen door opened and Kelly walked in. Maeve's eyes opened wide.

'Omigod!' she exclaimed. 'You've grown so tall! And so gorgeous.'

'Kelly, you remember Maeve,' said Dominique. 'We went to school together.'

'Hi.' Kelly nodded impatiently. 'Mum, can I go to the cinema with Anastasia? Her mum's taking us.'

'OK,' said Dominique. 'Do you have money?'

'Not enough,' replied Kelly.

'Here.' Dominique opened her purse and handed her a note. 'Buy popcorn for Anastasia. Tell her mum I said thanks.'

'Right. See you.' And Kelly ran out of the room again.

'I can't believe she's so grown up,' said Maeve.

'I know.' Dominique grinned. 'And that's why you shouldn't be so convinced you want to be me. When you have a ten-year-old child, you suddenly realise that your life is racing by.'

'Yes, but at least yours is racing by with a husband and a daughter,' said Maeve as she bit into another cookie. 'Whereas I . . . I'm still exactly where I was ten years ago. Except I've slept with a few fuck-wits in the meantime.'

'At least you didn't get pregnant.'

'No.' Maeve nodded. 'After you were caught out, I was excep-tionally careful.'

'I'm glad I was a warning to you. My mother would be pleased to know that.'

Maeve laughed.

'What's it like?' asked Dominique suddenly.

'Huh?'

'Sex. With different men. What's it like?'

Her friend looked thoughtful. 'I forgot that,' she said. 'You've only ever slept with Brendan.'

'I know. And I wondered – different men, different feelings?'

'Different techniques.' Maeve chuckled. 'Some of them are the passionate but sensitive type. Some of them are macho steamrollers. Some of them care more about their performance than anything. Some—'

'Crikey, Maeve, how many have there been?' Dominique inter-rupted her.

'Ah, not that many really. But none of them the right man.'

'I guess I'm lucky, so.'

'You don't know the half of it.'

But she did, of course. She thought about it after Maeve had gone. She thought about being a single girl looking for the right man and she wondered what that would be like. She told herself that she was lucky she'd found Brendan. And she looked at the clock and wondered what time he'd be home.

Chapter 11

Emma's mother died six months after she first went to the doctor. Gabriel's daily prayers hadn't been enough to stop the cancer spreading through her body. Nor had the chemotherapy, because by the time Maura had been diagnosed, the disease had already moved aggressively through her.

'She should have said something earlier.' Emma and Dominique were in the small hotel where the Walsh family had organised food and drink for the people who'd attended the funeral. 'There might have been some hope if she'd gone to the doctor sooner. And if she'd been more insistent about something being wrong.'

'Women don't generally make a fuss,' said Dominique. 'Especially mothers.'

'Mam wasn't the sort of person who liked fussing,' agreed Emma. 'She hated being ill.'

'How are you doing?' Dominique glanced at Emma's bump. It was only in the last month or so that she'd begun to look pregnant at all, but the stress of Maura's illness had taken its toll, because today she was pale and gaunt.

'Oh, I'm fine,' said Emma dismissively. 'I've been lucky, really. The baby hasn't been an ounce of bother.'

'You must be due any day now,' said Dominique.

'Next week,' said Emma. 'I was afraid it might come early. I had visions of giving birth by the graveside.'

'Hey, it's only me who goes in for birth drama.' Dominique grinned at her and Emma smiled faintly.

'And how's your dad coping?' added Dominique.

Emma glanced across the room. Her father was sitting in a corner, her two older brothers either side of him.

'We're worried about him, of course. He's in fair enough health himself, but him and Mam were together for nearly forty years. I can't imagine how alone he must feel now.'

'What are you going to do about him?'

Emma looked anxious. 'We don't want him to be on his own. He's not getting any younger, and this has aged him terribly. He's been staying with Johnny and Betty, but they can't really look after him full time. They're both working, and she's got three kids after all. Mark is going back to Germany after the funeral, so obviously he can't do anything.'

'Which leaves you.'

'I asked Greg whether he would mind if Dad came to live with us . . .' Emma sounded doubtful, and Dominique looked at her curiously.

'Does he mind? I can't imagine it somehow.'

'No, no, he was fine about it.' Once again Emma sounded dismissive, and then she looked at Dominique from tired eyes. 'As he always is.'

'He's a good guy, is Greg,' said Dominique warmly. 'You can depend on him in a crisis.'

Emma shrugged. 'You know, sometimes I think you married the wrong brother.'

'What?'

'Seriously,' Emma continued. 'Every time you talk about Greg, you go all gooey and sentimental.'

'No I don't. I just – well, like I said, he's one of the good guys.'

'I guess. Yes.'

Dominique was startled by Emma's lacklustre support of her husband.

'Is everything all right?' she asked. 'Only you seem out of sorts.'

'My mother just died,' said Emma starkly. 'Of course I'm out of sorts.' She sighed. 'Oh, Domino, I'm sorry, I just feel—' and then she broke off as Gabriel walked over to them.

Emma had asked Gabriel to come to her mother's funeral. He'd visited Maura unexpectedly a number of times while she was ill, and, as Greg had told Dominique a couple of weeks earlier, had been a real source of support to the whole family. Dominique had been pleased that her brother had helped them during a difficult time, although she had to admit to herself that she never felt entirely comfortable when Gabriel and Emma were together. Even though Emma was now married to Greg, she had too many memories of her friend sitting in her house, gazing longingly at her brother.

He sat down beside them and asked Emma how she was holding up. Emma replied, in a voice that was strained beyond measure, that she was fine but tired. Gabriel told her that it was natural. He asked after the baby, and then he talked about how good a woman her mother was and how her suffering was at an end.

Emma didn't speak while Gabriel talked. She didn't look at him either, but kept her head down, twisting her wedding and engagement rings round and round on her finger until he reached out and closed his hand over hers, forcing her to stop.

Dominique had never seen Emma so agitated before, and her heart went out to her friend. She knew that Maura's illness had upset her dreadfully – any time she'd met her over the past few months, Emma had been anxious and prone to tears – and she hoped that the birth of her baby would bring joy and happiness back to her life.

She wondered how much of what Gabriel was now saying he really and truly believed. All of it, she supposed, and yet how could anyone believe all of it? How could anyone believe in a kind and gentle God who allowed decent people like Maura Walsh to suffer terribly?

'I have to go,' he told Emma, taking his hand from hers. 'If you need anything, just call me.'

He stood up, and so did Dominique, but Emma remained seated on the red banquette.

'You've been a good friend to Emma,' he told Dominique quietly.

'I haven't done that much.'

'She told me earlier that you called around to see Maura every week.'

'It wasn't any big deal.'

'It meant a lot to her.'

'Well, it was probably more useful than the prayers.'

Gabriel sighed. 'You don't have to be so cynical.'

'I'm not. Just practical.'

'Whatever you say, Domino. Anyhow, I'd best be off.' Gabriel patted her on the shoulder and left the room.

Dominique turned towards Emma. Her friend's eyes were following Gabriel as he left. There was a raw pain in them that shocked Dominique. It was more than the pain of someone who had lost a parent, deep though that was. It was the pain of someone carrying a burden that could never be eased.

She couldn't, Dominique thought with deep concern, she just couldn't still have feelings for Gabriel. Not after so much time. Not when she and Greg had had a good marriage for so long. Not now.

'Would you like some tea?' she asked Emma.

'That'd be great.'

'I'm going to freshen up. I'll get it on my way back.'

'Thanks.'

Gabriel was standing in the foyer of the hotel when Dominique walked out of the lounge.

'I'm glad I caught you,' she said.

'What's the matter?' he asked.

'It's Emma,' she said.

'Is she all right?' His tone was suddenly anxious.

'I don't know.' Dominique's eyes searched her brother's face. 'What do you think?'

'She's hurt and grieving and so she's in pain,' Gabriel said. 'But she'll get over that.'

'It's just . . . she was watching you as you left.'

'And?' Gabriel looked at her warily.

'I just thought . . . I wondered . . .'

'What?' His expression was still wary.

'Oh, nothing.' Dominique had lost her nerve. She simply couldn't discuss Emma's feelings with her brother. He'd dismiss them, as he always did, and make her feel stupid for thinking that way. He'd be right. Emma was in emotional turmoil right now. She'd lost her mother, and her baby was due any day. Her hormones were probably all over the place. It was no wonder she felt burdened.

138

'Good.' Gabriel sounded relieved.

'Funerals, eh,' said Dominique shakily. 'They make you think, don't they? Sometimes thoughts you don't want to think.' This time her mind flitted to her own worries – wondering whether Brendan truly understood how she felt about having more children; afraid that her fear and her selfishness could harm their marriage.

Gabriel looked at her. 'Are you thinking any thoughts I can help you with?' he asked carefully. 'Anything, anyone in your life upsetting you?'

'There's no need to do the priestly thing with me,' she told him. 'I can manage without it, thanks.'

'I'm not being a priest, Domino,' said Gabriel. 'I'm being your brother. You never ask me for help with anything but you know I'm here if you need me.'

All of her life Dominique had found it difficult to separate Gabriel her brother from Gabriel the priest. Even now. She told him so.

'I wasn't always a priest,' he reminded her.

'You were always a bit of a saint, though. More than brother.'

'What about the time you climbed the apple tree and I got you down before Mam or Dad found out?'

'You were keeping the peace,' she responded with a sudden smile. '*And* you made me say three Hail Marys on my knees in the garden shed as penance.'

'Well, the time I got half killed by Dad for robbing sweets from the corner shop, then?'

'You never did!' Dominique was astonished. 'I don't remember that.'

'You just have a selective memory,' Gabriel told her.

'Rubbish,' she countered robustly. 'You were definitely saintly. Despite your criminal past.'

Gabriel laughed, and she smiled. Then she nodded and took a deep breath.

'What about Emma?' she asked abruptly.

'What about her?' His eyes darkened.

'I worry about how she might feel about you. Especially now. She seems so troubled, and I worry about what that might do to her and Greg.'

139

'Ah, Domino, don't be silly,' he said firmly. 'She loves Greg. She's having a baby. But she's gone through a difficult time and she feels a bit isolated down there in Cork without any of her old friends. She likes having someone to depend on.'

'She's made plenty of new friends,' said Dominique. 'She always has people around her. Besides, she should be depending on Greg, not you.'

'Sometimes we can't always depend on the person closest to us,' said Gabriel. 'Sometimes we need to reach out to someone else.'

Dominique stared at him. 'Are *you* all right?' she asked. 'In your isolated parish? Without someone close to you?'

'I have God,' he reminded her.

'So we're both OK then,' she said.

'Yes,' said Gabriel, and hugged her.

And for the first time in a long time, Dominique hugged him back.

Emma had her baby two days later, in Cork.

Brendan, Kelly and Dominique travelled down at the weekend to see the latest addition to the Delahaye family – an eight-pound, eight-ounce boy who was the image of Brendan, with his tuft of dark curly hair and his bright blue eyes.

'Good grief,' said Dominique to her husband when she saw him. 'Just as well I know you and Emma were never alone together. He's a mini you.'

'He's a fine figure of a man,' said Brendan, who was letting his nephew grip tightly to his index finger.

'He sure is.' Dominique felt her voice catch in her throat.

'D'you want to hold him, Domino?' asked Emma, who was sitting in an armchair. She was wearing make-up, but there were dark circles under her eyes that even copious amounts of Touche Éclat hadn't banished. 'He's the most placid baby in the world,' she added.

Dominique picked up baby Lugh and gazed at him while he stared at her from his wide eyes and then, as though he'd committed her to memory, closed them again.

'Please let me hold him,' begged Kelly. Dominique made her sit down, and then she put the baby in her daughter's arms.

'He's so cute!' cried Kelly. 'I wish he was ours.'

Dominique said nothing. She wished that she didn't feel so damn guilty every time she saw a baby. She wished that she didn't feel like the person who had prevented Brendan and Kelly from being part of a bigger family. They were fine the way they were. It wasn't her fault.

'Fair play to you,' Brendan told Greg as he slapped him on the back.

'Thanks.' Greg looked as tired as Emma, and slightly bemused at his new status.

June and Barry arrived with their three children and they all cooed over baby Lugh too. Then the children were told to go outside and play, while the adults sat around and talked.

There were two conversations. The men talked briefly about the baby, but quickly turned to sport and the ineptness of the county team selectors (a recurring conversation when they all got together). The women stuck to baby stories, with June dispensing lots of tips to Emma about looking after her new arrival. Dominique stayed quiet. She didn't feel that she had much to offer. Unless, she thought with a sudden spurt of amusement, Emma got immersed in depression too. Then she'd be the absolute must-know person among them.

She'd always found June irritating. Her older sister-in-law had a superior air and a way of making Dominique feel young and flighty, especially when she dished out her regular advice on childcare and running a home. She was also very glamorous. Unlike Emma, who was high-street fashionably stylish, June's wardrobe was heavy on designer names and chunky jewellery, and she usually wore lots of make-up and musky perfumes – Brendan had once commented to Dominique that you always knew when his sister had been around because her scent lingered long after she'd gone. Even though she didn't see her that often, Dominique felt intimidated by her.

'Anyway, now that you and Greg have the knack, maybe there'll be more little Delahayes in the future,' said June brightly to Emma, who glanced at Dominique.

'Oh, I dunno,' she said. 'Might take a leaf out of Domino's book and stop after one. It's better for the figure, don't you think?'

June looked appalled and Dominique stifled a giggle. Maybe June's right about some things, she thought. I can be very silly sometimes!

Brendan decided that they should stay in Cork for a few days. He wanted to look at a couple of sites and maybe have some discussions with the sellers.

As Kelly was on a mid-term break, Dominique didn't mind. She enjoyed being in Lily's house, where the atmosphere was always warm, welcoming and relaxing. Kelly loved staying with her granny and grandad too, because they indulged her endlessly and nobody ever told them to stop.

Dominique wanted to see Emma again before they headed off, so she dropped by on Saturday morning while Brendan, Kelly and Roy – the youngest Delahaye, who worked on one of the ferries but was at home on leave – went down to the port to watch the boats.

'We'll go to Carrigaline for lunch,' Brendan told her. 'If you want to meet us there, that'd be good.'

'Will do. Enjoy yourselves.'

She knew they would. Both her husband and her daughter loved being out in the open air, and there were plenty of nice walks around the town they could do together. Meanwhile she borrowed Lily's car and drove to Emma's house. Every time she came here, she wondered whether she and Brendan were off their heads living in Dublin when there was so much more space outside the capital.

Greg answered the door. He looked tired, and he hadn't shaved, but he smiled when he saw her.

'Hi,' he said. 'If you're looking for Emma, she's not here. She had to take her dad to the doctor.'

'Is everything all right?'

Greg nodded. 'To be honest, he's just fretting at the moment. He panics every time he coughs or sneezes in case it's something terminal, and then he frets about giving it to the baby.'

'Poor Norman.'

'Ah, hopefully he'll get over it. Both the hypochondria and Maura's death. Are you coming in?' Greg added.

'Will she be long, d'you think?'

'God knows.' Greg shrugged. 'You know what those Saturday-morning clinics are like. Why don't you stay for a while anyhow?'

'If I'm not interrupting you . . .'

'Not at all. I was just reading the paper and looking at my son every two minutes.'

Dominique laughed and followed him through the house to the sunny conservatory at the back. Lugh was in his pram in a shaded corner.

'Would you like some tea?' asked Greg. 'Or something stronger?'

Dominique looked at him in amusement. 'It's only eleven thirty,' she said. 'I haven't turned into one of those suburban housewives who down secret glasses of wine in the mornings. A glass of mineral water would be fine.'

She looked into the pram, where Lugh was sleeping happily, and then sank into one of the cushioned chairs. Emma's fashion sense, which worked so well in her clothes, was evident in the conservatory too. The fabrics were modern and bright, and instead of busy lizzies and geraniums, the mainstay of most conservatories, Emma had orchids and birds of paradise. It was also very neat. Dominique's own conservatory (added on by Brendan a few years previously) was part reading den, part playhouse and part office. It was impossible to sit down anywhere without moving a pile of papers, toys or the occasional hobnailed boot first.

'How's fatherhood?' she asked Greg when he returned with her water.

'It's good,' said Greg.

'Is that all?' Dominique's eyes danced. 'You look knackered. Is it harder than you thought?'

'No. No, Lugh's an absolute dote,' said Greg quickly. 'I never realised before how deeply you could feel about a child.'

Dominique nodded. 'Thanks to you, I feel the same about Kelly.'

'You would've come round eventually,' said Greg.

'Perhaps.'

'This is my first time alone with him,' Greg told her. 'I was a bit worried, but actually he's grand, just sleeping away there and not a bother on him.'

'Of course he is,' said Dominique cheerfully. 'Takes after his father. And you can see he's a Delahaye through and through.'

'Yeah, thanks.'

Dominique shot Greg a puzzled glance. She would have thought that he'd be more excited about the birth of his first child, but there was a strained air about him. As though he was holding something back from her. But they never kept things from each other.

'Will I get you another?' he asked as she finished her water.

'Actually, I'll take you up on the offer of tea.'

'OK,' said Greg. 'Won't be a minute.'

He disappeared, and Dominique walked over to the pram, and peered in. Lugh continued to sleep, his hands curled into two little fists beside his face. You couldn't help staring at babies, she thought. But even Greg's son, smelling of milk and baby powder, didn't make her feel like she wanted to go through it again. Perhaps, she thought, Lugh might go into the development business with Brendan. It could be Delahaye and Nephew instead of Delahaye and Son. Unless Kelly decided that she wanted a life of hard hats and boots. It was always possible.

She left the sleeping baby and sat down on one of the comfortable chairs just as Greg returned with the tea.

'Thanks.' She took the cup from him, stretched her legs out in front of her and rotated her ankle.

'Nice shoes,' he said as he noticed the soft pink leather and silver buckle of her stilettos.

'Stupid shoes,' she told him. 'I bought them on a whim and now I feel obliged to wear them. But the heels are too high. Emma would be able to wear them a lot more easily than me.'

'She's good with high heels all right,' said Greg blankly.

'An ability to carry off difficult footwear is a great reason to marry a woman,' Dominique joked.

'Why d'you think she married me?'

The question hung between them for a few seconds, during which Dominique wondered what answer he wanted her to give.

'Because she loves you?'

'Does she ever talk about me?' he asked.

'What sort of question is that?' Dominique frowned and then

shrugged. 'I guess girls always talk about the men in their lives. I talk about Brendan. Emma talks about you.' But not much, she realised. I don't talk about Brendan much and she doesn't really talk about Greg that much either. We don't share things. We don't moan about them. We tell each other that they work hard and that they're decent men. But we don't gossip. We keep it to ourselves.

What does Emma keep to herself? wondered Dominique. And what, when it comes down to it, do I?

'She never says terrible things about you,' she added lightly. 'In fact she usually comments on your good looks and manly charm and rabbits on about what a great husband you are.'

Greg said nothing.

'Is everything OK?' asked Dominique.

'Of course it is.' He shrugged and then smiled at her, and quite suddenly it was as though the cloud over him had lifted, and they chatted easily about babies and childcare and there were no undercurrents or tensions in his voice at all.

Dominique stayed for an hour, but there was no sign of Emma returning. And so, because she was meeting Brendan and Kelly for lunch, she had to leave.

Greg walked with her as far as the front gate, Lugh in his arms.

'You make a lovely daddy,' she said teasingly.

'Thanks.'

'Tell Emma I'll see her again before we head back.'

'Sure.'

She kissed Lugh on the forehead and smiled at Greg, who kissed her too, on the cheek, as he always did when they said goodbye. Dominique kissed him in return and then hurried to the car, because she didn't want to be late for lunch and she knew that Brendan and Kelly would be waiting impatiently for her. She put the car in gear and drove away from the house. In her rear-view mirror she could see Greg with Lugh in his arms, still standing at the gate, watching after her.

After lunch in Carrigaline town, Brendan, Dominique and Kelly returned to Castlecannon and sat on a low, crumbling wall overlooking the silver-grey sea, eating Cornettos. When Kelly got up to

145

skim stones across the surface of the water, Brendan asked Dominique if she didn't think that this was the most glorious place in the world. She nodded, and then said but maybe not so glorious if he was thinking of building houses all over it.

'Not houses,' he said. 'That's not what the site I'm interested in is about. It's a business park.'

'Here!' She looked horrified.

'No. Further inland. A great opportunity to work with local developers. A few of them have approached me already.'

'Don't you think you've got an awful lot on your plate?' she said. 'Houses, hotels, apartments, business parks . . .'

'The company is getting bigger,' he said. 'We need a prestigious headquarters. I want that to be here.'

'In Castlecannon?' Her voice was a squeak.

'Well, the business park wouldn't be here, I can't get the land. The best site is near Ringaskiddy.'

'And what about . . . We live in Dublin, Brendan. How can you have a headquarters here?'

'I want to put money back into this area,' he said. 'So we're going to move here, Domino.'

She stared at him. 'When?'

'In a year or so. When I have the house built.'

'What house?'

'There's another site.' He looked at her with excitement in his eyes. 'Overlooking the bay. It'll be fantastic.'

She looked at him hesitantly.

'You want to move everything down here?'

'Yes.'

'What about Kelly? And school?'

'For God's sake, Domino. There are schools outside Dublin, you know.'

'Of course I know that,' she said quickly. 'It's just a big decision. And you seem to have made it without talking to me.'

'It's my job to make the big decisions, and I'm talking to you about it now,' he told her.

She said nothing.

'I'm doing what's best for us as a family.'

'Are you?'

'Yes. And you'll be living a few miles from Emma. She's your best friend, isn't she? What more do you want?'

'*You're* my best friend,' she said. 'All I want is to be with you. To be a family and to be happy.'

'I know.' He smiled too. 'You're very easy to please, Domino.'

'Too easy?' she asked.

'Sometimes. But this is the right move for us.'

She nodded. 'I can see that. I just needed a minute or two to think it through.'

Brendan was right about moving to Cork, she realised. There was nothing to keep them in Dublin, and being in Cork would mean being closer to the Delahayes and to people who cared about her. There was nobody in Dublin who mattered to her in the same way as the Delahayes did. There never would be.

Chapter 12

Once the decision to move to Cork was made, Dominique was impatient for things to progress. She'd thought it would be quick, but there was a lengthy planning process to go through before the building could actually start. There was also the issue of who was going to do the building. She'd assumed that Brendan would build the house himself, but she quickly realised that she was being silly and that he would contract out the work. He was far too busy being the managing director of Delahaye Developments to actually lay bricks any more.

Brendan Delahaye was a businessman, not a builder.

This change was most clearly reflected in his wardrobe. When she'd first married him, Brendan had owned two navy suits, both of which he'd bought in a budget shop in Henry Street. Now he had ten. The latest two were from Louis Copeland, and one of the silk ties he'd bought to go with them had cost more than both his Henry Street suits put together.

He'd bought the most recent suit and tie for the launch of some new apartments he'd built on the Howth Road. It was, he said, the last of his city residential developments, and the two blocks of what the marketing brochure called 'luxury bespoke dwellings' had been built in what was once the garden of a Victorian detached house. Brendan had bought the almost derelict house and large garden two years earlier, after the elderly owner died. Now the site was totally transformed. Brendan had incorporated the façade of the old house into one of the apartment blocks, so that from the road it appeared as though the building was still a single house in a landscaped garden. It looked lovely, Dominique thought as she stepped out of the car and stood outside the transformed building, but she couldn't help feeling a little sad that the old house had actually been destroyed and that the façade was just an illusion.

She was the only person feeling sad, though. The launch of Larkspur was a perfectly managed PR exercise, and the interior hallway of the house, which had been turned into an atrium in the new building, was buzzing with local politicians and minor celebrities who'd been invited to add a bit of glamour to the occasion.

Dominique had been stunned when Brendan told her what had been organised for the evening.

'But . . . but it's just apartments,' she said in astonishment. 'Surely all you need to do is shove up a For Sale sign? After all, isn't almost everyone looking to buy a house at the moment?'

'Yes but we're providing something very different,' Brendan told her. 'Elegant living.'

'In an apartment block?' She stared at him.

'You're so stuck in the past,' he said. 'Things have moved on, Domino. It's not like a few years ago when people were happy just to get four walls and a tiling allowance for the bathroom. They want more. It's aspirational.'

'I don't get it.' She shook her head. 'It's still just a place to live.'

'But in a premium location,' said Brendan. 'Which means we can charge premium prices.'

She still looked doubtful.

'And so I want you to pull all the stops out on the glamour front for the launch,' he added. 'I want people to look at us and think that we're a golden couple and that we look fantastic and that if they buy one of my apartments they can look fantastic too.'

'Are you nuts?' she asked.

'I'm deadly serious,' he told her. 'I had a meeting today with the PR company and they think we can make a big splash with this. The prices are high, Domino. We want it to go well.' He took both her hands in his. 'This is the mega-deal. I sell these quickly and we're doubling our money.'

'They're still just apartments.'

'Please, Domino.'

'OK, OK,' she said. 'I'll do my best.'

'Good girl,' he said and kissed her.

She rang Emma to ask for advice.

'He wants me to look uber-glamorous,' she wailed. 'I don't do that sort of glam, Emma. You know that. I can afford to buy good stuff but I can't put together a look the way you can.'

'Why don't you come down for the weekend,' suggested Emma. 'I'll take you shopping and we'll find something that makes you look every inch the wife of a successful businessman.'

Even Emma thought of him as a businessman and not a builder any more, thought Dominique as she sat on the train the following Friday afternoon. Emma had seen how far he'd come but Dominique herself hadn't. Maybe things always appeared different when someone from outside looked in. Maybe when you were caught up in the day-to-day stuff you didn't always realise how lucky you'd become. She glanced at Kelly beside her, her nose buried in a copy of *Harry Potter and the Philosopher's Stone*, the book almost everyone at her school was reading. Kelly had been excited about a trip to Cork and the chance to see her cousins again. Dominique had thought that some time together on the train journey would be nice. She imagined having a girlie conversation with her daughter so that Kelly would know how cool her mum was and how much she cared about her. But in the end Kelly had begged her to shut up and let her read her book, and so Dominique had contented herself with flicking through a copy of *Hello!*, which she'd picked up at Heuston station with the idea of looking at the latest celebrity fashions as possible pointers.

Emma had said that she'd meet them at the train station, but it was actually Greg who was there when they got outside. Kelly rushed over to him and flung her arms around him, while Dominique waited for him to plant his customary kiss on her cheek.

'The traffic was terrible today and you know how Emma is about driving in traffic,' said Greg as he put their overnight bag into the boot of his Audi A3. 'So I offered to be chauffeur.'

'Thanks.' Dominique settled into the front passenger seat. 'How's things?'

'Not bad,' he told her. 'Norman is in great health. Lugh is

teething but he's not too cranky. Mam and Dad are enjoying life. What more could any of us ask for?'

His tone was cheerful, but Dominique glanced enquiringly at him. Greg's attention, however, was firmly fixed on the road ahead.

'Mam has invited us all to dinner tonight,' he added as he turned the car towards Ringaskiddy. 'And since my pretty wife isn't the world's best cook, we thought it would be a good idea to say yes.'

Dominique said that that was all right with her, and Kelly – whose book was open on her lap – piped up that it was all right with her too, before starting to read again.

As always, Dominique enjoyed the evening with the Delahayes. After dinner, as they sat in the living room, her gaze flickered over the large extended family. Everyone was doing their own thing. But all in the one room together. She liked it. She liked the warmth and the feeling of acceptance at the Delahayes' that she'd never felt in her own home. She knew that she was being unfair on her parents, because they were simply very different people to Lily and Maurice and it wasn't their fault that they weren't able to be as bright and bubbly as her parents-in-law, but she couldn't help thinking that she'd miss Brendan's parents a lot more than her own when they died. She was shocked at herself for having such a thought, and immediately clamped down on it for being so terrible.

'Penny for them,' said Greg softly as they sat side by side on the comfortable sofa.

'Oh, I was just thinking how cosy and nice this family is,' she said after a moment's pause. 'I was thinking how we share every-thing and how we all look out for each other and it's great.'

'I doubt we share everything,' said Greg. 'Not the way you think.'

'Maybe not everything,' she conceded. 'But we're still a big group of people who look out for each other no matter what.'

'What if one of us had done something unforgivable?'

'Nothing's totally unforgivable,' said Dominique.

'Do you really believe that?'

'I have to.' She grinned at him. 'I'm stuck with Gabriel's example. He's big into forgiveness. He'd be very disappointed if I wasn't too.'

Greg inhaled sharply and then released his breath slowly. 'But in real life,' he said grimly, 'outside the whole forgive-and-forget thing – could you forgive Brendan for . . . for . . . having an affair maybe?'

'Greg!' She looked startled and spoke more loudly than she'd intended, so that the others glanced across the room at them.

'Sorry,' he said. 'Bad example.'

'D'you think Brendan's having an affair?' Her words were muted but anxious.

'Of course not. I was just trying to pick an example.'

'Well it's not a good example,' she said crossly.

'Sorry,' he repeated.

'Anyway,' she said, 'what I really meant was that we all look out for each other. When we're in trouble we rally round. Remember when I was depressed? Everyone was great, even though I didn't realise it at the time. And when Emma's mam died? And when Barry lost his job?'

'It was easy for Brendan to rally round and give Barry a job,' said Greg. 'And him the successful entrepreneur.'

Dominique smiled. A few weeks earlier Barry had been made redundant and Brendan had immediately called his brother-in-law and offered him a place at Delahaye Developments, saying it would be good to have more family in the business.

'The Delahayes always look out for each other,' said Dominique. 'It isn't like that with the Bradys. They're not known for being good in a crisis.'

'Might depend on the crisis.'

'You're just being devil's advocate,' said Dominique sternly. 'I love being a Delahaye.'

'I'm glad.' The grim expression left Greg's face. 'I love you being one too.'

Dominique had never been shopping with anyone like Emma before. Her sister-in-law ignored the department stores and brought her to small boutiques with designer outfits and breathtaking price tags.

'Oh for heaven's sake!' she exclaimed when Dominique protested at the cost of the dress Emma insisted she try. 'You're rolling in it, Domino. Live a little, why don't you!'

'I'm not rolling in it,' she protested. 'And that's a wicked price for a dress.'

'Domino Delahaye, your husband is selling the most expensive apartments in Dublin city!' Emma told her. 'He wants you to look the part. He can pay for it.'

Dominique laughed. 'I suppose.'

'And that looks fabulous on you,' added Emma as she fingered the silver fabric. 'You'll totally wow them.'

'It's only a few local councillors and an ex-Rose of Tralee,' said Dominique. 'Hardly people who need wowing.'

'You've got to play the game. Make them feel important. And,' Emma added, 'this is an important event for Brendan. You need to treat it that way.'

Dominique looked at her sister-in-law and nodded slowly. Really, she thought, Emma understood it all so much better than she did. She always had. Perhaps – the thought came to her unexpectedly – perhaps it was a good thing that the first time Brendan had seen Emma had been at their wedding. If they'd met before that, maybe . . . She stopped thinking. She didn't like where it was leading.

'We're buying you some really good shoes, too,' said Emma after the dress had been carefully wrapped in tissue paper and placed in a carrier bag. 'High heels and no complaining.'

'Hey, I like heels,' Dominique said. 'I'm just no good at staying upright on them.'

'You can practise tonight,' Emma said. 'Wear them around the house. It's not just yourself, you know, Domino. You're representing the female face of the Delahayes. It's important you get it right.'

She knew she'd got it right when she came downstairs on the night of the launch. She'd taken to heart Emma's words about the importance of the evening for Brendan, and so as well as having her hair cut in a new, sleeker style, she'd also made an appointment at the local beauty salon for her make-up and a manicure. When she walked into the living room in her shimmering silver dress and her cripplingly high shoes, Brendan stared at her for a full ten seconds before giving an appreciative wolf whistle.

'You look stunning,' he said.

'Doesn't she?' Kelly was bouncing up and down on the sofa. She'd seen Dominique model the shoes and dress earlier and had thought her mother looked stunning too.

'Well, Mrs Delahaye,' Brendan smiled at her and offered her his arm, 'let's go and wow the crowds.'

'Anything you say, Mr Delahaye,' said Dominique as she walked unsteadily out of the door.

She'd totally underestimated the importance of the launch, Dominique realised after the first few minutes. She'd thought that the local councillors were irrelevant and that the media was unimportant. She hadn't thought that the pretty ex-Rose of Tralee would attract attention, or that the arrival of the interior decorator would be met by photographers. She kept telling herself that this was just a sales pitch for a block of apartments, but it didn't feel like that. It felt like a movie premiere.

Caryn Jacks, the PR girl, was everywhere, co-ordinating the photographers, arranging interviews with the press and making sure that people's glasses were topped up with champagne. She insisted Dominique talk to someone from one of the papers about life with a workaholic like Brendan, and then she made her pose for a photograph in the kitchen of one of the apartments. She continually told Dominique that she was fantastic and a real asset to Brendan, because everyone liked glamorous wives.

Dominique herself felt the same buzz as she'd felt when she played Judas Iscariot in the school production of *Jesus Christ Superstar*. People were looking at her and admiring her, and it was a good feeling. The journalists seemed to like talking to her (although she kept telling herself they weren't real journalists; they just worked for the property supplements, so it wasn't like a proper interview or anything), and she laughed and joked with them as she sipped the never-ending glasses of champagne about how fabulous the apartments were in comparison to her own house. Then she told them about the house that Brendan was building in Cork and how nice it would be to live near his family and how lovely they all were; and then someone asked her about their own family and she told them about Kelly, and before she knew what had happened they'd managed to learn about her post-natal depression and how she was better now and how much she loved her daughter and her husband and how sometimes, when you felt that you were in the very abyss, you could come out of it again.

She hadn't meant to talk so much and to say so many things, but the champagne had loosened her tongue and she hadn't been able to stop. And the journalists kept talking to her and the photographers kept taking her photo, asking her to pose at the window of the apartment, on the balcony and sitting on the marble worktop of the state-of-the-art kitchen, and she kept smiling at them and raising glasses of champagne, because she wanted to look good in the pictures for Brendan.

And so the next day the stories about the launch of the apartments ran alongside the story of Dominique Delahaye, the independent woman who was the wife of a successful man. And before she knew what had happened, she'd been asked on to the radio to talk about her marriage and her depression and share her wisdom with the listeners, and although she hadn't wanted to do it, she felt that perhaps she owed it to other women who might be going through a hard time to tell her story.

Later that month there was another story in the newspapers about how the apartments had all sold in the first week and how everyone had been utterly charmed by Dazzling Dominique Delahaye, and how inspirational she was to women everywhere.

The headline on the piece was 'The Domino Effect'.

Brendan was delighted with it. He cut out the article, framed it and hung it on his office wall, so that it was the first thing that anyone who came into his office saw when they walked through the door.

Chapter 13

The Domino Effect was what the PR girl, Caryn, called it too. People had seen Domino and identified with her and wanted to be like her, she told both Brendan and Dominique the week after all the apartments had sold out. Domino was a marketing phenomenon, she said.

Dominique couldn't understand it herself.

'I thought you'd be angry with me,' she told Brendan. 'I thought you'd be raging over the fact that I blabbed too much about us.'

'Well I wasn't very pleased to hear that I was forced into marrying you,' he said drily, 'or that you couldn't bear the sight of me after Kelly was born.'

'I didn't put it like that,' she told him. 'Really I didn't.'

'But it doesn't matter,' he continued, 'because it all worked out wonderfully and I've been asked about getting involved in a government housing regeneration project. I'm not sure it's something I want to do, but I'm delighted to have been asked . . . and it's nice to think that you've become an asset to Delahaye Developments at last.'

She blinked at that, wondering if he thought she'd been a liability before.

'It's the big step I've always wanted.' He beamed. 'The sale of the apartments was a key deal, and we've made a lot of money and I can do more stuff. We're big players now, Domino. Big.'

She didn't feel like a big player. But she was glad that he did. She knew how important it was to him.

Evelyn, Seamus and Gabriel had all been utterly gobsmacked to see the newspaper features about Larkspur and Brendan and Dominique.

Evelyn thought there was something distinctly trashy about being in the papers, and she certainly didn't approve of Dominique telling all of Ireland about her shotgun wedding and post-natal depression. It didn't matter to her that the neighbours were all congratulating her on how well Dominique had done; she thought it was tacky to talk about your life in public, especially when you were talking about times you would surely rather forget. She told Dominique that she'd better not get a big head because she'd nothing to have a big head about, and that there were more important things in life than appearing in the weekend supplements wearing a fabulous dress.

Seamus, who also spoke to her on the phone, agreed with Evelyn (as he always did) but added that he was glad that she seemed to be happy. Dominique was mildly surprised by her father's comment. She'd never thought that her happiness bothered him one way or the other.

Gabriel phoned her and told her that she looked amazing in the photographs but did she really think it had been a good idea to pour out her life story?

'No,' she admitted. 'I was a bit drunk at the time.'

'Dominique!'

'I'd had champagne,' she said defensively. 'I couldn't help myself. But Gabriel, I did good, I really did. When I went on that radio show and talked about how I felt after Kelly was born, they had a huge response. Loads of women suffer from post-natal depression and they think they're going crazy or that they have to go through it on their own. And they feel like I did, worthless and hopeless and terrible mothers weighed down with guilt. But the thing is, they're not, and I'm not either.'

'How does Kelly feel about it?' he asked. 'After all, she's hearing that she was a mistake and that you never wanted her.'

'That's not what she's hearing at all,' said Dominique. 'I sat down with her and told her that we hadn't planned to have her when we did and that I hadn't been well after she was born but that I love her more than anyone else in the world and will always love her. She doesn't remember how things were back then and we get on great now, so there's nothing to worry about.'

'Was it really that bad?' he asked. 'After she was born?'

'It was the worst time of my life,' she said simply.

'I tried to help,' Gabriel reminded her.

'Of course,' she said. 'Everyone did. And I'll always remember that.'

Everyone had tried to help, but it was only Greg who'd got through to her. She hadn't said that in the interviews, because that would have been telling them too much. All they needed to know was that she'd got better and that she loved her daughter and that her husband was the best damn builder in the country.

She was asked to become a patron of a charity that worked with women who suffered from post-natal depression, and she agreed. She also joined two other high-profile charity boards and became a regular invitee to various social events. She liked helping the charities. She enjoyed dressing up and going out with Brendan as guests at some of Ireland's most glamorous evenings. And she loved being Dazzling Domino Delahaye.

Brendan loved her being Dazzling Domino Delahaye too. Over the next few months, as they launched themselves on the social scene, they became known as the Dazzling Delahayes, which made him feel good. He was proud that all of his hard work over the past ten years had paid off and that he'd finally made the leap into the big league. Not yet the mega-league, of course. He wasn't one of those builders who had helicopters and stables of sports cars and who owned islands in the sun. But he was getting there. And it was Domino who'd helped him. He was glad, now, that he'd stood by her during her depression, when he'd seriously thought about leaving. It hadn't been because of Domino that he'd stayed, he knew that. It had been because of Kelly. From the moment she was born, he'd found himself totally beguiled by his lovely daughter. And there was no way he could have left her.

There had been times later when he'd wondered if he'd made the right choice. But now he knew that he had. Domino, his lucky charm, had worked her magic again.

It was a year later when they finally moved into the new house. They drove down from Dublin with the last of their bits and pieces in Brendan's brand-new van, and Dominique had to swallow hard to stop herself from crying. It was ridiculous, she knew. Cork wasn't that far away and it didn't matter to her where she lived, although it would mean that her recent appearances at charity dinners and fund-raisers would come to an abrupt end. There was a certain element of relief in this as far as Dominique was concerned, because although she loved the popularity, it was very tiring to feel that she had to be dazzling all the time. Nevertheless, she felt good about being asked to events that twelve months earlier nobody would have thought to invite her to, and it would be a wrench to leave much of that behind. She'd continue to do the charity work, but she couldn't see herself flitting up to Dublin every second week to live her socialite life. Her flame had burned brightly but it was time to move on.

The worst part, strangely, had been saying goodbye to her parents. When she'd first told them about the move to Cork, Seamus and Evelyn had simply said that it was disappointing that both of their children were at opposite ends of the country – something Dominique had never thought about before. The night before they left, Evelyn invited them over for dinner. She said that she was sure they didn't have anything worth eating in the house and that they might like a decent meal. Brendan had dithered about it because he'd planned to take his wife and daughter to a restaurant for a goodbye-to-Dublin dinner, but Dominique, still stunned by the invite in the first place, had said that it was the only time her mother had ever asked them to the house and she didn't think she could say no.

It had been an odd evening, with both her parents heaping praise on Brendan for his success and not tempering it by having a go at Dominique herself for any reason at all. Evelyn even showed her an article she'd cut out from one of the papers, entitled 'Women of Substance', which had included Domino.

'Mrs Treacey heard you on the radio,' she added. 'Talking about the counselling centre. She said you were very good.'

'Thanks,' said Dominique in surprise.

'I know I was a bit doubtful about it at first, but it's not a bad thing for women to know they can get help,' said Evelyn. 'Even if you're the one telling them.'

Dominique decided that her mother was actually paying her a compliment.

Evelyn had been warm with Kelly too, giving her an envelope with some money to buy herself 'something nice' when she got to her new house, which made her throw her arms around them and tell them that they were the best grandparents in the whole world. Evelyn had looked pleased and proud and Seamus had ruffled Kelly's hair and told her that she deserved it.

After that Dominique had found leaving Dublin harder than she'd imagined (she hadn't actually imagined it would be hard at all); but the sight of the new house, its pale pink walls bathed in the gentle light of the setting sun, had lifted her spirits. From the moment she opened the heavy front door with its Georgian-style fanlight arching over it, she felt that she really and truly was home. If she'd thought that Brendan had done a good job on the Terenure house, he had surpassed himself on Atlantic View. He had toyed with a number of names for their home, but, he'd said, it had the best views of the ocean in the country and there was no better name for it.

It was utterly magnificent. The floors were all timbered in white oak, while the fixtures and fittings were of such a high quality that Dominique couldn't help feeling that she was walking into one of Brendan's snazziest show houses.

'Well of course,' Brendan told her cheerfully when she said this. 'It *is* a show house. I want anyone who visits us to see just how good I can be.'

It was three times the size of their previous house and the location was spectacular. On the first morning, as Dominique stood at the bedroom window and gazed out over the green fields to the ocean beyond, she told Brendan that it was almost paradise. She was astonished that they'd been given planning permission to build it at all, she said, because its position on the top of a hill gave it unrivalled views down to the sea. Brendan had grinned at her and told her that it was always worth knowing the right people, and that the dinner he'd held with some local councillors before they'd started building had been a worthwhile investment.

Dominique settled into her new life much more quickly than she'd expected. Although she knew that the Delahayes were well known and liked in the area, she hadn't quite realised that, thanks to her media exposure, she was a minor celebrity here too. Her assumption that her social star would fade with her move was quite wrong, because along with Emma and June, she found herself part of a buzzing social scene and a trophy guest at some of the high-profile balls and dinners that were part and parcel of the local social circuit. One day, as she looked at herself in the full-length bedroom mirror before going out, Dominique realised that she had done what she'd always wanted to do. She'd found a look that suited her and that she felt comfortable with and she'd become popular. Now when she stood beside Emma she felt just as groomed and attractive as her sister-in-law, and it was a good feeling. It was strange, she mused, how it could take you so long to find yourself. But when you did, you became comfortable with who you were. And for the first time in her life, Dominique Delahaye knew that she was comfortable with who she was.

So the affair came as a bolt out of the blue.

She found out about it because she saw the message on Brendan's mobile phone. As she read it, she felt as though everything she had built up for herself was about to come crashing down around her. She read it over and over again, as though by doing so she could suddenly find a different meaning to the words that were tearing a hole in her heart. But it didn't matter how many times she read it. The meaning was plain.

She'd been a fool.

Brendan had a few different mobiles because he liked to use a variety of numbers depending on what part of his business he was dealing with. So it wasn't entirely unusual for him to leave a phone at home, and it was one of these phones that Dominique picked up when she went into the room he used as an office to get a writing pad for Kelly. Kelly wasn't allowed into the office, so Dominique had offered to get her one, and picked her way through the mess of hard hats, reinforced boots and rolled-up site plans thinking that no matter how much time he was now devoting to different business interests, he really was a bricklayer at heart.

The phone fell off the desk as she grabbed the writing pad. She didn't know why she looked at it. She never felt the need to check up on her husband. And yet, with the phone in her hand, she couldn't help herself scrolling through his messages. They were mostly short; things like 'See you Tuesday' or 'Meeting Friday', which were, Dominique was sure, work-related. And then she opened the one that made her blood run cold and had the potential to change her world for ever.

Hi hon, it said. *Really enjoyed last week, so sorry you had to leave. Miss you loads. You'll always be my Valentine.* There were about ten kisses and a smiley afterwards.

There was no name assigned to the number, which she didn't recognise. She sat down abruptly on the leather swivel chair behind the desk. She had always lived with the fear that one day Brendan would leave her. She'd expected it when she was first going out with him (especially when he met her parents); she'd thought it would happen after she found out she was pregnant; it had been a fear, along with so many other fears, during the dark months after Kelly's birth; and, she had to admit, it had been at the back of her mind all of the times he'd gone socialising without her as part of his so-called network-building. She'd worried that he'd find someone prettier, cleverer and more interesting to be with than her. But ever since she'd become Dazzling Domino those fears had eased. According to the magazines and newspapers, she was a confident woman, elegant and beautiful. She was a charity queen. She was an inspiration. How could he leave someone who was so great?

But Brendan had known her before she was dazzling and she was wrong to allow herself to think that the Domino Effect was enough to keep him in love with her. In the same way as she would always remember him as the man who'd sat at her table in American Burger, he'd always remember her as the girl he'd felt obliged to marry. Which might have worked out OK if she hadn't turned into the woman who refused to have more children. The woman who'd lied when she'd said 'not yet'. Who hadn't had the courage to admit that 'not ever' was the far more likely option.

She'd justified it by trying to convince herself that her feelings would change. There were, after all, lots of women who'd had difficult pregnancies, difficult births and even post-natal depression and who'd gone on to have more children and be happy. But she'd known that she just couldn't do it. She was a coward, she told herself, but she couldn't help it.

And so, in the end, she'd let him be the one to decide that his work was more important than having the family he'd always wanted. And she'd pushed all of her anxieties to the back of her mind and decided that it was the best thing for both of them. She'd thought that she was right, because even though she knew their relationship had changed subtly, their sex life had improved beyond measure. She'd done everything she could to make him feel that she was the only woman in the world for him. At the launch of Larkspur, when he'd been so wowed by her appearance, he'd made love to her twice when they got home and told her that he loved her and that she was wonderful.

But not wonderful enough.

She felt as though she'd been punched in the stomach. Her breath was coming in short gasps and she was finding it hard to focus. Her hands were shaking. She didn't want to believe that the worst had happened. She didn't want to think that he could possibly be seeing someone else.

She sat motionless in the chair for a few minutes. Then she stood up again, tucked the phone into the pocket of her jeans and went to give Kelly the writing pad. Her daughter was sitting at the desk in her room, her long hair pushed to one side as she studied the book in front of her.

'Here you are.' Dominique was surprised to hear her own voice sound quite normal.

'Thanks, Mum.' Kelly didn't look up from the book.

She was a good student, thought Dominique. Smart for her age. Very focused. Unlike her. More like Brendan, really.

She walked into their bedroom. It was a big room with long sash windows, which allowed plenty of light to stream inside. She sat on the double bed with its wrought-iron bedstead and ivory satin quilt and looked at the message again.

My Valentine. She wanted to laugh at that. Brendan didn't believe in Valentine's Day. He never sent her a card or flowers. He said that only suckers paid ten times the normal prices for roses on that one day of the year. But he did bring flowers home to her from time to time. She wondered now if they were to assuage his guilt.

She also wondered if Greg had known. She recalled the conversation she'd had with him when they'd talked about forgiveness and he'd asked if she could forgive an affair. He'd said that he'd picked it as an example and she'd believed him then, but now she wasn't so sure. Perhaps . . . the thought suddenly came to her . . . perhaps that was why Greg had occasionally seemed so distant with her lately. If he knew that Brendan was being unfaithful to her, he'd want to tell her. But he might also be conflicted because of his loyalty to his brother. Should she call Greg and ask him straight out? she wondered. Or should she talk to Brendan first?

She tried to think of how she might bring up the subject. Drop the phone on the table, perhaps? Ask him how he'd spent Valentine's Day? There had been a meeting that evening, she remembered now. With Matthew, who was still his accountant, and Ciara, who had taken over as his lawyer. Dominique had met Ciara a number of times. She was a well-groomed and intelligent woman, but hardly what anyone would regard as a babe. She was comfortably built, tall enough to carry a few extra pounds, with dark brown curly hair that she wore in a neatly cropped style. Not unattractive. But not a stunner either. He couldn't be having an affair with Ciara. If he was going to play away from home, he'd surely pick someone better-looking than his schoolmarm lawyer. So maybe the meeting on Valentine's Day had just been a meeting. Or maybe it had taken all of ten minutes and then Brendan had headed off to be with . . . with . . . Caryn, the PR girl, perhaps? She was altogether edgier-looking than Ciara. Younger, too. But Dominique couldn't see Brendan being interested in Caryn. She was too skinny. Brendan didn't like overly skinny women. So who?

It could be anyone. Dominique didn't know much about the people Brendan met when they weren't together. There was no need for her to know them or to meet them. But did she know this woman? Was she from Cork? Or Dublin? Was he in love with her? Were they, even now, having urgent conversations together, talking about the state of his marriage, discussing how it could all be ended? Was Brendan saying that he'd never really loved Dominique but, as this girl knew, had had no option but to marry her. Old-fashioned rules for old-fashioned times. He said that about planning laws sometimes. Did he think the same way about being married?

Divorce hadn't been available in Ireland when they'd got married, but it was now. The bitter campaign, in which posters with slogans like 'Hello Divorce, Goodbye Daddy' had been attached to lampposts along the streets, was still fresh in her mind. She hadn't given it much thought at the time. Her view had been that there was no point in forcing unhappy people to stay together. When a campaigner opposing the change had stopped her on the road one day, Dominique had pointed out that people split up whether or not divorce was available. And that it was unfair and unreasonable to expect them to remain legally tied to each other long after they'd physically moved apart.

She felt now that those words might come back to haunt her. She didn't want Brendan to divorce her. He was her husband and the father of her daughter and she didn't want anyone saying anything different. She didn't want him to think that he could simply leave them and set up a new home with a new wife and start a new family. But maybe that was what it was all about. Brendan had wanted a big family and she couldn't give it to him. He'd said that it didn't matter any more. He'd substituted bricks and mortar for children. But maybe he'd changed his mind. She felt sick at the thought.

She stared at the anonymous number as though by looking at it for long enough she could see the woman who sent the text. Should she send a message back in return? A warning, maybe. Stay away from my husband or else? Or else what? she asked herself. What can I do if he wants to be with Little Miss Valentine instead of me? What can I do to keep him?

She released her breath very slowly. Leaving would be a trauma for him too. It would be shocking publicity, because everyone liked her. Or, at least, they were supposed to like her. But did they really? And if Brendan got Caryn Jacks to spin some story about her . . . that was how PR people worked, wasn't it? Caryn had spun the Domino Effect story. She could spin something else, something that made Dominique appear a completely different sort of person. And people would feel sorry for him.

She squeezed her eyes shut. It wasn't about other people and what they thought. It was about her and Brendan. That was all. It was about how they felt for each other and why he might want to leave. The only reason would be that he loved this girl more than her and Kelly. Loved her enough to change his life completely. He couldn't love her that much. He just couldn't.

She opened her eyes again and scrolled through the rest of the messages. There weren't any more from the mysterious number. Maybe, she thought, the relationship, whatever it was, had already fizzled out. Maybe, whoever she was, she didn't really mean that much to him.

And maybe it hadn't. And maybe she did.

She said nothing when he came home that evening and nothing the following day either when he told her that he would be going up to Dublin and staying overnight. He had an apartment in Dublin, in a block that Delahaye Developments had built on Bachelors Walk. He'd brought her to town to see it and she'd laughed and told him that it was an apt address, and he'd laughed too and agreed that it was his secret bachelor pad. At the time, it had been piled full of folders, hi-vis jackets and Delahaye Developments calendars, and Dominique had thought of it more as an office with a bed in it than a bachelor pad. She might have been wrong about that. Now she thought of it as his illicit den. She pictured a large bed with chocolate-coloured silk sheets in the small bedroom, and a white leather sofa and zebra-skin-patterned rug on the living-room floor. Red lights everywhere and maybe a sideboard with a stash of drinks in the corner. She'd never actually seen how he'd decorated the apartment because she hadn't been in it since that day. There was no need. She hadn't spent a night in Dublin ever since she'd moved to Cork. She'd always wanted to come back to her beautiful home.

She couldn't believe she'd been so naïve as to assume he was faithful to her. He was a wealthy, attractive man who had an apartment in Dublin. Why wouldn't other women flock to him, lured by his money as much as his looks? How did she ever think that she'd be able to keep such a man to herself?

She didn't want her marriage to break up. She still loved him. And the truth was that even if he was seeing Little Miss Valentine, there was no reason to think that it was anything other than a casual affair. Brendan was a very passionate man in bed. She'd done her best to be equally passionate for him, but maybe it hadn't been enough. Perhaps those months when she hadn't been able to make love to him, when she'd turned away from him, had hurt him more than she knew. Maybe he needed to prove to himself that he was the kind of man that women wanted to make love to.

She shouldn't make excuses for him. He'd made vows to her and he hadn't kept them, although she acknowledged to herself that there was nothing in the text that implied he'd done anything more than spend an evening with its sender. Nevertheless, the sentiment was clear. Perhaps, though, it was *her* sentiment, not his.

She told herself she was clutching at straws. But she didn't know what else she could cling to.

She waited for the axe to fall, for him to tell her about Miss Valentine. She noticed now that he was cagey about where he was going and what he was doing. It had never bothered her before. She'd simply thought that he was busy with his things and she was busy with hers. After all, particularly in the last year, she'd found plenty to do, with her committees and meetings. And although things were more low-key in Cork than in Dublin, there was still lots for her to be involved in. But she couldn't concentrate for thinking of what he might be doing. It was driving her insane.

In the end she talked to Greg first.

He'd called over to Atlantic View to set up the new computer Brendan had bought for her as a birthday present. Neither she nor Brendan was very clued up about computers, but Brendan liked the idea of everything in Atlantic View being completely up to date. And he didn't want her messing with his own computer and maybe deleting important files.

'I wouldn't,' she said huffily, and he said better to be safe than sorry and bought her a computer for herself.

After Greg had finished installing the software, he came into the kitchen, where Dominique made him a cup of tea.

'I hope you'll have lots of happy hours playing Solitaire,' he told her.

She looked at him edgily. 'Why? You think I'll be stuck here on my own?'

'Of course not,' he replied. 'It's just that most people spend hours playing Solitaire on their computers.'

'Oh.' She shrugged. 'I guess that'll be me too, so.'

He knew there was something wrong. He always did. So he asked her and she, in return, told him about the text message and asked him if he'd known that Brendan was having an affair. If he'd been keeping quiet about it. She reminded him of the time he'd used the notion of Brendan having an affair as something that she'd be able to forgive, and reminded him, too, that he'd said it was just an example – had it been, she demanded, or had he known all along?

'Of course I didn't know,' said Greg. 'God Almighty, Domino, I would never have kept something like that from you.'

'Wouldn't you?'

'No.'

She was relieved at that. The idea of both Delahaye brothers keeping secrets from her was more than she could bear. A tear slid down her cheek.

'Don't cry.' Greg tore a strip of kitchen towel from the roll and handed it to her. 'I'm sure the two of you can work it out.'

'You mean that I'll forgive him?'

'Oh, Domino.' He took her into his arms and held her there while she cried. At last she pulled away and blew her nose in the piece of kitchen roll. 'I've always worried about the possibility.' She sniffed. 'Especially since he's become more successful. I've worried that there are women out there who admire him and want to be with him and be something for him that I can't.'

Greg looked startled.

'Too much information,' Dominique said wryly. 'Don't worry, Greg. It's not our sex life I'm talking about. It's just that he doesn't have to worry about any of them getting lost in a black fog and bursting into tears for no apparent reason.'

'Do you?'

'Not any more, obviously. But it's always there in the back of his mind. I know it is.'

'You're wrong, Domino. He loves you and he cares for you and you have to stop thinking about a time in your life that's done and dusted.'

'I heard him on the phone once. Maybe he was talking to a woman then. He said he hadn't signed up for it. That he'd had enough.'

'He was talking to me,' Greg corrected her. 'I told him that everything would be all right. And it is. You know it is.'

'So why is he having a damned affair?'

'Maybe he's not. Maybe you got it wrong.'

But she knew she hadn't. What she still didn't know was what the hell she was going to do about it.

Chapter 14

Kelly Delahaye ran down the steps of the local radio station. She pointed her zapper at the car, which was parked on the other side of the small car park, while at the same time answering her mobile phone and fixing the silver clip in her shining hair.

'Oh, sure,' she told her cousin Alicia, who had asked if Kelly would be joining their gang of friends at their favourite cheap and cheerful Italian that evening. 'I have to do this charity thing with Mum first, so if I'm late, go ahead without me. It's work experience. I'm going to try to interview some of her friends and then put together a piece about them.' She laughed as Alicia told her to have fun. 'Hardly fun,' she said as she got into the car, the mobile jammed between her shoulder and her chin. 'Most of Mum's events bore me to death. All those silly chattering women trying to outdo each other. I don't know how she puts up with it. She's not a bit like them really.'

She snapped her phone closed and threw it on to the passenger seat beside her. Then she started the car engine and moved forward slowly.

Kelly's car was a bright gold Micra that Brendan had bought her for her eighteenth birthday a couple of years earlier. Kelly had really wanted a motorbike (a Yamaha had been her bike of choice), but Brendan had put his foot down and told her in no uncertain terms that there wasn't a hope in hell of her getting a lethal weapon like a bike, no matter how vehemently she promised to be safe.

'It's not just you I'm worried about,' said Brendan. 'It's other road-users too.'

She'd been disappointed about the bike (and disappointed, too,

171

that the birthday present car had turned out to be a granny motor rather than something chic and sporty), but there was no doubt that the Micra was handy for getting around and a cinch to park in the city's overcrowded streets. It was, perhaps, a bit too easy to drive, but Kelly was hoping that if she managed to get as far as her upcoming twenty-first birthday without scratching it once, her father might rethink his position on something with a little more street cred.

She turned on to the main road that led towards Atlantic View. Kelly herself would have called the house something different – in her opinion, the name, though technically correct, was far too unimaginative. But then her father wasn't an imaginative person. What creativity he had was solely reserved for his building projects.

She hadn't been all that happy about moving to Cork at first. Leaving Dublin and her friends had been a terrible wrench, and none of her parents' efforts to cheer her up had made it any easier. Not the *Xena: Warrior Princess*-decorated room with its very own TV and PlayStation, nor the frequent trips to the local McDonald's (which Dominique had rationed very severely in Dublin) nor even the acquisition of a major new wardrobe had appeased her. It wasn't until she started school and began to make new friends that she finally felt as though she was fitting in. And, of course, when she brought other girls home and they saw all her gadgets, they were only too happy to be friends with her too.

She made quite a lot of friends, but she was closest to her cousin Alicia, older than her by a few months. Dominique had always called Alicia a sweet girl, and Kelly knew what she meant. Her cousin was gentle and kind and acted as a brake on some of Kelly's own madcap ideas. Kelly knew that Alicia was friends with her for her own sake too, unlike some of the girls in her class, who, she was sure, just wanted to nose around Atlantic View and play with her stuff. Alicia wasn't the sort of girl who was into stuff. Anyhow, her parents – though not as well off as Kelly's – were far more indulgent and generally bought her the newest of everything, so she had no reasons for envy.

Atlantic View was something to envy, thought Kelly, as she began the drive up the narrow, twisting road that led to the house. As far as she was concerned it was simply home, but there were times when she saw it featured in the glossy pages of style magazines and regarded it with a fresh perspective; those were the times when she realised that it was, as they always said, a very desirable property. She knew that was why so many women came to the charity events that Dominique hosted there. They all wanted to snoop around and say that they'd been invited to Dominique Delahaye's. It was a badge of social honour to get inside Atlantic View and to meet her mother, who was variously referred to, in those same glossy magazines, as Wonder Wife, Golden Girl and Dazzling Domino.

As far as Kelly was concerned, Dominique was just Mum. Kelly loved her with a protective ferocity that sometimes surprised even herself. She knew that her mother's life wasn't really a dizzying whirl of designer dresses, cocktail parties and jet-set holidays, although it was certainly true that after they'd first moved to Cork, the profile of the Delahayes had rocketed as Delahaye Developments grew and diversified. It was equally true that Dominique could have spent six nights a week out on the town if she chose. There was a time when that was exactly what she'd done, going to dinners and balls and shows with Brendan almost every night. But after a while they'd cut back on their socialising as Brendan concentrated even more on his business, and Dominique only went to events that she considered particularly worthwhile. Kelly remembered her mother telling her that being invited to so many things was great at first and it was nice to be popular. But she also said that not everybody liked you for who you were, that sometimes it was because of *what* you were. She'd looked resigned when she'd said those words, and Kelly – who knew exactly what she meant, because of her popularity in school being so closely linked to living at Atlantic View – agreed with her. These days Dominique was even more selective in her involvement with the charity circuit and preferred lower-key projects like painting the local community hall or sponsoring new kit for school sports teams. (To be fair, Kelly acknowledged, it was her dad who sponsored the kit, but her mum was the one who turned up at the school and made a big fuss of all the kids.)

Dominique was a voluntary director of half a dozen charitable groups. She kept completely up to date with everything they were doing and was a stern critic of projects that didn't meet certain criteria regarding fund-raising and outcomes, sometimes arguing vehemently with her fellow directors and demanding answers to searching questions. Kelly had been a little bit surprised to notice this harder edge develop in her mother, because until then she'd always thought that her dad was the tough businessperson in the family. But these days her mum was seen as successful too, even if, as her dad put it, she spent most of her time simply giving cash away, while he did his best to earn it.

It was tiring, she thought sometimes, to have parents who were seen as pillars of the community. It was a lot to live up to.

She circled past the catering vans parked in the driveway in front of the house and jumped out of the car. This afternoon's garden party was in aid of the children's hospital unit. Most of Dominique's charity functions helped children in some way, and Kelly thought that maybe that was why they were so popular. People liked helping kids. It gave them a good feeling inside.

She glanced at her watch. It was four thirty, and the party was due to start shortly. But she still had plenty of time to change into something more suitable than the scruffy jeans and T-shirt she was wearing before mingling with the crowd and trying to get interviews for the radio station.

'Hello, darling.' Dominique smiled as Kelly clattered into the hallway. 'Had a good day?'

'Were you listening?' asked Kelly.

'I heard some of it,' Dominique told her. 'I listened on my way to Stephanie's. Then we got caught up in the planning for next month's festival. I liked the talking-dog slot, though quite honestly I didn't understand a word he was supposed to be saying.'

Kelly's job at the radio station was temporary cover for the summer months. She worked as an assistant researcher, which actually meant general dogsbody, as the station was small and local and almost everybody had to do everything. She'd got the job through her college website and she was enjoying it tremendously. Kelly's ambition was to be a presenter herself some day, although, as she regularly told Dominique and Brendan, she wanted to do serious stuff too, not just sex-and-shopping items and being nice to not-very-famous local celebrities.

'Like me, you mean?' Dominique had grinned at her and Kelly had looked slightly abashed.

Today she planned to interview her mother about her charity work, and to talk to some of the women who came to the garden party, to ask them about their lives. Kelly knew that many people thought the charity circuit as vapid and pointless as some of the women who populated it, but the dinners and balls and parties did raise a huge amount of money. And surely that was better than nothing?

Dominique watched as Kelly skipped up the stairs to her room and thought, as she always did, that her daughter was the cleverest and loveliest girl in the whole world. Kelly was tall and slender and she walked with a sense of purpose that made her a noticeable figure. She was enjoying her media and communications studies at college, and she was enjoying the social side of her life too, being involved in lots of different societies and groups. Dominique knew that Kelly didn't suffer from the crippling insecurities that had swamped her during her own school years, and nor (as Dominique herself had) did she regard boys as some kind of mysterious race, impossible to understand. Kelly often had a boyfriend in tow, though she was equally happy when there was nobody special around. Dominique knew that her daughter was never fazed about her relationships and never spent hours hovering around the phone as she had when she'd first started going out with Brendan.

Not, of course, that Kelly needed to hover around the house phone when all of her communication was done either on her mobile or by email. Even though Dominique sometimes felt that the biggest difference between her and her outgoing daughter was self-confidence, she also knew that a major difference was that Kelly was never out of touch with anyone. Day or night she could contact a friend and spill her heart out – although Dominique would remind herself that that wasn't something Kelly appeared to need to do. Nevertheless, the option was there to be able to contact someone easily and never to be out of touch herself. Dominique thought that this was a good thing, although she did wonder how on earth her daughter would react if her mobile phone was ever prised from her grasp.

She walked out into the garden and surveyed the work of the caterers and party planners. The theme of today's event was Magical Childhood, and so the flower-filled garden had been turned into a fairy grotto, with coloured lanterns (though on such a glorious day it was far too bright to actually see them) and tiny models of elves and fairies clipped to trees and shrubs. Waist-high tables were strewn with rose petals – Dominique was thankful that the day was calm as well as hot, so the petals stayed where they were supposed to; and each table had plenty of golden envelopes into which she expected guests to place donations for the charity. Dominique had arranged for a jazz band and a singer too. She reckoned that it would be a great day and would go some way towards helping to fund some of the equipment the hospital so desperately needed.

She liked hosting charity functions. The first time she'd done it – a very small party to help fund-raise for the school sports facil- ities – she'd been shaking with nerves. But people had loved coming to Atlantic View and enjoyed the wine and canapés she'd provided, and afterwards Mrs Deegan, the school principal, had told her that it had been their most effective fund-raiser ever. And now, even though some of the events she got involved in were in the glitziest of venues and were reported on in the gossip magazines, she still liked the ones at her home the most.

It amazed her, when she looked back on it, how quickly she had become involved in so many different things. The charities covered a wide range of issues, and she was also involved in a post-natal depression support group in the area. What surprised her the most was the sense of purpose that being part of these organisations gave her and the amount of time and energy that she was prepared to put into everything she did. There had been a short period when it had all been about the glamour. But now the glitz had to be there for a reason, which was why she carefully considered every invitation she and Brendan were sent.

Brendan had told her that he'd try to get back to say hello to her guests later that afternoon. Her husband was always a big draw at the events because everyone liked to see a local person who'd done well for themselves. Recently he'd raised a lot of money from local investors for a building project in Barbados, promising them that they'd do well out of it too, saying that he wanted to spread the wealth around. He was known for being a generous employer and a sociable man, and even in middle age he was still tall and broad and very attractive. Dominique often told him, with some amusement, that the takings for the charities were always higher when he turned up because the women didn't want to disappoint him. They'd disappoint her, all right, she'd say with a smile. But when he went around the tables to collect the envelopes, she knew that there'd be an extra few bob in each one.

She glanced at her watch. He was in Dublin today, having spent a lot of time in the capital over the past few weeks at various meetings. He'd been grumpy the previous night about having to go to yet another, saying that it was sometimes hard to make the money men understand the value of what he was trying to achieve. He'd headed off early that morning, well before she'd woken, because he liked driving while the roads were empty. She'd texted him to remind him about the garden party, and he'd texted back to say that he hadn't forgotten but he wasn't sure about getting home in time. She'd made a face at that, because it would be nice if he could press the flesh and work his magic and charm a little extra out of all the women who'd turned up.

I'm so lucky, she murmured to herself. And I was so, so right not to throw it all down the pan by overreacting about Little Miss Valentine all those years ago. I did the right thing.

It was nearly a month after the discovery of the text before she told Brendan that she'd seen a message on his phone, by accident, and that it had seemed highly inappropriate to her. (It had taken so long because she'd had to practise saying the words 'highly inappropriate' over and over again until she was able to deliver them without a quiver in her voice.) An expression of horror, followed by denial, crossed Brendan's face. Because she'd expected as much, she was prepared for this too. She told him that she didn't mind if he'd made a mistake, that everybody did from time to time. But, she'd said, she didn't want him to make any mistakes that would threaten their marriage or hurt Kelly. She didn't want him to make mistakes that could come back to haunt them.

'You're right,' he said eventually. 'It *was* a mistake. You and Kelly are and always will be the most important people in my life.'

Hearing him say it was both a relief and a disappointment. There was a part of her that still hoped that she was the one who'd made the mistake, who'd got the wrong end of the stick and spent the last four weeks worrying needlessly.

'Does she matter to you?' She kept her tone as even as possible.

'No.' Brendan sighed. 'And it wasn't really what you think, either.'

'Oh?' Dominique felt a spurt of relief in her heart, but then she remembered that the message had called him *my Valentine*. There was no point in getting her hopes up.

'It was mostly texts,' Brendan said.

'Huh?'

'I met her at a business conference. She was fun and we got on well. We kept in touch by text. They were jokey at first and then I suppose they became, well, flirty.'

'She sent other texts? I didn't see any.'

'I usually deleted them. I thought I'd deleted that one too. It was harmless fun, Domino.'

'So you're saying you didn't sleep with her?' Dominique was incredulous.

Brendan looked as though he was going to deny it, and then his shoulders drooped. 'It happened,' he admitted. 'But that wasn't really what it was all about.'

Dominique tried not to think of him sleeping with another woman. It was too painful.

'It was about the messages,' he said. 'Silly messages at odd times during the day.'

'Silly messages?' Dominique couldn't help letting anger into her voice. 'I doubt that they were silly, Brendan. Erotic, I bet. And they clearly led to more . . .'

Despite her promise to herself not to cry, she choked up, unable to continue.

'It wasn't as bad as you think,' he protested. 'We didn't do half the things . . . and, Domino, I don't love her. She doesn't love me.'

178

'So *why?*'

'Because she was there.'

'Oh, Brendan.'

'I'm sorry. I was at the conference and I was missing home and she started talking to me, and I know it was wrong but I did it anyway.' There was a note of defiance in his voice. 'And . . .' he continued, 'she treated me as though I was an important person.'

'I treat you like an important person!'

'No you don't,' he said. 'You treat me like the person I always was. She treated me like a rich businessman.'

'You want me to treat you differently?' Dominique was confused.

Brendan sighed. 'Not really. It's just that with you, I'm always Brendan the Brickie. With her, I was Brendan Delahaye, entrepreneur. I was somebody.'

Dominique wasn't sure what to say.

'I know you probably think I'm silly and immature,' said Brendan. 'But it was nice to be . . . to be deferred to.'

'Oh my God,' said Dominique. 'You want a Stepford Wife.'

'Of course I don't,' he said. '*You're* my wife. I just wanted a bit of excitement.'

'Do we not get enough?' she asked. 'When we go to the dinners and the galas and stuff?'

'That's different.'

She felt a surge of panic rising within her. Was this how marriages ended? she wondered. Not with constant arguments and rows over stupid things but stuttering to an end because one or the other person felt there was no excitement any more?

'So what do you want to do about it?' asked Dominique.

'I'm sorry,' he said. 'I really am. It was a bit of fun, that's all.'

'And have you ever had this sort of fun with anyone else?'

A flicker of guilt passed over his face and she thought she was going to faint. Had there been scores of women? Because that would change things utterly, wouldn't it? One mistake could possibly be understood, but multiple text lovers was something very different.

'No,' he said. 'There was once or twice when I . . . when I thought about it, but no.'

'Do you love me?' asked Dominique.

He put his arms around her. 'You're my family,' he said. 'You and Kelly. You know how important my family is to me. And you, Domino, you're my lucky charm.'

'I don't feel very lucky,' she said flatly. 'And you slept with another woman. That shows how important your family is to you.'

'Please, please believe me when I say it really didn't mean anything. It was – oh, the opportunity was there and I took it and I know it was wrong. And I know that the texts were wrong too. I'm sorry, Domino.'

'Do you want to leave me?'

'Of course not,' he said. 'We work, Domino, you and me. You're the best asset I have. And you're still my lucky charm.'

It wasn't exactly what she wanted to hear. She didn't want to be his asset. Or even his lucky charm. She just wanted to be the person he loved.

'We're a partnership,' he told her.

She could see why he'd looked for text sex if he just thought of her as a partner. She needed to be more than that to him.

'What do you want?' she asked. 'Do you want me to come to all your events with you and then shag you in the hotel car park? Is that it?'

He looked startled. 'I wasn't quite thinking of it like that.'

'But now that I mention it?'

'Hey . . .' He smiled at her. 'We had some good times when we had sex in the open air.'

He'd stood by her when she was pregnant and stood by her when she'd gone through her depression. He didn't want to leave her. And the truth was that she didn't want to leave him either.

Everyone made mistakes, she thought, as she kissed him. It was what happened afterwards that mattered.

It was only when it was all over that Dominique realised how much time he'd been spending away from her and how many functions he'd gone to on his own. Going with him made her feel closer to him again. She was bright and chatty and back to her Dazzling Domino best. Sometimes, as they sat beside each other at a terminally boring dinner (she could understand why he'd looked for something to distract him in these cases), she would allow her hand to slide beneath the table and massage him while at the same time keeping up a conversation with the other guests. She knew he liked that very much. He came home earlier and more often too, and they would regularly go out to dinner or the movies together. On the way home he would sometimes divert into deserted laneways, where Dominique tried to treat him in a way that would make him forget thoughts of any other Miss Valentines who might be lurking in the wings. Deep down she thought that she'd outgrown the days when having sex in the car, or in a field, was an exciting thing. (To be perfectly honest, she preferred it at home in their bed with its crisp cotton sheets.) But if this was something that Brendan liked, then this was what she would do. And it wasn't that she didn't find it fun; it was just, she thought, that she'd become far too pampered these days.

She realised that there was more to it than sex. She knew that she needed him to be interested in her and what she did every day too, so that they would have different things to talk about and so that he would treat her as an equal. She became more and more involved in the management and operations of the charities she supported, and she made him get involved financially too. Sometimes her friends would sigh and say that she and Brendan were so lucky to have each other and that it must be great to have such a devoted husband. Dominique was confident that she had made it through yet another rocky patch in her marriage, and confident, too, that the worst would never happen now and Brendan would never leave her. He had too much to lose. And besides, he didn't want to go.

She'd never heard even a whisper about Miss Valentine on the social scene, even though it was a scene that was regularly rocked by rumours of infidelities among the people they knew. She was happy that there would be no such rumours about the Dazzling Delahayes. She knew that some women would think of her as weak for accepting Brendan's behaviour and forgiving it. But you had to forgive sometimes. You had to get over things and move on. Both of them had forgiving to do. Both of them had moved on. They'd made the right choice and Dominique, once again, was happy with the person she had become.

*　　*　　*

It was one of the warmest days of the year, and the women – it was usually mainly women – who'd come to the party were enjoying being able to show off their summer clothes as they moved through the garden like brightly coloured birds. Dominique herself was wearing a soft purple dress with white polka dots, though now, as the party was ending, she'd taken off her matching high-heeled sandals and was standing barefoot in the tinder-dry grass. Despite her dazzling status, she'd never really cracked high heels.

Kelly, in a strapless floral sundress, was interviewing Norah O'Connell, wife of a local businessman. Dominique watched as her daughter animatedly asked questions of the older woman for the piece that would be broadcast on the radio the following day. She knew that Kelly enjoyed what she was doing and that she desperately wanted a career in radio. Kelly was hoping that during the summer holidays she'd manage to get an exclusive scoop to bring to Countryside FM so that they'd realise how good she was. Dominique thought it was rather sweet that her daughter would think in terms of exclusives and scoops for what was really just a community service station, but she was impressed by Kelly's determination. Every day she saw her daughter scouring the newspapers and the internet for newsworthy items, and although she hadn't found anything yet, Dominique felt sure that eventually she would.

'Hey, Domino!' Emma walked across the grass towards her. 'I thought I'd better say goodbye. I've got to get home before Jia cracks up altogether.'

Dominique grinned at her. After Emma's dad, Norman, had died a couple of years ago, she'd had to find someone to help with her gorgeous but hyperactive son, Lugh. She'd been very fortunate in finding Jia, a Chinese girl with an abundance of patience, whom Lugh adored.

'He's going through a kung fu phase at the moment,' Emma added, 'and he expects poor Jia to know all the moves. Of course every time he comes at her, she just shrieks and runs away.'

Dominique laughed. 'He'll get over it.'

'I wish.' Emma's tone was heartfelt. 'I'm worn out by him, and Greg isn't much better. And Lily's a pet, but she's a bit old to be running after him all the time.'

'How did you and Greg manage to have such a bloodthirsty child?' demanded Dominique. 'You're both so charming!'

'If I didn't know better, I'd say he wasn't ours at all,' said Emma darkly. 'Oh, if only I'd had a lovely girl like Kelly.'

'You don't mean that.'

Emma groaned. 'At the moment I do. Lugh was great when he was younger, and hopefully he'll be great again when he's a bit older, but right now he's so difficult.'

'Kelly went through her obstinate stage too,' Dominique reminded her. 'And of course now . . . It's not all a bed of roses with girls.'

'What about now?' asked Emma.

'Now I look at her living her own life and doing her own thing, and I pray every single day that she gets it right and doesn't mess up. I'm terrified that she'll meet the wrong guy and fall for him and waste her life.'

Emma looked at her curiously. 'Is she seeing someone?'

'Oh, she has loads of friends who are boys,' Dominique replied easily. 'And she's not a bit devoted to any of them. But you know what it's like. One day it hits you, and then . . .' She shrugged.

Emma nodded. 'And then he's like a drug and you can't get enough,' she finished.

'Or you marry him.' Dominique smiled. 'And then you wonder what on earth it was you saw in him.'

'Do you think like that?' asked Emma.

'No. No.' Dominique spoke quickly. 'Not at all. But the mad passion doesn't last for ever.'

'If it was ever truly there in the first place.'

There was a sudden silence between the two women. Their friendship had never become close enough for them to share secrets about their marriages, even though both of them sometimes thought about giving advice to the other. But Dominique didn't want Emma Walsh feeling sorry for her, while Emma had never felt inferior to Dominique Brady and didn't want to give her any reason to think that she was other than perfectly happy all the time. Despite being related by marriage in the present, they could never entirely forget the pecking order of the past.

'Mrs Delahaye! Mrs Delahaye!'

Both women turned around. A photographer stood in front of them.

'Can I get a shot?' he asked. 'For the morning paper?'

'Of course.' Dominique put her arm around her sister-in-law's waist and the two of them smiled brightly for the camera. It was a picture that, in the following days, was used over and over again in the newspapers. And everyone who looked at it shook their heads as they gazed at Dazzling Dominique Delahaye looking radiantly confident beside her elegant sister-in-law, utterly unaware of the fact that her gilded life had already come crashing down around her.

Chapter 15

Brendan was in the back garden of their Dublin house. A few years earlier, he'd sold the Bachelors Walk apartment and bought the small but ideally located town house in Mount Merrion. It had been an excellent purchase. The entire family used the house whenever they came to Dublin, and Brendan himself always stayed there when he came to the capital for a business meeting. Today he'd had four of them and they'd been longer, tougher and significantly less successful than he'd either expected or hoped.

He glanced at his watch. He wondered how Domino's garden party was going. Probably a resounding success, like everything she did these days. She deserved her unofficial title of Ireland's Most Celebrated Hostess. She'd undoubtedly be pissed at him for not turning up. But she wouldn't say anything; she never did. Ever since the confrontation after she'd found that text message from Laura, she hadn't once nagged him or questioned him when he was away. He knew that she had decided to trust him. He admired her for that. And for the way that she'd treated him afterwards – their sex life had improved tremendously. There weren't many women, Brendan thought, who would have behaved like Domino. She was one in a million. Everybody loved her. He'd made the right choice to stick with her.

His lucky charm.

Until now.

Dominique was disappointed that Brendan hadn't made it back, though she knew that they'd raised a lot of money even without him there to charm her female guests. Nevertheless, she pushed her irritation with him to one side as she counted up the cash, sealed it in a manila envelope and placed it in the safe in his office. She'd bring it to the bank in the morning and then arrange with the hospital to give them the cheque. They wanted to have a photo shoot of the handover, and Dominique was happy to fall in with whatever suited them.

She closed the safe door and wandered outside again. The garden was back to its pristine state, although a few stray rose petals fluttered lazily across the lawn in the late-evening breeze. She sat down on the huge cushioned chair, which was carefully positioned to catch the dying rays of the sun. There was still quite some time to go before it would finally sink below the horizon. She enjoyed entertaining, but she basked in the quiet time afterwards, when she knew that a good job had been done and she was on her own again, able to lose herself in her thoughts.

Not that they were very exciting thoughts. Actually, sitting in the chair now, she wasn't thinking of anything at all. She was simply feeling content at being in the place she loved the most in the world, knowing that things had worked out for her and that she was lucky. She probably wouldn't have planned for her life to have taken the turns it had, but everything happened for a reason. She firmly believed that, just as she firmly believed that she had learned from both the good and the bad.

But hopefully there's nothing else I need to learn, she told herself. Hopefully I know it all by now.

Brendan hadn't come home by the time darkness fell and she went inside again. He hadn't even phoned, which left her feeling annoyed, mostly because his thoughtlessness was wiping out the warm glow of her day. She tried to call him, but his mobile was powered down. Nor was there a reply from the house in Mount Merrion.

Years ago she would have worried about him and wondered why he wasn't answering his phone, but these days she didn't. There were a million and one things that could have delayed him, a million and one things that he could be caught up in; and so she put him out of her mind and went to bed early, having told Kelly not to stay out too late. Kelly had laughed and said that she was meeting

Alicia and the gang, and that even though Joanna, Alicia's hell-raising younger sister, was coming along too, they wouldn't be out late at all and she wasn't to worry. They were going to spend the night at Alicia's, she said, because it was nearer town, and so she wasn't to expect her home.

Dominique, knowing that she was probably being overprotective but unable to help herself, asked Kelly to text her when they got back to Alicia's anyway, and Kelly looked at her in amused exasperation and said that she was an adult now and didn't need Dominique or Brendan worrying about her all the time. And Dominique said she knew, she was sorry, she couldn't help it, but mothers always worried.

She read a book until she got the text from Kelly at just after midnight, and then she turned out the light. She still hadn't heard from Brendan. This behaviour was typical of him when he was in the middle of a big project, but it always bothered her. She told herself that it was silly to expect him to call when he was preoccupied with work, but she wished he would all the same. Whenever he forgot about her like this, the memories of the Miss Valentine episode returned. He'd been busy and preoccupied then too, and she'd totally misread the situation. She didn't want that to happen again. And so she always fretted when he was out of reach for too long, but told herself that this wasn't obsessive behaviour and made herself refrain from ringing him to check up on him. It was hard, but worth it for him not to think of her as a nagging wife.

Nevertheless, she was still worrying as she lay in bed and heard the sound of the front door opening and Brendan's footsteps on the stairs. Usually she would call out to him if she was awake when he came home, because otherwise he slept in the bedroom across the hallway so as not to wake her. But she was annoyed with him for stressing her out on a day that had been important to her, and for not turning up at the event when he'd almost promised to be there, so she stayed silent. When she heard him go into the other bedroom, she turned on to her side, pulled the sheet around her and fell asleep almost immediately.

Dominique had slept badly in the years after Kelly's birth, but after moving to Atlantic View, she found that she slept much more soundly, even on the nights when Brendan wasn't with her. It had surprised her at first – she'd been afraid that in an isolated house she wouldn't be able to sleep at all. But the high walls and electronic gates, as well as their hi-tech security system, meant that she didn't jump at every creaking floorboard or worry vaguely at things that went bump in the night. And Atlantic View itself had a calming effect on her, which meant that she was rarely stressed going to bed.

So she had no problem falling asleep after Brendan's return but at about three in the morning she suddenly woke up with a start, her heart thumping in her chest. She had no idea what had woken her and she lay rigid in the bed for a few minutes. She thought of going in to Brendan's room and cuddling in beside him, but she told herself that she was being silly and that he was probably snoring his head off, which was the one thing that did keep her awake. She made herself close her eyes again and eventually she drifted off. This time she didn't wake until after eight o'clock, when she threw open the curtains and allowed the morning sun to flood into her bedroom.

She didn't bother putting her head around the door of the bedroom opposite to check on Brendan, because she knew that would wake him and he could do with the sleep. He'd been on the go almost solidly for a fortnight. (She'd forgiven him now for his lack of communication the day before and was feeling guilty at her selfishness in wanting him to fall in with her plans when he was clearly so busy.)

She went downstairs and made herself tea and toast smothered in the fruity marmalade that she bought every month from Deirdre Sullivan's organic farm a kilometre down the road. She brought her breakfast out to the patio behind the kitchen, thinking that it was going to be yet another spectacular day. She knew that she could happily spend all of it sitting in the garden doing nothing, but she couldn't truly relax until she'd brought the money from yesterday's event to the bank and called in to see the hospital administrator. Reluctantly, she made herself go inside and shower. She dressed in a slim-fitting white cotton dress, put her hair up so that her neck would be cool, and slid into a pair of bright pink sandals. Catching a glimpse of herself in the long bedroom mirror, she thought – if you didn't look too closely – she might still be taken for a woman in her early thirties instead of someone pushing forty. Forty had sounded incredibly old and past it when she was in her teens. Evelyn had been both physically and mentally middle-aged at forty. Actually, Dominique thought, Evelyn had always been mentally middle-aged. At least I managed not to turn into my mother, she told her reflection cheerfully. That's probably my biggest achievement in life!

She was picking up her keys from the hall table when the phone rang. She hesitated, wondering why it was that it always rang just as she was leaving the house, and thinking about not bothering to answer it. But if she left it ringing, then it would wake Brendan and he'd be in a foul mood, so in the end she picked up the handset.

'Hi, Domino.' It was Barry, her brother-in-law. 'Is Brendan there?'

'Still in bed,' she said. 'He wasn't home until the early hours.'

'I need to talk to him urgently,' said Barry.

'OK. Hold on.' Brendan was going to be woken whether he liked it or not. She placed the handset on the hall table and called out to him from the bottom of the stairs. There was no answer. She sighed, ran lightly up the stairs and pushed open the bedroom door.

The room was empty and the bed hadn't been slept in. She frowned slightly as she went inside and tapped at the door of the en-suite bathroom. There was no answer, so she pushed that door open too. Brendan wasn't in the bathroom either. Which meant that he hadn't come home at all during the night.

She shivered slightly. She'd been sure that she'd heard him. Convinced, in fact. Certain that she'd heard his footsteps on the stairs and the sound of the bedroom door opening and closing. How had she been so utterly mistaken? She thought for a moment, and then walked down the hallway to Kelly's room. But her daughter's bed hadn't been slept in either.

She went back downstairs slowly and thoughtfully.

'I'm sorry,' she said to Barry after she'd picked up the handset again. 'He's not home.'

'Where is he?'

'I was sure I heard him come home last night, but I must have been dreaming. So I suppose he's still in Dublin.'

'At the house?'

'I guess so. I don't know. What's wrong?'

She could sense the hesitation in her brother-in-law's voice.

'There's some stuff going on,' he said eventually. 'He was supposed to be here early this morning. I need to talk to him urgently.'

'I'll get him to call you as soon as I hear from him,' said Dominique.

'It's really, really important,' Barry told her.

'I'll make sure he rings you.'

She continued to hold the handset as she stood indecisively in the hallway. It wasn't like Brendan to be so completely out of touch. Whether or not he told her of his whereabouts, he nearly always told Barry. She hit the speed-dial button on the phone and was almost immediately connected to Brendan's voicemail.

'Is something wrong?' she asked. 'Call me.'

Then she rang the Mount Merrion house. The answering machine hadn't been switched on, so the phone rang out. She replaced the handset on its stand and went into Brendan's office, looking around as though something would give her a clue as to his whereabouts. She knew that her anxiety level was beginning to ratchet up a notch. She didn't want to think irrational thoughts like the first one that had flashed through her mind as the phone rang fruitlessly in the Mount Merrion house. That he'd found another woman. That he was leaving. That this time it was different.

She told herself not to be so stupid. Miss Valentine had been years ago, and nothing, absolutely nothing, since then had given her a moment for thought as far as affairs, virtual or otherwise, were concerned. He hadn't found anyone. He wasn't leaving. She needed to get a grip.

She suddenly imagined a completely different scenario: him lying on the floor of the house, unable to move, victim of some kind of medical emergency – a heart attack maybe; or perhaps he'd fallen down the stairs and broken a leg. Maybe he could hear the phone but not get to it. But, she told herself, that wouldn't happen to Brendan. Besides, he always had his mobile in his pocket. He'd be able to get in touch. Her thoughts turned to car crashes and fatal accidents. She was sure that she would have heard by now if he had been involved in a crash. Someone would already have been along to break that sort of news to her.

And so the thought that took root in her brain again was the one in which Brendan had found another woman, someone he wanted to be with so much that he was prepared to face not only her wrath when he eventually arrived home but the wrath of Barry Keane too. June's husband was notoriously short-tempered, and he wouldn't be at all amused if Brendan hadn't turned up to the office because of a woman.

Dominique left her bag on the hall table and went upstairs again. More deliberately this time, thinking about what it would mean for her if Brendan had begun an affair and wondering why it was that she couldn't rid herself of the idea. Did all women immediately suspect their husbands of infidelity if they couldn't get in touch with them? Or was it just her?

She strode into their bedroom and looked around her. Then she opened his bedside cabinet.

Lena Doyle, one of her circle of friends, had once confessed to searching through her husband's cabinet on a regular basis because he kept his private stuff there. Dominique had been horrified, thinking that everyone had to have somewhere to keep private stuff but then wondering what sort of things Brendan would keep hidden from her. He had better places than his cabinet, though, she thought as she opened it anyway. He had his office safe.

As she'd expected, the cherrywood cabinet was almost empty. All it contained was a packet of aspirin, a blister pack of the antacid tablets that Brendan occasionally needed to take, and a spare pair of the reading glasses he'd started wearing a couple of years earlier.

She went downstairs and back into his office. Perhaps, she thought, he'd left an itinerary on his desk with details of where he was going and what he was doing. He usually did this if he was going abroad, although he'd never before gone overseas without telling her. Over the last few years he'd dabbled in some foreign developments, such as the exclusive apartment resort near Biarritz, which had recently been completed. He'd brought her and Kelly to see the finished product, although, Dominique recalled, he'd said that it hadn't been as profitable as he would have liked. She and Kelly had stayed in one of the apartments for a week after Brendan had returned to Dublin and had enjoyed themselves immensely. There was the

Barbados project too, of course, but it was in the very early stages and she was absolutely certain that there was no way he'd have gone to the Caribbean island without telling her first.

Anyway, she thought now, he might not have headed off anywhere, but he hasn't left me any information on where he is either, and it's stupid of me to simply rely on being able to contact him by mobile phone and not know his actual whereabouts. He could ring me from the South Pole and say he was in Dublin and I wouldn't know any different.

She sighed. Brendan would turn up in his own good time. He always did. She could depend on him for that.

She was just about to leave the house for the second time when her mobile rang. If this was Brendan at last, she thought as she fished it out of her bag, she'd give him a bollocking for not being in touch.

'Are you in?'

'Emma?'

'Yes. Are you in?'

'I'm on the way out.'

'Don't leave. I'm coming over.'

'Why? What's up?'

'I'll be there in fifteen. Talk then.'

Her sister-in-law hung up and Dominique stared at the mobile. By now she was feeling really uneasy. What was all that about? Emma wouldn't normally keep her in suspense like that. Had they discovered Brendan's whereabouts? Were they afraid to tell her? Was it a woman? Was it a heart attack? Was he dead?

She told herself not to be so melodramatic, then went into the kitchen and poured herself a glass of filtered water, which she drank standing up and leaning against the kitchen wall. She was feeling far too edgy to sit down.

The gate buzzer sounded about ten minutes later. Emma certainly hadn't wasted any time in getting to Atlantic View, thought Dominique, as she released the lock. She opened the front door just as Emma drew to a halt in front of the house.

'Let's get inside,' said Emma.

'What on earth's going on?' demanded Dominique as she allowed herself to be hustled away from the door. 'Why all the drama?'

'Come into the living room.'

Dominique followed Emma into one of her favourite rooms of the house. It was decorated in pale cream and green and she found it supremely restful, with its panoramic views across her garden and down to the sea.

'Have you heard from Brendan at all?' asked Emma.

'No.' Dominique shook her head and then looked anxiously at Emma. 'Why?'

Emma took a deep breath and then spoke slowly. 'He hasn't turned up to the office today, although he was supposed to be there by ten. Domino . . .'

'What?' Dominique was really worried now.

'Oh, Domino! They've appointed a liquidator to the company. Delahaye Developments has gone belly-up.'

'What?' This time Dominique looked at Emma in utter disbelief. 'That can't be right. The company has made a ton of money over the past few years. It can't be in trouble now.'

'That's what I thought too. But June told me—'

'June?' interrupted Dominique.

'She was talking to Barry. He was there when the liquidator arrived. Apparently it's been on the cards for a while, but nobody's said a word. The company was struggling with its debts and couldn't borrow any more, so things started to go off the rails. The banks began asking for their money back. The thing is, Domino, a lot of the borrowings were guaranteed by Brendan's other companies and by him personally, and there seem to be some problems about that too, because the other companies weren't profitable either, and personally . . .' She broke off, not sure what to say next.

'But . . . but . . . he never said anything to me.' Dominique stared at Emma, her dark eyes wide with anxiety. 'I ask him from time to time how things are going, and sometimes he says better than others, but he's always been confident that everything was OK.'

'Maybe he didn't want to worry you.'

'Not telling me anything is far more worrying.'

'I know.' Emma's eyes were full of concern.

'Did you know?' demanded Dominique.

'No,' Emma said quickly. 'I only heard now. From June. She was spitting with rage and with fear and worried about herself and Barry.'

'She doesn't know where Brendan is?'

'No. She wanted to know if I did. Or if I'd been talking to you about it.'

'He must be with one of the banks,' said Dominique. 'He must be trying to negotiate a rescue package. Or maybe he's with Matthew.' She took out her mobile phone and began to scan through her list of contacts for the accountant's number.

'I don't think so.' Emma spoke carefully. 'He should have been at the company offices this morning. There was supposed to be an emergency meeting. It seems that today was make-or-break day.'

'Yes, but maybe he's trying to get the banks to . . .' Dominique's voice trailed off as the realisation of what was happening finally began to sink home. 'Oh my God, Emma. It's just not possible. People will lose their jobs . . .'

'Yes,' said Emma.

'I don't believe it,' said Dominique shakily. 'Not really. Brendan must be doing something. Trying to get money from somewhere. That's why he hasn't been home. That's why he hasn't been in touch. He would have told me if something was wrong. I know he would.'

'Domino, nobody has been able to contact him since yesterday afternoon, when he had a meeting with the bank. Apparently it didn't go well and he left in a rage. Nobody knows where he is.' She swallowed hard. 'Barry has called the guards.'

Dominique stared at her sister-in-law. 'Why?'

'Brendan's obviously known about the company's problems for a while,' said Emma uncomfortably. 'His own situation too. It must have been very stressful. We're concerned that . . .'

'That what?'

'Well, that he's gone away,' said Emma.

'Gone away?' Dominique looked confused. 'Where?'

'That's the thing,' said Emma. 'We don't know. But we need to find out. There's music he needs to face, Domino. And he can't escape that.'

* * *

194

When the phone rang again, Dominique nearly shot out of her seat. But it was Kelly. Dominique had tried calling her as soon as she heard from Emma, but Kelly's mobile had been switched off. Although she had left a message, Kelly had learned about her father's company as a breaking story on the radio. It had come in before her interview with Norah had been due to air, and Stephen, the producer, had asked if she'd interviewed Dominique the previous day as well. He was disappointed when she'd looked at him in disgust and said no.

'You've got to come home,' said Emma, who'd answered the phone before Dominique could pick it up. 'As quickly as you can.'

Kelly arrived at the house at the same time as Greg, who was also responding to a message left by Emma, and a few minutes before June, who had been at her parents' house.

'There are reporters outside the gate,' said June as she strode into the living room, a flurry of jangling bracelets and musky perfume. 'Here and at Mam's. Probably at ours too by now. Vultures every last one of them, shouting questions at us.'

'What sort of questions?' asked Emma.

'If there's any news on Brendan. If he's disappeared with company funds. If we're concerned for his safety. Asking about you too, Domino.'

'Mum?' Kelly sat down beside Dominique. 'Are we? Concerned for his safety?'

'No.' Dominique's lower lip trembled, but she spoke firmly. 'Everything will be fine. Your dad will be fine. He's sorting things out. I know he is.'

But *was* he sorting things out? she wondered. Or had he simply run away without saying a word to anybody? Yet that was so unlike him. He was normally able to deal with everything that life threw at him. He was dependable . . . Dominique felt her head begin to pound and she pressed her fingertips to her forehead.

'I can't believe he's done this to us.' June, who'd flopped down on one of the plump armchairs, was white-faced.

'He hasn't done anything to you yet,' said Dominique tersely.

'He's bankrupted us,' said June. 'All of us. Our whole lives are tied up in that company, and he's ruined us.'

'How could you be ruined, Aunt June?' asked Kelly. 'Uncle Barry

195

just worked there, didn't he? He got paid a lot of money for what he did. Surely you're all right?'

'Don't be cheeky with me, young lady,' said June. 'Barry was owed money by your father, who got him involved in God only knows what.'

'Yes, but—'

'You don't know what you're talking about, so don't try to defend him,' said June.

'June.' Greg, who was sitting on the other side of Dominique, spoke gently. 'This isn't the time or the place.'

'My brother always tried to be too damn flash,' said June angrily. 'He was too arrogant for his own good. Too convinced he was right. And look where it's left us.'

'Shut up, June.' Emma's voice wasn't one bit gentle, and both Kelly and Dominique jumped. 'If you can't be supportive, then get the hell out of here.'

The phone rang again. Everyone looked at it for a moment, but it was Greg who answered it.

'Yes,' he said. 'I see.'

He replaced the receiver and looked at Dominique and at Kelly.

'There's no sign of him in the house,' he said. 'No sign at all.'

Dominique wanted to feel relieved at his words. But all she felt was a further build-up of tension as she tried to imagine where he was and what he was doing. Or what he might have done. She shivered violently, and Kelly put her arms around her.

'So,' said Emma eventually. 'If he's not in Dublin, where on earth is he?'

'Maybe France?' Dominique raised her ashen face. 'In the apartments? London? Barbados?'

'We're going to have to talk to the liquidator,' said Greg. 'And the guards, too. He's got to be found.'

'What if he doesn't want to be found?' asked Kelly quietly. 'What then?'

But nobody had an answer to her question.

Chapter 16

Just because Brendan hadn't been in touch didn't mean that he'd deliberately disappeared without a trace, thought Dominique. Everyone was totally overreacting. He'd turn up. He always did. Although, she admitted to herself, when he did, this time he'd feel the full force of her anger for putting her and the rest of the family through so much worry.

He was probably stuck in a tense meeting trying to sort everything out to stave off this liquidation they were all talking about. He wasn't answering his calls because he didn't want to be disturbed and so his phone was off. He would emerge eventually and get in touch. Whatever had gone wrong, whatever the problems were, he would fix them. He always did.

She swallowed hard. But what if he didn't? What if the others were right? What if he'd gone for good? What would she do then? She couldn't bear the thought of losing him. She could live with the loss of the business, even with losing money, but she couldn't lose Brendan. Without him she was nothing. Not a charity queen, not Dazzling Domino, nothing. He was the foundation of everything in her life and she couldn't live without him.

He hadn't left her. He wouldn't have. Couldn't have. He'd call sooner or later. She just had to wait.

But waiting was hard, particularly when the story of the collapse of Delahaye Developments and its associated companies was now the main news story of the day and TV cameras and reporters had taken root outside the company headquarters in Cork and kept up a steady stream of speculation and conjecture.

'I don't know how they can say these things,' she said despairingly as one of the reporters suggested that Brendan had massive gambling debts. 'He's very cautious. He doesn't gamble. They don't know what they're talking about.'

Earlier, she'd phoned her parents to let them know what was happening. Evelyn sounded bewildered by what Dominique had told her.

'You mean you don't know where he is?' she asked for the fifth time.

'Exactly.'

'And nobody else does either?'

'No.'

'Say a prayer to St Anthony.'

'Huh?'

'He finds things. People too.'

Dominique knew that St Anthony was one of her mother's favourite saints. Any time she lost anything, Evelyn prayed to him. Being honest about it, Dominique often did herself. She didn't believe, and yet somehow once she had murmured a swift request to him to help her out, whatever it was she was looking for would turn up. But she used St Anthony for lost keys and other bits and pieces. Not for people.

'I'm telling you,' Evelyn said. 'St Anthony is the man. I'll do a novena.'

'Yes.' Dominique didn't have the strength to argue with her. 'Do that.'

'Do you need anything?' Evelyn asked.

Dominique shook her head slowly before speaking. 'No. Thanks.'

'Call me when you hear something.'

'Yes.'

'Dominique?

'Yes?' It was the easiest word to say.

'Brendan's a good man. I don't believe any of it.'

'Yes,' she whispered.

She hung up. She couldn't speak any more.

The phone rang incessantly throughout the day. Greg was the one who answered it for her. Sometimes it was reporters, sometimes it was Barry, or Lily, or one of Dominique's friends from the charity circuit. Stephanie Clooney, the chairwoman of one of the charities, told Greg that she had been in touch with the bank to tell them not to honour any cheques on the charity's account signed by Dominique.

Dominique stared at him. 'Why would she do that? Does she think I'd spend the money myself?' she asked, outraged. She wanted to phone Stephanie back but Greg told her not to bother, that she wasn't important in the whole scheme of things, and not to let herself get wound up by a silly woman.

'She's not a silly woman!' cried Dominique. 'I thought she was my friend.' She rubbed her eyes furiously. 'How can she possibly think . . .' The tears slid from beneath her fingertips.

'Come on, Domino.' Greg put his arms around her. 'Don't cry.'

She let him hold her for a moment. It was good to feel the strength of his arms, good to know that – as always – he was there for her.

After about the hundredth phone call of the day, Greg replaced the receiver and looked at Dominique anxiously.

'They're bringing the Fraud Squad in to look through Brendan's finances,' he said.

Dominique, unable to cry any more, looked at him blankly.

'It's a complicated financial situation,' Greg told her. 'The fact that Brendan has gone missing concerns them.'

'Daddy didn't rob his own company.' Kelly was defiant. 'People are trying to make him out to be some kind of master criminal. That's not true.'

'I know that,' said Greg. 'But you can't stop rumours and speculation.'

'I asked him,' said June fiercely. 'I asked him a few months ago how things were going, because I was reading in the paper about other people's financial problems, and he told me that everything was perfectly fine and that Delahaye Developments was a strong company.'

'Maybe everything *was* perfectly fine a few months ago,' said Greg.

'Oh, come on!' June's expression was full of disdain. 'Things don't turn around that much. If there was something wrong, it was wrong then and he knew it but—'

'Get out of my house.' Dominique spoke a little too loudly and startled even herself. 'Go on, June. Get out. Emma's right. You're not being supportive and you're just making things worse. All you're thinking of is yourself and Barry. You don't care about Brendan at all.'

'I'm thinking about myself and Barry and my *three* children,' retorted June. 'I have a family to worry about, you know.'

'And I don't?'

'Oh, come on!' June snorted. 'There's only you and Kelly and she's her daddy's spoiled princess, so nothing to worry about there, I'm sure she has a massive trust fund while the rest of us are destroyed.'

'June!' This time it was Greg who spoke. 'You're not being helpful. Really you're not. I know it's a stressful time for you. But at least you have your family around you. Brendan is missing.'

June looked at them defiantly. 'Brendan brought whatever it is upon himself. And he's missing with other people's money, something you're all conveniently ignoring. Barry and I are just innocent bystanders.'

'Domino and Kelly are innocent bystanders too.'

June opened her mouth and then closed it again.

'Please go,' said Dominique tiredly. 'I know you're upset. I know you don't mean everything you're saying. But you mean some of it and I can't bear listening to you right now. So go.'

'All right,' said June huffily. 'I need to talk to the children anyway. Barry is still holed up with Matthew and the liquidator or the receiver or whoever the damn hell is running the show now. He's the one taking all the flak, you know.'

Dominique nodded. 'Yes. I'm very sorry.'

'It's not your fault, Domino,' said Emma. She glanced at her watch. 'I'll go too, to check on things at home. Then I'll come back.'

'What about Lugh?'

'I'll bring him to Lily's, don't worry.'

'Thanks, Emma.'

'That's OK.' Emma gave her a sympathetic smile. 'I'll be back soon.'

The house seemed very empty after Emma and June had left. Greg suggested that he make some tea and went into the kitchen. Dominique sat on the sofa, staring unseeingly in front of her, while Kelly sent and received texts on her mobile phone.

'Are you worried?' asked Kelly. Her phone had briefly fallen silent.

'Of course.'

'What d'you think's happened to Dad?'

'I don't know.'

'What will happen to us?'

'I don't know that either.'

'I mean, you read about people losing everything. But that's not possible, is it? We're all right, aren't we? It's not our fault that the company has gone bust. I bet it's not Dad's fault either. And I don't believe he's robbed anyone. He wouldn't do that, would he?'

'Of course he wouldn't. When we find him, we can worry about the future of the company and everything else. Meantime, he's all that matters.'

'He's all right,' said Kelly. 'I know he is.'

'I know that too,' said Dominique, although what she didn't know was whether she was saying the words to comfort herself or to comfort her daughter.

The gardai came to the house. Detective Inspector Peter Murphy had a search warrant. Dominique had never seen a search warrant before. She looked at it in disbelief.

'Maybe we should get some legal advice, Domino,' said Greg. 'Before we allow the guards to tramp all over the house.'

'The warrant is valid,' said Peter Murphy. 'We're entitled to search the premises and that's what we're going to do. You may of course get legal advice – it's a good idea – but that won't make any difference to what we're doing now.'

'Let them search,' said Dominique to Greg. 'If they discover something that helps us find Brendan, that's a good thing.'

'Perhaps.' Greg looked sceptical. 'But—'

'It's OK,' she told the policeman. 'Go ahead.'

Dominique felt as though she was watching a TV drama as the gardai began to walk through the house. They were unfailingly polite and methodical about what they were doing, but they were systematically taking Brendan's office apart and removing files. All the time they searched, she wondered how she would react if they found evidence of another woman. She wished she hadn't stopped her own search at Brendan's almost empty bedside cabinet.

'Any chance of a cup of tea, Mrs Delahaye?' asked Peter, who had stayed in the living room while the rest of the gardai began the search.

She stared at him. He was a tall, lanky man with tousled sandy hair and light blue eyes.

'You don't have to make them tea, Domino,' said Greg.

'I will,' she said. 'It's something to do.'

She went into the kitchen. One of the gardai was looking in the cupboards. She ignored him as she filled the kettle and clicked it on to boil. Then she took mugs from the mug tree and put them on a tray. As she picked it up to carry it into the living room, she had a sudden flashback to the night when Brendan had called to her house to take her to the twenty-first birthday party. That was the night it had all begun, she realised. The night they'd made love in a field and the night she'd got pregnant. Everything that had happened in her life had happened as a result of that one night. Even this.

'Was your husband planning on going away, Mrs Delahaye?' asked Peter Murphy as one of the gardai came into the living room and spoke into his ear.

'I told you,' she said. 'He was in Dublin. He had a meeting.'

'He wasn't planning on going somewhere else? For a longer period of time?'

'No!' she cried. 'Of course he wasn't.'

'He doesn't have other friends he might stay with?'

'Friends? What sort of friends?' Dominique stared at him, and Peter Murphy shrugged.

Did he mean female friends? wondered Dominique. Women? Other women? Was that the way the police were thinking? That Brendan was having an affair? That he'd robbed the company to pay for it?

'Can you come upstairs with us?' Peter put his empty mug on the table.

She stood in front of Brendan's walk-in wardrobe, her eyes wide with shock. She'd looked in the bedside cabinet to see if she could find out where he was, but it had never occurred to her to look in his wardrobe, because he had clothes both in Cork and in Dublin and she'd assumed that he had whatever he needed with him. Yet almost all of his clothes were gone. The Louis Copeland suits, the Thomas Pink shirts and the Ferragamo ties had all been removed. The wooden hangers and tie racks rattled forlornly on the chrome rail. Dominique suddenly whirled away from the wardrobe and pulled at the drawers in the high chest beside it. Not everything had gone – there were a few T-shirts and jumpers still neatly folded – but she knew that there was more missing than was still there.

'This is insane,' she said. 'I can't believe he would . . .' and then she sat down on the edge of the bed and held her head in her hands, unable to take in what it might mean.

She was still sitting on the bed when Greg came upstairs. He walked into the bedroom and looked around.

'Everything all right?' he asked.

'No,' said Dominique.

'What's the matter?'

'Brendan's clothes are gone.'

Greg glanced at Peter Murphy. The detective was looking impassively at Dominique.

'When did he do that?' asked Greg.

'I . . . don't know.' Dominique was remembering the sounds in the middle of the night, when she'd been sure that she'd heard Brendan come home. Sounds of him coming up the stairs, going into the spare room. Vague sounds. But she would surely have heard him come into their own bedroom and take away all his clothes!

203

'What sort of person would you say your husband is, Mrs Delahaye?' asked Peter Murphy.

'A good person,' she told him. 'Really.' She shivered.

Greg took her hand in his and squeezed it comfortingly.

'He didn't say anything to you about going away?'

'No.'

He didn't have to have taken all the clothes last night, she realised. He could have done it any time. She never checked his things. She did all the laundry, but a woman from the village, Dolores, collected the ironing every week and returned it pressed and folded the following day. Dominique only ever looked in Brendan's wardrobe and chest of drawers when she was putting away the ironing. The wardrobe could, in fact, have been empty all week and she wouldn't have known.

'But he seems to have taken clothes with him,' said Peter Murphy.

'I know.'

'So . . . he said nothing to you?'

'I already told you!' she cried. 'I don't know where he is! I didn't know he'd done this. I . . .'

'Hey,' said Greg as she started to cry again. 'Don't worry. Everything's going to be all right.'

'I don't think so.' She took her hand from his and wiped her eyes. 'I don't know what's happening but I don't think anything's going to be all right. He's gone and I don't know where. And I don't know why either.'

What she did know, though, was that her worst fear had been realised. Brendan had finally left her. She was on her own.

The news about Delahaye Developments' collapse and Brendan's disappearance had gathered pace all through the day, so that it was the lead story on the evening bulletin. Dominique watched in numbed fascination as the news station's top reporter spoke animatedly to the camera while standing outside the locked gates of the company's office in the business park Brendan had built.

'. . . one of Cork's most prominent businessmen,' the reporter was saying. 'His wife, Dominique, is even better known on the Irish social and charity circuit, where she is responsible for large donations to various worthy causes.'

And then pictures of herself, arriving at a function in the city, wearing a long black evening dress with a demure neckline at the front but cut low at the back. She was talking to Brendan, laughing and looking up at him, and he was smiling back at her.

She felt her throat constrict. She remembered the night. It had been a fund-raiser for the local GAA club. Two of its members were on the county hurling team. Brendan was a big supporter of the club and sponsored them generously. Dominique had teased him that he'd rather be playing for them than paying them. He'd nodded and said that she was right.

She hadn't seen this footage before. She hated looking at photographs of herself, because then she would notice that her hips were too wide and her nose was too big and her lips were too narrow. She'd realise that the dress didn't look quite as wonderful as she'd thought when she'd put it on earlier and that her hair was slowly falling out of its style. But this time, as she watched the images on the screen, she didn't see anything of how she looked. All she saw was a woman who was smiling at her husband as though he was the most important man there.

'There's no suggestion,' the reporter continued, 'that Mrs Delahaye has been involved in any of her husband's activities, although the chairperson of one of the charities she is associated with moved quickly today to secure that organisation's funds. Mrs Delahaye is no longer a signatory on any of its accounts.'

Dominique was horrified. They were making out that in some way she was involved in something by saying that she wasn't! She felt sick.

'We're totally shocked.'

The reporter had moved to the town and was talking to the young girl behind the counter in the local Spar. Dominique knew her. Cathy Callery. Her father had gone to school with Brendan.

'I know Mr Delahaye well,' she was saying. 'He buys his paper here. And a sandwich sometimes. He's very down to earth.'

'A lovely man,' said another woman whom the reporter stopped in the street. 'Does a lot for the community.'

'I always thought there was something dodgy about him,' said a third. 'He dyes his hair.'

Dominique blinked in surprise. Brendan didn't dye his hair. It was hard to spot the grey in it, and it still retained a lot of its natural colour. Who was this woman who thought he dyed it? Why were they asking her questions at all? She knew nothing.

And then the camera location moved to outside the house. This time Dominique flinched as she saw the cluster of reporters' cars outside and the camera zoomed to the windows. She drew back as though they could see her.

'There have been a number of visitors to the Delahaye family home today,' intoned the reporter in a serious voice. 'Including members of the gardai. We have not been told whether foul play is suspected in the disappearance of Brendan Delahaye.'

'Will I turn it off?' asked Greg.

Dominique shook her head. They were showing pictures of both of them again.

'I need to know what they're saying.'

'You don't, Domino.'

'I do.'

There had been no word from Brendan by midnight that night. Dominique had left more than twenty messages on his voicemail and Kelly had texted him dozens of times without reply. Both of them were facing the fact that, wherever Brendan was and whatever he was doing, letting them know wasn't part of it. But they had never been part of it. He had obviously been planning this for some time. And Dominique still hadn't had the faintest idea what was going on.

Chapter 17

Greg was staying the night at Atlantic View. Dominique asked Emma (who'd returned after leaving Lugh with Lily and Maurice) if she was OK with that plan. Emma's glance flickered briefly between the two of them before she nodded and said that it would be good for Dominique and Kelly to have someone with them, and although she'd be happy to stay herself, it might be better all round if Greg was there. Especially if Brendan turned up.

'Because I'd flatten him,' she said. 'Whatever's happened, he should have called you.'

'Why would he call me?' asked Dominique hopelessly. 'He's left us. He's taken his clothes.'

'Maybe he can't phone,' said Kelly. 'Maybe he had to go away and that's why he took his clothes and now he's out of credit.'

'Sweetheart, the company pays his phone bill. He's not out of credit.'

'Maybe Uncle Barry pulled the plug on it. Or the people who are investigating the company.' Kelly looked defiant.

'I'm quite sure Barry might want to do that,' said Dominique. 'June's made it perfectly clear that things between Barry and Brendan weren't exactly rosy. But honey, even if for some reason he couldn't call us on the mobile, he could get to a landline, and the thing is . . .' her voice faltered, 'he's taken all his stuff.'

'I know.' Kelly sounded defeated. 'But that doesn't mean he hasn't got a plan. That doesn't mean he won't want to talk to us.'

'Maybe.' Dominique put her arms around her. 'I want him to talk to us too.'

*　　*　　*

Kelly eventually went upstairs to her room and fell asleep, fully clothed, on her bed. Greg and Dominique sat on the sofa in the living room. The TV was still on in the background but there were no more news programmes. The phone had stopped ringing. Dominique felt as though she was in an alternative reality, cut off from real life. Somewhere, away from them, Brendan was making plans. But whatever they were, they didn't seem to include her or Kelly. He had walked out on them without a word, knowing that his disappearance would be headline news. He had planned it. He hadn't given her any warning. And that was what she could neither forgive nor understand. Whatever had happened, whatever problems he had, surely he could share them with her?

'You OK?' Greg's voice broke the silence between them.

Dominique laughed shortly. 'Hunky-dory.'

'Domino . . .'

'He planned this,' she said. 'He planned it over time. He's left us.' She clenched her jaw. 'And he's ruined us too.'

'You don't know that, Domino.'

'I know that he's gone. I know that the company has gone bust. I think that's enough to be going on with.'

'I'm sure he's trying to work something out,' said Greg.

'I thought that too, at first. But now . . .'

'You need to sleep.' Greg heard the exhaustion in her voice.

'I can't possibly. I need to be awake in case we get some news.'

'Try, Domino. Nothing's going to happen now. Go upstairs and lie down.'

She shook her head. 'I can't. But you go ahead. There's no need for you to stay awake.'

'I'm not a good sleeper at the best of times,' he told her. 'Drives Emma nuts.'

'I guess we'll both be up all night, so.'

She closed her eyes. She didn't want to talk to anyone, even Greg, any more.

Barry Keane, June's husband, was the first to arrive at the house the following morning. He turned up shortly after seven, and by that time Dominique was awake again. She'd showered and changed her clothes and was dressed in a sleeveless linen top and Capri trousers, her dark hair still damp and caught back in a ponytail so that – despite her worried frown – she looked young and vulnerable.

Barry told them that the banks had appointed a receiver over non-payment of debts. That Matthew, the company's accountant, had given statements to the gardai, and that he himself would be going in to the offices later in the morning to assist the receiver. Additionally, said Barry, there were applications in front of the High Court to freeze Brendan's assets, because he owed a lot of people a lot of money. In particular there was an issue over the money he had raised from private investors for the Barbados deal. A separate company had been set up for this development, but there was no money in its bank account. The financial people were trying to trace it, but at the moment they didn't know where it was. And, of course, nobody knew where Brendan was either. However, Barry said, there was no actual evidence of a fraud yet. At the moment it was just bad management and an uncertain paper trail.

'Thanks, Barry,' said Dominique, when her brother-in-law had finished. 'You've been great. I appreciate it.' Then she smiled weakly and said that she needed to use the bathroom.

'I'll kill him,' Barry told Greg when Dominique left the room. 'He's messed up my life and my family and now he's fucked off with our money, even if they can't prove it yet.'

'Did you invest in the Barbados thing?'

'No.'

'Then he hasn't fucked off with your money, has he?'

Barry stared at Greg. 'Are you standing up for him?' he demanded. 'Whatever's happened, he's run away in disgrace. He's ruined us all.'

'He gave you a job when you were out of work,' Greg reminded him.

'He lied to me,' said Barry. 'He told me everything was fine, and it wasn't. I don't know what was going on with the company books. That wasn't my concern. But I'll tell you now, Dominique had better get herself a good lawyer, because he's left her and Kelly up shit creek, and there's sure as hell no paddles where that boat is.'

'I'll talk to her about it.'

'Talk to me about what?'

Dominique walked back into the room.

'I need to get hold of Brendan's solicitor again,' she said. 'I had no luck yesterday afternoon, but maybe she'll return my calls today.'

'She's helping the receiver too,' Barry told her. 'She arrived yesterday evening. She's acting for the company, what's left of it. Not for the family.'

'Do you have a solicitor?' asked Dominique.

'Yes. For me and June. We have to look after our interests.'

Dominique looked at him, concern in her eyes. 'You mean your interests might be different to mine?'

'Hey, Domino, we all have to look after ourselves. I have two daughters and a son as well as June to take care of.'

'Yes. June did point that out last night. I'm sorry that my husband seems to have messed up your lives.' There was a sudden sharpness in Dominique's voice. 'I'm sorry that you might think it necessary to make mine even worse.'

'Look, there's no need—'

Barry's words were interrupted by the sound of the gate buzzer, and all of them jumped and looked at each other.

'It can't be Brendan,' said Dominique quickly. 'He has a zapper.'

'Hi,' said a voice when Greg pressed the intercom. 'I'm here to see Domino. It's Gabriel.'

Dominique hadn't seen Gabriel in over a year. He'd spent a lot of the last twelve months in South America, working on a UNICEF project to bring safe water to the semi-arid regions of Paraguay. She'd been astonished when he'd told her his reasons for going. But she'd told him that it was up to him to make his own choices.

He looked older but happier, she thought now. His handsome face was tanned, and his black hair was still without the slightest hint of grey. His dark eyes seemed even darker and they were full of concern for her. He was wearing a pair of faded Levis and an olive-green T-shirt.

'Hey, Domino,' he said, opening his arms wide and pulling her into his embrace. 'I was in London all week and I'd planned to come to Ireland for a visit. Mam phoned me yesterday. I got a flight this morning.'

'Oh, Gabriel.' She hugged him fiercely in return. 'It's good to see you.'

And, surprisingly, it was. She'd never expected to be relieved to have her brother beside her, but she'd been feeling under siege by the Delahayes. Emma and Greg were being nothing but supportive, but June and Barry had their own agenda, and she knew from what Greg had said last night that Lily, Maurice and Roy were absolutely stunned by the news and more anxious about Brendan than they were about her. When the chips were down, she'd thought earlier, it might not be easy for Greg and Emma to stay friendly either. They were lucky, because Greg had never got involved with the company, and so, unlike June and Barry, they weren't worried about their immediate future. But she still didn't know how things might evolve. And even though she couldn't honestly believe that Greg would ever desert her, it was nice to know that she had someone who was totally on her side. Who wasn't a Delahaye.

'Mam is worried sick about you,' said Gabriel. 'She was talking about coming down, but it's been a bit of a struggle for her lately, what with her hip replacement and everything, so I said I'd come.'

'I called her,' said Dominique. 'I told her everything was OK.'

'Everything isn't OK,' said Gabriel. 'Of course it isn't. Your husband is missing. There's trouble at the company. You need support.'

'Thanks,' Dominique told him shakily. 'Greg's being a great support already. And Emma will be here soon too.'

Gabriel turned towards Greg, who'd stood to one side as brother and sister hugged.

'Good to see you,' he said.

Greg nodded briefly. 'Difficult circumstances.'

'Yes.' Gabriel's voice was calm. 'Thank you for being here for Dominique.'

'I'm always here for her,' said Greg. 'We all are.'

Dominique glanced at both of them. They were acting like strangers, she thought, although perhaps it wasn't all that surprising. It was a long time since they'd met. And Greg, knowing about Emma's unrequited teenage love, had never really hit it off with Gabriel. Besides, he didn't trust priests, he'd told her. They were

211

too damn sure that they were right about everything. She'd nodded at that. She thought very much the same herself.

'Would you like tea or coffee?' she asked them.

'I'll make it,' said Greg. 'You probably want to talk to your brother.'

'Thanks, Greg.' She shot him a grateful look. As she sat down on the sofa, Kelly walked into the room. She was dressed in cargo pants and a sleeveless T-shirt and wearing make-up. She looked at Gabriel in surprise. Gabriel repeated his reasons for coming and she nodded.

'Mum needs someone else,' she agreed.

'And you too,' said Gabriel. 'You look tired, Kelly.'

'I'm fine.' Kelly twisted her hair into a plait and secured it with a ribbon. 'I'm going to work.'

'Work!' Dominique stared at her.

'I'm scheduled for the lunchtime show,' said Kelly.

'Nobody will be expecting you to go in,' Dominique told her. 'And you should be at home with the rest of us.'

'I know. But I'm going in anyway. I can't sit around here listening to you and the others fighting. When you have news, you can text me.'

'We're not . . .' Dominique shrugged. 'What if there are reporters trying to harass you?'

'Hey, Mum, I work in the media.' Kelly gave her the ghost of a smile. 'I can deal with reporters.'

Dominique's faint smile echoed her daughter's. 'I'm sure you can. But . . .'

'I have to get out,' Kelly said. 'I really do. I can't sit around all day waiting.'

She picked up her keys and left the house.

'She's a credit to you,' said Gabriel.

'I did my best.'

'All anyone can do.'

'Is there anything you want me to do for you?' asked Gabriel.

'I don't know.' Dominique frowned. She told him about the visit of the gardai and the missing money, and mentioned the need for her to get some legal advice.

212

'Actually, I might be able to help you on that,' Gabriel told her. 'I have a friend who works in law. I'll give him a call.'

'That'd be great.'

'Don't worry, Domino. Between us we'll get to the bottom of it all.'

As Kelly drove through the front gates, she thought that this must be what it was like to be a celebrity. A cluster of reporters and photographers scattered when she revved up the car and burst on to the main road. She supposed they were probably already writing a story about the spoiled princess of Atlantic View.

At the radio station she was greeted with a mixture of surprise and sympathy. Dan Connolly, the station manager, told her that she was great to come in but that she was part of the biggest story in the area.

'Local radio, local interest,' he said. 'Can we interview you, Kelly?'

'All right,' she said, and so she found herself in the tiny studio opposite Mona Corry-Jones, whose mid-morning programme was almost required listening in the region.

'My father is an honourable, decent man,' said Kelly in response to Mona's questions. 'And if he's missing, it's because he's trying to put a deal together to save jobs and save the company.'

'Delahaye Developments is already in receivership,' said Mona. 'It's too late to save it.'

'If anyone can do anything, my dad can,' said Kelly.

'Wouldn't it have been better if he'd stayed?' asked Mona. 'Faced the music and tried to assist the receiver?'

'Probably,' admitted Kelly. 'But I'm sure he has his reasons.'

Dominique heard the interview as she drank her fifth cup of tea of the day. Her heart was in her mouth wondering both what they might ask and what Kelly might say. But in the end she thought her daughter handled herself extremely well, and she sent her a text to say so.

The media continued to call the house. There was also another call from Stephanie Clooney, who told Dominique that she'd been asked by some of the other charities to let her know that they'd accept her resignation from their boards; and one from Brendan's solicitor, Ciara, who said that she didn't know where he was and that she hadn't spoken to him in over a week. Detective Inspector Peter Murphy contacted Dominique to ask if Brendan had turned up (would she tell him if he had? wondered Dominique); and Lily arrived at the house looking as though she'd aged ten years since Dominique had last seen her only the week before. Emma, who was with her, stared in disbelief at Gabriel Brady.

'I thought you were in South America,' she said.

'Until last week,' he told her. 'I was in London when I heard the news, so I came straight over.'

'You look well,' she said after a moment's pause. 'Obviously your time away suited you. As do your clothes.'

Gabriel glanced down at his jeans and T-shirt.

'It was a decision I had to make,' he told her.

'Better late than never.' There was a hint of a challenge in her voice.

'But not easy,' he said. 'Not easy at all.'

The decision Gabriel had made, to the absolute astonishment of everyone who knew him, was to leave the priesthood. He told them all that he had been struggling with his conscience for a number of years and that he'd come to the very difficult conclusion that he'd been mistaken in his vocation.

Evelyn, naturally, had been devastated by his announcement. Having a son in the priesthood had always been a source of comfort to her.

'But what are you going to do?' she'd wailed as he sat with her in the living room, trying not to look at the photographs of his ordination that were hanging on the wall.

'I've taken a job with UNICEF,' he said. 'Working on irrigation projects. I'll be abroad for a while.'

He'd stayed with a friend in Donegal while he'd been in Ireland but had visited Dominique for two days, explaining that he'd made a mistake about the priesthood and that he couldn't carry on the pretence any more.

'Is it because of a woman?' she asked immediately.

'No.' Gabriel was dismissive.

'A man?' She looked at him doubtfully, and he smiled faintly.

'No,' he repeated. 'I just realised one day that I did the wrong thing for reasons I thought were the right ones at the time.'

'What reasons?'

'I thought I was special. I thought that this meant I was right for the priesthood.'

'But everyone said that you were a great priest.'

'I know. I was good at parish work. I liked it. But after a while I realised that I wasn't being true to myself or to the people around me. I think . . .' he hesitated, 'I think I needed to belong to something. And I do believe a lot of what the Church teaches. I believe that it works for good in many, many places. I know that there have been scandals. It's not because of them that I left. It's because of me.'

'You've wasted a lot of your life.'

'Not wasted.' He smiled at her – the smile that she'd always called his priest's smile. Half knowing, half accepting. But not a priest's smile, she realised now. Just Gabriel's normal smile. 'Not wasted,' he repeated. 'I liked the studying. I liked the work. But I was mistaken about the rest.'

Dominique said nothing. It was the first time in her life she could remember Gabriel ever admitting to being mistaken about anything.

Greg spent a lot of his time on the phone trying to find out exactly what the receivership meant for Dominique and Kelly, and what was going on with the Barbados money.

'I knew nothing about Barbados,' said Dominique. 'Other than that he was raising funds for it. But I've no idea what the project was.' She shrugged helplessly. 'I've no idea about any of it really. I should have listened a bit more. I used to know everything that was going on, but as the company got bigger and bigger, it all seemed to be so complicated, and there were advisers and accountants and lawyers and everyone else, so . . . I stopped asking. But I should've asked. Then I'd be able to tell you all about bloody Barbados!'

'It's the worst part from Brendan's point of view,' Greg told her.

215

'He raised a lot of money from people in the area and at the moment nobody can account for it.'

He then reeled off a list of names that left Dominique white-faced.

'And what's the worst part from mine?' she asked. 'Given that robbing our neighbours sounds like the absolute worst that could happen.'

'Well . . .' Greg looked uncomfortable. 'The bank can't give you any money out of Brendan's accounts. Most likely it will break up the company and sell it. And it can repossess the other properties too.'

'But not our house?' Dominique looked anxious. 'Surely they can't take our house.'

'There's a mortgage on it,' said Greg uncomfortably. 'I don't think they'd want to turn you on to the street or anything, Domino, and there haven't been any defaults on your payments yet, but obviously there will be and that could be a problem.'

'And the others?' She pressed her fingers to her forehead. 'Oh, Greg, I know it sounds mad for me to be asking about my houses as though I'm a property mogul or something, but . . . Is there a mortgage on Mount Merrion? And the apartment in France?'

'I don't know,' he admitted. 'Gabriel's friend gave me the name of someone in the city. We'll contact him now. You need someone working for you, looking after you and Kelly.'

'Brendan always looked after me and Kelly,' said Dominique disconsolately. 'He . . . he . . .' She blinked away the tears that threatened to fall. Then she got up and walked out of the room, banging the door behind her.

Chapter 18

People were looking at them with undisguised interest, Kelly realised as she sat in the city coffee bar, sipping lattes and nibbling on warm muffins with Alicia and Joanna. The other customers were actually prodding each other and pointing towards them as though they wouldn't notice. And every so often a burst of raucous laughter would erupt and Kelly would wonder if it was directed at her. In the week since her father's disappearance, the story had stopped being national news, but it was still a hot topic locally and there was a lot of anger over the collapse of the company. Not just from the people who'd lost their jobs, but from others who felt that Brendan had given the community a bad name. The other issue was the missing Barbados money. Kelly was absolutely convinced that her father wouldn't have stolen it, but she knew things looked bad for him. People would ultimately forgive the failed company, she thought. But they'd never forgive him if he'd simply robbed them.

At work, Kelly's colleagues were outwardly friendly but, since her interview, the station had also run a short piece on the rise and fall of Delahaye Developments, which had included a fairly unflattering profile of Brendan and had called Dominique a glamorous socialite as though she'd never done a day's work in her life. And although they'd said that it was nothing personal, Kelly had been angry and hurt by the piece. She'd felt like walking out, but then decided that that would be giving in.

'Our mother's going ballistic,' Alicia told Kelly as she broke a piece off a cinnamon muffin and popped it into her mouth. 'She totally blames your dad for everything.'

'So do I,' said Kelly tightly.

'Yeah, but Mum blames Aunt Domino too,' Joanna added. 'She says there's no way she couldn't have known what Uncle Brendan was up to and she should've stopped him. But that she egged him on because it meant more clothes and jewellery and stuff.'

Kelly gritted her teeth. 'You know my mum's not like that,' she told her cousin. 'And she wouldn't have had a clue about what Dad was doing.'

'Yeah.' Joanna nodded. 'But our mum says you can't live cheek by jowl with someone and not have an inkling of what's going on.'

'Well your dad worked with him!' cried Kelly. 'He probably spent more time with him than Mum. So he should've known too.'

'It wasn't my dad's job to know.'

'It wasn't my mum's either!'

'Hey, girls.' Alicia held up a hand in warning. 'There's no need for us to argue among ourselves. Certainly not in public.'

'Right, Miss Goody Two-Shoes,' said Joanna.

'C'mon.' Alicia brushed her soft blond hair out of her eyes and looked at her cousin and her sister pleadingly. 'We're all in this together.'

'What exactly are you in?' asked Kelly. 'I mean, I know the shit that I'm in. Mum is meeting this lawyer guy again that Uncle Gabriel has set her up with and she's totally stressed over the money part of things as well as everything else, but I can't see what your problem is.'

'It's the second time Dad's ended up without a job,' said Alicia. 'He's not getting any younger and his employment prospects aren't great. We don't have as much saved as we should have either. His investments aren't doing well and Mum is giving him terrible grief. He can't cope with it, I know he can't.'

'Yeah, well, me and Mum could be out of our house, and how are we supposed to cope with that?' Kelly felt her eyes sting with sudden tears. 'That's what they're meeting to talk about. We could lose Atlantic View.'

Her two cousins looked at her with sudden, silent sympathy. Whatever else, they knew that they still had a home and both

218

their parents. It was looking increasingly likely that Kelly would end up with one parent and nowhere to live.

Dominique was sitting in the office of Colin Pearson, her new solicitor. The offices were in one of the stately old buildings along the Mall in Cork city, and the dark blue carpets and cream walls were vaguely comforting. Gabriel's legal friend, who worked in Dublin, had recommended Colin as the absolute best person in Cork to help her. He was younger than her, with a shock of dark brown hair and a square face that was immediately sympathetic, though it could also mould itself into an intense hardness when he was making a point. He had already simplified things for her so that she knew where she stood.

'As far as I can gather, there is no evidence at this point that your husband has actually defrauded anyone,' said Colin calmly. 'Just because they haven't found where the Barbados money is invested doesn't mean that Brendan simply took it, although the lack of clarity is, of course, worrying. The collapse of the company – which is a private company, so there are no outside investors – is a commercial matter. But the problem for you is that many of the company's borrowings were secured on personal guarantees from your husband.'

'What about our home?' Dominique looked at him anxiously. 'Our home is OK, isn't it?'

Colin's response wasn't as reassuring as she'd hoped. Brendan had recently remortgaged the house, and Dominique was also liable for the repayments.

'Don't you remember signing the documents?' asked Colin.

'Sure I do. But I didn't realise what was going on. Brendan often got me to sign things.' Dominique rubbed her forehead. 'You're looking at me and thinking that I'm a very stupid, gullible, trusting woman, aren't you?'

'Hey, you were married to the guy for twenty-odd years,' said Colin. 'Of course you trusted him.'

Dominique felt her eyes flood with tears.

'I'm sorry,' she said hastily as she pulled a tissue out of her bag. 'I can cry at the drop of a hat right now.' She blew her nose.

'You're right, we were married for a long time and I totally trusted him.'

'I'm sure you had no reason not to.'

'I behaved like a stupid, silly trophy wife!' cried Dominique. 'Everything was going fine and I never asked any questions, no matter what Brendan was doing. I'm a fool.'

'Of course you're not,' said Colin.

'I feel terrible, too, because if it's all down to the business problems, he was going through all this on his own and he didn't feel he could tell me.'

'Do you think there's more to it than business worries?'

Dominique thought about the newspaper stories, which were getting more lurid and fantastical by the day, and sighed. One had implied that Brendan, knowing his business empire was in trouble, had fled to the Caribbean with a mystery millionairess. She'd felt nauseated when she read it.

Colin was looking at her sympathetically.

'Who knows,' she replied. 'What I can't understand is why he just walked out without saying anything and left us to face the music. And the bloody neighbours. And the damn reporters, who think it's perfectly all right to camp on my doorstep and shove microphones into my face or Kelly's. It's not right. It's not. And they think that we're happily living a great life, but we could lose our home! Brendan was supposed to protect us. That was his job. Not getting caught up in all sorts of mad borrowings and dodgy deals. Just keeping us safe. That's all we wanted.' She choked back another sob.

'I'll be meeting with the bank's solicitors as soon as possible to see if we can come up with a settlement,' said Colin. 'I'll call you when I can.'

Dominique nodded and blew her nose again. All she wanted was to go home, get into bed and pull the cover over her head. She wanted to block out everything that had happened and was going to happen. She wanted to retreat into a place where no one could find her.

'Mrs Delahaye?'

She blinked as she realised that Colin had spoken.

'Are you OK?' he asked.

'Yes,' she said after a moment. 'Yes. I'm . . . I'm fine. I was just
. . .' She sniffed. 'Sorry. Thank you, Colin, for everything you're
doing.'

'You're welcome,' he said as he offered her a tissue from the box
on his desk.

Emma called Greg at work.

'Any news for Domino?' was the first thing he said.

'I'm not phoning about bloody Domino!' she cried. 'There are
other priorities in our life, Greg. I phoned to say I was dropping
over to Lily later and I might be late home. But not to panic, I'm
not running away without a word. I won't leave you and Domino
to sob on each other's shoulders.'

There was silence on the line.

'Greg?'

'I'm sorry,' he said. 'I didn't mean it to appear as if Brendan and
Domino were the only people on my mind. It's just that they're at
the forefront of it just now.'

'She is, certainly.'

'Emma, I'm just trying to help her.'

'I know.'

'There's no need to get upset with me. I'm not getting upset
with you, am I?'

Emma thought before she spoke. 'You've no reason to be upset
with me,' she said finally.

'Oh, good.' Greg's voice was grim. 'That's very nice to know.'

Emma could feel the start of a headache niggling behind her
right eye as she got out of the car in front of Lily's house. She
didn't know whether it was due to her conversation with Greg
earlier, or because these days it was stressful visiting Lily. Her
mother-in-law had been drained by Brendan's disappearance. It
seemed as if she'd shrunk before their very eyes, losing her normal
positive and cheerful outlook on everything, and suddenly looking
her age.

But she seemed a bit better today, thought Emma when Lily

opened the door. There was some colour in her cheeks and the circles around her eyes weren't quite as black as before.

'We're in the kitchen,' said Lily.

'We?' Emma looked at her enquiringly. 'Who's we?'

'Gabriel called,' Lily told her. 'He came to offer some non-priestly advice and comfort. Which was nice of him.'

Emma felt her heart skip a beat. 'Good advice, I hope.'

'Ah, well, he might not be a priest any more but he's still big into forgiveness.' Lily sighed. 'As though I wouldn't forgive my own son! It's just . . .' she pushed open the kitchen door, 'it's hard to feel anything but worry right now.'

Gabriel was sitting at the table. He looked at Emma in surprise. She was wearing a plain white top and a short red skirt that made the most of her long and still shapely legs.

'Hello,' she said, pulling out a chair and sitting at the opposite end of the table. 'I didn't expect to meet you here.'

'I thought it would be nice to see Lily,' said Gabriel. 'And Domino is supposed to be dropping by, so I was waiting for her too.'

'It seems funny to hear you call her that,' said Emma.

'I like it. It suits her.'

'She used to call you Gorgeous Gabe,' Emma remembered. 'We all did. But never to your face.'

'Would you like tea?' asked Lily.

'I'll make it.' Emma stood up again. Her niggling headache was still pinned behind her eye. Tea might help, she thought.

'No, no.' Lily sounded almost like her old self. 'I'll do it. Why don't you and Gabriel sit in the garden? It's a shame to be inside on a lovely day like today, and there haven't been any of those awful photographers around lately.'

'Photographers?' asked Gabriel.

'Trying to catch Brendan coming back to the house. I can't enjoy my own garden for them, the feckers.'

'They snoop around Briarwood too,' said Emma.

'It's ridiculous.' Lily grunted as she filled the kettle. 'Why can't they leave us alone?'

'Well,' said Emma, 'shall we?' She pushed open the door and went out to the garden. Gabriel followed her. Emma glanced around before they sat down at the old wooden garden table with its equally old chairs.

'Brendan wanted to buy her a fancy granite set,' Emma remarked. 'Like the one at his house. But she preferred this.'

'It's grand,' said Gabriel. 'I prefer it too.'

'This is awkward,' said Emma after they'd sat in silence for over a minute. 'It's the first time we've been alone together in a long, long time.'

'The past is the past.' Gabriel's voice was quiet.

'Do you always talk like that?' Emma was irritated. 'In clichés, and sounding like you're speaking to someone who doesn't understand English?'

'Of course not.'

'No.' She laughed shortly. 'Of course you don't. And I suppose that since you're now an ordinary member of the public and not blessed by God or anything, you don't really get the opportunities to lecture people any more either.'

'I never lectured people,' said Gabriel.

'You lectured me.' She looked at him through her long dark lashes. 'About what clothes I should wear. About how I should behave. About temptation.'

'Years ago,' said Gabriel. 'And I was wrong about that.'

'Not entirely,' said Emma. 'You were wrong about a lot of other things, though.'

'How are you and Greg doing?' Gabriel changed the subject.

'Do you really want to talk about me and Greg?' she asked.

'How is this thing with Brendan affecting you?' said Gabriel.

'Oh, that's all anyone wants to talk about really. The Domino and Brendan saga.'

'I'll talk about whatever you like,' said Gabriel.

'It's not affecting us in the financial sense.' Emma answered his question. 'Greg never worked for Brendan, even though Brendan offered him jobs a number of times. He asked him if he wanted to be involved in the Barbados deal too, but Greg said no.' She shrugged. 'They quarrelled a bit over it, but I'm glad that Greg stuck to his guns. Everyone knows who we are around here, and although loads of people are being really nice about it – to our faces, anyway – they're unbearably curious and totally convinced there's more to things than we're saying. There's stories about Brendan having a secret life with dozens of women – they called their house in Merrion his love nest, which upset Kelly dreadfully, because she stays there any time she goes to Dublin. Then there's a rumour that Domino is actually hiding Brendan in a secret room in the basement of Atlantic View and that they plan to skip the country when the heat dies down. Most people seem to think he's left already, having robbed the company blind, and is now holed up in the Seychelles or somewhere. Opinion is divided on whether Domino and Kelly will disappear in the middle of the night to be with him.'

'It's tough,' agreed Gabriel.

'And people want to believe the worst. There are still those who think that Brendan was so ashamed of losing everything that he killed himself. Though I guess if he was going to do that he wouldn't have cleared his wardrobe out first.'

'I guess not,' agreed Gabriel.

'The thing is . . .' Emma looked at him uneasily and massaged her temples, 'there's a part of me that thinks it wouldn't be a bad thing.'

Gabriel said nothing.

'If he killed himself, there'd be an end to all this. People would be sympathetic. It would be horrible for Domino and Kelly, but they'd get over it and they could move on instead of clinging to a broken past.'

Gabriel looked at her from his dark eyes. 'Emma . . .'

'None of us can go on like this, angry with each other and angry with Brendan and worried about what will happen,' she said.

'Who are you most angry with?'

Emma stared at him.

'I don't know,' she said shortly. 'Who should I be most angry with, Gabriel? Out of all the people in my life, who?'

'You should try not to be angry at all,' he said.

'You're the one who brought up the subject,' she told him. 'And yes, I'm angry with you, Gabriel.'

'Why?'

'You know damn well why! You're not a priest any more. Now – when it's too late. When it's messed with your life.'

'You shouldn't be angry about that,' said Gabriel. 'Really, Emma. It's not worth it.'

'You think?'

'I know it's not,' said Gabriel.

'Easy for you to say.' Emma snorted. 'Easy for you to swan off to the Amazon or whatever and be your wonderful, caring layman self.'

'Please, Emma.'

She looked at him unhappily. 'You messed up your life and you sure as hell allowed me to mess up mine,' she said. 'Everyone else is going on and on about Brendan and what he's done and how he's ruined their lives, but it's you that did it to me, Gabriel Brady, and you know it.'

'I thought we'd dealt with all that a long time ago, Emma. I thought you were OK. I thought you and Greg were happy together. That's what you told me—'

'And that's ironic, isn't it?' she interrupted him. 'I bet you've ministered to loads and loads of people and they all said that you were great, but me . . . You thought I was OK just because I said so.'

She suddenly covered her eyes with her hands and her voice shook. 'Why is it everyone always thinks that? When you're pretty and popular as a kid, everyone expects you to be OK for ever. Everyone assumes your life is going to be great. But for someone like Domino, it's different. Everyone always worried about Domino or talked about Domino. The teachers always give more attention to the quiet ones at school. And it's been nothing but attention for her ever since, what with her getting pregnant and getting married and getting depressed and getting rich. And now getting – well, whatever. But nobody ever worries about me.'

Gabriel watched her as she cried. He swallowed hard and then took her hands in his. He was still holding them gently when the back door opened and Dominique stepped outside.

Gabriel didn't let go of Emma's hands as he smiled at his younger sister, who was staring at him and her sister-in-law with dismay in her eyes.

225

'It's just all become a bit much for Emma at the moment,' Gabriel said. 'It's difficult for everyone, Domino. Not just you.'

'Emma's husband hasn't disappeared,' said Dominique shortly.

'That's not the point,' said Gabriel.

'No,' said Dominique, her glance shifting between her brother and her sister-in-law. 'It's not.'

Emma slid her hands from Gabriel's. 'How were things at the solicitor's?' she asked.

'As you'd expect. No money. No husband. No hope.'

'Oh, Domino.' Gabriel looked sympathetically at her. 'I'm so sorry. But maybe it can still all work out.'

'Yeah, right. I'll pray for that, will I?'

Emma rubbed her temples again, and Gabriel looked at her. 'You all right?' he asked.

'Headache. All day.'

'I'll go and see how Lily is getting on with the tea,' he said. 'You'll feel better with a cup of tea.'

He walked into the house and Emma laughed shortly. 'A cup of tea! I need max-strength paracetamol,' she said. 'And probably Xanax too.'

Dominique was silent.

'What?' Emma looked at her with eyes that were too bright.

'What is it with you and Gabriel?' Dominique asked. 'Even now? Why were you holding hands?'

'Oh for heaven's sake,' said Emma. 'You've spent the last few weeks holding hands with everyone who comes into your house. There's nothing wrong with me and Gabe holding hands.'

Dominique thought there was everything wrong with it. But she didn't know how to say that to her sister-in-law without sounding paranoid.

'I'd better go,' she said abruptly.

'Why?'

'I just . . .' She shook her head. 'I've things to do.'

She turned away from Emma and walked back towards the house.

Chapter 19

Gabriel and Lily were setting a tray with tea things. Dominique said that she couldn't stay, that she needed to get home. She told Lily that she'd see her again soon and bring her up to date on any new developments.

'I can't stay either.' Emma had followed Dominique to the house. 'I have a rotten headache, Lily, and I really need to get home.'

'But . . . what about your tea?' Lily looked after the two of them as they strode through the house, and then back at Gabriel.

'Emotions are running high,' he said as he poured boiling water into the teapot.

'They never did before,' Lily told him. 'We were always relaxed before. We always had time for a cup of tea and a laugh together.'

Neither Dominique nor Emma spoke until Dominique unlocked her car door.

'What's the matter with you?' asked Emma.

'What's the matter with me!' Dominique laughed shortly. 'My life is in ruins and you . . . Emma, I think you're playing some kind of dangerous game with Gabriel. You always fancied him, and—'

'And what?' Emma interrupted her. 'He didn't fancy me, did he? Wasn't that always the point? Didn't he head off and become a priest?'

'But now he's not,' said Dominique cautiously.

'And you think that I'm going to leave Greg for him, is that it? Just because you caught us holding hands? Grow up, Domino.'

'He's not the right person to be offering you comfort,' said Dominique.

'Why shouldn't he?' asked Emma. 'Anyway, you're one to talk. You're perfectly prepared for Greg to hold your hand and give you comfort!' There was an edge to her voice.

Dominique stared at her. 'What are you saying?'

'You have a relationship with Greg that I don't,' said Emma. 'You always did and you always will. You wrap him around your little finger and you don't care how it makes me feel. You always want to be number one. In his affections and everyone else's too.'

'That's complete nonsense!' cried Dominique.

'It's always about you, Domino,' Emma continued. 'It always will be. Your problems are always bigger than everyone else's. Just like everything in your life!'

'That's not true. How can you possibly think that way?'

'You don't know what anyone else is thinking or feeling!' said Emma. 'All cocooned in your Dazzling Domino world. You didn't know your husband was a crook. And that he was going to leave you.'

Dominique was unable to speak.

'I didn't want it all to go wrong for you,' said Emma. 'But maybe now you know what it's like.'

She got into her car and slammed the door shut. Then she drove off.

Dominique realised that she was shaking. She opened her own car door and slid into the driver's seat. It was a few minutes before she felt able to start the engine and move off.

She clipped the gate on the way out of the driveway.

There was a single red car parked on the verge outside the gates. Dominique knew that it belonged to one of the reporters covering Brendan's disappearance. She knew that the paper he worked for was the one running with the story that Brendan was actually back in Atlantic View and that she was hiding him from the public. She wondered if the reporter really believed this, or whether he was bored out of his mind fruitlessly staking out their house.

As she zapped the gates open, he got out of his car and took her photograph. Dominique eased up the driveway and into the house. When she got out of the car, she looked at the long scrape on the driver's door, courtesy of her brush with Lily's gate. A few weeks ago she would have been horrified by it. Now, she didn't care. She went into the kitchen, opened the fridge, took out a carton of fruit juice and a disposable glass and walked back down the driveway. She waved at the reporter, who was watching her with interest.

'Here,' she said, handing him the juice. 'It's a hot day and you must be dying of thirst.'

'I'm OK,' he told her. 'I have a supply.'

'Whatever,' she said. 'You can take it anyway.'

'Doesn't your husband need it?'

She smiled faintly. 'I don't know. You are, honestly, wasting your time. He's not here.'

'He might come back.'

'And who says I'll let him in if he does?'

The reporter's eyes narrowed. 'Are you divorcing him?'

'I don't think you realise my situation. I don't know where he is. I don't know if he's dead or alive.' She sighed. 'My whole life is a mess and I can't tell you what I'd do if he turned up. But what I can tell you is that he's not here now.'

'Well, my job is to stay here until he shows up one way or the other,' said the reporter.

'You'll be spending a lot of time in the car, so,' Dominique told him. 'And you'll miss a lot of other good stories in the meantime.'

'You know, I can't make up my mind about you,' said the reporter.

'Oh?'

'You're either terribly smart or terribly unlucky.'

'Brendan used to say I was his lucky charm,' she said. 'But I guess I wasn't so lucky after all.'

'Do you miss him?'

'I was married to him for twenty-odd years,' said Dominique. 'What the hell do you think?'

It was written up as an exclusive in the paper.

'The End of the Domino Effect. Dazzling Domino Delahaye reveals that she was Unlucky Charm for Missing Husband.'

She read it the following afternoon with Kelly.

'Did you really say that stuff?' asked her daughter.

'Yes. Though not exactly in the way they've printed it.'

'Oh, Mum. You should've had more sense than to talk to a reporter!' Kelly cried. 'You know it never turns out the way you think. Even I struggled on the radio, and I'm experienced.'

'I don't care,' said Dominique, who was unexpectedly amused by the fact that Kelly thought of herself as an experienced newshound. 'I didn't realise at first, and then, when I thought about it, I just didn't care.'

'"The elegant Mrs Delahaye is looking older",' read Kelly out loud. '"Her eyes are tired and the pain of her ordeal is clearly etched on her face."'

'Actually, the ordeal is having to drive past that guy every day.'

'"But she is still as beautiful as ever, and thoughtful, as evidenced by her concern for my well-being."'

'I didn't want him to dehydrate outside my front gate,' said Dominique. 'Things are bad enough without having reporters flake out in front of the house. They'd blame me for that too.'

Kelly couldn't help smiling.

'Oh, Kelly.' Dominique suddenly started to laugh desperately. 'It's just so mad, isn't it? It's like we've stepped through a door into a weird parallel universe and I don't know what I'm supposed to do or how I'm supposed to behave.'

'You're doing great,' said Kelly.

'I wish,' said Dominique. She hugged her daughter. 'I'm glad I have you.'

It was early evening when Kelly came downstairs, a card in her hand. Her face was pale, and when Dominique saw her she jumped up instantly.

'What?' she asked.

'I found this.' Kelly's voice was just above a whisper. 'It was in the middle of the book I'd been reading. I'd left the book in my tote bag and I hadn't bothered to open it since . . . since everything started.' She handed the card to her mother. It was a twenty-first birthday card, covered in pink flowers and sliver glitter.

Dominique opened it slowly.

Hi, Kelly, Brendan had written. *I'd planned on stuff for your*

21st but it hasn't worked out like that. I'm going to try to fix things. If I'm not there for your birthday, I hope you have a wonderful day. Love always, Dad.

When she'd finished reading it, Dominique looked at her daughter.

'That's it?' she said. 'He didn't leave anything for me?'

Kelly handed her the book.

'Huh?' Dominique's expression was puzzled.

'Flick through it,' said Kelly.

Dominique did as her daughter instructed. Between each page was a crisp new fifty-euro note. She gasped.

'How much is in there?' asked Kelly.

It took some time to extract all the notes and then count them, but when she'd finished, there was a stack worth five thousand euros.

'Oh.' Kelly's eyes were wide.

'He always had some cash,' said Dominique slowly. 'That's how things were when we were starting out. He paid for everything in cash and he got paid in cash.'

'This helps,' said Kelly. 'We can pay the bills, Mum.'

Dominique didn't tell her that, as a household, they had easily spent that much – and often more – in a month. It was a relief, though, to see actual cash in front of them. Although this money was clearly for Kelly. From her father. For her birthday.

'He says he hopes to be back,' said Kelly.

'I know.'

'So maybe he'll fix things.'

'Maybe.'

'But maybe leaving the money means he won't ever be back. Maybe . . . maybe he decided that it was all too much and . . .' Kelly swallowed hard, and her eyes flooded with tears.

'Oh, honey!' Dominique put her arm around her. 'Don't think like that.' She took a deep breath. 'Your dad wouldn't have taken all his clothes if he'd planned anything . . . fatal.'

'I guess not.' Kelly's voice trembled. 'Do you think he misses us?'

Dominique was staring at the card again as though she could see more than the printed words.

'I'm sure he does.'

'I know he's done a terrible thing, Mum. I know that people blame him for everything. But I want him to be all right.'

'So do I,' said Dominique softly as she dropped the card on the table and put both arms around Kelly. 'So do I.'

But as she looked at the pretty pink card lying in front of them, all Dominique wanted to do was to kill him for making their daughter cry.

Greg called by the house on his way home from work. For the first time in her life, Dominique didn't really want to see him. Emma's words were still too raw in her mind. She recalled all the times that Emma had made amused comments about her and Greg and how well they got on with each other. Had she thought then that Dominique was trying to steal her husband from her?

It was hard for Dominique to explain to anyone, least of all Emma, the connection she had with Greg. As far as she knew, Emma still didn't know about his bout of depression and the reasons behind it. Dominique hadn't told her, because it wasn't up to her to say anything. But it wasn't something that Greg should have kept from her. Dominique shouldn't know one of his secrets when Emma didn't.

She worried, too, about having interrupted Emma and Gabriel together. There seemed to have been an unspoken communication between the two of them, an unexpected tenderness in the way that Gabriel was holding Emma's hands. It made Dominique feel profoundly uncomfortable.

'. . . money of your own?'

Greg's question pushed thoughts of Emma and Gabriel out of her head. She'd filled him in on her solicitor's visit and said that by the end of the week she expected to know where she stood in relation to the house. Then he'd started talking, but she hadn't really been listening.

'Sorry?' she said.

'I should've asked before,' Greg repeated, 'but do you actually have money of your own?'

Dominique thought about Kelly's five thousand euros, now in the safe in Brendan's office, along with the pieces of expensive jewellery that he'd bought her over the years.

'We have a bit of money,' she told him hesitantly. 'We'll be fine for a short time, and I can also sell my diamonds and stuff. Thank God he bought me lots of fancy jewellery.'

'I guess. But it's a shame to have to sell it.'

'What chance will I have of ever wearing it again?' She smiled ruefully. 'Colin seems really competent, so I'm hoping that I'll have a clearer picture of how we're fixed by the end of the week.'

'Right.'

'I also gave him the money that we raised from my last charity do to give to the hospital. After all the hassle I got from Stephanie Clooney, I was really anxious to get rid of it, but I didn't want to go to the bank myself. I had a nice phone call from the director of the hospital saying that she knew I was under pressure and that I could send in the money when I had time, but I also got a call from someone who was at the event saying that she would be contacting the hospital to ensure that they got the money, because otherwise she was going to sue me for raising money under false pretences.'

'No!'

'I can see her point,' said Dominique. 'We raised a few thousand. I guess she's thinking that could keep me in expensive tights for a few weeks.'

'Domino!'

'Maybe I'd think the same,' she said ruefully. 'If I was her.'

'You're being very nonchalant about it all of a sudden.'

'Totally not,' she said, suddenly serious again. 'But oh, Greg, I can't bear the weight of misery all the time. I have to find something . . .'

Greg nodded.

'Brendan left a card.' Dominique had to tell him that much.

'A card?'

'For Kelly's twenty-first.' She ran upstairs to Kelly's bedroom and fetched the card.

'Perhaps you should show this to the gardai,' he said when he'd read it.

'I thought that,' said Dominique. 'But it's a personal card to Kelly. I can't bear the thought of that detective reading it and quizzing her about it. Besides, they searched the house and they missed it. It wasn't our fault it was in Kelly's bag.'

Greg nodded again.

'D'you think he's abroad somewhere?' asked Dominique.

Greg shrugged. 'Probably.'

'Doing what?'

'Trying to raise money, I suppose. Trying to find a way out.'

'He can't come back here still owing money. He'd be lynched.'

'I know.' She thought again about mentioning the five thousand euros, but it was better that Greg didn't know. In the great scheme of things it wasn't that much, but maybe he'd feel obliged to tell the liquidator or something, and the thing was that she and Kelly needed that money. She wished fervently that she'd kept her own personal account instead of putting everything into their joint account. Brendan had told her that it was simpler for them to have just one account. And as he was the one paying the bills, she'd agreed.

'Why won't he talk to me!' she cried suddenly. 'Why won't he answer his bloody phone?'

Gabriel had been staying with her at Atlantic View, but when he arrived back that night (he said that he'd gone into the city and had something to eat and taken in a movie), he told her that it was time he left.

'I think you'll worry about me if I stay,' he said. 'And you don't need more worry right now.'

'I shouldn't have to worry about you,' she said. 'Or Emma.'

'I know. And there's no need.'

'Gabe, you know Emma always fancied you. It's not a good idea for you to be around her.'

'Don't you trust her?' asked Gabriel.

'Yes. No. I don't know.' Dominique sighed. 'Oh, Gabe, I don't know who to trust any more. And I can't bear to think that something else might go wrong because you're here.'

'I promise you, nothing will.'

'You can't promise that,' said Dominique. 'Nobody can.'

He left the following day. He went back to Dublin to spend a couple of days with their parents, and then he returned to Paraguay. As far as Dominique knew, he didn't see or talk to Emma before he went.

Colin Pearson came to Atlantic View after his meeting with the bank's solicitors. Kelly was there too. Dominique said that they both needed to know where they stood for the future, no matter how bleak it was. Colin talked for a while about the companies and the mortgages and the loans and the missing money, and Dominique felt herself grow more and more tense as she realised just how badly Brendan had miscalculated in the running of his business. She couldn't help thinking that the lure of making big money had always led him towards getting involved in more and more elaborate schemes, when perhaps it might have been better to let one or two of them go.

'He should have told me,' she said miserably when she saw that some of his biggest losses had happened the previous year, at a time when they'd gone to the Maldives on holiday. 'We didn't have to go away. Not that saving money on the holiday would've helped much,' she added with grim humour. 'But still.'

'It's simple enough,' said Colin when she asked him to summarise everything. 'The banks will get back some money when they break up the business and sell the properties. They're not involved in the Barbados deal. That's all down to local investors and has nothing to do with you, Mrs Delahaye. But as far as the properties go . . . well, your house will be sold and the truth is that you won't get anything from it.'

Dominique stifled a despairing gasp.

'I tried to persuade them that you didn't know what was going on and that as you weren't a director of the company you weren't aware of the borrowing structure. You might be able to sue them for advancing money against the house. But it could be a tortuous process. Nevertheless, it might be worth doing, because that way you could retain your home or perhaps get a portion of the value.'

'No,' said Dominique after she'd sat in silence for almost a minute.

'If you don't do anything, you'll lose the house,' said Colin. 'I really think you should consider—'

235

'I love this house,' said Dominique shakily. 'But it's never going to be the same again, even if Brendan does return.'

'It's possible that the banks might make a settlement with you. They don't want to be seen to be throwing people on to the streets.'

'There's a lot of people who probably think I deserve to be thrown on to the street.'

'You have to live somewhere.'

'No,' she said again.

'You can also apply to have funds made available to you from Brendan's assets.'

'Like I'm someone else he owes money to?'

Colin nodded.

'I can't.'

'You haven't done anything wrong, Dominique,' he said. 'You should—'

'I don't care!'

'But—'

'I did do something wrong. I didn't ask any questions. I believed everything was great. So I don't want anything. I don't want people saying that I came out of it all right when they've lost everything.'

'Really, Domino . . .' He'd never called her that before. Always Dominique. Sometimes Mrs Delahaye. It sounded strange coming from him.

'I wouldn't feel right,' she said stubbornly.

'You're entitled to—'

'Absolutely nothing.' Her voice was fierce. 'I was a fool. Brendan was a fool. I don't want anything from the mess.'

'You have to think about your daughter, too.' He glanced over at Kelly, who hadn't spoken as Colin had outlined their position.

'I can get a job,' she said.

'And you will, I hope, when you graduate,' Dominique told her. 'But in the meantime, you can keep on with your studies. We'll find somewhere else to live and *I'll* get a job. We'll be fine.'

'What sort of a job?' asked Kelly.

'I'm a good organiser,' said Dominique. 'I'll find something.'

'Maybe nobody around here will give you a job.'

'I'll get a job,' repeated Dominique firmly. 'And I'll sell my damn jewellery. And Colin, I was thinking that maybe we could sell the contents of the house, too. After all, the bank doesn't own the plasma TV or the Waterford glass or anything else and they could bring in quite a bit of money.'

'You're being incredibly strong,' said Colin. 'You know that at one time you were worth millions, and now . . .'

'I never felt as though I was worth anything like that,' said Dominique. 'So it doesn't really matter in the end. And I'm not being strong at all. This is my worst nightmare. I'm faking it, that's all.'

Chapter 20

Dominique felt as though she was living in another world. Every day when she woke up, the sun had risen and the sky was blue (or at least blue for part of the day; it was summer in Ireland after all, and so grey clouds also featured prominently); and every day she did ordinary things like taking a shower and cleaning her teeth and sometimes even having breakfast. In the first few days following Brendan's disappearance she hadn't been able to eat at all, but it shocked her that now she was, at least occasionally, beginning to feel hungry again. Yet even as she did these ordinary, everyday things; even as she listened to the radio or filled the kettle or loaded the washing machine with laundry, she would suddenly stop and tell herself that her husband had gone and she didn't know where. That her house was about to be sold. That she didn't have a job. That she was practically broke. That their family's name was mud. At that point she would begin to tremble and would have to sit down and take deep breaths to steady herself.

She would tell herself that eventually people would forget about Delahaye Developments and that she wasn't totally penniless; she would try to convince herself that she would find a job and that Brendan would come back. But she was never sure about any of these things and when they might come to pass. And when she stood in her beautiful garden with its wonderful views of the Atlantic Ocean, she couldn't quite bring herself to believe that all of this had really happened and that she would have to leave. This was her home. This was where she had felt the happiest in her whole life. And, despite what she'd said to Colin Pearson, this was where she wanted to stay.

She'd hoped that the bank would struggle to sell the house.

After all, it was a trophy home, not within the financial reach of the average house-hunter, and although its location was superb, it was a little remote for some people. Maybe, she thought, she'd be here for a lot longer than she expected.

But when Jerry Kavanagh, the local estate agent, arrived at the door and told her that he had people lined up to view the property and that he also wanted to put a For Sale sign up in the garden, she realised that everything was real and not part of some dream that she could simply forget.

'I'm sorry, Domino,' said Jerry.

'That's all right. You have to do your job.'

She knew Jerry and his wife Melody well. Jerry's agency had been involved with the selling of some of Brendan's developments and Melody was on one of the same charity boards as Dominique herself. Or one of the boards that Dominique had been on. Because after the phone calls from Stephanie Clooney, she had resigned from that board and from the others she was involved with, including Melody's. A part of her had hoped that the women she knew so well would contact her and say not to be silly, that none of this was her fault and that they'd love to have her stay on. She'd pictured a girlie get-together in which they'd down a few glasses of wine and the women would offer her loads of support and tell her that they'd always be there for her. There had been a couple of awkward phone calls from the people she'd been closest to. But nobody wanted to be seen with Dominique Delahaye these days. She wasn't good for the image of the charities. And it seemed that the women concerned were afraid that somehow her misfortunes would rub off on them too. The husbands of some of them, she knew, had also invested in the Barbados project, which made it hardly surprising that they didn't want to see her. She received a selection of cards thanking her for her work in the past and wishing her well for the future, but no invitations to lunches. And certainly no invitations to girlie get-togethers.

'Melody asked me to pass on her best wishes,' said Jerry.

Melody had been at Dominique's final garden party. She'd laughed and joked with Dominique and told her that her garden was looking particularly lovely and that her polka-dot dress was stunning and that she did the absolute best events in the county.

Both Jerry and Melody had also been to dinner with Brendan and Dominique a week before that. Brendan had picked up the tab for a memorable meal at Ballymaloe House, which had been accompanied by the most expensive wines the restaurant had to offer.

'I hope she's well,' Dominique said in response.

'Ah, you know Melody.'

'Yes.'

Melody considered herself to be a very sensitive person. She complained regularly of being stressed and upset, although as far as Dominique could see, there was little in her life to stress or upset her. Actually, Dominique thought, Melody was as sensitive as an old boot.

'What are you planning to do, Domino?'

Dominique wondered which of the two of them was the more embarrassed by her current situation.

'I haven't decided yet,' she said.

'Is it true that all your money is gone?' There was a note of incredulity in his voice.

'If I had money, I'd keep the house,' she said.

'It's hard to believe that he did this.'

She was working very, very hard not to cry. It was ridiculous, she told herself, to want to blub every time she had to talk about it. But she was damned if she was going to let Jerry Kavanagh see her sob.

'Well he did. And Kelly and I are dealing with it.'

'I saw Kelly in town the other day. She seems in good spirits.'

'Like me, she's doing her best.'

'Well, lookit, I'll just go and put up this sign, and I hope it makes a good price,' said Jerry.

He wasn't the worst in the world, thought Dominique, as she thanked him. It was hard for people to take in. She knew that.

It was especially difficult for her when people started making appointments to view the house. She was sure that half of them only wanted to poke around and check it out so that they could say that they'd looked over the place. She imagined them prodding her comfortable squishy sofas, criticising her choice of tiling in the bathrooms

241

and saying that Atlantic View wasn't up to much after all. She pictured them peering at the paintings on the walls, wondering how valuable they were. (Not very. She'd bought most of them in local galleries, and although they were lovely, none of them had cost a lot.) Her stomach churned when she thought of people standing at the door to her bedroom, looking at the enormous bed with its expensive linen and saying to themselves that she was sleeping alone in it now. She told herself that she was being paranoid, but she knew that she wasn't really. Everyone loved nosing around other people's houses. And everyone loved seeing pride come before a fall.

She couldn't stay there any longer. So the day before the first open day, when the house was free to all and sundry to look at, she and Kelly packed their bags and moved in with Lily and Maurice.

Lily welcomed her warmly and told her to go to her usual room. Dominique couldn't help smiling a little at that; she hadn't stayed at Lily's since the days when Brendan's main business had still been house extensions and attic conversions and they'd been living in Terenure.

Kelly, who'd had plenty of sleepovers at her grandmother's even after they'd moved into Atlantic View, knew that she'd be sleeping in Roy's old bedroom. Brendan's youngest brother was now the captain of a cargo ship and currently somewhere in the middle of the Atlantic and well away from the family drama, though still keeping in touch with them all.

'I thought we might send out for food tonight,' said Lily. 'I don't feel like cooking and Maurice likes the local Indian, even though he says it gives him shocking heartburn these days and the doctor is always telling him to go easy on the spicy food. Still, he's lasted this long, so I don't think a few chillies will kill him.'

This time Dominique smiled properly. She got on well with Maurice who, in his eighties, was still a fun-loving man. Though not so fun-loving these last few weeks.

I could kill you, she told Brendan mentally. I could kill you for what you've done to me and what you've done to them. I don't care how terrible things were for you. Running away wasn't the answer.

Living with her parents-in-law was harder than Dominique had expected. More people called there than had to Atlantic View, and she was constantly having to put on a brave face when one or other of Lily's elderly friends knocked at the door. They would smile at her and ask how she was and then go into the kitchen or living room or garden for a chat with Lily. Dominique couldn't help thinking that Lily's friends were a lot less judgemental than her own and considerably more forgiving. But then Lily had grown up here with all of them. They were friends for life. Hers hadn't been.

Lily had resumed going to her weekly bingo nights, and although she invited her daughter-in-law to go along with her, Dominique said that she preferred to stay home with Maurice. She admired Lily's strength in socialising again. But she couldn't do it herself. She still thought everyone was pointing fingers and talking about her.

'It's yesterday's news, Mum,' said Kelly one afternoon. 'People have moved on.'

'I really don't think so,' Dominique responded. 'Didn't you see the piece in the paper at the weekend? All about the people who've lost their money because of your dad?'

'They haven't lost anything yet,' said Kelly stubbornly. 'And the guards haven't pressed charges either, so people are wrong to think Dad has done something wrong just because he isn't here to defend himself.'

Dominique wondered when Kelly's faith in Brendan would shatter. Her own faith in him was practically gone.

Kelly was tired of it all. Tired of the talk and tired too of sudden silences when she walked into a room. Tired of caring and tired of trying not to care.

She wasn't as upset as her mother about the company or about their changed circumstances, precarious though she knew they were, but she wasn't able to think about her father without being totally conflicted. It was all very well, she thought, for him to leave a card and money for her but that wasn't what she wanted. She wanted him back, to face their problems together. He used to bang on and on about them all being a family and being strong together. But he clearly didn't believe it himself.

She didn't feel the same sense of responsibility that had affected both her grandmother and her mother. She knew that lots of people had depended on her father for their jobs and she was very sorry for them, but her view was that businesses failed all the time and you couldn't blame any one person. Sure, her father should have managed things better, but all his life he'd employed people and helped them and she didn't think it was right that everyone was coming down on him so hard now. The situation with the missing money was more problematic, but she didn't for one second believe he'd stolen it.

Her friends hadn't cut her off in the same way as her mother's seemed to have. They'd been a bit embarrassed at first, but then they'd begun to rally round and had posted messages of support on her Bebo page. She and Alicia had agreed that not everyone was truly supportive and that some of the comments were actually quite bitchy, but the majority of her friends were still friends. They accepted that you made mistakes. Dominique's friends didn't. Which meant that Kelly was in a much better situation than her mum.

Greg and Emma were in the conservatory. Jia, who had taken to dropping by, even on her day off, had taken Lugh for a walk, leaving them unexpectedly on their own.

'Have you been talking to Domino?' Greg looked up from the crossword he'd been doing for the past thirty minutes.

Emma folded the paper she'd been reading and shook her head.

'Not today,' she said. 'Why?'

'I wondered whether she'd made any decision about where she was going to live.'

'She's OK with Lily for the time being.'

'She's going out of her mind at Lily's.'

'How d'you know that?'

'I can see it.'

'You always could,' said Emma drily.

'Don't start,' said Greg. 'I'm worried about her, that's all.'

'And you always were.' Emma's tone was still dry. 'Just as she always worries about you.'

'What's this all about?' he asked. 'Why are you being so narky?'

'Stress,' said Emma succinctly.

'There's an offer on Domino's house,' said Greg. 'I presume the bank will accept it. As far as they're concerned, the sooner they get their money back the better. So that leaves her homeless.'

'Not homeless, just living with Lily. So no change there.'

'It's a strain for both of them.'

'Maybe,' conceded Emma, putting the paper to one side. 'But there's nothing we can do about it. Unless . . .' She looked at him enquiringly. 'You weren't thinking of inviting her and Kelly to stay here, were you?'

'No,' said Greg, although he sounded doubtful.

'Oh, for God's sake.' Emma got up, her body crackling with sudden anger. 'I know this is a disaster for everyone, but we're not that involved, Greg. We had nothing to do with Brendan's businesses, thank God. We don't need to be the ones to take them in. For any reason.'

'It's hard for them,' said Greg. 'Domino's doing her best but she's struggling at Lily's.'

'I don't want her struggling here.'

'I thought you were her friend.'

'Yes. But I'm also realistic. She has to stand on her own two feet, Greg. She never did before. And you can't always be the one trying to catch her before she falls.'

'I'm not—'

'Oh, don't start.' Emma snorted. 'This whole situation has given you the chance to be Domino's saviour again.'

'No it hasn't.'

'If only Brendan hadn't got her pregnant and rushed to marry her, you might have met her and enticed her away from him and everyone would've been happy.'

'Emma!'

'Even at her wedding,' continued Emma, 'when she introduced me to you, you were lusting after her.'

'No I wasn't,' said Greg sharply. 'I spent most of my time with you, didn't I?'

'Yeah, right. After she shoved me at you. You probably didn't want to refuse her.'

'And back then, of course, you were lusting after the brother.' Now his tone was dangerous. 'Perhaps you still do.'

'Don't go there,' said Emma. 'Just don't.'

'I should've realised.' Greg shook his head. 'Domino said it herself. Hey, Greg, was what she said. Why don't you take my friend's mind off the fact that my gorgeous brother is a priest?'

Emma said nothing. She was remembering that too. And remembering the fact that she hadn't wanted anyone to take her mind off Gabriel at all. But then Greg had smiled at her and asked her to dance, and she'd known what Dominique had meant when she called him Gabriel-lite, because he was almost as handsome as her brother and had the same watchful calmness about him too. She'd thought she'd found someone special that day. She'd been pleased when he'd asked her out. And she hadn't hesitated for a second when he'd asked her to marry him.

'But of course he isn't a priest now, is he?' Greg looked challengingly at his wife.

'You're being very stupid about this,' said Emma. 'You're talking about the past, and he's thousands of miles away.'

'Not far enough.'

'Are you deliberately trying to provoke me?' demanded Emma. 'Have you finally decided to wreck our marriage?'

The two of them stared at each other, aware that she had suddenly crossed a line.

'I don't know,' said Greg slowly. 'I don't know what I'm trying to do, Emma.'

'Then forget about it. Forget about him.'

'I've never lived up to him, have I? In any respect.'

'It's not a question of that.'

'Isn't it?' He glared at her.

And then the phone rang. They ignored it for a moment, but its insistent shrill didn't stop.

Greg picked it up.

'Hi, Domino,' he said after a moment. 'Yes, sure, I can pick some stuff up from the house for you.'

Emma laughed shortly at his words, then walked out of the room, slamming the door behind her.

Atlantic View was sold. There was a big banner across Jerry Kavanagh's sign in the garden with the word emblazoned on it.

Dominique had driven up the road to see it when Colin Pearson phoned her with the news. Excellent news, he said, because the purchaser had bought the contents too. They had been valued separately and Colin had been arranging for them to be auctioned when he'd been told that the prospective buyer was also interested in them. Although the amount raised for the contents was a lot less than the actual value, Dominique had cried tears of relief when Colin had called with the news. A year ago she wouldn't have considered the cheque he handed her to be a lot of money. Now it was her lifeline.

The buyer was a retired golfer, Colin told her, who was separated from his wife and awaiting the finalisation of their divorce. He wanted space and privacy and Atlantic View fitted the bill perfectly. Buying the contents meant that he could move in straight away, which was what he wanted to do. Dominique pictured him standing on the rolling lawns, looking out towards the sea and practising his pitch shots, as Brendan had often done. Brendan wasn't a keen golfer, but he gave it a go because it was a businessman's game. Dominique knew he would have preferred Atlantic View to have been bought by a proper sportsman – a footballer or a hurler, not a boring old golfer in an argyle jumper, ridiculously bright trousers and a sun visor. But she was just glad that someone had stepped up to the plate and bought it at all.

She pressed her zapper and the gates opened. She'd forgotten to give the zapper to Colin, but she planned to drop it in to him the next time she went in to Cork. Now, though, she wanted to walk around the grounds one last time. It seemed unbelievable to her that a few months ago she had owned all this. She had been envied and admired. She had been someone other people wanted to be. Now it was owned by some ancient golf bore and she was skulking around like a trespasser.

'Can I help you?'

She jumped in surprise, her heart thumping.

'Can I help you?' The man who had appeared from around the side of the house repeated the question. He was tall and rangy, with cropped fair hair and bright blue eyes in a tanned face. He was wearing faded Levis and a loose cotton shirt. Too young to be the retired golfer, Dominique thought. He could be anywhere between thirty-five and forty-five. It was hard to tell. Perhaps he was the golfer's agent. Or maybe even his son.

'I'm sorry,' she said. 'I shouldn't be here.'

'No, you shouldn't,' he told her, brushing his hand through his short hair. 'How did you get in? The gates were locked.'

She held up the zapper and he frowned.

'I should've given it to the auctioneer sooner,' she said.

'You lived here?' He looked astonished.

She nodded.

'You're Dominique Delahaye?'

She nodded again.

'You're a lot better-looking than your pictures,' he told her.

She supposed she shouldn't be surprised that a complete stranger knew who she was. The pictures had been plastered all over the papers every time there was a story about Brendan.

'Thanks. I think.'

'You must be feeling bad about this.' He waved towards the house and she shrugged.

'What can I do?' she asked. 'The banks want their money and this is the only way they'll get it.'

'But I'm sorry you've lost your home.'

'It doesn't feel like home any more now anyway.' There was a slight catch in her voice. 'And I guess the new owner will change things once he moves in.'

'Actually, I don't have time to change much right now.'

'You're the *golfer*?' She was unable to keep the surprise out of her voice.

'Yes.'

'My solicitor said a *retired* golfer,' Dominique told him. 'You don't look retired to me.'

He grinned at her and his blue eyes twinkled. 'D'you know, I'm going to take that as a compliment.'

Dominique blushed. 'I didn't mean . . .'

'We don't all last till we totter along the fairway using our clubs as walking sticks,' he told her in amusement. 'I retired early because I tore ligaments in my shoulder. I don't play much these days.

Can't, to be honest. So I design courses instead.'

'Oh,' she said. 'I'm sorry. I don't know much about golf. My husband used to play from time to time and occasionally dragged me to golf dinners. But that's as much as I know.'

'Oh dear.' He laughed. 'The dreaded golf dinner. You won't have got a great impression from them.'

She couldn't help smiling a little. 'Not entirely.'

'Boring, unattractive, style-free, sexist misogynists?' he suggested.

She looked startled.

'That's what my former wife used to call us.'

'Not you, surely?' The words were out before she could stop them. Because in a million years she couldn't call the man in front of her unattractive. The jeans and shirt weren't a riveting style statement, she supposed, but they looked damn good on him. As for the rest . . . well, she probably wouldn't get the opportunity to find out. But she'd give him the benefit of the doubt.

He grinned. 'Glad I've made a good first impression.'

'You bought my house,' Dominique said. 'That was bound to make a good impression. Are you a big cheese in the golfing world, Mr . . . ?'

'Paddy. Paddy O'Brien.' He held out his hand and she shook it. 'A minor cheese, I'm afraid. I never won anything big, though I managed to make a living from it for a while.'

'A reasonably good living.' She glanced at the rolling gardens of Atlantic View. Even with a deeply discounted price, it had been an expensive purchase.

'Yes,' Paddy agreed. He looked at her sympathetically. 'I truly am sorry that you had to sell your house.'

'Oh, well . . .' She swallowed. She wasn't going to cry in front of the new owner.

'And I wish we could have met under happier circumstances,' said Paddy.

'I *hated* having to sell the house,' she confessed. 'But thank you for buying the contents as well; that lifted a burden from me.'

'It lifted a burden from me too,' said Paddy. 'I needed somewhere I could move straight into and I don't have time right now for interior decorating and furnishing and all that palaver. But . . .'

He paused.

'But what?'

'Well, if there's anything in particular that you didn't want to sell . . . anything you want to take with you – please do.'

She looked at him in surprise. 'Thank you. That's really kind of you. But I don't want anything. Honestly.'

'Are you sure?' asked Paddy. 'If you change your mind, just let me know.'

'I will. Thanks again.'

'So what are your plans?' He looked enquiringly at her.

'None yet,' she told him. 'I haven't been able to make any until the house was sorted.'

'I actually meant, what are your plans for right now,' amended Paddy. 'I wondered if you'd like a drink, a cup of tea or anything.'

'Oh.' Dominique looked at him in confusion. She was so used to thinking about her long-term future that she didn't consider the short term any more. She would have loved something to drink, because she was hot and thirsty, but she couldn't possibly be a guest in her own house. 'No thanks. I'd better get going.'

'You'll be OK, right?'

'Sure,' she said. 'Sure. I'm thinking of moving away,' she added.

'Where?'

'I don't know yet.'

She didn't. The idea of moving away had only just come to her. She hadn't thought of it before, but the idea of living near Atlantic View when somebody else owned it was painful.

'Well, look, I hope things work out for you.'

'Thanks.'

'Dazzling Domino.'

'Sorry?'

'That's what it said in the photo caption.'

'That's generally what they used to call me,' she admitted. 'But these days it's usually Deserted Domino. Or Downcast Domino. Or sometimes Dopey Domino, which is probably the most accurate.'

'He was a fool.'

'You don't know him,' said Dominique. 'You're making assumptions from what you've read.'

250

'Oh.'

Dominique hitched her bag on to her shoulder. 'I'd better be going. That was the last of the zappers, so there won't be any more unexpected visits from me.'

'Did you want to go inside one more time?' asked Paddy. 'Was that why you came?'

She hesitated.

'It's not a problem,' he said.

'No. Thanks.' She shook her head. 'I couldn't have gone in. I don't have keys. It's not my house any more. I just wanted . . . but it doesn't matter. Better if I go now.'

'OK, then.' He held out his hand again. 'It was nice meeting you.'

'You too, Mr O'Brien,' said Dominique as she opened her car door.

'See you again sometime,' he said.

'I doubt that,' she told him.

'Pity,' he said.

She smiled at him and drove away. She didn't look back.

Chapter 21

Detective Inspector Peter Murphy came to see her again. They sat in Lily's living room while he told her that as yet they'd had no luck in tracing Brendan but that they were sure he'd eventually turn up. The world was a much smaller place than it had once been, he reminded her, as if she didn't know that already, and it would be hard for him to stay missing for ever. Meantime they had an open file on the Barbados money, but until the complex web of inter-company transactions was unravelled, they couldn't forward a file to the Director of Public Prosecutions because they still hadn't uncovered any criminal actions. The fact that the money wasn't in the account that had originally been opened didn't mean it had been fraudulently misappropriated, the detective told her.

'So all his investments could be perfectly legitimate,' said Dominique. 'And he hasn't scarpered with the lot despite what everyone is trying to make out.'

'It's always possible,' said Peter, although he sounded highly sceptical. 'The whole set-up is very complicated.'

'I don't know anything about it,' she said. 'I've never known anything about it and I really and truly can't help you.'

'Would you?' he asked. 'If you knew where your husband was, would you tell me?'

'But I don't know,' said Dominique, 'so that's a stupid question.'

'You've had no communication with him at all?'

Dominique looked at him curiously. 'Do you have my phone tapped?'

He laughed. 'No.'

'I wish he would get in touch with me,' she said fervently. 'I'd tell him what a total tosser he is to have landed us in this mess.'

'The word is that you've no money,' said Peter. 'That he left you in the shit too.'

Dominique sighed. 'Brendan used to build house extensions, for God's sake. Bigger kitchens for people. Bigger living areas. He made a lot of money doing it. He should've stuck to it.'

'I like you, Mrs Delahaye,' said the detective. 'Please tell me if you hear anything from your husband. The sooner we find him, the sooner everything will get sorted out.'

'Sorted out for who?' Dominique knew she was going to cry, and she grabbed a tissue. 'Every time I think things are getting better, they just seem to get worse.'

Lily wanted the whole family together for Sunday lunch. Dominique told her that it would be far too much work for her, but Lily snorted and said that she'd get in some cold meat and salads and bake some bread herself. Dominique insisted on doing the shopping, because she knew that Lily found it a strain to hold her head high every time she went out. She found it a strain herself.

She stood in the queue at the supermarket checkout, her eyes studiously on the contents of her shopping trolley. Even though she told herself she was being paranoid, she couldn't shake the feeling that people were looking at her and making comments about her all the time. When they leaned towards each other and spoke, she was sure they were saying that she had a cheek to show her face in the town, given that her husband had ripped off half the county. But the girl at the till – young and bored – didn't give her a second glance as she packed her groceries and handed over her money.

Maybe I only think people are looking at and talking about me, thought Dominique as she walked back to her car. Maybe it's all in my head. Then she took a deep breath as she saw Stephanie Clooney and her husband in the parking bay beside her. She was ready to greet them when Stephanie pointedly turned away from her.

Not looking at me, and talking about me but not to me, thought Dominique. And it's not in my head after all.

* * *

Nobody enjoyed lunch, even though Lily had done her best and the table was groaning under the weight of food. But not one of them was hungry and there was still only one topic of conversation among them, although they avoided it until the two youngest children had left the table. Alicia, Kelly and Joanna hadn't come to lunch, saying that they were meeting friends. Dominique was glad. She wouldn't have liked her daughter to hear the contempt in Barry's voice as he said that Brendan deserved to go to jail. Or June's scathing remark that it was Dominique's expensive lifestyle that had driven Brendan to robbing friends and family.

'You're being really hard on Domino,' Greg told them. 'You can't blame her for what Brendan's done.'

'Oh, we all know that you'd support her no matter what,' said June scornfully. 'You've got a very soft spot for Domino, haven't you, Greg? You've quite enjoyed being her knight in shining armour. But then she enjoys you being there. She has you wrapped around her little finger. And more.'

There was a sudden taut silence around the table. And then Emma – who hadn't spoken to Dominique since the day she'd seen her with Gabriel at Lily's – pushed her chair away and stood up.

'You're a poisonous cow,' she told June as she walked out of the room.

Greg looked helplessly after her.

'Are you going to stay or go?' asked June waspishly. 'Who needs you more? Your wife or your sister-in-law?'

Barry put his hand on his wife's arm.

'For God's sake!' Maurice spoke, startling them. 'It's not right, everyone fighting.' He stood up. 'I'm going outside for a smoke. I don't like this.'

'Neither do I,' said Dominique shakily. 'I'm sorry. Sorry for everything.'

'It's not your fault,' said Greg. He got up from the table and left the room.

'God in heaven!' Barry turned to June. 'Why do you open your big fat mouth like that?'

'Because you won't,' said June. 'If you'd opened your mouth

sooner, then maybe Brendan wouldn't have run away with our money.'

And June also walked out. Barry looked at Lily and at Dominique, then shrugged his shoulders and followed her.

'I'm so sorry,' said Dominique again. 'Somehow I've managed to bring this down on your head, Lily.'

'Is it true?' asked Lily sharply. 'Is there something going on between you and Greg?'

'No!' cried Dominique.

'They have their troubles, those two,' said Lily.

'Not because of me,' Dominique told her. 'Really. I've never . . . there's never . . .' She buried her head in her hands. When she eventually got herself under control, she realised that she was the only one sitting at the table. Lily had gone too.

She didn't know what she was going to do or where she was going to go. She wanted to get far away from the Delahayes and everything to do with them. She couldn't believe that they had all turned against her, that in some way even Lily was blaming her for what had happened. She didn't know what to say to Kelly. How to work things out. But she knew that they had to leave as soon as possible.

Emma and Greg were at home. Lugh had gone to bed. The silence between them was as taut as a piano wire.

'It isn't working, is it?' asked Emma eventually. 'Even after all this time. June has a point.'

'I don't know why June needs to be so spiteful,' said Greg. 'She was always a bit catty, but she's getting worse with every passing day.'

'She's just saying what everyone thinks.'

'Do you think it?' asked Greg. 'Do you truly think that I care more for Domino than you?'

'I wouldn't be surprised,' said Emma bitterly. 'But then you'd feel entitled, wouldn't you?'

'You don't know me at all, Emma. You should. But you don't.'

'I thought we had it worked out,' she said. 'I thought we'd be happy.'

'Did you?'

'I wanted us to be.'

Greg said nothing.

Emma watched him. She had nothing left to say herself.

Colin sold Dominique's jewellery for her. He did it quietly and discreetly and gave her a cheque afterwards that she lodged in her newly opened personal bank account. Between that and the furniture money, the financial pressure was off for the time being. The cash that Brendan had left them, less what she'd contributed to Lily and Maurice, was tucked away in the bottom drawer of her dressing table.

The previous year, Dominique and Brendan had made elaborate plans for Kelly's twenty-first birthday. It was to have been the biggest bash that Cork had ever seen. They'd booked a marquee, caterers and entertainment and had planned to invite half the county.

Now, despite the cash Brendan had left – which wouldn't have covered half the cost anyway – neither Kelly nor Dominique was interested in or able to throw such a party. Dominique had cancelled everything, feeling that it wasn't just Brendan who'd let their daughter down. By not being involved enough in what was going on in his life, she had too.

Kelly said that it didn't matter about the party. Anyway, she told Dominique, she'd had a bash for her eighteenth. How many times, she asked, did she have to be reminded that she was getting older?

Dominique smiled at that and hugged her and told her that she loved her. And that they would celebrate her birthday together.

So, for the first time since Brendan had left, Dominique and Kelly went out to dinner. They chose Kelly's favourite place, the popular vegetarian Café Paradiso, where they had risotto and tofu and shared a bottle of Pinot Grigio. Dominique handed Kelly a present of a silver chain and locket, which Brendan had given her as a wedding present and which Kelly immediately fastened around her neck.

They had never eaten out together like this before. There had been family celebrations, of course, with Brendan and sometimes an assortment of other Delahaye relatives. But they had never gone

257

to a restaurant together for dinner on their own. The realisation hit Dominique, as she sat across the table from her, that Kelly wasn't a child any more. She didn't look at all childlike now, in her figure-hugging amber dress and with her tousled hair cascading around her heart-shaped face. She looked like a grown-up. Dominique wondered how that had suddenly happened. How one day Kelly had been a tomboy running around the garden, and now she was a serene beauty attracting admiring glances from total strangers. What did seem a total lifetime away was the time when Dominique hadn't even been able to look at her, when she hadn't cared about her one little bit. Now, in the midst of their family crisis, it was Kelly who was the constant, most important person in her life.

'That was the best birthday meal ever,' said Kelly as they waited for their coffees to arrive.

'Oh, Kelly . . .'

'I mean it,' Kelly said firmly. 'The party would've been fun, of course. But this was nice. The two of us together, ignoring the sideways glances of people who can't believe we've had the nerve to have a night out! Putting on a united front. It was good for us, Mum. Really.'

Dominique sighed. 'Just not what we originally had in mind for today.'

'Who cares?' asked Kelly. 'I liked being out with you. I really did. And I love my locket.'

'Thank you,' said Dominique.

'No,' said Kelly seriously. 'Thank you, Mum, for doing your best even though it's been tough.'

Dominique swallowed hard. 'It's going to get tougher.'

'Oh?'

'We need to move out of Gran and Grandad's. We can't stay with them for ever.'

'I know that, but I like being with them,' Kelly said.

'I do too. But it's hard on them, and we're a constant reminder that your dad messed up.'

'It's not something that's easy to forget,' said Kelly darkly.

'I realise that. But I guess we have to . . . move on.'

'Where do you want to go?' asked Kelly.

'I don't know yet. We should both think about it.'

Kelly nodded slowly. 'I don't want you to feel that you have to do things for me.'

'Like what?'

'Anything, really. I'm not sure.' She shrugged easily. 'If you have plans or ideas, they don't have to include me.'

'Kelly! Of course they do.'

'I'm an adult now.' She grinned. 'I'm twenty-one. I have to map out my own life. I don't want you to think that you have to do it for me.'

'Of course not,' said Dominique. 'I understand how you feel. But I'm here for you, Kelly, no matter what. We have to get through this together.'

'I know. I know. And we're doing that, aren't we?' Kelly smiled at her. 'You're the best mum in the whole world.'

Dominique swallowed the lump in her throat at her daughter's words.

'Were you happy?' Kelly asked suddenly. 'You and Dad? Did you love each other?'

'Sorry?' Dominique looked startled.

'You always looked great together,' said Kelly. 'You looked like the perfect couple. I was so proud of you. But did you love each other?'

'We were good together. But there were some things we kept from each other. People do. Unfortunately, his business worries were one of those things.'

'I asked if you were happy,' said Kelly. 'I asked if you loved each other. Not if you were good together.'

Dominique looked up and thanked the waiter, who'd placed their coffees on the table. She stirred hers, even though, as she didn't take sugar, there was no need to.

Had they loved each other? From the start? She'd married for love, but had he? Right now, of course, she didn't love him, but that was because she was so angry with him. But if all the problems of the last months hadn't happened, if they were still together, would she be answering Kelly by saying that of course she loved Brendan? Would she be confident that he loved her equally in return? Had their marriage been a happy one?

259

She'd been happy. As a couple, they'd overcome her depression and his infidelity. He hadn't left her and she hadn't left him. They'd supported each other for better or for worse, just as they'd promised in their wedding vows. So he must have loved her and she must have loved him, because otherwise they wouldn't still be together. Not, of course, that they actually were right now.

Kelly might look like a grown-up, but she didn't need to know Dominique's own uncertainties.

'I loved your dad very much. We were very happy. I still love him,' she said firmly.

'And if . . . when he comes home . . . will you forgive him?'

'Uncle Gabe would be very annoyed with me if I didn't,' said Dominique.

'Uncle Gabe is an idiot,' said Kelly.

Dominique was startled.

'Well, he came rushing home and then he went rushing away again, and he seems to be on another planet altogether half the time.'

'He spent so much time being a priest that he struggles to be an ordinary person,' said Dominique.

'I s'pose.'

'He does his best. We all do.'

'Even Aunt June and Uncle Barry?' Kelly looked wickedly at her. 'Well . . .'

'It's screwed up our whole family, this thing with Dad, hasn't it? It's made us all look at each other differently.'

Dominique nodded.

'He'll come back,' said Kelly.

'I'm sure he will,' said Dominique, although that certainty was slipping further away every single day. And, whether she loved him or not, her desire to see him back was slipping further away too.

She couldn't stay with Evelyn and Seamus in Dublin. She'd come too far to return to her parents' home, even if she wanted to. And, tense as it had been at Lily's, it would be even worse at Evelyn's, with her mother lighting candles and praying at every available opportunity. Besides, Kelly couldn't move to Dublin. She was due to go back to college in a few weeks; her whole life was in Cork.

A couple of days later, Kelly made her own decision.

'I spoke to Alicia today and we've decided to move in together,' she told Dominique.

'What?' Dominique was surprised at her daughter's statement. 'Where?'

'Student accommodation,' said Kelly. 'With two other girls in college. It won't be that expensive, and I thought that maybe you could give me some of the money Dad left to help pay for it. I mean, I know I have some money from my job at the radio station, and a bit of savings too, but . . .'

Dominique looked thoughtful.

'Is this something you want to do? Or are you doing it because you want to be independent and not have me worrying about you?'

Kelly grinned at her. 'Both of those things. But yes, I want to do it too. So does Alicia. Her mum is driving her nuts.'

'Huh.' Dominique snorted. 'Her and everyone else.'

'She's not a very nice person, is she?'

'I suppose she's stressed.' Dominique always did her best not to bad-mouth any of their relatives in front of her daughter, even though she thought June was a poisonous bitch.

'And we're not?'

Dominique smiled. 'Somehow, we're dealing with it better.'

'She was banging on at Alicia about us having a hidden stash of money. I thought she meant the five grand, but she was just talking about money generally. She's convinced that you have access to millions.'

'Her and the rest of the county,' said Dominique wryly.

'And she keeps calling me the trust-fund princess, even though I told her that I don't have one.'

'Your dad planned to build you a house.'

'The best-laid plans . . .' Kelly sighed. 'He was . . . is an awful fool.'

'But you're not,' said Dominique. 'You have best-laid plans of your own.'

Kelly nodded. 'I need to do this. I want to. So does Alicia.'

'I certainly won't stop you,' said Dominique. 'I'm glad you're independent and I'm glad you feel this is something you can do.'

'But I don't want you to be on your own and unhappy,' said Kelly.

'I haven't made a decision on anything yet,' Dominique told her. 'But you're not to worry about me at all. Honestly.' She hugged her daughter. 'We're going to be fine.'

'I know,' said Kelly, and Dominique hoped that they were both right.

Dominique wanted to look for him. She'd always known that she wanted to look for him, but now, with Kelly having decided to move in with her cousin and friends, she felt that she could make her own decision. She would use some of their money to find him. She would confront him. After that . . . well, she didn't know. But she did know that the only way for her to move on was for him to come back. She was certain of that.

Chapter 22

She went to London first. Brendan had travelled there frequently and she knew that he generally stayed at a small boutique hotel in Kensington. It was discreetly expensive, but, by the standards of the capital, not outrageous, so she didn't feel too bad about staying there. A restored Edwardian building, it had a small marble foyer, an oak-panelled reception area and rooms that were reassuringly comfortable and relaxing.

That was the thing, thought Dominique as she sat in the hotel bar a couple of days after her arrival: Brendan liked being seen as a hugely successful businessman, but the truth was that when he travelled alone, he didn't splash the cash half as ostentatiously as people might have expected. It was only when they were together that they put on the Dazzling Delahaye display of flashy jewellery and expensive clothes. Brendan liked having money, but she'd always felt that he had, in many respects, remained down to earth. And despite its obvious comforts, this was a down-to-earth sort of hotel.

She looked around her as she sipped a herbal tea. The only people in the bar were businessmen in expensive suits and highly polished shoes speaking in low tones about whatever it was that businessmen talked about. None of them looked like builders, but then Brendan hadn't looked much like a builder in the last few years, because it had all been about suits and highly polished shoes for him too. It was a long time since he'd sat in the kitchen in a grimy T-shirt and mud-caked boots.

He wasn't staying in the hotel. She'd asked at reception the day she arrived but the pretty Bulgarian girl had shaken her head and said that there was no one of that name booked in. Dominique had asked if she could check the last time Brendan had been a guest, but the receptionist had refused, saying that she couldn't give out that information. And when Dominique had shown her a photograph of Brendan and asked if she recognised him, the girl had contacted her supervisor.

Dominique explained that he was her husband and that he was missing, but the supervisor said that she didn't recognise him and reminded Dominique that they had lots of visitors and it would be difficult to remember them all. Dominique rather thought that the whole idea of staying somewhere quiet and discreet was so that people *would* actually remember you; then she suddenly realised that, despite everything he'd ever told her, it was perfectly possible that Brendan had stayed here with a woman and that the receptionist's memory lapse was part of the hotel's service. So she thanked her and walked away, wishing that she didn't feel like crying again. She was fed up crying over Brendan.

There was no point in trying to meet any of his business contacts in the city. Barry had been in touch with them since Brendan first disappeared, and nobody had heard from him at all. Dominique didn't know any of them herself. But she'd walked past their offices on the off chance that she'd see him there anyway. She hadn't gone in to any of the tall glass buildings, which looked grim and forbidding beneath London's grey skies. She'd stood outside and imagined him hurrying up the steps to meet people inside. It was a different picture of Brendan to the one she usually had. She wondered whether he'd been nervous going to see people in these imposing buildings. Whether his heart had thudded in his chest as he'd mounted the steps. She wondered if any of them had been involved in the businesses that had gone so terribly wrong. She wanted to ask them, but she didn't even know the questions to ask. She realised that coming here had been very, very stupid. But she hadn't really expected to find the answers here. London had been the first place on her list, but the place where she'd had the least hope of finding him. She might have better luck in Biarritz.

The thought had come to her as she'd boarded the flight to London, and came to her again now as she alighted at the airport in Biarritz, that she had never travelled on her own before. It was a shocking reminder of how little she'd done without Brendan. She had, of course, been to lots of different places with him – they'd travelled to Paris and Rome and Madrid together; and they'd gone to New York and Los Angeles, the Maldives and Barbados too. But she'd never gone anywhere on her own. She'd never had to deal with dragging her own luggage off a carousel or looking for a taxi or finding a suitable hotel. All those things had been done for her. Now, if she was being totally honest with herself, Dominique had to admit that she was quite enjoying travelling solo, even though she told herself that it was pathetic to think that a woman of her age was excited about making sure she caught her flight and her connecting train or bus on time. If I'd done the gap year thing, like Kelly, she thought, this would all be a bore. But as it was, she actually found it quite liberating.

Although she knew that she should be feeling miserable and alone, she was shocked to realise that she was beginning to feel a lot better than she had in ages. She thought perhaps that being away from Cork and from the cracks that Brendan's disappearance had triggered in the Delahaye family was allowing her to relax a little. What surprised her more than anything, though, was that she was happy to be by herself. She'd suddenly realised that over the last twenty years, she had never spent much time on her own. Her life had revolved around Brendan and Kelly and she'd spoken to them or seen them (one of them at least) every single day, checking to see what they were doing, where they were going, when they'd be home and what they needed from her. There had never been a time when she was only responsible for herself, when the twenty-four hours of a day were hers to fill whatever way she desired. Perhaps trekking around Europe looking for her errant husband wasn't what she would have chosen as a way to occupy herself, but it was something very different. And travelling on her own was sort of fun, even though searching for Brendan wasn't supposed to be fun. It was a serious thing.

But it was hard to feel serious when you'd just stepped out of the small beachfront hotel in Saint-Jean-de-Luz, the quaint town near Biarritz where Brendan had been involved in the building consortium, and seen the blue water of the Atlantic Ocean tumbling on to the wide crescent of beach. One of the reasons Brendan had chosen to build here was because of the ocean. He liked to think that Cork and Saint-Jean-de-Luz were linked by the same stretch of water. He said that it was more meaningful than being involved in a development on the Mediterranean coast. (Although as it turned out, he'd also had a finger in the pie of a development in Benalmadena, so it wasn't all about meaningful building; it was about the money too.)

Dominique had chosen her hotel at random. When they'd come before, they'd stayed in the apartments, but of course she couldn't stay there now, so she'd picked somewhere inexpensive but immaculately clean, and decorated in the slightly mad way that some French hotels had, which meant that both walls and ceilings were covered in a busy floral wallpaper. It was all slightly overwhelming, but different, which only added to her guilty delight at being away on her own.

She walked from the hotel past a little terrace of pretty white-washed holiday houses, each with a different-coloured door, and reached the bustling seafront, where the sun glittered off the blue water and children played happily on the white sand. She strolled along the promenade, checking out the people who were sitting outside the cafés as she walked. Brendan wasn't really a beach person – she remembered him on their honeymoon in Majorca, burned to a crisp after just a few minutes in the sun, banished to the shade of the bar while she acquired a tan for the first time. He'd been so good about that too, she remembered. He'd never complained that he was bored, waiting for her to toast herself brown. (Something she never did these days, of course.) He'd been good about so many damn things. But everything was overshadowed now by his disappearance.

She eventually sat down in one of the promenade cafés herself and ordered a *citron pressé*, which she sipped slowly as she continued to scan passers-by. She hadn't yet decided what she'd say to Brendan if she saw him. Sometimes she thought that she'd lose her temper completely. Other times she imagined herself throwing her arms around him and telling him that everything would be OK. In London, losing her temper had seemed the more likely outcome. Here, in the warmth of the sun, she couldn't bear the thought of a confrontation. It was easier to imagine him apologising to her and telling her how sorry he was, easier to imagine forgiving him and telling him that she still loved him.

But did she? That question had nagged at her ever since Kelly had asked it. She had always thought that she did. Sometimes she thought that she'd loved him too much, that he mattered more to her than she mattered to him. She certainly used to love him. But now, after all this, did she still?

Her heart missed a beat as she spotted the man climbing the stone steps from the beach to the promenade. He was wearing navy blue shorts and a navy blue Nike baseball cap pulled low over his eyes. His bare shoulders were smothered in sun cream. He carried a white polo shirt. He stood at the top of the steps and she held her breath. Then he took off the baseball cap and swept his hand over an almost bald head. It still took a moment for her to realise that he wasn't Brendan. A moment to realise that she didn't have to make up her mind just yet about whether she still loved him or not. She ordered another glass of lemon. She was getting to like its bittersweet taste.

Later that night, sitting on the terrace of the hotel, she was chatted up by a fellow guest. She didn't realise what was happening at first (it was, she reminded herself, a long, long time since anyone had even attempted to chat her up), so she was dismissive of the attractive tanned man who sat at the adjoining table and asked her if he might borrow the newspaper that lay beside her but which she wasn't reading. She figured out what he was saying because he'd gestured at the paper, not because she understood his rapid French. She'd done quite well at French in school, but she'd hardly spoken it since, even though she realised she still recognised many of the words when she saw them in print. She nodded to the man and he thanked her and asked her something else, but she shrugged, whereupon he switched to perfect English and asked her if she was staying in the town.

'Only for a few days,' she replied.

'Perhaps you would like to join me for dinner tomorrow evening?' He smiled at her.

Dominique was stunned. In her whole life nobody had ever asked her on a dinner date before. Which, she thought, was rather pathetic. (When she'd gone out to eat with Brendan while they'd been dating, it was always to places like American Burger, or inexpensive Chinese restaurants, never to places with starched linen tablecloths, silver cutlery and napkins. She'd only started eating at places like that with him when they'd been out with clients or partners.) Still, flattering though it was to be asked, she didn't intend to be picked up by a perfect stranger. Besides, what if she saw Brendan while she was in the restaurant? What would she do then?

'I'm sorry,' she said. 'I'm busy.'

'Well then, can I buy you a drink now?' he asked.

She was going to say no, and then she thought, what the hell, and said yes. She stayed chatting to him for nearly two hours, while he talked about the fact that he was in town on business and that he lived in Paris and that he travelled around France a lot and that he was divorced with two little girls whom he adored.

'Do you miss them?' she asked.

'Of course. But I have a good relationship with my ex-wife and I see them a lot so it is not so bad. Worse, I think, if I was still there and everyone was unhappy.'

She nodded.

'I've talked a lot about me,' he said. 'But you have said very little about you.'

She had no intention of telling him anything at all. So all she did was smile and say that she had nothing interesting to talk about but that it had been lovely to listen to him. Then she said that it was getting late and she should be going to bed, and he said, 'All alone?' in a way that made her realise that she didn't have to be all alone.

What would it be like? she wondered. A one-night stand (or maybe even a two-night stand; she planned to stay in Saint-Jean-de-Luz for a couple of days) with a man she hardly knew. Casual sex. And maybe he'd stay in touch by text afterwards.

'All alone,' she said, even as he looked at her enquiringly.

And then she drained her wine glass and went to bed.

*   *   *

Her luggage went missing on the flight to Malaga but she didn't really care; she bought herself some toiletries and some inexpensive summer clothes at a beachside shop and spent two days around the pool before being reunited with her stuff again. She wasn't really expecting to find Brendan on the Costa del Sol – he'd only come here once before, to check out the Benalmadena development, and she knew it wasn't a place he'd choose to visit again – but there was still a sense that people with something to hide, people on the run, often fetched up on the sun-soaked coast. And as much as she really and truly didn't want to think of her husband as a criminal, and much as she knew he preferred cooler temperatures, she felt that she had to check it out.

The major flaw in her plan, of course, was that the Costa was teeming with late-summer visitors and that it would have been a miracle if she'd picked a single person out from the hordes that flocked to the beaches by day and the bars by night. After eventually retrieving her luggage in Malaga, she'd gone on to Torremolinos, then to Benalmadena and finally to Marbella and Puerto Banus, where she'd shown his picture at some of the bars and restaurants and asked if anyone remembered him. The wall of silence that greeted her made her realise that she might not be the first person ever to come looking for someone in this part of the world, and that most people kept their mouths shut. She remembered the TV detective dramas that she loved to watch, and that sometimes showing photos and asking about people had unintended consequences, and she suddenly felt alone and vulnerable and didn't want to stay any longer.

She couldn't get a flight out for two days, and so she returned to Malaga and stayed at an inexpensive hotel close to the airport. Now that she'd decided to leave, she wanted to get home as soon as possible. She phoned Kelly and told her that she missed her and was looking forward to seeing her again. Kelly told her that she'd missed her too and then said that she had sorted out the student accommodation with Alicia and her other two friends, and Dominique suddenly felt as though she was unnecessary in her daughter's life. She told herself that she was being silly and that Kelly had always done her own thing before, and that she herself was doing her own thing, wasn't she, by skittering around haphazardly looking for Brendan – the whole trip, she thought, had been as ill thought out as anything she'd ever done in her life before. She knew now that she hadn't really expected to find him, that it had all simply been an excuse to get away.

And now she was going home. And she'd have to face whatever needed to be faced when she got there.

It had all been a waste of time and money, and yet, she thought as the plane came to a stop at Cork airport terminal, it had been strangely cathartic. She hadn't found Brendan, but she had learned that she was perfectly capable of managing on her own. She'd learned that she had reserves of strength that she'd never quite believed in, because she'd always felt that someone who'd once been unable to get out of bed to face the day ahead of them couldn't possibly have inner strength.

But her life was still a mess. And she still had no idea how she was going to cope in the future, inner strength or no inner strength.

Then she saw Kelly waiting for her and a smile broke out on her face. Only now, seeing her in front of her, did she realise how much she'd missed her daughter during her few weeks of independence. As she hugged her close, she realised that she was very, very glad to be home. Even if she still didn't have the faintest idea where her husband was and what on earth he was doing.

Even if everything and nothing had changed.

Chapter 23

There was a letter waiting for her when she arrived back at Lily's. It was from her old friend Maeve Mulligan.

Dear Dominique, she'd written. *I hope this reaches you. I'm working on the assumption that people in Castlecannon know where you are. I'm sorry we lost touch after you moved to Cork, but I know you've been busy becoming a style icon and socialite because I've seen your picture in magazines. I never would've thought it back in school, when you were so worried about your spots! Naturally I've read about the other stuff too and I'm very sorry that this has happened to you. I thought that perhaps you might like to meet up, have a chat, remember old times. If you don't want to, that's fine of course. But I'd love to get together with you again. Don't worry, I'm sure things will turn out OK. Love, Maeve.*

Dominique felt her eyes fill with the dreaded tears again as she re-read Maeve's letter. It was what she'd wanted before, from all her friends in Cork. Someone to support her unconditionally. Someone who wasn't judging her or criticising her or making assumptions about her. Someone who knew her as Dominique Brady, not Dazzling Domino Delahaye.

Maeve had written her mobile number on the letter. Dominique called her.

'How are you doing?' Maeve's voice was warm.

'Not so bad,' said Dominique. 'I've been away. Sort of looking for Brendan and sort of . . . well, just getting away.'

'I understand that,' said Maeve. 'It must be tough for you.'

'A bit.' Dominique was determined not to sound like a victim. 'But, sure, I'll get over it.'

271

'Why don't you come up to town?' asked Maeve. 'We could do dinner, that sort of thing.'

'I'd love to.' Dominique's tone was heartfelt.

'Next week?' suggested Maeve.

'Perfect,' said Dominique. 'Oh, Maeve, I just can't wait to see you.'

Most of her social interaction seemed to be by phone these days. She took calls from Colin, her solicitor, and from her new bank manager, Nicholas, who was friendly and approachable and helpful about how best she could manage her limited resources. She was also phoned by Lena, one of her old charity group friends, to say that the annual gala ball was taking place in Jurys this year and that she was sorry Dominique couldn't attend. Dominique was both touched by Lena's phone call and hurt by the fact that one of the reasons she wasn't attending was simply that she hadn't actually been invited.

'I hope you're keeping well,' Lena said, and Dominique replied that she was fine, absolutely.

'Well, all the best.'

It was clear that Lena felt she'd done enough by ringing her in the first place, and Dominique was grateful that she had.

And then she had the phone call from Greg, asking her to meet him in Cork. He needed to talk to her.

'Have you heard from Brendan?' Her voice was anxious.

'No,' replied Greg. 'But we do have to have a chat.'

They met in a small café off Patrick Street. Dominique was struck by the fact that Greg looked pale and drawn, and she realised how much of an impact Brendan's disappearance had had on everyone in the Delahaye family.

'You look great,' Greg told her. 'Tanned and healthy.'

'I don't feel great,' she assured him wryly. 'I still feel as though my whole life is balanced on an eggshell.'

He smiled. 'You're doing well, though.'

'I'm coping,' she agreed. 'I suppose you have to, don't you?'

He nodded.

'And you?' she asked. 'You're looking a bit tired, Greg. Are you OK?'

She knew from the expression on his face that he wasn't.

'Emma . . .' He cleared his throat. 'Emma and I have split up,' he said.

'Oh, Greg, no.'

'Oh, Domino, yes.' He shrugged. 'It was inevitable, wasn't it? Eventually.'

'Why should it have been inevitable?' she asked.

'Because you and I both know that Emma was never really in love with me,' said Greg.

'Is this because of what June said?' asked Dominique. 'I know she's your sister, but she can be a terrible bitch.'

'She stirs it up all right, but Emma . . .'

'Emma loves you, Greg. I know she does.'

'Sometimes there are things about the people that we're closest to that we only think we know,' said Greg. 'Like with you and Brendan.'

Dominique nodded slowly.

'So what are you going to do?' she asked.

'I've moved out,' he told her. 'Got a place in town for the time being.'

She didn't know what to say.

'I'm meeting a solicitor this afternoon.'

She reached out and took him by the hand.

'I'm very, very sorry,' she said.

'It's ironic, isn't it?' His hand tightened around hers. 'I thought I was being a support for you, but all I was doing was undermining my own marriage.'

Dominique said nothing.

'And the worst part is that she isn't entirely wrong. I do love you, Domino.'

'Not the way she thinks,' Dominique told him quickly. 'You saw something in me that reminded you of someone else, and it's always been there.'

He smiled faintly. 'Perhaps. But I envied Brendan from the moment he brought you home.'

'Greg, please . . .'

He released her hand. 'I'd do anything for you, you know that.'

'You already have,' she told him. 'You gave me my life back all those years ago.'

'So that Brendan could wreck it.'

'No.' She sat up straighter in her chair. 'I'm not going to let that happen.'

He stared at her. 'You're strong, Domino. Stronger than me now.'

'I'm not strong at all,' she assured him. 'But I'm damned if I'm going to be miserable for the rest of my life. And you shouldn't be either, Greg Delahaye. You should try to save your marriage. But if you can't do that, then you have to get on with things. That's what I'm going to do. Well, what I'm trying to do, anyway.'

He laughed. And then looked up as Jennie Knight, a neighbour of Lily's, stopped beside their table.

'Glad to see you're both well,' said Jennie. 'Glad to see that the Delahayes are looking after each other.'

She walked out of the café. Dominique groaned. It probably hadn't been a good idea to meet Greg in a place where Cork county's biggest gossip could bump into them. And get the wrong idea entirely.

Dominique knew that she'd have to speak to Emma, so she called over to Briarwood.

'You know,' said Emma as soon as she saw Dominique.

'Yes.'

'I knew he'd tell you. That's why I didn't bother myself. I guess there's nothing about our relationship you don't know.'

'Plenty,' Dominique said.

'Oh, please.' Emma shook her head. 'I bet he tells you every-thing. He's in love with you.'

'Emma, I swear to you, even though he cares about me, there's nothing between us that should ever worry you.' Dominique put Greg's own words out of her mind. He was only a little bit in love with her. And that was only because Emma wasn't enough in love with him. 'We never, ever talk about you and him.'

274

'Don't you?' There was an extra edge to Emma's voice, and Dominique looked at her curiously.

'Of course not.'

'I wonder why it is I don't entirely believe you.'

'Emma, I swear to you – if there's some deep secret about your lives that you're afraid Greg's told me . . . he hasn't!' She raised her hands in despair. 'I admit that we're close. But he doesn't tell me everything. And whatever feelings he has for me – whatever feelings I have for him too, when it comes to it – are perfectly innocent.'

'What else can you say?' demanded Emma.

'It's true,' said Dominique. 'What he feels for me is all tied up with that girl he was in love with years ago and the baby . . .' Her voice trailed off as Emma stared uncomprehendingly at her.

'The baby?' whispered Emma. 'What baby?'

Dominique looked at her, horrified by what she'd just said. She'd totally forgotten that Emma knew nothing about Greg's teenage love.

'I'm sorry,' she said shakily. 'There *is* no baby, but he thought there was . . . There was a girl . . . It was ages ago, Emma, and—'

'And whatever it is, you know about it but I don't.' Emma rubbed her head with her hands. 'Now d'you see, Dominique? He tells you stuff he doesn't tell me.'

Greg should have told her, thought Dominique. How could he expect his marriage to work when he was keeping such important secrets from his wife?

'I haven't seen him in a week.' Emma sighed. 'He said it was over and just disappeared. Family trait, obviously. When the going gets tough, the weak piss off without telling anyone. Well that's fine, because I don't care that he's left. I just wish he'd had the decency to tell me whatever it was he told you.' She rubbed the back of her neck. 'When did you see him?'

'Yesterday.'

'At least you're telling the truth about that,' said Emma.

Dominique's expression was wary.

'I met Jennie Knight at the shops,' said Emma. 'She told me she'd seen the two of you in Cork together. Holding hands.'

'That woman is as bad as June!' Suddenly Dominique herself was angry. 'Of course I held his hand. He's very upset.' She sighed. 'I've known you for a long time, Emma. If I was having some kind of relationship with Greg, I'd be honest about it and tell you. But I'm not.'

'I held hands with Gabriel and you practically accused me of having an affair with him,' said Emma tightly.

Dominique didn't know what to say. She knew that Emma was right.

'Did you ever turn him down?' asked Emma.

It was a question Dominique didn't want to answer. It was too close to the truth, even though she was utterly certain that Greg didn't really love her. He saw parts of himself in her; he wanted to fix her life because he thought that way he could fix his own. But he was wrong.

'Or is the other story doing the rounds true instead – that you've heard from Brendan and you're going to meet him in exile?'

'Emma! This is all nonsense.' Dominique was frustrated. 'I don't know where Brendan is, and if I did, I certainly wouldn't be going to meet him.'

'Liar! You've spent the last few weeks looking for him!'

'That's different.'

'In the same way you and Greg are different?'

'Make up your bloody mind!' cried Dominique. 'Either I'm rushing off to live a new life with my criminal husband or I'm having an affair with my brother-in-law. You can't have it both ways, Emma.'

'Can't you?'

Dominique knew she was wasting her time. There was a gulf between herself and her sister-in-law that right now she simply couldn't bridge.

'When you want to talk seriously, you can give me a call,' she said as she gathered up her things. 'I can't do this any more.' She walked out of the conservatory, leaving her friend staring out over the garden.

She wasn't expecting to hear from Emma any time soon.

*   *   *

276

She also called to see June, although it was the last thing she wanted to do. Her sister-in-law was scathing about Dominique's reason for calling – to see that she was OK with Kelly and Alicia's student accommodation plans. June said that at least it meant the two girls had a roof over their heads, which was more than she and Barry would have soon, because they were selling their house. They couldn't afford to stay, June said, now that Barry didn't have a job. In fact, she added, her whole marriage was under strain because of the situation Brendan's actions had put them in. Dominique listened to her sister-in-law and then left without saying another word.

She was shattered by her visits to June and Emma. She was tired of feeling responsible for everything. And she was fed up that everyone was using her as a punchbag for their understandable rage at her husband.

Maeve met her at Heuston station. Her old school friend looked smart and cheerful, wearing a fitted red jacket and DKNY jeans, her dark hair cut into a flattering bob. Dominique felt a wave of relief when Maeve smiled at her and hurried towards her, flinging her arms around her and hugging her.

'I'm so glad you came,' said Maeve.

'I'm so glad you asked me.' Dominique was choking up again. She swallowed hard a few times before smiling at her friend.

'Let's go,' said Maeve. 'We've lots to catch up on.'

Maeve was living in an old Victorian house off the Howth Road. Five years ago, she told Dominique, she'd met Kevin Dalgleish, a physiotherapist, and they'd moved in together.

'Getting married?' asked Dominique.

'When his divorce comes through.' Maeve grinned. 'He was broken in for me.'

'Maeve!'

'It's true,' said Maeve. 'Sharon knocked all the hard edges off him.'

'So why did they split up?'

'They married young.'

Dominique sighed. 'A hazard, I agree.'

'He has two of the nicest kids you could ever meet,' Maeve told her. 'And the split with Sharon was relatively amicable. So it's not pistols at dawn or anything.'

'All the same,' mused Dominique, 'it's getting harder and harder to find unattached men.'

'Are you looking?' asked Maeve.

'God, no.' Dominique laughed hollowly. 'It's just that every couple I know seem to be either on the verge of breaking up, broken up, or part of a new relationship. Emma and Greg. June – Brendan's sister – and her husband.'

'That's life,' said Maeve.

'Yes.' Dominique sighed. 'I didn't think it would be, though.'

'So what do you plan to do, post-Brendan?'

Dominique had filled Maeve in on the entire story, although she'd left out the part about Greg saying that he was a little bit in love with her. No point in making herself sound like the chief marriage-wrecker herself.

'I have to move out of Lily's,' she replied. 'That's always been the plan, but I'm not sure yet where to go. A city, I think. I need to get a job and I'll never get one around Castlecannon. Besides, I don't feel comfortable there any more.'

'Move back to Dublin,' said Maeve easily.

'I've been thinking about it,' admitted Dominique. 'I like the thought of getting away from everyone. Especially the Delahayes. But that would mean leaving Kelly, and I don't know if I could do that.'

'She's going to be in her flat, isn't she?'

'It's not the same. Besides,' added Dominique, 'it's probably more expensive to live here, and I need to be careful with money.'

'Hey, you always were in the past. Like me. Did we ever own anything that didn't come from Dunnes or Penneys back in those days?'

'True.' Dominique grinned suddenly. 'But I've become accustomed to my glittering life and choosing designer over high street.'

Maeve laughed, then looked at her friend quizzically.

'If you're truly interested in coming back to Dublin, I know somewhere you could stay,' she said.

'Oh?'

'I have a house in Fairview,' said Maeve. 'I rent it out. The tenants are leaving next month.'

'A house?' asked Dominique in surprise. 'I didn't realise you were into property.'

'I bought it a few years ago,' said Maeve. 'But then I moved in with Kevin. So we rent it out.'

Dominique nodded.

'I'd love to rent it to you,' said Maeve. 'I know you'd be a good tenant.'

'This isn't some kind of charity offer, is it?'

'Of course not,' said Maeve. 'I'd be charging you the proper rent.'

'Let me think about it,' said Dominique. 'I need to talk to Kelly, too.'

'Sure,' said Maeve easily. 'Let me know.'

She went to see her parents while she was in Dublin. She walked up the garden path of the house in Drimnagh, realising that the last time she'd been there, everything in her life had seemed perfect. She'd even felt a bit condescending, visiting her parents in their small terraced house. Pride well and truly had come before a fall, she thought as she rang the bell. Just like her mother so often said.

When she and Brendan had first started making big money, she'd offered to help her parents move to a bigger house in a better neighbourhood, but Seamus had looked at her in astonishment and asked her why on earth they'd want to uproot themselves from the place they'd lived in all their lives. Evelyn had told her that they were happy in their home and happy with their lot. As you should be, she'd said, which had annoyed Dominique at the time.

The small garden was, as always, perfectly maintained, the grass carefully cut, the borders weeded and the flowers at exact intervals. The house, when Evelyn opened the door, smelled, as always, of Pledge furniture polish and roses. Dominique noticed that her parents had recently replaced the downstairs carpets with a wooden floor.

'Easier to keep,' Evelyn said.

Dominique had offered to get Brendan to do the floor for them

279

years ago, but they'd refused. Back then, Evelyn had wanted to stick with her Axminster.

'So how are things?' Evelyn asked when they sat down in the kitchen. 'Any news on him?'

Dominique shook her head.

'I still can't believe it,' said Evelyn. 'I know he wouldn't have been my choice, but he worked hard and I thought things would work out.'

It wasn't right, thought Dominique. It wasn't right that her parents were worrying about her. She knew they were worried by the way Evelyn was polishing her varifocal glasses, not looking at her but instead concentrating on ensuring that the lenses were smudge-free before putting the glasses back on her nose.

She hadn't changed much, thought Dominique. In her seventies, she was greyer, of course, than she'd been. But her clothes were the same style as she'd always worn (today she had on a tweed skirt and yellow cardigan), and she hadn't changed her hair either – the colour was silver-grey, but Dominique knew that she was still going for her weekly wash and set at the salon in the village. I thought she was old at forty, Dominique remembered. I was right then. But it suits her now.

'I'm doing a novena,' Evelyn told her.

'Thanks.'

'Father Moran said a Mass for you last Sunday, too,' added Seamus.

'Thanks,' said Dominique again.

She didn't think the novenas and Masses would make any difference. But if they made her parents feel better, then that was a good thing.

'How's Kelly?' Seamus asked.

'In great form,' said Dominique. 'Living with Alicia and two friends and very happy.'

'Hardly happy,' said Evelyn. 'Her father's missing.'

'As happy as she can be.'

'And Lily?' asked Evelyn. 'I spoke to that poor woman on the phone a couple of weeks ago. She's having to carry a terrible cross.'

'Obviously it's a difficult time for her,' Dominique said. 'But she's doing her best.'

'And you?' asked Seamus gently. 'How are you?'

'I'll be all right,' replied Dominique.

'It's nice to see you,' said Seamus.

'You too.' Dominique realised that she meant what she was saying.

There was a silence around the table, and then Evelyn stood up.

'Tea and cake,' she said as she put her arm around Dominique's shoulders and squeezed them. 'I made an apple tart.'

'Lovely,' said Dominique, and she meant that too.

'Of course you should go and live in Dublin,' said Kelly when Dominique got home again and told her about Maeve's proposal. 'I'm fine here, Mum. I don't need you hanging around.'

'Great,' said Dominique drily.

'That didn't come out quite the way I meant.' Kelly looked apologetically at her mother. 'What I wanted to say was that I'm doing my own thing and I'm OK with that.'

'How's Alicia?'

'Upset,' said Kelly. 'There are some terrible rows going on at home, so she's glad to be out of it. She's terribly afraid that her parents will split up.'

All the Delahaye marriages down the tubes, thought Dominique, even though she'd find it hard to blame Barry for leaving June.

'I hope they don't,' she told Kelly.

'Would you take Dad back if he turned up now?'

'It would be very difficult,' replied Dominique slowly.

'He did his best for us.'

'I know.'

'I still want to know where he is.'

'So do I.'

Kelly twirled her burnished hair between her fingers.

'Do you think he has someone else?'

Dominique said nothing.

'Did he leave us for another woman?' asked Kelly.

'I don't think so,' Dominique replied. 'I think the collapse of the businesses was the main thing.'

'Was he having an affair?' asked Kelly.

'Why would you say that?'

'Men do stupid things. Even fathers.'

Dominique sighed. 'I know.'

'Was he?'

'That I don't know.'

'Why is it so hard?' demanded Kelly. 'How is it that you can love someone and hate them at the exact same time?'

'One of life's many mysteries,' said Dominique.

'The new owners have moved into Atlantic View.' Kelly changed the subject abruptly.

'Oh?' Dominique had never mentioned meeting Paddy O'Brien.

'I saw a furniture van there last week.'

'You'd think they'd have enough furniture, what with all the stuff they bought from us,' said Dominique ruefully.

Kelly grinned. 'I guess they had their own, too.'

'I guess so.'

'I still think of it as our house.'

'It's hard not to.' Although, since coming back from her futile trip to find Brendan, Dominique didn't feel the same attachment to Atlantic View any more.

'Maybe I'll become a famous radio broadcaster and one day I'll have enough money to buy it back,' said Kelly suddenly.

Dominique laughed. 'If you earn enough money, then you should buy your own place,' she told her. 'There's no point in looking back.'

'Do you believe that?'

'Almost,' replied Dominique. 'Almost.'

Chapter 24

Old friends were best, thought Dominique as she stood in the bedroom of the Fairview house, the contents of her two suitcases laid out on the bed in front of her. People who had known you all your life understood who you really were. Maeve had always known that she wasn't Dazzling Domino at all, just an ordinary person who'd wanted to lose her spots, get married, have a family and live happily ever after. Maeve knew that the big house and the diamond rings and the glittering social functions weren't important. Maeve knew what really was.

Which was why, a couple of hours after she'd left Dominique to her own devices at the house, the doorbell had rung and a Pizza Express delivery guy had handed her a twelve-inch bacon and pineapple with extra cheese, which had always been her favourite. Dominique had texted 'thanks' to her friend, and Maeve had replied that she was welcome, and then Dominique had thought that they actually were getting old because she hadn't done any text abbreviations and neither had Maeve. It was so unlike getting texts from Kelly, which took her ages to decipher.

The aroma of pizza still wafted around the house, but it was a homely smell. Dominique was already feeling relaxed here, liking the small but cosy rooms and the old-fashioned pine kitchen. The entire kitchen, she'd thought as she sat on the edge of the square wooden table chomping on a slice of pizza, would've fitted into one of her walk-in cupboards in Cork. Downsizing, she reminded herself. They were all doing it. Greg and Emma. June and Barry. Kelly and herself.

Greg and Emma had both met with solicitors and were moving

ahead with a divorce. Because they hadn't been affected financially by the collapse of Delahaye Developments, their future financial arrangements were all based around Lugh. Dominique hadn't spoken to either of them in the last few weeks, but she knew from her conversations with Lily that Emma was hoping to keep Briarwood for Lugh and herself, while at the same time accepting that perhaps they'd have to sell it and move somewhere smaller.

June and Barry were still living together in Abbotsville, their family home. Again, according to Lily, they had so far been incapable of deciding anything about the future of their marriage. Their house was up for sale, but so far there was no interest in their custom-designed home at the price they wanted. Probably no interest at a hundred grand less, Lily had grunted. June always overvalued things.

Kelly had done her bit to add to her cash flow by selling her Micra. She'd bought a Vespa instead, which she rode to and from college. Dominique was terrified at the idea of her daughter whizzing around on a scooter, but Kelly had assured her that it was a cinch to ride and safe as anything. Dominique had traded down on her own car too. She'd sold her sporty silver Audi and bought a Ford Fiesta.

She picked up a backless white dress and slid it on to a hanger. There wasn't enough room in the wardrobes for all of her clothes. When she'd first moved out of Atlantic View, she'd thought about donating some of them to a local charity shop, but she hadn't been able to pluck up the courage to walk inside. In the past, she'd often given dresses and skirts to Angie's Angel Boutique, but Angie was another person who'd cut her dead in the street one day, and she wasn't inclined to leave clothes with her now.

She was glad to be able to lose herself in the anonymity of a city again. And tomorrow, she hoped, would be the start of a whole new life, because Kevin, Maeve's adorable partner, had arranged a job interview for her, and she was determined that she would get it.

As she drove along the narrow country roads that led to the Glenmallon Golf & Country Club, she wished the Fiesta had the Audi's inbuilt satnav. She didn't know this area at all well, and the sheeting rain was making driving conditions difficult. The thought of having to do the drive every day, especially in heavy commuter traffic, was daunting. But it would have to be done and, she muttered to herself, she had no right to be in the slightest bit iffy about it when she was lucky to have the opportunity to get work at all. Especially when it was thanks to someone she'd only just met. Kevin was the physio at the golf centre and he'd told her that they were looking to hire someone urgently as cover for the receptionist there, who was about to go on maternity leave.

'I'm sure you'd be well able to do it,' he'd said encouragingly, although Dominique wasn't quite so certain. It occurred to her, as she yanked the steering wheel hard left, having almost missed the turn, that this was only the second time in her life that she'd ever gone for a job interview, and that she had absolutely no decent skills or experience whatsoever.

The only proper paying job she'd ever had was being a waitress at American Burger, which she'd originally believed was a stopgap until she got something better. But that hadn't happened. She'd done the books for Brendan, but only for a short time. There had been a lot of hard work involved in her charity functions, but it still wasn't the same as having a real job. Nobody would have shouted at her if she'd made a hash of a coffee morning or a garden party. It wouldn't have mattered to anyone except herself – and, of course, the charity.

Now, for the first time in over twenty years, she was going for an interview. And she was scared witless. As she drove slowly up the long curving driveway to the hotel and clubhouse, she could feel her heart thumping erratically in her chest. The manager, Paul Rothery, had told her to come to the hotel reception and ask for him. Dominique hurried up the weathered steps, protecting her hair from the rain with her big leather bag, and stepped into the beautifully restored country house. She blinked a couple of times in the light from the huge chandelier that hung in the hallway before giving the receptionist her name and saying that she had an appointment with Paul. The pretty blonde smiled at her and told her to take a seat. But not before Dominique had seen the flicker of recognition in her eyes. There had been another piece about Brendan in the paper at the weekend, and a photograph captioned 'Deserted Domino', which had been taken as she'd left Atlantic View for the last time. (Well, she thought with inner amusement, the second-last time, because nobody had learned about her secret return trip, when she'd bumped into the new owner. She hoped he was enjoying living there even on a day like today, when the storm clouds would have rolled in from the ocean and the rain would thunder against the wide French doors.)

She perched on the edge of one of the reception area's high-backed upholstered chairs and waited until the manager arrived.

Paul Rothery was around the same age as her; tall, dark-haired and with a long, narrow face.

'Mrs Delahaye,' he said, holding out his hand to her. 'Dominique. It's a pleasure to meet you.'

'You too.' She was so nervous she could hardly speak, and she knew that her palm was damp with perspiration. She reminded herself that it didn't matter that she had no specific experience for this job, because she was a good organiser and had arranged charity balls that had been resounding successes. Nevertheless, she was still shaking like a leaf as she followed him into a small, but equally elegantly furnished room.

'I knew your husband,' Paul said after he'd made some general conversation. 'Not well, but I met him a number of times.'

'Oh.'

'He was involved in a lot of good work.'

'I thought so.'

'Have you heard from him at all?'

Dominique shook her head.

'I have to admit that I agreed to interview you partly because I was intrigued,' he said. 'I thought that you'd left the country.'

'Really?'

'To live abroad with him. I'm sure I read that in one of the papers.'

'Oh well,' she said, as dismissively as she could, 'you know what the papers are like.' She tucked a stray lock of hair nervously behind her ear. 'I'm sorry to hear that you're not taking my application for the job seriously. I didn't realise it was just because you knew my husband. I don't want to waste your time.' She stood up.

'No, no.' Paul waved at her. 'Sit down, for heaven's sake. I apologise. I didn't mean to offend you.'

Dominique hesitated, then sat down again.

'Do you play golf?'

'No.' She shook her head. 'Brendan was a member of a local club, but to be honest, he wasn't that into it and neither was I. Though we did go to the Ryder Cup one year.'

'Nice.'

They hadn't seen much golf. They'd spent most of the time in one of the hospitality tents, where Brendan had been networking with other businessmen.

She wondered if it was worth talking any more to Paul Rothery. She wanted this job. She hadn't been sure at first. But suddenly it was important to her. She didn't want to be rejected. She needed the work and she wanted to think that she hadn't wasted her time during her marriage. She was a good organiser and surely that was what you needed to be to do this job well. Yet if all Paul Rothery really wanted to know was what her life was like since Brendan left, or whether she had some inside knowledge of his whereabouts, then there was no point in staying.

He started to ask her about her knowledge of computer programs like Word and Excel. Feeling that these, at least, were sensible questions, she assured him that she used them regularly. (She was grateful, then, for the time she'd spent composing letters and keeping accounts for her charity boards.) And then she said, quite abruptly, that she knew she could do the job, that she wasn't a flighty, inexperienced kid, and she really wanted to know whether he was serious about giving it to her or not.

'I'm sorry,' said Paul. 'I didn't mean to imply that you were inexperienced. Or indeed that I was being too curious about your private life.' He stood up. 'Come on. I'll bring you over to the clubhouse.'

The clubhouse was a five-minute walk along a covered walkway from the hotel. In contrast, it was a modern building, although sympathetically built to blend in with both the hotel and the surrounding countryside. It was warm and bright inside and decorated in a contemporary style. As he walked, Paul talked about the responsibilities of the job – making bookings, scheduling tournaments, helping with the organisation of private functions (at this last comment, Dominique smiled. Piece of cake, she thought). However, she was suddenly nervous again as Paul brought her over to the oak reception desk and introduced her to Agnes, a bubbly brunette who looked as though she was about to give birth any second.

'I'm not due for another three weeks,' said Agnes cheerfully. 'But obviously I'm going to have a monster.'

Dominique remembered how she'd felt at that point in her pregnancy. Terrified and exhausted. She doubted she'd looked as chirpy as Agnes.

'So,' said Paul after he'd shown her around and they'd returned to the hotel. 'The job is only for the duration of Agnes's maternity leave. I don't have any positions after that.'

'That's fine.'

'My wife was at a charity auction you organised,' said Paul.

'Really?'

'She said that it was one of the best-planned events she'd ever been at.'

Dominique couldn't help feeling a glow of satisfaction. 'I'm glad.'

'We run a lot of events here at Glenmallon,' he told her. 'But they're always within a strict budget.'

'I'm very good with strict budgets,' she assured him. 'Especially these days.'

'You can start tomorrow?'

'Yes,' she said.

'OK then.' Paul smiled. 'Welcome on board.'

Dominique had never felt anything like the pride she felt now. She couldn't believe how excited she was at landing a job. Even if it was just maternity cover. Even if it wasn't the most exciting job in the world. It was hers, and she'd earned it.

She rang Kelly, who was equally excited and who said that it was a good thing that the Delahaye women were making their own way in the world. Dominique suggested that she come and visit her soon – she said that she was missing her madly already – and Kelly reassured her by saying that she was delighted to have a place to stay in the capital and she'd be up the following week. When Dominique ended the call, she felt uplifted. And happy. Happier than she'd felt in a really long time.

She was shaking with nerves as she pinned a name badge on to the front of her white blouse. The staff at the country club were expected to wear navy suits and white blouses, and since Dominique already had an appropriate suit and plenty of blouses, she didn't need to borrow from the store. Her Louise Kennedy suit was well cut and very stylish, and she knew that she looked the part (Agnes told her so when she turned up), but she was utterly, utterly terrified that she'd make a bags of it and that they'd despise her for being completely hopeless.

By lunchtime, though, she realised that she knew what she was doing, and at the end of the day she sighed with relief.

'You'll be grand,' said Agnes. 'The guys like you.'

Which was true. Dominique had been happy and cheerful with everyone who'd turned up to play and had given them all a word of encouragement before they went out to tackle the picturesque course. She'd imagined that there would be a lot of members who were the terminally boring business types that Brendan knew and she was right. Golf seemed to attract them. But there were also younger men too, and a high proportion of women, including – Agnes said – a young girl with prospects of being a top professional. Glenmallon was a progressive club, Agnes added. No fuddy-duddiness. No rules about women only having associate membership. None of that rubbish.

Dominique admitted to herself that she would have taken the job even if Glenmallon's policy had been to keep women totally out of sight and never let them near the course. But she was glad that it was a nice place to work. And glad, too, that nobody had recognised her or looked at her twice as though they should know who she was. With her hair tied back (company policy) and wearing the navy suit, she blended in anonymously and perfectly.

Agnes had twigged who she was, although not until mid-afternoon, because that was the first time she'd heard Dominique's surname. Dominique had caught the glance of sympathy that Agnes had shot at her, but the other girl had then spoken cheerfully.

'It didn't click with me before,' she said. 'Why would it?' And then she added that she was glad Dominique was getting on with her life and that men were all bastards, except of course Richard, her husband, who was actually quite perfect.

Agnes left for her maternity leave at the end of the week, by which time Dominique felt totally on top of what she had to do and had also met Meganne and Sorcha, who both worked on the clubhouse reception desk too. They'd told her that they sometimes switched shifts and hoped she was OK with that, and she said that she was; they also said that they were delighted to have her working with them. Neither of them reacted to her name, which relieved Dominique. Not everyone, she told herself, gorged on news about missing businessmen and deserted wives.

Which she wasn't any more, she decided. She was a working woman. Her marital status was totally irrelevant.

Kelly came to Dublin the following weekend. It rained incessantly and they spent all day Saturday on the sofa in front of the TV, watching old movies. On Sunday they visited Evelyn and Seamus for dinner. Afterwards, as Dominique drove her back to the train station, Kelly said that it was very different to dinner at Lily and Maurice's but that Evelyn wasn't a bad cook.

'She's improved,' said Dominique. 'She was crap when I was younger.'

'Genetic, so.' Kelly grinned wickedly at her. 'You're not much better.'

'Get away with you, you ungrateful wretch.' Dominique laughed. 'What about my famous steak and kidney pie?'

'I'll give you a shout during the week,' Kelly promised as they pulled up outside the station. 'Let you know when I'll be back up again.'

'I have to work next weekend,' Dominique reminded her.

Kelly nodded and grabbed her bag. Then she kissed Dominique on the cheek.

'See you soon.'

'See you soon,' repeated Dominique as her daughter strode confidently away from her.

The following Saturday morning, she saw Paddy O'Brien. At first she didn't recognise him. He was dressed in a navy jumper and dark trousers, rather than the jeans and casual shirt he'd been wearing in the garden of Atlantic View. But he stood out among the group of men he was with, taller than them by far, and she suddenly realised who he was.

They were all going out to play a round, and it wasn't Paddy who came up to the desk but Paul Rothery.

'It's a free round,' he told Dominique. 'That man there . . .' he pointed to Paddy, 'is the course designer. So he's seeing how it's holding up.'

'Fine,' she said, her eyes following Paddy as he said something to one of the men in the group and they all laughed.

'Everything going all right?'

'Perfectly.'

It was as they were trooping through the atrium of the clubhouse that she saw Paddy looking at her, a faintly puzzled expression on his face. And then he smiled slightly and nodded in recognition and she nodded back at him. She was still surprised at seeing him here, still couldn't quite take in that the man who had moved into her house was now someone she might see at work. Although she'd hardly see him that often, she reminded herself. Cork was two hundred and fifty kilometres away, after all!

Four hours later, when they returned, he came over to the desk.

'I couldn't believe it was you at first,' he said.

'Bit of a shock, I'm sure.' She smiled her new efficient smile at him.

'What on earth are you doing here?' he asked.

'Working.'

'Here? Full time? You're living in Dublin now?'

She nodded. 'I needed to get away from Cork.'

'I understand.'

'How's Atlantic View?' she asked.

291

'It's a beautiful house. I haven't spent much time there, unfortunately.'

'Why not?'

'I've been travelling. The course design takes me abroad a lot. I was just seeing how this place has matured.'

'And how has it?'

He smiled. 'You'd want to ask the players that.'

Suddenly she grinned at him. 'I heard someone say yesterday that the fifteenth was nothing more than the jaws of hell biting you on the arse.'

This time he roared with laughter.

'And the par four sixth?' Her eyes twinkled. 'So not a par four apparently. A truly difficult drive with the dog-leg, and the green slopes too much.'

'My goodness, you've certainly learned a lot since I last met you.'

'To be honest, I'm just parroting what I hear.'

'So you haven't been converted?'

'I've played golf on the Wii in the games room,' she told him in amusement. 'I was terrible at it. But honest to God, Paddy, there are an awful lot of posers in this game.'

'Oh dear,' said Paddy. 'You've had plenty of experience of them?'

'Every time I went to a golf event before, it was always to hang around the sponsors' tent with Brendan. And it was so phoney and patronising that I couldn't really take to it. But I'm trying.'

'I'd be scared of my life to patronise you,' he assured her. 'And I bet most of the other guys would be too.'

'You'd be surprised,' she said darkly.

'Oh well, can't win 'em all.' Paddy's voice was philosophical as he glanced at his watch. 'Fancy a drink?'

Dominique looked at him in surprise.

'I can't,' she said. 'I'm working.'

'Fancy a drink when you've finished?'

She grimaced. 'I don't think I can do that. I'm not sure that Paul would be too pleased to have me quaffing pints with the punters.'

'I'm not a punter,' said Paddy. 'I'm the designer. And I'm . . . Well, we know each other, after all.'

'He'd probably like it even less if I was drinking on the premises with people I know. Not that we actually do know each other, Mr O'Brien.'

'I feel I know you,' he said. 'I'm living in your house, after all.'

'Your house now,' she said.

Paddy shrugged. 'Would you like to have a drink with me? If he doesn't mind?'

Dominique looked at him uncertainly. Their banter had been spontaneous. She'd been trying to be friendly and not let the circumstances of their last meeting bother her. And they hadn't really, because he'd been so friendly. But having a drink with him was different. Having a drink implied a friendship and who knew what else. The last time she'd worked somewhere and had a drink with a customer, she'd married him! She smiled to herself. She was being very presumptuous in thinking that Paddy O'Brien was being anything other than super-polite and kind to the woman whose house he'd picked up for a song.

'I can't have a drink,' she told him. 'I've got my car and it's a good forty minutes' drive back to the city. So thank you, but it's not possible.'

'And I'm supposed to be having dinner with the guys later anyway,' he said, 'so it's probably not a great idea. How about tomorrow?'

'I . . .'

'In town. You can get a cab.'

'Well . . .'

'Or somewhere close to you,' he said. 'So's you can walk. I don't mind.'

'I'm working tomorrow as well,' she said. 'Sorry.'

'I'm going back to Cork the day after,' said Paddy.

'Oh well,' she said.

'I would've liked that drink.'

'Maybe another time.'

'Indeed.'

She smiled her bright receptionist smile at him, and kept smiling as he walked away. Even if it had been possible, she wouldn't have gone for a drink with him. He was a nice guy and she was perfectly

293

entitled to go out with him, but she wouldn't. Not because she was still married to Brendan or in love with him or anything. But because she didn't want to get entangled with men, nice or not. She was doing fine on her own. And she didn't want any man, no matter who he was, messing with her newly constructed life.

Chapter 25

'The next time he asks you, you should go.'

Maeve was sitting in the living room of the Fairview house with her. They were both drinking hot chocolate and had been watching *Strictly Come Dancing* on TV. Dominique loved *Strictly*. It was comfort viewing.

'Leaving aside the fact that I don't want to get involved with any man, I certainly don't want to get involved with the man who bought my house,' she told Maeve. 'How weird would that be in my already weird life?'

Maeve grinned. 'Slightly odd, I agree. But Kev says that Paddy O'Brien is a really nice guy.'

'Don't care.'

'Ah, come on, Domino.'

Dominique picked a marshmallow from the bag in front of them and dropped it into her hot chocolate.

'What you're really asking me to do is move on, Maeve, but I can't.'

'At some point you have to.'

'Maybe. But I'm nowhere near that yet. I know Brendan's out there somewhere. I know that one day he'll get in touch . . .' She swirled the marshmallow in her chocolate with a long-handled spoon. 'I wake up every day and I think: this is the day. He'll phone. He'll text. He'll email me. Something.'

'What if he doesn't? What then?'

'He will,' said Dominique fiercely.

'But you can't live the rest of your life waiting,' said Maeve. 'You've got to—'

'Move on. And I have. But not the way you're suggesting.'

Maeve sighed. 'OK, what if we accept that you still don't have closure and you can't put it behind you yet. You still need to build up a network of friends outside of that totally dysfunctional Delahaye crew.'

'They're not dysfunctional.'

'Excuse me?' Maeve snorted. 'Your husband does a runner. Your brother-in-law has more issues than a weekly magazine. June is a narky cow. And Emma Walsh was, is and always will be a self-obsessed narcissist.'

Dominique laughed despite herself. 'Funny. I always thought it was my own family that was dysfunctional, what with the pictures of the Sacred Heart and St Dominic scattered around the place and my mother spending more time on her knees in church than anywhere else.'

'Admittedly the religious motif was a touch strong in your home,' agreed Maeve. 'But your parents are good-hearted.'

'Maybe a bit more so now,' agreed Dominique. 'But remember what they were like when we were younger. It was their way or no way, and I hated it.'

'Things change.'

'Over time. To be fair, my mother's been very supportive about Brendan. More than I ever expected. Although deep down I can't help wondering if she doesn't think I deserve what's happened.'

'Domino!'

'I know, I know. I'm being as self-obsessed as Emma. Who, by the way, is actually a nice person when you get to know her, even if we're currently not speaking.'

Maeve grinned. 'Never mind, you still have me.'

'Thankfully,' said Dominique. 'I'm sorry that we were out of touch for so long.'

'Partly my fault,' said Maeve. 'I was off doing my London thing. And when I came back, you were someone else entirely and it was like we had nothing in common any more.'

'But now that I'm a deserted wife, we have?' Dominique looked enquiringly at her friend.

'Now that you're back to being yourself, we have,' amended

Maeve. 'So listen to my advice. Chill out. Have a drink with Paddy O'Brien.'

'I just told you why I can't.'

'You're not betraying Brendan,' said Maeve. 'Maybe one day he'll show up, but in the meantime you've got to live your life.'

'Paddy might want more of my life than I can give.'

'Unless you go out with him, you'll never know,' said Maeve.

She thought about her friend's words a couple of weeks later when she answered the phone at the golf club and heard Paddy's voice.

'How's it going?' he asked.

'Pretty good,' she told him.

'I'm in town next Wednesday,' he said. 'Not coming to the club, though. Wondered if you fancy a drink in the city centre.'

Would it be moving on? Or would it just be a pleasant interlude in her isolated personal life? Until now she hadn't socialised in Dublin with anyone other than Maeve and Kevin. Understanding though they were, she didn't want to be a permanent gooseberry in their lives. But would going out with Paddy start something she couldn't stop? Or was she over-analysing a simple request for a social drink?

'OK,' she said after a pause during which he didn't speak at all.

'Great.' He sounded pleased. 'Seven thirty? Shelbourne?'

'That's fine.'

'See you then.'

She hung up. Her heart was thudding wildly in her chest. She felt like a teenager again.

She was late home on Wednesday, so getting ready for her drink consisted of changing out of her navy suit and into a pair of tailored black trousers and one of her many cream silk blouses. The sensual extravagance of the fabric caressed her shoulders and she knew that she didn't really want to return to buying cheap clothes. She had to treat the expensive ones she had as the investments she'd once told Brendan they were.

The sound of the doorbell ringing startled her. Surely Paddy hadn't decided to call to the house? He couldn't have. She hadn't even told him where she lived. She ran lightly down the stairs and opened the door. Greg stood outside. Her eyes widened in surprise.

'Hi,' he said.

'Hello.' She opened the door a bit wider and he stepped into the narrow hallway. His eyes narrowed as he took in the silk blouse and her loosely brushed hair.

'You're looking great,' he said.

'Thanks,' she said as she glanced at her watch.

'Are you going somewhere?' he asked. 'Is this a bad time?'

'Surprisingly, it kind of is,' she told him apologetically.

'Oh.'

'I'm sorry. It's just a stupid thing I've arranged.'

'Oh,' he said again.

'But don't worry,' she said. 'We have time to talk.'

He looked around as she ushered him into the tiny living room, taking in the half-filled bookshelves and the faded upholstery of the slightly too large sofa.

'Would you like tea?'

He shook his head.

'Why are you here?' she asked.

'Does there have to be a reason?'

She looked at him, her head to one side. 'No. But I'm sure there is.'

'I came up to town,' he said. 'I haven't seen you in a while. I thought it would be nice to drop by.'

'You should have called and let me know,' she told him.

'I never did before,' he reminded her. 'Whenever I came to Atlantic View, you were always there.'

'Not always,' she corrected him.

'I knew where you were, though,' he said. 'And now, the way things have changed, I don't.'

'Does that matter?' she asked. 'I thought we were OK.'

Greg leaned forward and put his face in his hands. 'I was never OK,' he said.

'Greg!' Dominique was taken aback by the utter desolation in his voice. She moved beside him on the sofa and put her arms around him.

'I'm such an idiot.' His voice was muffled. 'I always thought I was helping you. Now I realise that I was helping me.'

She said nothing as she continued to hold him against her.

Eventually he straightened up and she took her arms away.

'I'm sorry,' he said. 'I guess it's all been a bit fraught the last few weeks. Emma and her solicitors are being difficult, and all this divorce talk is doing my head in. I hate being away from home and from Lugh. I miss them. I miss everything. I hate the way it's all changed. And I hate not seeing you.'

'Greg . . .'

'Oh, I know. We're just friends. Close friends. Closer than any other friends we have. I understand that. I do. It's just that I feel everything is slipping away from me, and I want to grab hold of something and keep it but I can't.'

'I know how that feels,' she said. 'It's how I've felt every single day since Brendan disappeared.'

'It's how I've felt since Emma and I split up,' said Greg bleakly. 'Despite her . . . despite what . . . despite everything, I wish we weren't getting a divorce.'

'Have you told her that?'

'What's the point? She doesn't love me. She never loved me, Domino. Never.'

'That's not true.'

'It is, you know. Maybe she loved me for a time, but not for long enough.'

Dominique sighed. 'She told me she loved you. I'm sure she meant it. And saying that was unusual for Emma. She always had men falling at her feet and she never felt the need to tell them that she cared.'

'She thought there was something going on between you and me,' said Greg. 'And I kind of encouraged her to think that because—'

'Greg!' Dominique looked horrified. 'You *encouraged* her to think we were having an affair?'

'Not entirely.' He looked shamefaced. 'It was to punish her for Gabriel.'

'Why would you punish her for something that's entirely in her head?' demanded Dominique. 'For God's sake, Greg, wasn't it a very stupid and dangerous thing to do?'

Greg rubbed his face again and looked at Dominique through tired eyes. 'It wasn't . . .' He swallowed hard and was silent. He didn't speak for almost a minute. 'I've fucked up big-time,' he said despairingly. 'I'm not cut out for this revenge lark. I've lost everything and everyone.'

'No you haven't,' Dominique told him. 'There are plenty of people who care for you. Including me.'

'But you're going out.'

'No.' She shook her head. 'I'll stay.'

'Oh, Domino.'

He looked so miserable, so desolate, that she put her arms around him again. He held her close to him, and then he kissed her. On the cheek at first. Then his mouth moved towards hers so that he was kissing her on the lips. And she was kissing him back, thinking that it was nice to kiss someone again and that Greg's kisses were much softer than Brendan's. Which was how she'd always imagined they would be.

Her mobile beeped. She pulled away from Greg and looked at it. It was Paddy, saying that he would be slightly delayed but that he'd be in the bar as soon as possible. She pushed her tousled hair out of her eyes and tapped out a reply: *So sorry. Sudden emergency. Will have to cancel.* Then she turned to Greg. 'Maybe it should always have been us,' she said as she unbuttoned her blouse.

He fell asleep on the sofa. She observed him as he lay there, his expression, even in sleep, anxious. She was worried about him. She understood the feelings of helplessness and worthlessness that could take over your life. She remembered how she'd felt all those years ago; how a fog had seemed to creep into her brain and lethargy had taken over her mind and body. It had been awful. And it was Greg who had brought her out of it.

It had happened to Greg before, too. But she didn't know how to solve things for him as he had for her. She didn't know how to make it right. She couldn't pretend to him.

'I'm not in love with you.' She whispered it to herself. There had been a time when she'd thought, perhaps, she might be. Or that she could fall in love with him. It had been a guilty secret

300

she'd kept buried deep within her. And now she knew that it had been a figment of her imagination. That when she'd felt emotionally connected to Greg, it had been for a whole heap of reasons, none of which were that she was in love with him and wanted to spend the rest of her life with him.

She'd been attracted to Greg because she'd seen in him the same sense of unease with the world that she knew was in herself. Yet he always seemed to cope so much better than her, and she'd hero-worshipped him. But he wasn't a hero at all. Just an ordinary guy who was doing his best like everyone else. And his best hadn't turned out to be good enough.

Sometimes, no matter how hard you tried, it never would be.

He was awake and sitting at the kitchen table, a mug of coffee in front of him, when she came downstairs the following morning.

'Hi,' she said cautiously.

'Good morning, Domino.' He smiled ruefully at her. 'Thanks for the use of your sofa.'

'Any time,' she told him. 'How are you feeling?'

'A bit of an eejit, to tell you the truth,' he replied. 'I shouldn't have come here last night.'

'I'm glad you did. We needed to . . . we needed to have closure on something.'

'And have we?'

She nodded. 'I think so.'

She'd slid the silk blouse from her shoulders as she'd sat beside him the previous night, and then he'd unhooked her bra and held her breasts in his hands and told her that she was the most beautiful woman in the world. He'd kissed her again, and she'd kissed him back, and it had been passionate and exciting. She'd felt light-headed with Greg's arms around her and Greg's lips on hers. It had always been Greg, she'd thought then, not Brendan. She'd married the wrong brother, that was all. Greg understood her in a way that Brendan never had. Greg would always be there for her. He wouldn't walk out on her. Locked together, holding each other tight, she couldn't quite believe that this was happening, that she was swamped with desire and passion for the first time in ages.

301

Because although she'd tried to keep lovemaking with Brendan as exciting as possible, the truth was that something familiar could never be the same as something new. This was different, she thought. This was the way it used to be. This was exciting and forbidden and dangerous. And all of those things made her tremble.

Then, abruptly, Greg had pulled away from her and stared at her. She'd stared at him too. Her brother-in-law. The man she'd always cared about. The man she'd always depended on. Her friend. Her friend's husband. Her husband's brother. Suddenly she'd shivered.

He'd told her he was sorry, that he couldn't do this. Even though he wanted to, he couldn't. It was weird and strange and felt so wrong, even though he wanted it to feel so right. He couldn't believe he was saying this to her. He'd always wanted to do this with her. But it wasn't going to happen.

And she'd nodded slowly and said that she couldn't do it either but that she wished she could. She said that she was a bad, bad person to be thinking the way she was thinking, and he said no, she wasn't, because he was thinking that way too. He'd looked at her anxiously and then she'd leaned forward and kissed him again. But this time the passion wasn't there. This time it was the sort of kiss that she'd always given him.

She'd got up from the sofa and put on her blouse again and told him that he could stay the night.

Then she'd gone to bed alone. And she'd cried, even though she hadn't really known what she was crying for.

'Are you OK?' he asked now.

She nodded. 'It was all very . . .' She shrugged helplessly. 'Are we both all right?'

'I hope so,' he said. 'You're my friend, Domino.'

'So why?' she asked. 'Why did we nearly wreck it all?'

'I don't know. It seemed right, and then . . . then, in an instant, it just seemed horribly wrong.'

'The thing is . . .' she looked at him steadily from her brown eyes, 'it wouldn't really have been wrong. You're getting a divorce. Brendan has left me. There was nothing to stop us sleeping together.'

'That's what I said to myself,' he agreed. 'And yet . . .'

Dominique sighed. 'I know. I know. There are some things that are impossible to put out of your mind.'

'I'm very sorry,' he said.

'So am I.'

'I kissed you because I was still trying to get back at Emma,' said Greg.

'I know. I was trying to get back at Brendan.'

'Christ,' he said. 'What a pair we are.'

'Everything's turned upside down on us,' she told him. 'We're not thinking straight.'

'Totally,' he said. 'I came to you because I was so damn miserable. And I thought that maybe the two of us . . . Well, it seemed like a way it could all work out, didn't it? You and me. Together.'

'But it's not the right reason to be together. The feeling that someone – anyone – is better than no one at all. It wasn't the right reason for me to stay with Brendan, and it's not the right reason for us either.'

'You stayed with Brendan because you were afraid to be on your own? Is that the only reason?'

'It's the easy reason, isn't it?'

'You and Brendan had a good marriage,' said Greg. 'Everyone said so. The Dazzling Delahayes.'

'And you know that it nearly came unstuck,' she reminded him. 'Only I did my best for that not to happen. And to be fair to Brendan, so did he.'

'I envied you,' said Greg. 'I envied your closeness over the last few years.'

'We obviously weren't close enough,' Dominique pointed out. 'Otherwise he would have told me what was going on and he wouldn't have left like he did.'

She looked at the wedding ring she still wore on her left hand. 'I was always afraid that one day he'd leave. I just didn't think that it would turn out like this.'

Chapter 26

It was when she heard that Paddy O'Brien's divorce had finally come through that Dominique thought about throwing a party. It surprised her that the idea had come into her head, because a few months earlier she wouldn't have thought that she'd want to have parties ever again. But over the last few weeks she'd got to know Paddy better, and she'd suddenly thought that it might be a fun thing to do. That it would be something she'd enjoy. And, more importantly, something he'd enjoy too.

Paddy had laughed when she'd asked him. She was relieved that he'd laughed, because she'd been afraid that he'd call her interfering and refuse to have anything to do with it. But when she'd talked about it, a wide grin had split his face.

'You're a gas woman,' he'd told her. 'You really are. I'd never have thought of that.'

She was glad that Paddy thought of her as a gas woman. She'd worried, after she'd stood him up by text message, that he wouldn't have time for her at all. She would have understood perfectly if he'd refused to have anything to do with her. Especially if he'd known that she'd stood him up to almost make the biggest mistake of her life.

He'd replied to her text asking if everything was all right, but she hadn't responded until the following day, after Greg had gone home. She'd thought about texting again, but instead she phoned him. She told him that Greg had turned up in a very distressed state and that she hadn't felt able to leave him. She said nothing about sliding her silk blouse from her shoulders and kissing her brother-in-law. There was only so much understanding anyone who'd been stood up by text could take. But she did say that she'd always been very close to Greg and he'd helped her through some bad times, and that he'd needed her that night and she hadn't been able to leave him.

'I thought perhaps that Brendan had turned up,' said Paddy. 'I was worried about you.'

'I don't think Brendan's ever going to come back,' said Dominique. 'And even if he did, there's no need to worry about me.'

'You don't have to be so independent,' said Paddy.

'I do,' she said.

She thought she heard him sigh. And then he said he'd see her around sometime.

She hadn't expected much after that conversation. She felt that Paddy might see her as more trouble than she was worth. And she could understand that. She was sorry that she'd messed up whatever it was that had been between them, but she'd got to a point – one she'd never expected to reach – where having someone in her life wasn't the most important thing to her any more. She didn't value herself only because of the man she was with. It hadn't been like that before. She hadn't felt good enough being Dominique Brady; she'd had to be Domino Delahaye, wife of Brendan, to be worth knowing. But now she didn't care. She was still Domino, but she was herself again. And she was learning to live with that.

All the same, she was very pleased when a few weeks later Paddy turned up at the golf club and came over to the reception desk.

'What are the chances,' he asked, 'that you'll be able to meet me for a drink sometime within the next three days and that you won't be distracted by broken-hearted brothers-in-law or other stray people descending on your doorstep needing your sympathetic nature?'

She smiled. The sunny smile of her younger self, which made her cheeks dimple.

'Pretty good,' she assured him.

'Right,' he said. 'I have to warn you that I give up after multiple rejections, so if you don't make it this time, I'm not sure how many other invitations I can issue.'

'No matter who might arrive at my front door, I'll turn up,' she promised him. 'It doesn't matter what sob story they come up with. I'm all sympathised out right now.'

'I hope not,' he said. 'I like your sympathetic nature.'

Meganne, who'd been checking out the function room, walked back to the reception desk just as he left.

'Was that Paddy O'Brien?' she asked.

Dominique nodded.

'We haven't seen him here in over a year, and now twice in a few weeks,' she said. 'It would be great to think he'd drop by more often.'

'Why?' asked Dominique.

'Why?' Meganne's eyes widened. 'Haven't you seen that man? Would you not want him wandering around the place all the time? Those eyes! That bum!'

Dominique laughed.

'Everyone here loves him,' Meganne told her. 'He's great.'

'I'm meeting him for dinner.' Dominique hadn't intended to say anything, but she couldn't help herself.

'No way!' Meganne stared at her. 'But I'm *so* not surprised. Dominique Delahaye and Paddy O'Brien! You'll make the loveliest couple!'

Dominique laughed and told her that they were just going to dinner. It was no big deal. But she could see that her colleague thought it actually was.

They met in a small restaurant off Grafton Street, where the food was good and the atmosphere mellow. Dominique found herself instantly relaxed in Paddy's company and was amused by his stories about his career both on and off the course.

'I was devastated when I had to retire,' he said, as he placed his knife and fork on his now empty plate. 'I didn't know how I'd get on with my life. But it's worked out wonderfully for me.'

She nodded.

'And how's it going for you?' he asked.

'Better than I expected now,' she replied. 'Obviously difficult at first, but I suppose time does heal an awful lot. Except, of course, until I know what's happened to Brendan I can't really put it completely behind me.'

307

He nodded. 'I read a lot about it all. A lot about you.'

'Some of it true,' said Dominique wryly. 'And some of it complete shite.'

'The stuff about your depression after your baby?'

'Absolutely true. It was a long time ago, though. My baby is a stunning grown-up now.'

'The charity work?'

'The thing about charity work,' Dominique told him, 'is that so many people despise the women who are involved, and yet it does mean a lot.'

'And then all that stuff about your husband.'

'Hard to miss that, of course. Some of it true, but most of it bollocks.'

'Obviously I'd read a lot before I bought your house. Then after I met you, I read a lot more.'

'Can't blame you for that.'

'I know that the bits about you and him being in cahoots are rubbish.'

'There'll always be people who believe differently.'

'It must be very tough.'

Dominique thought for a moment. 'What's tough is knowing that Brendan is out there somewhere and that he hasn't even tried to get in touch with me. That he was able to walk out of my life without a second glance. I did so much to make everything right for him . . .' She smiled faintly at the querying look on Paddy's face. 'After my depression I was afraid he'd leave me and I wanted to be sure that he wouldn't. So I never interfered and I never asked the questions that perhaps I should have asked. I let myself get caught up in being Dominique Delahaye and I forgot that there's more to life than being someone's wife.' She shrugged. 'Realising that about myself was tough. And not knowing what he's doing is difficult, too. It's . . . it's like having a splinter in your finger. You can't ignore it. It hurts all the time. Brendan's still my husband, and not knowing hurts every day. But the rest of it – well, losing everything was scary, but in the end it wasn't everything because,' she grinned, 'you bought my furniture and I sold my jewellery and my car and so I ended up with some cash, which was a good security blanket. And then I got the job and, you know, it's all OK really. I was lucky.' She took a sip of her drink. 'He always called me his lucky charm.'

'He was lucky to have you,' said Paddy.

Dominique shrugged. 'Oh, I don't know. I think maybe I was the wrong person for him really. He needed someone stronger, someone to challenge him. I never did.'

'You're very hard on yourself.'

She shook her head. 'No. I have to be realistic, that's all. Anyway,' she took another sip of her drink, 'it must have been just as hard for you.'

'Huh?'

'When your wife left you. When you had to give up golf.'

She'd heard about the break-up of Paddy O'Brien's marriage from the girls at the golf club. It had been a whirlwind romance but the marriage had been nearly as short-lived. They had no children.

'Our lives were going in opposite directions,' he said. 'That's why our marriage broke up. Oh, and the fact that she was bonking her personal trainer. Those things tend to undermine a relationship.'

Dominique looked at him sympathetically.

'I was more gutted about having to give up golf, to be honest,' he admitted. 'I had dreams about being a top pro. Foolish dreams, probably. I was never that good. But in the end it's turned out OK, because I like course design and it's given me a good living.'

'Survivors, then,' she said. 'Both of us.'

'I'll drink to that.'

And they clinked their glasses together.

She met him for dinner again the following weekend. And again a few days later, when he invited her to a concert at the O2. She'd said she liked classical guitar, he reminded her, and this show was supposed to be wonderful. It was. She really enjoyed it. And enjoyed the drink with him afterwards.

Then he went to South Africa for a fortnight, and she missed him.

When Maeve asked about her relationship with Paddy O'Brien,

309

Dominique replied that it wasn't so much a relationship as a friendship. Maeve looked disgusted at that and said that Dominique didn't need a friend, she needed a lover. And Dominique laughed and said that a lover was the last thing she needed in her life right now. That love clouded your judgement. She was fine just the way she was.

But she kissed him when he returned from South Africa. It had been the first time since she'd married Brendan that she'd kissed someone other than a Delahaye on the lips. And she'd liked it.

'God Almighty, it's just a party. You don't need to renovate the whole house!' Maeve, who'd called to see Dominique the week before the party, looked around in her astonishment. Dominique had already asked if she minded her doing a bit of DIY around the place, and Maeve had said not at all, but if she was doing anything permanent to let her know, because she'd pay for it. At which Dominique had guffawed and told her not to be silly; that anything she wanted to do was for her own enjoyment.

'D'you like it?'

'It's lovely,' said Maeve as she took in the fresh paintwork and the delicate curtain poles over which Dominique had draped swathes of muslin. 'You have an eye for this, Domino. I wish I'd seen Atlantic View in real life instead of through the pages of glossy magazines.'

Dominique smiled. 'I wish you had too,' she said. 'It was the loveliest house in the world.'

'Do you miss it?'

'Sometimes,' admitted Dominique. 'But this is where I live now and I'm really happy here.'

'I'm glad to hear it,' said Maeve. 'We're happy having you as our tenant.'

'I'll try not to let the party-goers trash the place,' Dominique told her lightly, and Maeve laughed.

'I guess we're all well past our trashing days,' she said. 'Though you, Dominique Brady, have a glow about you that's knocked about ten years off you.'

'Rubbish.' Dominique adjusted the muslin.

'Totally glowy,' said Maeve. 'And all thanks to our Mr O'Brien.'

'I enjoy myself with him,' admitted Dominique. 'He's good fun.'

'About time you had a bit of fun,' agreed Maeve. 'I hope he's good in bed too.'

'Maeve Mulligan!' Dominique felt herself blush.

'Don't tell me you haven't slept with him yet?' Maeve looked astonished.

'We've been out together fewer than a dozen times,' said Dominique.

Maeve roared with laughter. 'Did Brendan have to wait that long before he struck lucky?'

'Of course not.' Dominique was flustered. 'But it's different with Paddy. Like I said, Maeve, he's a friend.'

'My poor delusional Domino.' Maeve smiled at her. 'Whatever you say, sweetie. Whatever you say.'

She could feel the old buzz of excitement returning as she arranged the party, even though it didn't need the kind of strategic planning that either her charity events or her work at Glenmallon called for. This was a much more casual affair altogether. Nevertheless, she wanted everything to be perfect. And that was why she had arranged for caterers and why she'd set up a spreadsheet to keep track of everything that needed to be organised, even though she really could've done it all in her head without breaking sweat.

She looked around her now. The house looked great and so did the back garden. Well, not a garden exactly. At the time the houses had been built, the paved area behind them would have been simply called a yard, but nobody used that phrase any more. Courtyard, she thought, although that implied something grander and bigger. The sun was slanting into it, keeping the flagstones warm, dappling through the bamboo grasses that had been planted in one corner and brightening the flowers in the raised bed along the side wall. Dominique had set up a bar beside the bamboos, hoping that the weather forecast, which had been for a clear fine day and an equally clear night, was accurate and that people could spend most of their time outdoors. Out of all of the parties she'd planned, she'd always felt the outdoors ones had turned out to be the most fun.

She peeped inside the fridge, conceding that the caterers had done a good job with the food and that the selection was excellent.

The wine chiller was really handy too. It was touches like that, Dominique thought, that made a good company great. If she'd still been part of the charity circuit, she'd have been giving them lots more business in the future.

The doorbell rang. It was Kelly, who was staying with her for the weekend, but who'd visited her grandparents for the afternoon. Dominique had invited Evelyn and Seamus to the party but they'd declined.

'Not because I don't want to come,' said Evelyn when she spoke to Dominique on the phone. 'But because your dad isn't really up to crowds of people any more.'

Dominique hadn't really expected them to come, but she'd been touched by her mother's excuse. Years ago, Evelyn would have considered a party to be a waste of time and money. Actually, thought Dominique, she probably still did, but at least she didn't say so out loud.

'How's it going?' Kelly's voice was exceptionally bright and cheerful.

Dominique knew she was cheerful because her latest boyfriend, Charlie, was staying with them for the weekend. Kelly had been going out with him for three months, and it was the most serious relationship she'd ever had.

'But don't worry,' Kelly had said to Dominique the first weekend she went away with him. 'I won't do anything stupid like get pregnant and ruin my life.'

'Getting pregnant with you didn't ruin my life,' Dominique told her calmly. 'My life is still a work in progress.'

'I didn't mean . . . I wasn't talking about you!' Kelly looked dismayed.

'I know you didn't,' said Dominique and hugged her.

'Has Charlie arrived yet?' Kelly asked her now as she came into the house. Her boyfriend hadn't come with her on the visit to Evelyn and Seamus but had gone into town instead.

'No,' said Dominique. 'So you've plenty of time to make yourself gorgeous for him.'

Kelly pulled a face. 'He has to love me for how I am,' she said, which made Dominique laugh.

'How were Gran and Gramps?' she asked.

'Oh, great.'

This time Dominique could hear a slight hesitation in Kelly's voice.

'What's up?'

'Up? What d'you mean?'

'Something's up. I can tell.'

Kelly sighed. 'How do mothers do that?' she asked irritably.

'Mammy radar.'

'Well I hope I get it too. I'll make my kids' lives a misery.'

Dominique laughed. 'So?' she said. 'Tell me.'

'Uncle Gabe was there too.'

'Gabriel?' Dominique was taken aback.

'He got back to Ireland yesterday.'

'You're joking.'

'Now why would I joke?' demanded Kelly.

'I know, I know. It's just an expression. What's he doing here?'

'Holidays, I suppose.' She looked at her mother thoughtfully. 'I know you and he had a bit of a falling-out,' she said, 'but why don't you ask him along tonight?'

'Did you ask him already?'

'No,' said Kelly. 'It's your party, Mum. But you haven't seen him in ages and it's silly to row.' She looked sideways at her mother. 'He did try to be kind to us after Dad disappeared.'

'I know,' said Dominique. 'It's just that Gabriel has his own way of doing things and it's not necessarily mine.'

'What did you row over?' asked Kelly.

'It was a tense time back then,' said Dominique, not answering the question. 'We all said things that maybe we shouldn't.'

'Was it to do with Aunt Emma?'

'Why would you say that?'

'I don't live in a bubble, you know,' said Kelly. 'There's always tension between you and Emma when Gabriel is around.'

'It's not important,' said Dominique.

'Well, will you ask him?' Kelly looked enquiringly at her mother.

'I'll call him,' said Dominique, although she had no intention of asking Gabriel to a divorce party.

Especially as Emma would be there.

*   *   *

She hadn't spoken to Emma in weeks, and she'd hesitated before sending her an invitation. Her contact with all of the Delahayes had lessened, although she still rang Lily once a week. But their conversations were usually short and not the rambling, gossipy ones they'd once had. She spoke to Greg, too, but ever since the night he'd called to her house, she'd felt the closeness she'd once had with him slowly erode. It seemed extraordinary to her that, after a night when they had been closer than ever before, this should be the case, but it was.

She both regretted and was grateful for the distance between herself and the Delahayes. They had been such a huge part of her life for so long that it was strange not to see one or other of them every day. It was particularly odd not to see Emma, to whom she'd been closest. As Emma had once said to her, they were both Drimnagh girls in the wilds of Cork. They should stick together. Not having seen her for a while had made Dominique less emotional about Emma, her marriage to Greg and her ill-defined feelings towards Gabriel. She was sorry that she'd rowed with her, and she wondered how the other girl was doing, still in the thick of things.

So when she was drawing up her guest list, she picked up the phone and called Emma, who was astonished to hear from her.

'A party?' she'd said. 'What sort of party?'

Dominique had explained it to her, and Emma, though at first surprised, had said that she'd love to come.

'I'll stay with Johnny and Betty in Rathfarnham,' she said, 'and get a cab over to you.'

'That would be great,' Dominique told her. 'It'll be good to see you again.'

'Yes,' said Emma. 'You too.'

Dominique didn't want her reconciliation of sorts with Emma to be tarnished by Gabriel's presence. She didn't know whether Emma and her brother had got in touch after the breakdown of her marriage, and part of her didn't want to know. But the idea of the two of them together in her house, either gazing soulfully at each other or lugging around past baggage, was too much.

She rang her parents' house, but Evelyn told her that Gabriel had gone out.

'He won't be back till late,' she said. 'He was meeting someone.'

'Say hello to him from me,' Dominique told her mother as she pushed the thought that Greg could be meeting Emma to the back of her mind. 'And I'll be in touch.'

She felt as though she'd been let off the hook. She'd done the right thing and still got the result she wanted. She hadn't had to talk to her brother and she hadn't had to invite him to her party.

Not my party, she reminded herself, as she went outside to look at the sky again. Paddy's party. Something I have to remember.

Kelly had compiled a party playlist and was transferring it to her iPod. Dominique left her to it and went upstairs to get changed.

She stood in front of the wardrobe, but she already knew which dress she was going to wear. It was the purple polka dot, the one she'd worn to the last party she'd ever hosted, on the day that Brendan had disappeared. She hadn't been able to wear that dress since – hadn't really had the occasion to either – but now it seemed the appropriate choice. She was back, and so was her dress. Not the same as before, of course. She wasn't Dazzling Domino any more. But neither was she the crying, despairing wreck that she'd been. She was still Dominique Delahaye, because she could never go back to being Dominique Brady. But now she was Dominique Delahaye on her own terms. With a new sense of who she was and what was important to her, and with her own friends and her own house and her own job. She was still working at the golf club. Agnes had decided not to return after her maternity leave, and Paul had immediately offered the full-time position to Dominique, who was both efficient and popular. He told her that she was one of the most organised people he'd ever met, which always made her smile, because in the last few months she hadn't really considered herself to be organised at all. More hopeful, she thought, hopeful that things wouldn't go pear-shaped, but prepared for the fact that they might.

'Hey, Mum, are you going to be in there for ever?' Kelly banged on the bedroom door. 'I thought I took ages, but you've been in there for hours.'

315

'Not hours,' said Dominique as she opened the door. 'It takes longer when you get to my age.'

'Oh, Mum,' breathed Kelly. 'You do look lovely.'

And Dominique smiled, because she'd taken a lot of time to become Dazzling Domino again, in how she looked if not in how she felt. The purple polka dot clung to her body (thinner now than she'd been the last time she wore it) and her dark hair fell in loose waves around her face. Her make-up was simple, but she'd blended, toned and concealed in all the right places so that her skin appeared smooth and flawless. Her big dark eyes were emphasised by her smoky eye shadow and long-lash mascara.

She was wearing sparkling drop earrings and a silver pendant with a small diamond stone. The pendant was the one piece of her expensive jewellery that she'd kept. She'd bought the earrings in Boots for less than a tenner.

'How do you do that?' demanded Kelly. 'How do you manage to look as though you've just stepped out of a magazine?'

'Depends on the magazine.' Dominique grinned at her. 'And, as you pointed out, it takes hours. Whereas you, my sweet, look totally fabulous and it only took you ten minutes.'

'A bit more than that,' said Kelly, who was carrying off a layered look in shades of green that Dominique knew she'd never be able to do herself.

'The thing about it is that you are young and therefore automatically lovely,' said Dominique. 'But then you always do look great, you wretch.'

'Dazzling Delahayes.' Kelly grinned at her.

'And why wouldn't we be?' asked Dominique cheerfully as she ruffled her daughter's hair.

It was a dazzling party, too. Maeve and Kevin arrived first, followed by some of Paddy's friends, and then Paddy himself turned up with a huge bouquet of flowers for Dominique, although she was hard pressed to find a place to put them. Charlie, Kelly's boyfriend, who was studying chemistry at college, was being barman for the day and enjoying himself hugely making cocktails for anyone who wanted.

The sun continued to shine, and even though the yard was now in shadow, the air was warm. Kelly's party playlist was in its mellow phase and so was excellent background music to the conversation that buzzed both inside and outside the house. I'm good at parties, thought Dominique as she listened to it. I really am. And a key part of it is getting the right mix of people. It's nice that I can do that with people who are my friends.

She looked around her. There were some notable absentees this time, like June, who'd once been at almost all her parties but who (unlike Emma) she simply couldn't bear to see again. Greg was looking after Lugh so that Emma could come, which meant there was no chance of him dropping by as he might have done in the past. Emma herself still hadn't arrived. But the major absentee, even though he hadn't always turned up to her events, was Brendan. And she couldn't help thinking about him. No matter how much she'd wanted this party to be different to all the others she'd ever had, the ghosts of the past were still with her.

I wonder if everyone's lives are this complicated, she asked herself as she handed around some of the nibbles that Lizzie Horgan had left earlier. I wonder if we all seem to be sailing along on the surface while we're madly bailing out the water underneath.

Emma arrived twenty minutes later. Although she looked as stunning as ever, her careful make-up couldn't conceal the fact that her face was thinner, which really didn't suit her.

'Thank you for asking me,' said Emma. 'I've missed you, Domino.'

'I've missed you too,' Dominique said as she hugged her fiercely. 'And look who's here!'

Emma pushed her way through a knot of people to where Maeve was standing admiring Charlie's antics with the cocktail shaker. The two girls squealed as they saw each other (although as Maeve told Dominique afterwards, 'God knows why I squealed, I was never that friendly with her') and both declared that the other hadn't changed a bit.

'I bloody hope I have!' Maeve cried, and Emma smiled at her.

Dominique was delighted that Maeve was able to take the strain of Emma from her shoulders. Even though she was pleased to see

317

her sister-in-law again, she knew that if she'd had to talk to her herself, they'd have ended up thrashing through Delahaye relationships, and that was something she wasn't interested in today. It was Paddy O'Brien's party, not an occasion for Delahaye drama. Meanwhile she was keeping her fingers crossed that Gabriel truly did have the good sense not to show up. It wasn't a day for the Bradys to have a go at each other again either.

She glanced at her watch. It was time to crack open the bottles of champagne. Dominique still loved the bubbling fizzy drink, which always seemed to promise better things. She went into the house and retrieved the bottles, then made sure that Charlie had the glasses ready.

She stepped up on to the small yellow-brick wall that enclosed the flowerbed and clapped her hands.

'Ladies and gentlemen,' she said. As she spoke, she remembered all the other times she'd done things like this. Always, perhaps, for better causes and better reasons, but none that were important to her personally. Not like today. Because even though they weren't celebrating her divorce, she was celebrating a sense of liberation that she hadn't realised she needed.

'Ladies and gentlemen, I'd like to thank you all for coming here today.'

Among the guests, she could see Emma leaning against the back wall of the house, Paul Rothery from the hotel and golf club beside her. Kelly and Charlie were both behind the bar, holding hands. Her neighbours from either side had been invited too, and were watching her. Maeve and Kevin were standing side by side. Paddy was smiling.

'We're here to celebrate a divorce,' she said. 'Which sounds a bit strange, given that it's the end of something rather than the beginning. Yes, it means that a marriage is over. And that's always sad. But it also means that two people have decided that they need to change their lives. And sometimes, hard as it is, we have to do that.' She cleared her throat. 'You all know that my life has changed a lot over the last while. Not all of it was welcome.' There was a small murmur of acknowledgement. 'But even when change isn't welcome, we have to get on with it. No point in trying to hide.'

She took a deep breath. 'So for helping me not to hide, I'd like to thank all of you who are here. Most especially Kelly, the best daughter in the world.'

Everyone applauded, and Kelly blushed.

'However, we're not here because of me.' She grinned suddenly. 'We're here to party! So I'd like to thank Paddy for not saying no to the idea of celebrating his divorce and for being a really good friend to me over the past few months. I hope he has a very happy time as an officially single man. I can vouch for the fact that being single again is not as bad as people make it out to be.'

Charlie began filling glasses with champagne.

'So!' cried Dominique when everyone's glass was full. 'Paddy O'Brien!'

'You do make me laugh.' Paddy handed her a glass of champagne for herself. 'Parties, speeches and stuff like that. You're good at it, though.'

'I thought it would be nice for you,' she said.

'It was.' He smiled at her. 'And you're right. I didn't think I needed to do anything to mark the divorce, but actually it makes me feel better inside. I think it could be that whole closure thing they talk about.'

She nodded. 'It's good to be able to close the book on things sometimes.'

'Which you haven't entirely been able to do yourself,' he remarked.

'One day,' Dominique promised him. 'Soon.'

'Are you going out with him?' asked Emma when Paddy disappeared into the house for a while.

'We're friends,' said Dominique. 'That's all.'

'Another male friend.' Emma shrugged. 'You do make a lot of them, Domino.'

'Not really,' said Dominique.

'Greg is still your friend, isn't he?'

'I talk to him occasionally. I haven't seen him in weeks.'

'Must be weird for you.'

'No,' said Dominique carefully. 'Greg was good to me when I

319

really needed it and he'll always be a friend, but I don't need to lean on him for support any more. Maybe I did that too much when he was married to you. If that's the case, I'm sorry. And maybe . . .' she hesitated and then continued, 'maybe we were closer than you'd expect. But he loved you, Emma. He told me that many times. I'm sure he still does.'

'Not enough,' said Emma.

'That's what he thought about your feelings for him,' Dominique told her.

'Huh.' Emma snorted.

'I'm truly sorry you've split up,' said Dominique. 'I'm sorry about a lot of things.'

'You've changed,' said Emma.

'And you're surprised by that?' Dominique smiled faintly.

'I guess not.'

'Can we get over everything?' asked Dominique.

'I can,' said Emma. 'Can you stop being so judgemental?'

Dominique had never considered herself to be judgemental before. But she realised that she was. Just like her mother had been. It was a shock to think that she was like Evelyn in any way.

'Yes,' she told Emma firmly. 'I can.'

Kelly changed the playlist and people started dancing.

'Come on!' Paddy grabbed Dominique by the waist. "Let's Twist Again".'

'I'm so, so bad at dancing!' she cried.

'Not a bother on you,' he assured her as he twirled her around in the lights of the Chinese lanterns.

'Way to go, Mum!'

They were all gathered around, watching Paddy and Dominique dance. She was hot and breathless, laughing as she twisted this way and that, lost in the sheer fun of the music and the movement.

She wished that this moment, when everything in her life seemed almost perfect, could go on for ever. But as the music stopped and she collapsed, exhausted, on to one of the wicker chairs in the yard, she knew that nothing was for ever.

* * *

320

After midnight there were only a few people left, and with the exception of Charlie and Kelly, who were still listening to music in the yard, they'd all moved inside the house. Kevin and Maeve were stretched out on the sofa. Paddy was slumped into one of the armchairs. Emma was in the armchair opposite. Dominique was in the kitchen making coffee.

She carried the tray into the living room and handed around the mismatched cups. Then she perched on the high-backed kitchen chair she'd dragged in to the living room.

'I'll sit there, you should relax.' Paddy got up from the armchair.

'It's OK,' said Dominique. 'If I collapse into that chair, I'll never get up again. My legs are falling off me from all that dancing.'

'You need to work on your fitness,' he said sternly.

'Yeah, yeah.' She grinned at him and then looked startled as the doorbell rang.

'I'll get it,' said Paddy. 'Maybe the neighbours have come back for more.'

Dominique chuckled.

'You have nice neighbours,' remarked Emma. 'Which is important when you're so close to them.'

Dominique wondered whether the comment was meant to be a jibe at her current impoverished state. But as she was mentally telling herself not to be so hypersensitive, Emma laughed.

'Remember the Johnsons next door to us?' she said. 'With their fake leprechauns in the garden and them blasting out the céili music at all hours? Drove my mother nuts.'

Dominique smiled. 'And poor Feena, who was so hopeless at Irish dancing but her mother made her go all the time?'

'Any girl less suited to ringlets I've never yet met. They were like demented springs bobbing around her head.' Maeve, who remembered the Johnsons too, nodded.

'Still,' said Dominique, 'with all that practice she might've ended up on *Riverdance*.'

The three girls chortled and Kevin said that they were being very unkind. And then Emma said that girls were unkind sometimes but other times they were good and supportive of each other. Maeve and Dominique smiled at her words.

At that moment, Paddy walked back into the room. Everyone turned to look at him. And at the man who had followed him.

He was tall and broad. His face was tanned, although there was a narrow white scar on his right cheek, and his dark hair was more grey than black. He was wearing a cotton shirt and blue jeans.

They all turned to look at Dominique.

They saw the shock on her face.

They saw her mouth his name.

'Hello, Domino,' said Brendan. 'It's me. I'm home. I'm sorry I was away so long. I hope you can forgive me.'

Chapter 27

She was trying to identify her strongest emotion.

Shock, she supposed. She'd always been convinced that one day she'd see him again, but she hadn't expected it to be today. She hadn't expected him to turn up out of the blue with no warning.

Relief was there too. Relief that he was finally home and that all the parts of her life that had been in suspended animation while he was away could now be tidied up. Although that also made her fearful, because she didn't know exactly how they would be tidied.

And anger. She knew that she was angry. Angry at him for the past and for the present, and angry for the future too.

Nobody was saying anything at all, and the silence would have been total if it wasn't for the muted sound of Katie Melua wafting in through the open patio doors. And then Kelly herself stopped it and stepped inside the house. She walked slowly across the room to him, her eyes never leaving his face. At last she stood in front of him. They looked at each other in silence, but it was Kelly who spoke first.

'I'm so glad to see you, Dad,' she said and threw her arms around him.

Dominique watched as he hugged her tightly in return. He held her for almost a minute before he loosened his grip on her and turned to face Dominique herself.

'You utter shit!'

It was Emma who spoke. Dominique turned towards her, startled, as in one fluid movement she got up from the chair and hit Brendan sharply across the face.

'Emma!' gasped Dominique.

'It's all his fault,' cried Emma. 'All of it. And he has the nerve to walk back in here as though nothing has happened.'

'I'm not trying to pretend nothing has happened.' Brendan rubbed the side of his face. 'I'm here to fix it.'

'Fix it!' Dominique spoke for the first time. Her voice quavered. 'You can't fix it, Brendan.' She stood up too, although her legs were shaking. 'It's too late for that.'

'I've made mistakes,' he admitted. 'Big ones. But I want to put things right.'

'I can't . . .' Dominique was light-headed. She staggered slightly, and then felt a hand steady her.

'Sit down,' said Paddy.

Brendan looked at him and his eyes narrowed.

'Who the hell are you?' he asked.

'This is Paddy.' Dominique remained on her feet, Paddy's hold supporting her. 'You've met Maeve before, although it was a long time ago. This is her partner, Kevin. And that . . .' she indicated Charlie, who'd followed Kelly into the house, 'that's Kelly's boyfriend.' She couldn't quite believe that she was making introductions as though they were all meeting up at a social event.

'Paddy?' Brendan looked at her and then at the other man.

'Paddy O'Brien,' said Paddy, not answering the question in Brendan's eyes.

Kelly was still standing close to her father. Dominique hadn't yet touched him.

'We should go, Domino,' said Maeve.

'If that's what you want,' added Paddy.

Once again Brendan looked at him questioningly, and once again Paddy said nothing.

'I'm sorry, Domino,' said Brendan. 'I know I messed things up. I know I let you down.'

Dominique realised that she wouldn't be able to speak without crying.

'You left us,' said Kelly.

'I didn't have a choice.'

'Of course you did.' It was Emma's voice. 'You had a choice to tell your family exactly what was going on but you didn't take it.

324

You had a choice to be honest but you decided not to be. You fucked up all our lives, Brendan Delahaye, and you have a damn nerve showing your face here – and making the dramatic middle-of-the-night entrance too! Was that so's Domino would be home? So she couldn't ignore you like she should?'

Maeve glanced at Dominique, who was still unable to speak.

'Emma, right now I think you should come with Kevin and me,' she said. 'I think Domino and Kelly need to be on their own with Brendan.'

Emma looked as though she was about to argue with Maeve, but then she shrugged.

'But we all need to know what's going on,' she said as she picked up her bag.

'You'll know,' said Maeve. 'Right now, though, Dominique and Brendan and Kelly need to be left to themselves.'

'Will you be OK, Domino?' asked Paddy.

She nodded wordlessly.

'Well, look, thanks for organising the party and everything.' He leaned towards her and kissed her lightly on the cheek. 'When you've got yourself together again, perhaps you'll give me a call.'

She nodded again.

'What made you come home?' Emma turned to Brendan again. 'Why now?'

'Emma . . .' Maeve looked at her impatiently.

'It was time,' said Brendan. 'I talked to Gabriel and I knew it was time.'

'Gabriel?' This time both Emma and Dominique were looking at him in astonishment.

'I was in Panama,' said Brendan tiredly. 'I met him there. He came back with me yesterday.'

Dominique was the only one who saw the sudden tightening of Emma's jaw.

'Come on, Emma,' said Maeve. 'Let's go.'

'Gabriel is here? In Ireland?' she said to Brendan, who nodded.

Maeve took her by the arm. 'Come on,' she said again.

Emma allowed herself to be led out of the room. Dominique watched them leave. Then she turned to face her husband. Kelly

325

was still standing beside him, and Charlie was now holding her hand. Brendan hadn't moved from the centre of the room. He was looking at Dominique anxiously.

'Say something,' he said at last. 'Say you forgive me.'

'Hey, Dad, we need to know a lot more about everything before we can do that.' Kelly's voice was suddenly hard, and she moved away from him, allowing Charlie to put his arm around her. 'We love you and we're glad you're back and you're OK, but you can't just waltz back into our lives and ask forgiveness when you haven't told us exactly why you left in the first place.'

'I left to protect you,' said Brendan.

'You should have *stayed* to protect us,' Kelly said.

'I couldn't,' said Brendan. 'It was better for you that I was away.'

Dominique caught her breath but still said nothing.

'It was a decision I had to make,' said Brendan.

'It was a bad decision to go away without saying anything.' It was Kelly who spoke again, while Dominique continued to stand silently, her hands balled into fists at her sides.

'I didn't have time. When things go wrong they go wrong very quickly. I had to get out of the country before I got caught up in all sorts of complicated investigations and God knows what else.'

'You mean before you were arrested?' Dominique's voice, when she finally spoke, was faint and shaky.

'People can be very quick to judge. And they can make mistakes. When it comes to money, they want to find someone to blame, and I was an easy target. I could only help myself by being away.'

'That didn't help us,' said Dominique.

'Believe me, it did,' Brendan told her.

'So why are you home now? And why didn't you call me yesterday?'

'We arrived late last night into Shannon. I didn't want to call you then. We only got up to Dublin this evening. Gabriel went to see your parents and I left my stuff at a B&B. Then I went to see my solicitor.'

'Before calling me.'

'I didn't want to *call* you. I wanted to see you.'

Dominique looked at the clock on the wall. 'You left it late.'

'I heard about the party.'

'So you decided to gatecrash at this hour? You're my husband, Brendan. You should have come to me before anyone.'

'Gabriel said—'

'I'm sure he said a lot of things, but right now I only care about what you're saying. And why you've come here.'

'I had to come home.'

'And did Gabriel persuade you that everything would be all right when you did?'

'No,' said Brendan. 'I know that I've caused a lot of trouble and that I can't fix everything. I know I've let down a lot of people. I can't rescue the company. But I can do my best to fix some things and restore our good name. And we can start again, Domino. You and me and Kelly.'

'What kind of fantasy land are you living in?' Dominique's voice trembled. 'Because of you we *have* no good name. Nothing you do can change what we've gone through over the last year. Nothing! It blew the family apart. It nearly killed your parents. Kelly and I . . .' She swallowed hard. 'You left us on our own, without a word, with no money . . . well, nothing worth speaking of.' He'd left the five grand, she remembered. Pocket money as far as he was concerned.

'I planned to get money to you,' he said. 'But it all got too complicated. I couldn't transfer it into our account because I was afraid that there'd be a court order to freeze it. I was hoping that I could sort everything out really quickly. Access cash I had abroad. But it turned out to be harder than I thought.'

'And in the meantime our house was repossessed and sold!'

'I didn't think that would happen,' said Brendan. 'I thought you'd get legal advice and that you'd be able to stall the banks.'

'How could I?' she demanded. 'They were breathing down my neck for money.'

'You could've cut a deal,' said Brendan.

'No I couldn't!' cried Dominique. 'I couldn't keep my house when everyone else had lost their savings or, even worse, their jobs.'

'I was shocked when I read about the house,' said Brendan.

'But you didn't phone. You didn't email. You didn't care.'

'Of course I cared! I was desperate to get in touch. You don't know how desperate. But I was afraid that if I called you I'd be traced and I'd be dragged back before I could get my hands on the money . . . Look, Domino, it was all very complicated and it needs a lot of explaining. I can't expect you to understand—'

'I understand that you left me to face the music,' said Dominique. 'I understand that perfectly well.'

'I didn't think it would be as tough as it was.'

'Well what the hell did you think would happen?' demanded Dominique. 'That everyone would just say, "Oh, it's fine, it doesn't matter"? We had an awful time. We took the flak for you.'

'And I feel terrible about it,' said Brendan, 'but the important thing—'

'Is that you left us,' Dominique told him. 'You walked out on us. We meant nothing to you.'

She turned away from him and left the room.

'That's not true.' Brendan's voice followed her as she went up the stairs. 'You're my family. You and Kelly. Everything I've ever done, I've done for you.'

Maeve, Emma, Kevin and Paddy had walked to Fairview Strand to hail a couple of taxis. Maeve, Kevin and Paddy were all travelling northwards; Maeve and Kevin to their house in Clontarf and Paddy to the Glenmallon Hotel, where he was staying the night. Emma was going to Rathfarnham, to her brother's house, and so in the opposite direction.

'We'll wait until you get a cab,' said Kevin as they stopped at the rank. 'I'm sure there'll be one any minute, but we don't want to leave you here on your own.'

'Thanks,' said Emma.

The four of them stood in silence. At last Paddy remarked, with studied casualness, that Brendan's return had been very dramatic.

'Typical Brendan,' Emma said. 'He always had a touch of the theatrical about him. That's why the media loved him.'

'And Domino?' asked Paddy. 'Was that why she loved him too?'

'No,' said Emma shortly. 'She loved him because he married her

328

when she was pregnant and rescued her from her religious maniac parents.'

Paddy looked startled and Emma shrugged, while Maeve shifted uncomfortably beside Kevin.

They were all relieved when a cab drew up at the rank.

'See you again, Emma?' asked Maeve as her old friend got into it.

'You never know.' Emma smiled suddenly, and Maeve remembered her then as the girl she'd once been, the prettiest girl in the class, and the most confident. 'Another old school reunion might be fun. Though not quite so exciting in the end.'

'Where to, love?' asked the cabbie.

Emma gave him the address. Then, sitting back in the rear seat, she opened her mobile phone. She scrolled through the list of names in her address book and stopped at G.

Then she pressed the dial key.

Greg Delahaye had spent the morning sailing. He'd sailed a lot when he was younger; he and Roy, his younger brother, had been members of the local sailing club. Brendan had never been interested in the water. Greg had enjoyed sailing, though he'd grown away from it even as Roy had made it his career. Now, since his separation from Emma, he was spending more time in boats again. Being out on the water calmed him. In the last few weeks he'd managed to douse the flames of anger and resentment that had been part of his life ever since the day that Brendan had disappeared (though that wasn't entirely accurate; he'd been full of anger and resentment ever since his teens, ever since the whole episode of his lost baby). He'd found that spending time on the sea was the best way to think things through. His brother's desertion had impacted on him in ways he hadn't expected. First of all there had been the shock at discovering he was missing. And then the shock of learning about the business. Then – and this was what Greg had struggled with so much – there was the sudden realisation that Domino was on her own. And that she was depending on him.

Greg knew that he had always been a little bit in love with Domino. He'd fallen for her the first time he'd seen her, getting off the train with Brendan, her pose confident but her eyes scared. She'd reminded him, if he ever needed reminding, of his teenage sweetheart, but she'd been a stronger, more determined person than Maria. He'd been attracted to her but he had never, back then, thought about her in any way other than as his brother's fiancée. It had been when she'd fallen into her depression that he'd been scared for her, wanting more than anything to help her. He'd been pleased and proud that he'd been able to help and that she knew it. And even though, at that stage, he was married to Emma, he liked to think that another woman depended on him too.

What is it in me, he wondered, that makes me want to feel needed all the time? Why do I look for unhappy women and try to fix whatever's wrong? Because that was what I did with Emma, too.

He'd asked Emma out because Domino's brother Gabriel was a priest. Greg didn't have time for priests, never had. Especially after what had happened with Maria. A priest had been to their home after she lost the baby. He'd spoken to Maria and somehow made her believe that what had happened had happened because she'd sinned with him. She'd hated Greg for it. And he'd hated the priest. So putting one over on Gabriel by asking out the girl who fancied him was a good thing as far as he was concerned.

Having a long-term relationship with her hadn't been part of his plan. But he had discovered that he liked being with her. She was fun and sparkly and quite unlike any girl he'd ever known before. The sense of sadness he'd got from her at the wedding, which he'd assumed was because of Gabriel, simply wasn't there. She'd dismissed what she'd said about Gabriel before, told him that she'd been silly, and then kissed him in a way that made him think she was telling him the truth. And he'd started to fall in love with her because she was a beautiful, fun girl and it was about time he started seeing beautiful, fun girls instead of having unsatisfactory one-night stands, which was how his love life had been up till then.

The relationship with Emma hadn't always gone smoothly. There were times when she was sweet and lovely and easy to be with and other times when she was impatient, prickly and difficult to talk to. When she was unhappy, he didn't seem to be able to cheer her up in the way that he was always able to cheer up Domino. He felt

330

guilty about that, because he should surely be able to make his wife smile. Yet in some ways she was a more complicated person than his sister-in-law. Domino was easy to please. Emma was definitely a more high-maintenance woman. But he loved her.

He'd been delighted when she finally got pregnant, but what should have been an exciting time for them had coincided with her mother's illness and with her getting in touch once again with Gabriel Brady. For spiritual comfort, she'd told Greg at the time, not that he'd ever believed that, not even for an instant. He'd asked her about her feelings for Gabriel, and she'd smiled at him.

'My feelings for Gabriel,' she replied calmly, 'are the same as yours for Domino.'

Which always bothered him.

He'd never really thought very much about his feelings for Domino. Never put them into context. Never wondered how Emma saw them. If she ever asked him, he always used to say that he felt a bit sorry for her, rushed into marriage to Brendan, having the baby, everything being so difficult, and then, suddenly, thrust into the spotlight, which he didn't think she liked very much. (Emma would snort at that and say that he was wrong. Domino was an exhibitionist, she always had been.)

When he'd gone to Domino's house in Fairview, it had been with the intention of making love to her. He'd been sure that she would want it too. He'd thought that he was entitled to sleep with her. Emma had left him, after all. Brendan had left Domino. It seemed to him that they themselves were the one constant in a changing world.

But it hadn't happened. He still couldn't understand it. It wasn't because he'd had any qualms about getting into bed with her, but at the precise moment when Domino slipped her blouse from her shoulders, he hadn't wanted to make love to her at all. She had been, he realised, his fantasy woman. Perhaps his revenge woman too. Maybe she felt the same way because she hadn't wanted to make love to him either. The decision had somehow surprised both of them.

But not making love to Domino wasn't what made him still miss Emma. He had missed his wife from the moment she'd left him.

He knew that he was as much to blame as her, because he'd pushed her into leaving. He'd made it almost impossible for her to stay, what with his jealousy and his sense of martyrdom and all the things that he felt made him an especially sensitive person but didn't really. He wanted to blame Emma and Gabriel for what had happened to his marriage, but the truth was he could just as easily blame himself.

He shook his head. He'd always believed that one day he'd become a mature and responsible adult who knew exactly what he wanted from life and worked hard to achieve it. He thought he'd be like his own father. But he was a mess, really. He hadn't succeeded at anything.

'Dad?'

Greg had been gazing back at the land as he tried to bring order to the thoughts that competed for space in his head. But now he turned his attention to the dinghy and to his son, who was sitting watching him, an impatient expression on his face. And when Greg looked at Lugh, he knew that he was wrong about one thing. He had succeeded at least in having a great kid.

'Sorry, what?' he asked.

'You're not listening to me.'

'I know. I should've been. What's up?'

'Can we go a bit faster?'

'Faster?' Greg grinned at him.

'Yeah, Dad. When I go out with Uncle Roy, we zip around the place.'

'You mean your Uncle Roy is a better sailor than me?'

'He's the captain of a ship,' said Lugh solemnly.

'True,' Greg acknowledged. 'I'm only a pale imitation.'

'Ah, you're all right,' said Lugh.

Greg laughed and adjusted the trim so that they were skimming across the water. Whatever happens with Emma, he thought, I always have Lugh. And that's a good thing.

He loved his son. He loved being a father – even if he was now a part-time fixture in Lugh's life. That was one of the main issues in his divorce negotiations with Emma. He wanted to spend as much time as possible with his son. Emma was currently being difficult about it. He knew that it was just a ploy, but it was wrong that time with their child had become a negotiating tool.

He'd been happy when Emma said that she was going to Domino's party and that she'd be leaving him to look after their son. He'd also had to admit to being slightly miffed that Domino had asked Emma and not him. But the important thing was that he now had time to be with Lugh, and he was determined to make the most of it.

And so, after sailing together, they went for a burger and chips in Lugh's favourite burger place, and then to the shops, where Greg bought him a new waterproof jacket and Lugh hugged him and told him that he loved him, which made Greg feel calmer than he had in ages. They went home happy and contented together, Lugh almost asleep from the exertions of the day. Greg had agreed to look after him at the family home rather than at his apartment in the city centre, and although it was difficult, at first, to go inside and remember that this had once been his home too, he felt warm and secure sitting in the familiar living room with his boy.

It had been a good day, he thought, after Lugh had eventually gone to bed (much later, Greg knew, than normal; his son had got his second wind once he stepped inside the door) and he'd sat down in front of the TV to watch the news. He and Emma needed to get together and resolve their differences in a less aggressive way then they were doing now. He knew that their solicitors were just doing their best and earning their money, but the truth was that no matter how things had turned out, he and Emma both cared for Lugh. They'd managed to arrange this weekend without having a major fight, so surely they could sort out the rest of their lives the same way?

Probably being a bit optimistic, he told himself as he opened a beer. But you never knew.

His phone rang. He saw Emma's name and sighed. Checking up on me, he thought. Doesn't trust me. Typical Emma.

'Hi,' he said as he answered it. 'Everything's fine. Lugh's in bed, we had a great day.'

'I'm glad,' she said.

'Good party?' he asked.

'Until the end,' said Emma. 'Because that's when Brendan showed up.'

There was silence for several moments.

'Greg?' said Emma.

'You're not serious!'

'Very serious,' said Emma. 'And I suppose that now he's back, there's more shit heading in the direction of the fan. Particularly when they hear about it in Cork. So I think you'd better be prepared.'

Emma closed her phone, then opened it again. This time, when she scrolled through the Gs, she selected Gabriel Brady's number.

Chapter 28

Kelly and Charlie were in the back yard again. Despite the fact that the night air was warm, Kelly had pulled on a black jumper with overlong arms and was hugging it tightly around her body. Charlie's arm was around her too, keeping her close to him.

'Are you OK?' he asked after they'd sat in silence for over a quarter of an hour.

'Yes.'

'Are you sure?'

She pulled the jumper even tighter around her and nodded.

'Because I know this has been a shock for you.'

Kelly inhaled deeply and then exhaled again. 'No more than the shock of him leaving in the first place,' she said. 'No more than the shock of learning that the company had gone bust. No more than the shock of having to sell our house. I'm used to shocks by now, Charlie. It's just a shame that it's always my dad giving them to me.'

He squeezed her shoulders sympathetically.

'I love him,' said Kelly. 'But I'd quite happily kill him.'

'Your mum probably has first dibs on that,' said Charlie.

'She loves him too.' There was resignation in Kelly's voice. 'She'll forgive him. She always has before.'

Domino sat on the end of the double bed while Brendan stood near the window. She felt it was somehow inappropriate for him to be in her bedroom, yet she didn't want to talk to him downstairs, not while Kelly and Charlie were still there. So she hadn't asked him to leave, and he seemed to dominate the small room – she'd forgotten how big and how strong he was. Handsome too, although his much greyer hair was disconcerting.

'Explain it to me properly,' she said.

'I made a mistake,' he told her.

'Everyone makes mistakes,' she said. 'They don't run away because of them. And if you'd stayed – well, maybe things wouldn't have worked out too badly. It's been a tough time for a lot of businesses, you know.'

'I'm not in the too-big-to-fail category,' said Brendan. 'I would have got roasted. And it wasn't just a question of falling prices.' He explained that as various parts of his businesses had come under pressure he'd moved money around them even though all he was doing was robbing Peter to pay Paul. And that some of the cash hadn't been properly accounted for. Like the Barbados money which hadn't all gone into the development project there.

'OK, OK, I agree it's complicated!' cried Dominique. 'And you didn't feel able to stick it out.'

'I couldn't bear it,' he confessed. 'It was like my whole life was being destroyed in front of me. I was worried about us, our future. I didn't know what to do. I had money overseas but not easily accessible. I knew that the guards would get called in and I was afraid that if they started poking around I'd have even more problems with the overseas money. So I left. To protect our assets and to protect you.'

'You mean, you sneaked home in the middle of the night, took your stuff and went. Like the proverbial thief in the night. And left us totally unprotected.'

'Domino . . .'

'You'd planned it for a while,' she continued. 'Because all your things were gone and there was no way that you'd just decided what to do that day.'

'I knew it was getting dicey. I wanted to be prepared.'

'And you didn't think for one second to confide in me? To tell me what was going on?'

'I intended to,' he said. 'Originally, I planned . . . well, I planned for us all to go away together until I could sort things out. You and me and Kelly.'

She stared at him, her eyes wide open.

'Away? Where?'

'I thought we could go to the apartment in France. You two could live quietly while I tried to liquidate my investments.'

Dominique shook her head slowly. 'People thought you were in the Maldives,' she said. 'They thought we were going to join you there. There was stuff in the papers about your champagne lifestyle. Oh, and some of them thought there was another woman too.'

'You should know better than to believe that,' said Brendan.

'I don't know what to believe any more,' she said tiredly. 'The guards came to our house with a search warrant. They might still arrest you.' Her brown eyes creased with worry.

'That's what I'm hoping to avoid,' he told her.

She rubbed her forehead. 'Did you know what was happening to us when you left?'

'Not at first. Then I was able to Google it and I saw the news reports.'

'Right. So you read what people were saying.'

'I knew it wasn't true.'

'They suspected me and Kelly of being in cahoots with you. Of planning to run away and live an exotic life of luxury based on money you'd stolen. It all sounded quite glamorous, actually. There was nothing about hiding out in France while you tried to find the money you'd stolen.'

'I didn't steal it.' Brendan was suddenly angry. 'I made a mistake and it went wrong.'

'You took it from one company and put it into another and you shouldn't have.'

'But I didn't do it for myself!' he cried. 'Can't you understand that? All I wanted was to make a profit for everyone. And when it was going wrong, I needed to protect our interests. That's why I went to Panama. That's where I'd invested most of our personal savings.'

'Why in God's name did you put it in Panama?' she asked. 'Why not closer to home?'

'Well . . .' He looked guilty.

'What?'

'It was from our early days,' he told her. 'When I was still mainly doing small work. Taxes in this country were scandalously high, and I wanted to . . . to hide a bit of money.'

'Oh, Brendan!'

'Everyone was doing it,' he protested. 'You know that. All I did was do some work for cash. Off the books.'

'You never did that when *I* was keeping the books,' she said.

'No.'

'You wouldn't have done it if I'd stayed keeping the books.'

'It was practically obligatory back then,' he told her. 'I never would have made any money otherwise. And don't get on some kind of moral high horse with me, Domino. You liked the life we had.'

'Yes, but—'

'Everyone was doing it,' he repeated. 'They still bloody are – you see it all the time, whether it's politicians or businesspeople, working the system, making some money.'

She sighed. He was right. She remembered the days of the black economy, where more work was done outside the system than inside. She just hadn't realised that she was part of it.

'And so have you got this money now?' she asked. 'Are you going to be able to pay everyone back?'

'It still isn't that simple,' he told her.

The money had been invested in high-risk funds and the stock markets had fallen sharply, wiping a lot of it out. He'd hoped to use this money to bail out the Barbados investors, but he couldn't.

'When all this happened, I was close to losing my mind,' he told her. 'Regardless of what happened to the companies – and I was devastated by that – I couldn't bear to think that people I knew, people who were friends, had lost money. I hadn't thought that could possibly happen.'

'You were always too damn optimistic,' she said.

'And then I was mugged. Properly mugged.' His hand went to the scar on his face. 'My own fault. I was walking in a bad neighbourhood and I was jumped on. The same thing that could happen in any city, I guess. And I stupidly tried to resist, which made things worse.' He took off his shirt and showed her another scar on his back.

338

'But in the end I was lucky. Something happened to disturb them. They took my wallet, my cards . . . I was left with nothing.'

Dominique wasn't sure what to say.

'I'd never felt so down in my life,' Brendan continued. 'I couldn't believe it had come to this. I was Brendan Delahaye. I was a successful businessman. And here I was, lying on my back in the mud in Panama City with blood pouring down my face like some clapped-out nobody. It was like I'd stepped out of my life.'

'What happened then?' She stared at the scar, wanting to touch it, to trace the line of it on his face.

'I eventually made it to my hotel. I had some money in the safe there – well, I wasn't using credit cards, because I was afraid they'd be traced. I sat in my room and flicked through this magazine, and I saw an article about UNICEF and a water project in Paraguay. There was a picture of Gabriel. And contact details. So I phoned him.'

Dominique said nothing.

'I told him what had happened and he said he'd come straight away. He was a great comfort. I said that I was in Panama to get money back I'd invested. That a lot was lost but that some was tied up in . . . well, complicated accounts. That I needed to stay to work things out. And Gabriel told me I was wrong. That to work things out I had to come home.'

'Gabriel!' Dominique shook her head at Brendan's words. 'Gabriel persuaded you to come back? What made him think he could persuade you to do anything?'

'I like Gabriel,' said Brendan defensively. 'He helped me to get my head together.'

'Converted you to the whole happy-clappy I'm-a-good-person routine, did he?' Dominique was scathing. 'He can talk, when he's probably responsible for wrecking your brother's marriage!'

'What are you talking about?'

'Emma and Greg are getting a divorce,' she told him.

Brendan looked at her in shock.

'Well it's not surprising. Gabe practically instigated it, what with all the hands-on comfort he was giving Emma when you left.'

'Why would he have to comfort Emma?'

'Because our fucking lives were destroyed by you!' It was the first time she had ever sworn at him. 'Don't you get it? You threw a grenade into the heart of our family and walked away. Everyone else got caught up in the explosion. June and Barry are separated too – or at least they would be if they were able to sell their house. June blames me completely and utterly for everything, because she thinks it's all down to my Dazzling Domino lifestyle, which I made you give me! Your father has hardly left their home since the day it happened. Lily has to make a big effort to go out because she's so ashamed.'

'She has nothing to be ashamed about. She did nothing wrong.'

'How thick can you possibly be?' demanded Dominique. 'You talked about it yourself. Our good name. Well, for people of your parents' generation, that's probably the most important thing they have. How d'you think Lily feels when she goes out and knows everyone is talking about her son? Are you just totally insensitive? Are you?'

'Of course not.'

'You used to understand!' cried Dominique. 'You used to see every point of view. You were the one who told me not to argue with my parents, to try to get on with them. But you left it all behind, Brendan, in some mad rush to be the most successful, the richest, the . . . oh, I don't know.' She slumped suddenly, the fight draining out of her. 'We all would've stood by you. But you left.'

'You mean you're not standing by me now?' he asked. 'You're going to head off with your . . . boyfriend? That's what he is, is he? That guy who was going to call you or whatever?'

'Oh, give me a break.' Dominique could feel the tears beginning to roll down her cheeks. She didn't know whether they were tears of anger or of sadness. 'You have a damn nerve waltzing back into our lives without any warning and expecting us to take up where we left off.'

'I'm not expecting that,' said Brendan. 'Of course I'm not. But you're my wife, Domino, and we've been together a long time. We work well together. The Dazzling Delahayes. We can make it work again. I know that I put you through hell, and I'm sorry about that. I didn't think, though, that you'd fall into the arms of the first guy who came along.'

'Don't be stupid.' Anger, thought Domino. That was what the tears were. She was angry with Brendan. Angrier than she'd ever been before, even when she'd found out about Miss Valentine. 'I didn't fall into anyone's arms. Paddy is a friend, that's all. And I needed friends because you weren't around to help me.'

'I thought you'd be able to work things out,' he said. 'I thought you'd get decent legal advice and you'd be OK in the house and that you'd manage until I came home again.'

'Well you thought wrong,' retorted Dominique. 'I did get legal advice, but I couldn't stay in the house. And I *have* managed, though maybe not the way you thought.'

'I got everything wrong,' said Brendan blankly. 'You, the house, the business. I thought I knew what was best. And I thought Googling would keep me in touch. I thought if I saw all the reports I'd know what was going on. But I was wrong. Completely wrong.'

'Yes,' said Dominique. 'We finally agree on something. You were.'

Emma asked the taxi driver to go to Drimnagh instead of Rathfarnham. She got out of the cab, paid the fare and then stood for a moment on the pavement outside the Brady house. The last time she'd been here had been the time she called around dressed like Madonna, hoping to persuade Gabriel Brady that there were far better things for him to think about in life than being a priest. He'd been totally impervious to her charms then. She flushed a little as she remembered. She'd thought he'd like how she looked, but he'd told her, in his quiet, reserved voice, that it was too trashy for her. She'd been hurt and embarrassed by his comments and for the first time in her life had asked herself why she was actually bothering with Gabriel Brady. And yet, even as she'd gone home, angry with him, she'd been wondering when she'd see him again. Besides, he'd been right. Afterwards she'd toned down the make-up, invested in skirts that came closer to her knees (though not too close; she was proud of her shapely legs) and tops that hinted at more than they actually showed. Her style had become more subtle. And that, in the end, had been what had snared Greg Delahaye.

341

He'd said it to her once. He'd told her that she was the most sophisticated, elegant girl he'd ever met. A proper grown-up, he'd called her, a comment that made her feel good inside. Gabriel Brady had always treated her as a child. Greg knew that she was a woman.

The front door of the Brady house opened and she saw Gabriel framed in the orange glow of the hall light. She walked slowly up the pathway.

'Hi,' she said.

'Emma.' He looked awkwardly at her. They hadn't seen or spoken to each other since the day in Lily's garden when she'd argued with Dominique.

'Are Mr and Mrs Brady in?' She didn't want to see Domino's parents.

'It's very late,' Gabriel reminded her. 'They've gone to bed.'

It seemed odd to follow him into the house. It was like stepping into the past. Her heart beat faster. She hoped that Mrs Brady wouldn't come downstairs to see what was going on. She'd always been a bit scared of Dominique's mother.

'So,' she said as she sat at the kitchen table, remembering all the times she'd sat there before, not really interested in talking to Dominique but hoping to seeing her brother, 'you brought Brendan back.'

'He needed to come home,' said Gabriel. 'He was miserable.'

'How did you find him?'

'He found me.' Gabriel explained how Brendan had discovered his whereabouts in the magazine.

'That must have been a shock.'

'Yes,' said Gabriel.

'Why wasn't he arrested when you got home?'

'There isn't a warrant out for his arrest,' said Gabriel. 'As yet, there isn't a criminal case against him. And there may not be. He's managed to get some funds together, although I don't know how much. He just didn't know the best way forward.'

'Was it your idea he should turn up tonight?' asked Emma.

'He'd planned to call on Domino today, and then I learned about the party from Kelly. So I told him to wait. But Brendan thought she'd be in a better mood after a party, more inclined to listen to him. He said she always liked parties. To be honest, I think he was a bit surprised that that was what she was doing. He was hoping she'd be sitting in, on her own.'

'Waiting for him?' Emma made a face.

'I suppose so.'

'Men are such fools,' she said. 'You all think that's what we do. Sit around and wait for you.'

'That's a bit harsh.'

'It's bloody true. We have lives, you know.'

'I know that.'

'Domino has done great things without Brendan. She's got a job and a house and a boyfriend.'

Gabriel looked surprised.

'Oh, yes,' said Emma. 'She's found someone new. Paddy. I met him tonight. He's lovely.'

'I don't believe she has a boyfriend.'

'Why? You don't think she's attractive enough?'

'Brendan's still her husband and she loves him.'

'Gabriel! Brendan left her. He betrayed her. He shamed her. Why the hell would she still love him?'

'She's always loved him,' said Gabriel, 'because he stood by her.'

Emma shook her head. 'Is it a male thing to think that just because you once did the right thing, a woman will forgive you for every wrong you do in the future?'

'Forgiveness is important,' said Gabriel. 'It's the most important thing of all.'

The atmosphere between them changed suddenly. Emma said nothing, but looked down at the table, her long chestnut hair hiding her face.

'And between us?' she asked eventually. 'Who has to forgive whom?'

'I'm sorry.' Gabriel spoke again and she looked up. 'That was unfair of me, Emma.'

'Greg and I are getting a divorce,' she told him abruptly.

'Why?'

'Because he doesn't love me,' she said. 'It doesn't really matter, you see, how I feel about him. He doesn't love me. And I can't blame him for that.'

343

'Emma . . .'

'He tried to forgive me.' She swallowed hard. 'He tried very hard. But it was asking too much.'

'Forgiveness is—'

'Oh, don't tell me how important forgiveness is again. You're talking about theoretical forgiveness. It's a lot more difficult in real life.' She took a tissue out of her bag and wiped her eyes. 'God knows, I've never really forgiven him for caring as much as he does for Domino. So why the hell would he forgive me for sleeping with her brother?'

Emma Delahaye had slept with Gabriel Brady when she was pregnant with Lugh. It had happened on one of her first visits to Dublin to see her mother. Following the lunch with Dominique when she'd told her about Maura's illness, and having got Gabriel's phone number from her, she'd called him and he'd been sympathetic and understanding. He'd told her to tell him the next time she was coming to town because, he said, he'd make a trip too, to see her. She could do with extra support.

She knew that it was Gabriel's job to be supportive and caring, but it was balm to her ears to hear him sound so concerned on her behalf. Of course, Greg was concerned about Maura too, and always supportive, but at that time much of his concern seemed to focus on the fact that she was pregnant. She shouldn't worry too much in case it affected the baby. Getting stressed wasn't good for their unborn child. He never seemed to think that getting upset or stressed wasn't good for her!

She'd phoned Gabriel two weeks later. They'd met at the Clarence Hotel, after Emma had spent the afternoon with Maura. She had reserved a room there because she hadn't wanted to spend the night in her parents' house. Later, she'd wondered if she'd always planned to take Gabriel to it.

She'd used it to get ready to meet him, changing from her comfortable Levis and ballerina pumps into a slim-fitting dress in her favourite shade of lilac and delicate high heels on her feet. Even with the dress's tailored fit she had no trouble getting into it, because she'd barely put on any weight at all so far in her pregnancy. Her stomach was rounder, she knew, but a casual glance wouldn't have given her away. Of course in the end Gabriel had got a good deal more than a casual glance at her, but as he hadn't a clue about naked women, he'd no idea that she was pregnant either.

He'd walked into the hotel, where she'd been sitting at a table sipping plain water, because she'd suddenly gone off both tea and coffee. She'd put her hair up, securing it with an amber clip, knowing that an up-do made her appear even more slender and elegant. Gabriel Brady was a sucker for the slender, elegant look. Maybe, thought Emma, it was because it was more in line with the original Madonna rather than the singing superstar version.

Gabriel had gone for a different look too. He wasn't wearing his priest's collar but was dressed instead in jeans and a checked cotton shirt over which he wore a brown leather jacket. Emma was surprised by his casual appearance.

'People treat you differently when you're in uniform,' Gabriel explained. 'It's nice to be an ordinary person from time to time.'

'You look like a total rock star,' she said.

He laughed. 'When you said the Clarence, I thought we might bump into some of the U2 gang.'

She grinned at him. 'You'd fit in perfectly. Well, maybe you're a little too clean cut for Bono and the Edge, but you look great to me.'

'And so do you,' said Gabriel. 'You're absolutely glowing, Emma. I'm glad that you're not getting too stressed about your mum.'

She told him about Maura's recently confirmed diagnosis and his eyes softened.

'I'm sorry,' he said. 'You must actually be very stressed indeed. You've got to remember to take care of yourself, Emma.'

'You never know how things will turn out,' Emma said. 'I'm staying positive for Mum's sake and for mine.'

'Good for you.'

It was then that he put his arm around her. Then that she felt the touch of his fingers on her bare arm. And then that she knew, without a shadow of a doubt, that she wanted to bring him back to the bedroom overlooking the Liffey. She felt sick with the desire of wanting him, of always having wanted him. She knew that what she felt was wrong on more levels than she could count, but she couldn't help herself. From the moment she'd first set eyes on Gabriel Brady, he'd been the one she wanted, and the one she couldn't have. Today, for the first time, she thought that maybe she could. And it wasn't just about the sex, she told herself. It was about how he made her feel. Gabriel saw her as a person to be cherished; not a person to be cherished just because she was carrying his baby. Ever since she'd got pregnant, she'd felt like an incubator as far as her life with Greg was concerned. He treated her as though she was a precious cargo-carrier, but he'd forgotten that she was a person too. She wanted to feel like a woman again, someone desirable and beautiful and someone who – as had been the case in her teenage years – could have any man she chose.

Gabriel didn't take his arm away from her shoulder. Even when he loosened his grip on her his fingers were still brushing lightly against her bare skin. And as she turned the conversation around to him and his parish in Rossanagh, he continued to hold her.

'It's not the back of beyond,' he said. 'But it can be lonely at times.'

'Lonely?' She looked up at him with a half-smile. 'I didn't think you were the lonely type, Gabriel. I thought you had God.'

'Sometimes God isn't quite enough.' He shook his head. 'Sorry, I shouldn't say that. I don't mean it.'

'Hey.' She put one of her fingers to his lips and quickly took it away again. 'You don't have to justify yourself to me. I'm sure you can't be a saint all the time.'

'I do my best,' he said.

'Oh, Gabriel. You're making life very difficult for yourself. Nobody's perfect.'

'I have to try.'

'No you don't. You're a person, Gabriel, not a machine.'

'I have an inner strength,' he told her.

She laughed. 'You're fooling yourself, Brady.'

'I have,' he assured her. 'I just have to tap into it.'

A large group of shoppers, carrying bags and chattering loudly, clattered into the bar and began ordering drinks.

'Maybe I should go.' Gabriel looked at his watch.

'Please don't,' she said. 'Not yet.'

'This place is filling up and—'

'Talk to me a bit more,' said Emma. 'I need to talk. I really do. Everything's so difficult these days. Come up to my room and we won't be disturbed.'

'I don't think . . .'

'Oh, for heaven's sake,' she said impatiently. 'You're a priest. It'll be fine. Like confession.'

She knew it wouldn't be fine. She knew it as she stood in front of the mirror and took the amber clip from her hair and saw the look in his eyes as her chestnut curls tumbled past her shoulders. And then she turned to him and put her head on his chest and then raised her face and kissed him, losing herself in the gentleness of his lips and the faint scratch of his stubble on her cheek and the touch of his fingers again but this time as they eased the zip of her dress downwards and slid it softly from her shoulders.

It takes two, she'd said to herself afterwards, as they'd lain together in the tangled sheets. I know I wanted to do this, but so did he. If he hadn't, it wouldn't have happened. And, she thought, it was a relief that it finally had. Wanting to make love to Gabriel had been a part of her life ever since the first time she'd seen him. Although, she reflected as she lay beside him, he'd been wildly inexperienced and desperately clumsy and none of it had been as erotic and sensuous as she'd expected. It was difficult to believe that with someone as damn sexy and masculine as him, it wouldn't be the best sex she'd ever had.

'That was amazing.' Gabriel finally spoke. 'I never realised . . .'

'That the sins of the flesh could be so great,' Emma finished for him.

'Something like that.'

She sat up in the bed and looked down at him.

She'd never known a man as handsome as Gabriel Brady. He looked like a poster boy for an aftershave ad as he stared up at her. The words of the Chinese proverb her mother used to quote drifted into her mind. *Be careful what you wish for* . . . She felt a sudden pain in her chest, and for a moment thought that she was having a heart attack. And then she told herself that it was probably just heartburn. She'd been suffering terribly with it ever since she'd got pregnant.

Gabriel closed his eyes. 'I'm so sorry,' he said. 'This . . . this was wrong. I shouldn't have given in to it.'

'Give yourself a break,' she said. 'You couldn't help it.'

'Of course I could,' he said. 'I did before.'

Who she wondered, who had he managed to resist before?

'All the times you came to our house.' He opened his eyes and looked at her. 'Dressed in the way you did, looking so very, very sexy and gorgeous. I was able to resist you. Easily.'

So he had noticed the effort she'd made for him back then. The thought cheered her.

'I was able to put you out of my mind because I had more important things to think about,' he said.

'And now?' she asked.

'I've been going through a hard time. I suppose my defences are low.'

'What sort of hard time?'

'It's nothing I shouldn't be able to deal with,' he said. 'It's lonely sometimes in Rossanagh, that's all. Isolating. And I've been feeling that lately. So I let myself be tempted by someone who cared about me. But by giving in to personal gratification and forgetting that there's something more—'

'Don't start larding on the Catholic guilt and worrying about it being a sin,' Emma told him. 'It was something we had to do. Something good for both of us.'

'It *was* good.' Gabriel sighed. 'But not in a good way.'

'I've always wanted to make love to you,' she told him. 'So that's why it was good for me. But also because I've always liked you, Gabriel. You know that.'

'You've been a temptation to me too,' he said. 'I thought I'd always be able to resist you. I thought I was strong enough.'

She sighed. 'I'm a person, not a temptation. I did this with you because you usually make me feel like a person. Now, though, I'm beginning to feel like the devil's mistress.'

He sat up. 'I have a vocation,' he told her. 'And you have a husband.'

She didn't say anything about the fact that she was going to have a baby. She hadn't thought about the baby while they'd been making love, but she thought about it now. Nonetheless, she wasn't going to tell him. That knowledge would send his moral compass spinning out of control.

'Are there consequences?' he asked. 'For us?'

She'd been tempted to say that there were always consequences.

'Not this time,' she told him, and then got out of bed. 'Go in peace, Gabriel, to love and serve the Lord. Don't worry about me. I'll be fine.'

He'd phoned her and texted her and sent emails to the house, all of which told her that she was a special person and that God would look after her. Greg had seen the texts and emails; there was nothing in them that would have let him know that she'd slept with the person sending them. She knew that Greg was pissed off that Gabriel was sending so much stuff, and he complained to her that he was trying to convert her into some kind of Holy Joe.

Emma, struggling with her feelings of guilt about her afternoon in bed with Gabriel, and suddenly worried that the priest might feel the need to confess his sin to her husband, started snapping at Greg, telling him that he was deliberately trying to be unsupportive, comparing him unfavourably with Gabriel, who, she said, was simply trying to comfort her.

'Easy to do that at the other end of the country when he doesn't have to live with you,' said Greg.

'What's that supposed to mean?'

'Well I doubt that even the saintliest man in the world could put up with someone who's become as self-obsessed as you.'

'I'm not self-obsessed.'

'You bloody are,' said Greg. 'Going off into your own little world, telling me that you're meditating, not letting me near you . . .'

'I don't feel like it right now,' she said.

It had been over a month since they'd made love. The last time had been the day after she came home from Dublin, the day after she'd slept with Gabriel. Making love to Greg was a totally different experience. He took time exploring her body, kissing her gently and caressing her and then moving rhythmically with her so that they cried out at the same time. He was good in bed, Emma thought. Gabriel had been like a teenager by comparison.

She hadn't expected to feel guilty. When she'd planned to sleep with Gabriel, she'd been completely able to justify it to herself, telling herself that they would have done it before she'd married Greg if only Gabriel hadn't been so hung up on the whole becoming-a-priest thing. And that was a relic of old times now, surely. Admittedly, the Catholic Church still demanded celibacy of its priests, but Emma was utterly convinced that it was a vow many of them broke. Hadn't there been scandal after scandal in the nineties when it had been discovered that priests (even a bishop, for heaven's sake) had fathered children? No, she thought Gabriel had always been living an impossible life.

Yet back in Cork, with Greg in the bed beside her and the knowledge that she was carrying his baby, Emma couldn't help the waves of guilt washing over her. She had been wrong to deceive Greg. If she'd wanted to sleep with Gabriel, she should have left her husband first.

If it was an option, if Gabriel was available, would she leave Greg for him now? Would she leave someone who was a considerate and tender lover for someone who hadn't a clue – always provided that he wanted her in the first place? Gabriel could learn about sex, of course. But would he? And it wasn't just about sex, Emma acknowledged to herself. It was about the family. She was, after all, going to be part of a family with Greg. Two parents and their child. What the hell would she be with Gabriel?

She allowed herself to think of all these things before remembering that Gabriel hadn't said anything about giving up the priesthood for her. And she wondered if the sins of the flesh, which he'd enjoyed so much with her, would be enough to make him want to change his life for ever. She wondered if he'd think she was worth it.

She didn't see him again until a month before her mother died. Maura had been in a hospice at that point and Gabriel had called to see her. He'd been sitting by her bed when Emma had walked in, and had stared at her in stunned amazement.

Afterwards, he met her in the coffee shop and looked at her anxiously.

'Why didn't you tell me?' he demanded.

'Why should I?'

'We've been in touch for months,' he said. 'You should have said something.'

'It wasn't relevant,' she said.

He continued to look at her, and suddenly she realised what was bothering him.

'It's not your baby, Gabriel,' she told him.

'How can you be sure of that?' he asked.

And then she told him that she'd been pregnant when they'd made love, and an expression of utter revulsion had passed over his face as he'd put his cup back on the saucer with a hand that was shaking.

'You had no right . . .'

'Oh, shut up, Gabriel,' she snapped. 'Don't start lecturing me on what's right or not.'

'What happened between us was incredibly wrong.'

'I know. But you liked it.'

'That's not the point.'

'You wanted to know when we could meet again,' she pointed out. He'd sent that text to her the week after they'd both returned home.

'I'm struggling with this,' he said. 'I've been struggling with it since it happened. The physical stuff. And how I was feeling. Everything.'

'I've been struggling too,' she told him. 'I'm the married woman after all!' She reached out and touched his hand, and he jerked back from her as though she'd hit him.

'Look, it's not that I don't . . . It's just . . . inappropriate,' he said urgently. 'Emma – we can't . . . it's not right. It will never be right.' And then he'd got up and walked out, leaving her to finish her tea under the curious gaze of the two women who'd been sitting at the table opposite them.

He hadn't sent any more texts or messages. Then Maura had died. And her funeral had been a strain for Emma in more ways than one. There was no way Gabriel couldn't be there. Norman had wanted him to come. And Emma had wanted him there too, because his absence would have been noticed.

351

On the evening of the funeral, she and Greg were alone in the living room of her parents' house (Norman had gone to bed) when she suddenly started to cry. Greg had hugged her gently and told her that it was a difficult time and that she'd been brilliant with her mother and it was time for her to let it all out.

She'd cried harder, and then, unable to stop herself, had told him about Gabriel.

He'd stopped hugging her after that.

And even though, after Lugh was born, he told her that it was in the past and that he wasn't going to talk about it, he never again hugged her in the way he'd hugged her before. And even though he'd made love to her, it had never been the same either.

When Emma had learned from Dominique that Gabriel had given up the priesthood, she'd waited for him to call her. She'd wondered if his leaving had been because of her and their night together. She'd both wanted to hear from him and dreaded it. But he hadn't got in touch with her. Which left her feeling hurt. And relieved.

She didn't love Gabriel Brady. She'd realised that after they'd made love in the Clarence Hotel. Because she'd realised that they hadn't made love, they'd just had sex. Not even very good sex. The irony of it all, she supposed, was that in sleeping with Gabriel, she'd realised just how much she loved Greg. But in confessing to Greg what she'd done, she'd managed to betray his trust in her for ever.

She'd been a fool, she knew that. Wanting what she couldn't have, making sure she got it in the end. And then finding out that it hadn't been worth it.

Now she looked at Gabriel Brady, the ex-priest, sitting in front of her, his handsome face worried and concerned.

'Are you sure your marriage is over?' he asked.

'Would anyone in their right mind blame Greg for leaving me?' she asked. 'I was unfaithful to him. I was the one who messed it up. And why? To fulfil a whim.'

'Sleeping with me was a whim?' asked Gabriel. 'Nothing more?'

'Gabriel, I seduced you that day. I wasn't thinking about anyone

352

other than myself. I was a horrible, selfish person and I deserved what I got.'

'But . . .'

'And you know what?'

'What?'

'I think maybe I thought that it would be OK because you were a priest and, in the end, you'd stop me. And I could have told myself that I'd really tried to make you love me and failed.'

'So you're blaming me?' He looked puzzled.

She shook her head. 'Oh no. It was my own fault. But I was stupid and foolish and I forgot that I was only one person in a whole tangle of people's lives. Maybe I thought that sex with you would be so wonderful that nothing else would matter. That the two of us would walk into the sunset in some great love story. But that wouldn't have happened, because I was pregnant! So I guess what I'm trying to say is that I got it wrong, Gabriel. I messed up. I've been punished for it. But part of the punishment is people like Domino suspecting something and not knowing exactly what. I want to tell her what happened, I want to tell her that it's never going to happen again, and I want your permission to do that.'

Gabriel looked at her anxiously.

'I don't want to tell anyone else. Just Domino.'

'Fine.'

'And I want . . .' Suddenly the tears spilled from Emma's eyes. Gabriel watched her but he didn't touch her. 'I want you to forgive me.'

'I thought forgiveness was all theoretical?'

'Oh shut up, Gabriel,' she said. 'I don't want you to forgive me personally. Just, you know, do the confession thing. Absolve me.'

'I can't,' he said. 'I'm not a priest.'

'It doesn't matter,' she said. 'All I want is for you to tell me that everything's going to be all right.'

Gabriel nodded slowly, then took Emma's hand and squeezed it gently.

'Of course it's going to be all right,' he told her. 'I promise.'

Chapter 29

Kelly made coffee for herself and Charlie and they drank it outside.

'I should head off,' he said as he put his empty cup on the ground. 'You and your folks need to be together.'

'There's nowhere for you to go,' Kelly told him.

'Of course there is.' Charlie grinned. 'I can head over to Damien Rafter's place in Drumcondra. It's only a half-hour's walk.'

'I thought this would be such a good night,' said Kelly. 'It *was* such a good night until Dad turned up. I was happy that you were here, that you were going to stay.'

'You all need your space to sort things out,' Charlie said. 'I'm in the way.'

Kelly nodded. 'Call me?'

'Of course,' he said.

He kissed her and went inside. He slung the backpack he'd left in the hallway over his shoulder.

'Call me,' she said again as he opened the front door.

'Will do.'

He stepped outside and on to the street. Then he walked away. Kelly closed the door.

She wondered if he'd bother to call her. After all, he must surely think her family was completely nuts. And he was probably right.

Another thing to blame her dad for.

She heard the bedroom door open and her mother come down-stairs.

'Is everything all right?' Kelly asked tentatively.

'Depends on what all right means,' said Dominique. She went

into the kitchen and Kelly followed her. The table and countertops were strewn with empty glasses and disposable plates.

'I should tidy up.' Dominique picked up a glass and rinsed it under the tap.

'Don't be silly,' Kelly told her. 'Where's Dad? What's he doing?'

'Having a shower,' said Dominique.

'Huh?'

'He said he needed to clear his head.'

'What's he planning to do?'

Dominique left the kitchen and went into the living room, where she sat down on the sofa and stared at the empty grate.

'He seems to think that he can just . . . well, he thinks he's come home and that we can put everything behind us.'

'He thinks this is home now?' Kelly, who'd followed her, glanced back towards the untidy kitchen.

'No, not that. Just that . . . well, that he's back and we're together and that's the way things are going to be.'

'And are they?'

'You're being very mature about all this.' Dominique didn't answer her daughter's question.

'Not really,' said Kelly. 'I'm in a daze, to be honest. But I suppose we always talked about him coming home, and now he has. So I wondered if you'd forgiven him already.'

Dominique sighed. 'It's more complicated than that.'

'You're a very forgiving person,' Kelly said.

'You think?'

'You forgave me when I wore your Dries Van Noten dress without telling you and spilled red wine down the front.'

'I think I grounded you for a while after that.'

'Yes. But you forgave me.'

'This is rather different.'

'I'm going to bed.' Kelly rubbed her eyes. 'I can't get my head around everything right now.'

'OK,' said Dominique. 'Where's Charlie?' she added, suddenly realising that Kelly's boyfriend wasn't there.

'He thought we needed our own space.'

'He's right about that, I guess. He's a nice boy, Kelly. I like him.'

'Yeah, he is.' Kelly got up from the seat beside her mother. 'Which is why he'll probably steer clear of me from now on. See you in the morning.'

It was twenty minutes later before Brendan came downstairs again, his hair still damp and tousled from his shower. Dominique had spent the time packing the used glasses into the boxes that Lizzie Horgan had left for her and putting the disposable plates into black plastic refuse sacks. She was tying up the last sack when Brendan walked into the kitchen.

He looked around it, his practised eye taking in the badly chased electrical work on one wall and the damaged skirting below.

'Gabriel told me that one of your friends is letting you stay here,' he said.

'I'm renting it,' she told him sharply. 'I pay for it every month out of my salary. She's not "letting" me stay.'

'What are you doing that's paying you a salary?' he asked.

She told him about the job at Glenmallon.

'You got that all by yourself?'

'Why do you sound so surprised?' she asked.

'A job,' he said. 'I never thought of you supporting yourself by getting a job. I didn't think you were that sort of person.'

'You don't know what sort of person I am,' she said abruptly. 'You never did. And I had a job before I met you. I supported myself then, didn't I?'

'I'm sorry.' He walked over to her and put his hand on her shoulder. 'I didn't mean to belittle you.'

'Didn't you?'

'Don't give me such a hard time, Domino,' said Brendan. 'Please.'

She looked up at him, astonishment in her eyes. 'What do you want from me?' she demanded. 'Instant forgiveness? For me to fall on my knees and thank you for coming home?'

'Of course not. But . . .'

'You broke my heart,' she cried.

'I never meant to.'

'Will you go to jail?' she asked.

'I don't know. I spent a lot of time talking to Ciara about it

357

yesterday and we're going to have a meeting with the guards . . .'

Dominique shuddered.

'. . . but she's hopeful that they don't have a strong enough case for fraud. There are issues in court, of course, about judgements against the companies and that sort of thing, but that's entirely different.'

'Can you pay them back?'

'Who?'

'The people in Cork? With the difficult-to-find Panama money?'

'I'm hoping to come to some arrangement,' he said. 'I need to talk to Ciara about that too. Anyway, you've got to look at it like this, Domino. If I'd done the Barbados investment by the book I probably wouldn't have to pay them back because property prices have fallen. This way they might get something. So in the end they're better off.'

'That's not the point.'

'Perhaps not. But it's the truth.'

'You should never have left the way you did.' Dominique tacitly accepted that he wasn't entirely wrong about the Barbados deal. 'That's what hurts me more than anything. That you didn't tell me what was happening.'

'You didn't need to know that sort of stuff, Domino. I was afraid of the effect it would have on you.'

'What were you afraid of?' Her voice was steely. 'That I'd get depressed again? You know that was a completely different situation. I can't believe you're even speaking about it.'

'I was afraid you'd do nothing but worry. And want to talk endlessly about it. And I couldn't. I just couldn't.'

'I did nothing but worry anyway. If you'd told me, I might have been able to help,' she said.

'What could you have done? Hosted a charity dinner where people put money in a gold envelope for us?'

Dominique caught her breath.

'Let's face it, honey, you're beautiful and you're kind and you've been a wonderful asset to me in the last few years, but you know jack-shit about finance. I don't think you could've come up with a solution when I couldn't.'

'I'm not the one who had to skip the country because I made

a mess of my business,' she said tightly. 'And I found solutions for me and Kelly all by myself.'

'I'm sorry.' He looked at her contritely. 'I didn't mean that you couldn't cope. I just . . . Well, look, I'm back now and we can do more than cope. I promise you. We'll sort this out and then, who knows, there will be plenty of opportunities for me. I just have to get back down to it and make things work. And I will, Domino. You know I will. With your support, I can do anything.'

'Oh, Brendan . . .'

'You can't walk away from me now.' He looked pleadingly at her. 'You've got to give me another chance.' She stared at him. And then she allowed him to put his arms around her and hold her tightly against his chest.

Greg phoned the following morning.

Dominique was asleep in the main bedroom. She'd shown Brendan to the tiny box room with its foldaway bed, saying that this was the best she could do, that she had the main room and Kelly was in the guest room. He'd started to object but then, suddenly, had given in, telling her he appreciated that she needed time to come to terms with everything. She'd said that she certainly did need time and that she was very tired now. She'd left him in the smaller room, gone to her bedroom and lain down, fully clothed, on the bed. It was a long time before she undressed and crawled beneath the covers, but she didn't nod off until the sky had begun to lighten with the oncoming dawn. Then she'd fallen into an uneasy slumber, dreaming that she was searching for Brendan again but never finding him.

The sound of the phone ringing took a while to penetrate the fog of sleep, and it wasn't until she heard Brendan's deep, gravelly voice from the hallway that she realised that the events of the previous night had really happened and that he was home.

'We'll come down today,' he was saying as she rubbed the sleep out of her eyes. 'I can't wait to see everyone.'

She was out of bed and brushing her hair when he came up the stairs and poked his head around the door.

'Sleeping Beauty,' he said. 'That was Greg. I told him we were going to Cork.'

'When?' she asked, even though she'd heard him on the phone.

'A couple of hours. I want to see Mam and Dad.'

'Have you spoken to them yet?'

'I told Greg to tell Mam I'd talk to her in person. I don't want to have an unsatisfactory phone conversation with her.'

'And where are we going to stay in Cork?' asked Dominique.

'At Mam's, I guess.'

'You don't think that people will know you're back?'

'Nobody does yet,' he said. 'The media aren't half as savvy as people think.'

As they drove through Abbeyleix on their way to Castlecannon, having stopped at the B&B to pick up Brendan's bag on the way, Dominique's mobile rang. It was Greg again.

'Hi,' he said. 'How're you doing?'

'OK.'

'Bit of a shock?'

'Yes.'

'Well, look, I know Brendan was going to go to Mam's, but I've asked them to come to Briarwood instead. You should too. We're out of the way of prying eyes here.'

'Why aren't you at your apartment?' asked Dominique.

'Looking after Lugh,' explained Greg. 'Emma asked me to stay here. She phoned last night. She'll be home later.'

'Oh, OK.'

She relayed the conversation to Brendan, who frowned.

'I want to go home, not to Greg's place.'

'Maybe afterwards,' she said. 'When we see how the land lies.'

'Is everyone meeting at Greg's?' Kelly, who'd been texting Alicia and Charlie on her phone, piped up from the back seat. She hadn't wanted to come to Cork, but in the end had decided that she should be where the action was. She wanted to look after her mother. Dominique was very pale, and the shadows under her eyes were huge. Kelly knew that she too was very conflicted about Brendan's return. Kelly herself had her own life and was living with Alicia and didn't have to worry about her dad. But it was different for her mum, who'd had to change everything, absolutely

360

everything, and now was faced with having to change it all back again.

It wasn't realistic of her dad to waltz back into their lives as though nothing had happened, she thought. But no matter what he'd done, they simply couldn't just abandon him.

It was raining steadily by the time they arrived at Briarwood, and they hurried quickly past Maurice and Lily's car, which was already parked in the driveway. As they stepped into the porch, Greg opened the front door.

'Hi, Domino.' He hugged her quickly and then kissed Kelly on the cheek. 'Hi, Kells.'

Then he looked at his brother.

'Well,' was all he said.

'It's good to see you,' Brendan said. 'I've missed you.'

'We've all missed you,' said Greg. 'But maybe for lots of different reasons.'

'Are you going to give me a hard time?' asked Brendan.

'No,' said Greg. 'Mam might, though.'

But Lily didn't give Brendan a hard time at all. When he walked through to the conservatory where both she and Maurice were sitting, she burst into tears. He came over to her and put his arms around her, and she held him close to her and patted him on the back over and over.

'I'm sorry, Ma.' Brendan had tears in his eyes too. 'I've let you down. I never meant to.'

'Why?' asked Maurice.

'It all went wrong, Dad. Things spun out of control and I couldn't stop them.'

Dominique sat in the corner, Kelly beside her, and listened as Brendan went through it all again. She wondered how many times she'd hear it, hear his excuses, hear that it had all been a mistake. She knew it had. She knew that Brendan hadn't deliberately set out to bring down his company or lose money. She could understand how he'd got caught up in a spiral of events. But running away, leaving them. That was entirely different. That was a choice.

Chapter 30

It wasn't long before they heard the crunch of tyres on the gravel and then the ringing of the doorbell. This time it was June and Barry who walked into the conservatory, followed by Greg.

'You thieving bastard!' said June furiously before she'd even taken off the short red jacket she was wearing. 'You've ruined us with your stupid, stupid schemes.'

Brendan flinched, but he let his sister and her husband rant at him about the mess he'd made of everything. Gabriel Brady had warned him that people would want to lash out and had told him to be prepared for it. Brendan had taken it from Dominique as best he could, but it was harder to take from his angry sister without losing his own temper.

'How could you think that running away was the best thing to do?' Lily asked her son when June had finally run out of things to say. 'Didn't I bring you up better than that?'

Brendan pushed his hands through his hair. 'Yes, Mam,' he said. 'It was just that everyone was pressurising me and I didn't know what to do. I couldn't cope.'

'You could have talked to any of us,' said Greg. 'We would've helped out.'

'I couldn't,' said Brendan fiercely. 'I was the success of the family. I couldn't . . .' His voice trailed off and he suddenly looked defeated.

Dominique watched as his jaw tightened. She could see that he was struggling to keep himself under control. She got up from the wicker chair where she'd been sitting and stood beside him. Then she put her hand on his arm.

'I understand that,' she said. 'I truly do.'

'Do you?' he whispered.

She nodded. 'It's like a crushing weight, isn't it? When you can't see a way out. It's impossible to deal with.'

He slid his hand into hers. 'Thank you,' he said. 'Thank you for being here.'

'We're all here for you,' Greg told him. 'You and Domino and Kelly. You know that.'

June snorted, and Barry prodded her in the side.

'Can we agree?' asked Lily. 'That as a family we're behind Brendan? That we'll support him in whatever lies ahead?'

Brendan looked at his brother, his sister and her husband.

'Of course we will,' said Greg. 'You know we won't throw you to the wolves, Brendan. But I'm damned if I'm happy about what's happened.'

'I understand,' said Brendan. 'I really do. And thank you.'

'I'm not saying I'm happy either,' said June.

'You don't have to,' Brendan told her. 'Just don't . . .' He sighed.

'I can't forgive you for what you did,' said Barry. 'But I've never said anything bad about you and I won't now.'

'Thanks,' said Brendan again. 'Thank you all. And Domino, most of all, thank you for understanding.'

Dominique said nothing.

'I'll support you, son,' said Maurice. 'But you've got to knuckle down. Take whatever punishment you get.'

'Of course.' Brendan turned to Kelly. 'What about you, honey?'

Kelly looked up from her mobile phone, where she'd been reading a text from Charlie, relieved that the events of the previous night hadn't, as she'd feared, stopped him from getting in touch with her again.

'You know I'll always support you,' she said. 'I'm so glad you're back, Dad. But I'm struggling with the desertion thing.'

'I know,' said Brendan. 'I knew as soon as I'd gone that it was a mistake, but then I couldn't come back.'

They heard the crunch of tyres again and exchanged anxious looks.

'The papers haven't heard already, have they?' asked Lily tremulously. 'I don't want all that stuff to start over.'

'I don't think so.' Greg walked out of the conservatory. A moment

364

later he returned, his face dark and brooding, followed by Gabriel and Emma.

'Gabriel.' Lily got out of her seat and put her arms around him. 'It's good to see you.'

'You too, Lily,' he said. 'I hope you're well.'

'Better,' she replied. 'Better for knowing that Brendan is back, even though things will be tough.'

'Of course,' said Gabriel. 'But sometimes you have to face your troubles.'

'Indeed you do,' said Greg tautly. 'What are you doing here, Brady?'

'Emma asked me to come down with her,' he said. 'After Domino's party—'

'Party?' June looked at Dominique curiously. 'You were having a party? In Dublin?'

'A small party,' Dominique said.

'Glad to hear that you weren't pining for your husband, anyway.'

'June!' Barry looked at her in annoyance.

'I'm just saying!' June's voice was filled with injured innocence.

'It was a party for a friend of hers,' said Emma.

Dominique shot her a glance.

'Domino is perfectly entitled to throw parties,' said Greg. 'She couldn't put her life on hold for ever; nobody can.'

'It was a great party,' said Kelly. 'With loads of really nice people at it.'

'Kelly, the party isn't exactly relevant right now,' said Dominique. 'What we need to focus on is what happens to us as a family. The whole family,' she added hastily. 'Not just you and me and Brendan.'

'I thought we'd agreed we were standing by him,' said Lily.

'We are,' said Greg.

'That's good to hear,' Gabriel told them. 'Look, I know there's been a lot of disunity among . . . among all of us, and maybe for lots of reasons, but this is a time for everyone to support each other.'

'Absolutely,' said Lily spiritedly.

Although the rest of them still looked far too angry for her liking. And much to her surprise, Greg looked the angriest of all.

* * *

The return of Jia, who'd taken Lugh and some of his friends swimming for a couple of hours, was the signal for the gathering to split up. Lily, Maurice, Barry and June departed together, leaving Greg, Emma, Gabriel, Dominique, Kelly and Brendan behind. Kelly asked Lugh if he'd like to play a game on his PlayStation, and he nodded eagerly.

'Thanks, Kelly,' said Dominique as her daughter led her cousin out of the room.

'Would anyone like anything to eat?' asked Emma.

'Maybe a sandwich?' suggested Gabriel.

'I'll see what I can manage.' Emma went into the kitchen. After about a minute, during which nobody said anything, Dominique got up and followed her.

'Why on earth did you bring Gabriel here, Emma?' she demanded when she'd closed the kitchen door behind her.

'He got Brendan home,' said Emma. 'Surely he's entitled to know what's going on?'

'I would've told him what was going on,' said Dominique. 'He's my brother, after all.'

Emma took a deep breath. 'I need to talk to you about Gabriel,' she said. 'Not right now, though. Sometime when there's just you and me.'

Dominique's shoulders sagged.

'I'm not sure I want to hear whatever it is you have to say.'

'I need to tell you all the same,' said Emma.

'All I really want is for things to be the way they were before,' said Dominique dismally. 'When everything was perfect.'

'It was never perfect,' said Emma. 'And you know it.'

The three men were sitting silently in the conservatory.

Greg was staring out over the garden, watching a pair of swallows as they swooped between the trees. Gabriel was reading the information label stuck in the potted plant on the table beside him. Brendan was studying his fingernails and picking at his cuticles.

'The hurling team did well this year,' he said eventually. 'I kept an eye on them on the internet.'

Greg turned to face him. 'They got lucky,' he said shortly. 'They didn't deserve to win some of their matches.'

'Better to be lucky than smart,' said Brendan.

'Yeah.' Greg nodded. 'I guess so.'

'I ran out of luck myself,' said Brendan. 'Everything I'd touched had turned to gold and I thought it would go on for ever.'

'Nothing is for ever,' said Gabriel. 'Not good times. Not bad times. But if we have people who love us and care about us we can cope. And that love and care stays with us always.'

'That is, of course, the kind of hypocritical shite I'd expect from you, Brady,' said Greg. 'You know you're talking bollocks as usual. And that's no help to anyone.'

Brendan looked at his brother in surprise.

'You're being very harsh,' he said. 'Gabriel told me some home truths. I'd got myself into a mess and I didn't know how to get out of it. He helped me and I'll always be grateful to him.'

'That's Gabriel for you,' said Greg. 'Always ready to help the Delahayes. Always ready to dip his toe in the murky family waters. Not only his toe, of course.'

Brendan stared at his brother and his brother-in-law, aware that there was a simmering anger between them.

'What's the matter?' he asked.

'Ah, your brother has some issues with me,' said Gabriel. 'We've never really dealt with them. I was hoping, Greg, that we could have a talk later, just you and me.'

Once again Brendan stared at both of them.

Then Greg laughed bitterly. 'You want to give me the opportunity to do what I didn't before?' he asked. 'Punch your lights out?'

'Why on earth would you want to do that?' asked Brendan.

'That hypocritical bastard slept with my wife.' Greg felt the years of pent-up anger erupting and he couldn't stay silent. 'Which I think gives me a very good reason to deck him.'

Brendan's jaw dropped while Greg glared at Gabriel, his body tense.

Two things had enraged him the night Emma told him about her unfaithfulness. The first was that he'd shaken hands with Gabriel Brady earlier in the day and thanked him for the support he'd given

367

to Emma and her family in the difficult days of Maura's illness. The second was that he realised that Emma had been pregnant with his child when she'd betrayed him with the priest.

'It wasn't great with him, you know,' she'd sobbed after her confession. 'It was just . . . he was my dream man, Greg. In my head, anyway. I needed to . . . I had to . . .'

'You didn't have to do anything with that hypocritical git!' He'd spat the words at her. 'What you had to do, Emma, was stay faithful to me. But you couldn't.'

'It'll never happen again.'

'No,' said Greg. 'It damn well won't.'

He'd wanted to throw her out of the house there and then, but how could he when she was pregnant with the baby he so desperately wanted? She'd been utterly repentant afterwards, trying really hard to make things right. But it was impossible. He'd trusted Emma. He'd trusted Gabriel. And they'd made a fool of him.

Now Greg could feel the rage coursing through him. He'd almost slugged Gabriel when he'd opened the door to them, but Emma had hurried past saying that it wasn't the time or the place for arguments and that Gabriel had a right to know what was going on in his sister's life. And Greg had been too stunned to stop her, or him. Then he'd thought that he didn't have any damn right to stop him anyway, because the house was Emma's now, not his. Another thing to blame Brady for. It was his fault that they were getting a divorce.

'You slept with Emma!' Brendan stared at Gabriel with a mixture of disgust and disbelief. 'You slept with my brother's wife?'

'It was a long time ago,' said Gabriel.

'Is that why you and Emma have separated?' Brendan turned to Greg.

'Yes.'

'Oh, come on, Greg. You can't entirely blame me for that,' said Gabriel. 'There's a lot more to it than one night with me. You made her life a misery.'

'Excuse me?'

'She always felt you cared more about Domino than her. You looked out for her in a way you never looked out for your own wife. As though somehow Emma was perfectly capable of managing

368

on her own but Domino wasn't. And after the . . . the incident with me, you never stopped blaming her. Yes, I behaved dreadfully and disgracefully and that's something I've had to live with and something I can't ever forgive myself for. But you made her feel perpetually guilty, and nobody can live like that.'

'Of course I care about Domino. She's part of our family and she went through a really bad time and she matters to me,' said Greg, aware that Brendan was looking at him tensely. And aware, too, that neither he nor Gabriel knew about the night he'd come to Domino's in Dublin. He suddenly felt a rush of the guilt that he knew Emma must have felt when she'd told him about Gabriel. But, he reminded himself, he'd done nothing in the end, while Emma had utterly betrayed him.

'Emma felt guilty because she *was* guilty,' he told Gabriel. 'And just because she came clean about it doesn't exonerate her.'

'You should have broken up with her then, if you couldn't live with it,' Gabriel told him. 'You should have told her to leave. You could have left yourself. But you didn't. You told her that you forgave her but you punished her every single day afterwards.'

'She slept with you!' cried Greg. 'When she was pregnant. She deserved to be punished.'

'For ever?' asked Gabriel.

Greg clenched his jaw.

'If you forgive somebody, you forgive them unconditionally,' Gabriel said.

'Is this one of your sermons?' asked Greg. 'Forgive and forget? Have a group hug? Offer each other the sign of peace?'

'This family needs some peace,' said Gabriel.

'Yeah, well, you've helped a lot.' There was derision in Greg's voice. 'You know what would give me peace, Brady? Giving you what you deserve!' He took a step in Gabriel's direction.

'Greg!' exclaimed Brendan as he caught his brother by the arm. 'For God's sake!'

The three men stared at each other, the air between them crackling with tension and anger.

And then Emma walked into the room carrying a tray of sandwiches, followed by Dominique with the pot of tea.

Chapter 31

The two women immediately sensed the suppressed aggression in the room.

'What's going on?' asked Domino.

'Everything,' said Greg. 'The shit has finally hit the fan.'

'Huh?' Dominique put the heavy teapot on the low glass table.

'It's all out in the open, Domino. Emma's sordid secret. Her night of passion with Gabriel. Don't tell me you hadn't guessed that they'd slept together?'

'You what?' Dominique looked at Gabriel in shocked disbelief. 'You actually slept with Emma? When?' And then she turned to her sister-in-law. 'Is this what you wanted to talk to me about? To tell me that I was right all along?'

Emma's grip tightened on the tray she was holding, although everyone could hear the rattle of the cups against the saucers as her hands shook.

'You've been talking about it?' she said to Greg, her voice barely above a whisper. At the same time, Gabriel took the tray from her before she let it drop. 'In front of Brendan? How could you?'

'You were the one who brought him into our house, Emma. You knew what would happen.'

'I can't believe you'd betray Greg like that.' Brendan stared at her.

'Oh, you can talk about betrayal all right, Brendan Delahaye!' Emma's voice was stronger this time. 'When you've betrayed everyone in the entire family!'

'What I did was completely different,' said Brendan. 'I know it was wrong, but . . . God Almighty, Emma – sleeping with Domino's brother!'

'You never strayed yourself?' asked Emma. 'All those times you were away from home being the big important businessman? And these last months, while you were globetrotting? There was never a girl waiting for you in a bar somewhere ready to offer a bit of comfort in a foreign country?'

Brendan looked furiously at Emma while Domino watched him carefully.

'There were no women,' he said. 'I promise you, Domino.'

'And you believe him?' asked Emma. 'He has form, after all.'

'Emma . . .' Dominique looked helpless.

'You cheated on Domino, didn't you?' Emma shot at Brendan. 'So you've got a damn nerve being critical of me.'

Dominique exhaled sharply.

'You told her about that?' asked Brendan. 'You shared private things about our marriage with someone else?'

She looked at Greg, and then at Emma. Greg must have told her, because Dominique hadn't ever discussed Brendan's affair with her sister-in-law. It hadn't occurred to her that he would share something so personal about her life with his wife, although she knew she wouldn't have kept similar information from Brendan. And he hadn't told her about Emma sleeping with Gabriel. She thought he'd told her everything. But she was wrong. Nevertheless, she wasn't going to let Brendan know that it was Greg she'd confided in, not Emma.

Before she could say anything in reply, Kelly walked in and almost physically recoiled at the atmosphere that permeated the room.

'What's going on?' she asked.

'Family stuff,' said Gabriel.

'Not good family stuff,' Kelly said. 'I can tell that from just standing here.'

'Stuff that maybe would have been better left unsaid,' said Greg.

'Stuff about my dad?'

'No.' Emma's voice trembled. 'About all of us. About things we've done wrong.'

'What sort of things?' asked Kelly.

'They don't matter.' Gabriel's voice was firm. 'We all do stupid things, Kelly. Wrong things. You know that. But what we have to do is to forgive ourselves and forgive everyone else too.'

'That's convenient,' said Greg. 'The great Catholic get-out clause. Confess your sins, ask for forgiveness and feel so much better, eh, Brady?'

Kelly looked anxiously at him. She could hear the anger in his voice.

'Gabriel is right, Greg,' said Dominique. 'We could play the blame game for ever but it won't get us anywhere.'

'So what's going to happen now?' demanded Greg. 'A group confession and general absolution from the ex-priest?'

'I think we've done the confessing,' said Brendan. 'We have to move on. Hard though that clearly is.'

'Easy to say when it suits you,' remarked Emma.

'We need togetherness,' said Gabriel.

'Yes.' Dominique nodded.

'But there's no togetherness any more,' said Greg. 'There can't be, can there? Somehow we've managed to blast it all apart.'

'I suppose this is all my fault too,' said Brendan bitterly. 'Everything would've been hidden or glossed over if it wasn't for me.'

'In which case, maybe you've done us all a favour, Dad,' said Kelly. 'OK, so I don't know what grim secrets you're talking about, although they're probably not as grim as you think really. Things hardly ever are. But hiding them doesn't help, does it?' She shook her head. 'I used to be proud to be a Delahaye. I thought it was a good name to have. But now . . .'

'Oh, don't you start on our good name.' Brendan's anger had subsided and he suddenly sounded defeated. 'I know all about how I've dragged us into the mud.'

'Maybe we let you,' said Kelly.

'That's sweet of you, honey,' said Brendan. 'But, hell, I'll accept the blame for everything if it makes you all feel better. For Emma and Gabriel's problems. For Greg's. For June and Barry and Alicia and Joanna and Mossie. For Mam and Dad, and your other grand-parents too, Kelly.'

'And Lugh,' added Kelly. 'He knows there are terrible things going on. He's very upset by it all.'

'I know.' Emma choked back a sob. 'We've been crap parents,

Greg and I. We've probably messed up Lugh for ever and he'll have a terrible life because of us.'

'Blame me,' Brendan reminded her bitterly as she walked out of the room. 'I'm the one who deserves it, after all.'

You couldn't live your life at high tension for ever, thought Dominique as they drove back to Dublin. Kelly had nodded off in the back seat of the car and Brendan was silent as he sat at the steering wheel. No matter how awful things were, there was always a moment when something ordinary happened and it brought you back to the fact that you had to get on with it.

The ordinary thing that had happened in the case of the Delahayes was Lugh running into the living room and asking his father if it was OK to watch *Top Gear*. They were reviewing a Lamborghini that night, he said, and he wanted to see it on the big TV. Lambos were his favourite car, he added, and it was important to hear Clarkson's view on it. He didn't appear to notice anyone else in the room at all.

Greg had said that it was absolutely fine to watch whatever he liked, at which Lugh said, 'Cool,' and turned on the TV. Emma returned, her eyes red, and the adults looked uncertainly at each other, nobody quite sure what was going to happen next.

Then Gabriel said that it was time for him to go.

'Where?' Dominique asked.

'I'll go into the city,' he said. 'Get a hotel. And go back to Dublin tomorrow. After that . . . Well, I'll be heading back to Paraguay.'

'I'm going too,' said Greg, without looking at Gabriel.

'You don't have to,' said Emma.

'I don't live here any more,' he reminded her.

'I know. But for tonight . . .'

'No,' said Greg.

'Not for me,' Emma said. 'For Lugh. He needs you.'

Greg hesitated.

'Please,' begged Emma.

Greg shrugged helplessly and glanced at his son, who was absorbed in the TV programme. Then he sat down beside him.

'Can I call a cab from here?' asked Gabriel.

374

'There's a number beside the phone in the kitchen,' Emma told him.

'We should get back too,' said Dominique. 'We can drop you into town, Gabriel.'

'Would you mind?'

Dominique glanced towards Brendan and Kelly.

'Yes,' she said.

'We could drive you to Dublin if you like,' offered Brendan.

'No thanks.' Gabriel shook his head. 'I'd prefer to get the train in the morning.'

'Are you sure?' asked Brendan.

'Absolutely.'

They picked up their jackets and left. Nobody embraced, although Kelly gave Lugh a hug. He kissed her hurriedly and then turned back to the TV, engrossed in the dream of driving a Lamborghini.

There was silence in the car as they drove to the city and left Gabriel outside a Jurys hotel.

'I know you don't think much of me,' he said to Dominique as he got out of the car. 'I never meant to hurt anyone.'

She got out too and stood beside him.

'I once asked you if you left the priesthood because of a woman,' she said. 'You told me you didn't.'

'That was the truth,' Gabriel told her. 'It wasn't because of Emma. It was because I knew I couldn't live without that sort of closeness any more.'

'Do you love her?'

He shook his head. 'Which makes it all the more despicable that I slept with her.'

Dominique shrugged. 'Loads of people sleep with people they don't love.'

'That's different,' said Gabriel.

'I know.'

'I thought you suspected,' said Gabriel. 'I thought that was why you were so anxious about her.'

'I didn't know you'd slept with her, but I was always afraid something might happen,' admitted Dominique. 'Whenever you were together . . . I could feel the tension. I was afraid of how things might turn out. Afraid you'd do something you'd regret.'

'Of course I regret it,' said Gabriel. 'Although that sounds unfair on Emma. I regret being the cause of the trouble between her and Greg. I regret being weak.'

'Welcome to the real world,' said Dominique wryly.

'I wanted to make amends,' said Gabriel. 'I thought that bringing Brendan home would make up for things, though obviously not for Greg and Emma. I'm not sure that's exactly what you wanted either.'

Dominique hesitated, and then smiled faintly at her brother. 'I'm glad he's back. I couldn't move on until he came back.' She hugged Gabriel briefly and then opened the car door. 'You did the right thing there anyway, Gabe.'

'Thanks, Domino. Take care.'

'You too.'

She got into the car and watched him walk into the hotel. Then she sat back in the passenger seat as Brendan drove slowly down the street.

Emma insisted that Lugh go to bed directly after *Top Gear* finished. He complained that his dad had let him stay up much later the previous night, and Emma told him that dads did that sort of thing but that mothers were much stricter and he had to go upstairs right now.

Lugh asked for Greg to put him to bed. When he was finally snuggled down beneath his duvet, and Greg had read him a chapter from a Young James Bond book, he yawned and said that it had been nice to have his dad and his mum both at home again, and that he knew they were getting a divorce but was it possible they could live together anyway?

'I don't think so,' said Greg.

'I wish you could.'

'I know.' Greg kissed him on the forehead and went downstairs again.

Emma was curled up in one of the big armchairs. She looked pale and thin and her hair hung limply in front of her face.

Greg sat down and looked unseeingly at the TV.

'I know you can't forgive me,' said Emma. 'I've lived with your mistrust for years. I guess that's why when Gabriel came back I wanted to see him. I wanted to know whether I had feelings for him.'

'I don't care, Emma,' said Greg dully.

'I *do* have feelings for him,' she said, which made him glance at her. 'But they're feelings of guilt, not feelings that I want to be with him.'

'It's OK,' said Greg. 'I understand that.'

'And I'm sorry if those feelings made you want to be Dominique's support system.'

Greg hit the mute button on the TV remote control.

'Maybe they did, maybe they didn't,' he said. 'I don't know, Emma. I don't know why I did some things and I don't know why you did the things you did. But it doesn't matter. The result is still the same.'

'You're being very hard.'

'You're not trying to save our marriage, are you?' He laughed harshly. 'It's too late for that.'

'I was thinking of Lugh,' said Emma.

'He wouldn't be happy if we were together and sniping all the time.'

'Could we be together and not snipe?'

'Emma – all of our married life I've felt that I was your second choice. When we first got married I didn't mind. Actually, I thought I was being sort of noble, rescuing your heart from the evil priest. But I was wrong.'

'I thought I was being noble in rescuing your heart from the unreachable Domino,' said Emma.

'No you didn't.'

'I knew you cared about her.'

'When I asked you to marry me it was because I loved you,' said Greg.

'When I said yes it was because I loved you too. And I wanted to share my life with you. Everything in my life. Well, of course, in the end I didn't. The thing is, Greg, you didn't share everything with me either.'

'What?' he asked. 'What didn't I share?'

'Something you shared with Domino.' She shrugged. 'It had nothing to do with me and Gabriel. I only found out recently. But it made me see that she has a place in your heart that I don't.'

'I haven't the faintest idea what you're talking about.'

'Your baby,' she said.

'My baby?' And then the realisation dawned. She wasn't talking about the night he'd called to Domino's house in Dublin, miserable, depressed and looking for love. She was talking about Maria and the child she'd lost.

'Emma, that was years ago. And I only told Domino about it to explain why I understood her depression.'

'But you never told me.'

'It didn't matter to you.'

'How do you know what matters until you tell me?'

He nodded slowly. 'If you want to know . . .'

'Yes,' she said. 'I do.'

So he told her about Maria and her pregnancy and she listened to him without saying a word.

'It's no great secret,' he said.

'You should have shared it all the same. And I might have understood more.'

'Too late now,' he said, aware that he was still keeping secrets from her and that he would never, ever tell her about kissing Dominique and wanting to make love to her. There were some things that should stay buried. Some things that she would never understand. They were getting divorced. There was no point in hurting her any further.

She nodded. 'We're going through a tough time right now. Whether or not we can live together any more, we have to stop blaming each other.'

'I think that's what happens in divorces.'

'We didn't have a successful marriage,' said Emma. 'Let's try and have a successful divorce.'

He couldn't help smiling at her. 'That's a great way of putting it.'

'Thank you.' She smiled in return.

'OK then. So can we leave both Dominique and Gabriel out of it?'

'Absolutely,' said Emma.

'No more talking about them?'

'No. Although I have a horrible feeling there's still lots of talk about Domino to come.' Emma, suddenly relaxed, folded her legs beneath her body in the armchair. 'The papers will have a field day with Brendan and she's sure to be in the firing line.'

'I won't be rushing to support her, if that's what worries you,' said Greg. 'Besides, she has someone else now, hasn't she?'

'Paddy O'Brien?'

'She likes him, doesn't she?'

'Maeve told me that she just thinks of him as a friend. I told her that Domino had too many friends who were men.'

'Not that many,' protested Greg.

'One too many as far as I was concerned,' said Emma. She got up from the chair. 'My reasons for what I did with Gabriel were inexcusable. But I always envied your relationship with his sister.' She opened the door. 'Good night,' she said. 'And thanks for staying.'

'You're welcome.' Greg heard her close the door again. He stared straight ahead, not seeing the pictures on the TV screen in front of him at all.

They arrived back at Fairview at two in the morning. Kelly woke up when Brendan pulled up outside the house. Dominique looked around her before she opened the front door.

'I'm convinced photographers are lurking in the bushes,' she explained.

'Like at Atlantic View.' Kelly yawned and walked into the house.

'There were photographers in the bushes at Atlantic View?' said Brendan questioningly.

'In the bushes, at the gate, on the road outside your mum's house . . . Everywhere,' said Dominique.

'Was it hell?' asked Brendan.

'What do you think?'

'I'm sorry.'

'I know. And don't bother saying you're sorry any more,' said Dominique as she hung her jacket on the coat rack. 'I'm going to bed. You can sleep in the box room again.'

'Domino . . .'

'Look, Brendan, I'm going to support you during the next few weeks. I owe you and your family that much. I owe it to Kelly, too. But right now I don't want to sleep with you. In fact you've got to be pretty grateful that I'm letting you stay here in the first place.'

'I am grateful, of course I am,' he said. 'And I know we can work this out, Domino. For the long term.'

'Right,' she said, and went upstairs to the bedroom, closing the door very firmly behind her.

Chapter 32

The news that Brendan was back in the country had filtered through to the media by the following day. He went to see the guards with his solicitor, Ciara, while Dominique headed off to work. Kelly stayed in bed. Although she was awake when both of her parents left the house, she went back to sleep again afterwards. She didn't have the strength to face another day just yet.

Brendan and Ciara spent nearly two hours at the offices of the Bureau of Fraud Investigation in Harcourt Street. There were reporters outside as he left, but Brendan ignored them and got into a waiting taxi. He directed the driver to Dominique's house in a roundabout way, just in case anyone was following him. He'd got used to doing things like this while he was away, although it made him feel like the criminal he so fervently believed he wasn't. And after his talks with the guards, he was beginning to hope that they didn't think so either. Ciara was optimistic too. Stupid maybe, criminal not, was what she'd said. And unlucky, of course, in the way things had conspired against him.

The house was deserted when he eventually arrived back. He knew that Dominique was at work, but he wasn't sure where Kelly was. Dominique had told him that their daughter had originally planned to spend a few days in the capital, and Brendan supposed that if she'd changed her mind she would've stayed in Cork the previous night, but he had no idea what she wanted to do now.

It was strange to be in the house on his own. He wandered through the small rooms, picking up things he didn't recognise – new books and magazines, a framed photo of Dominique and Kelly that had obviously been taken after he'd left, a DVD of a newly released movie. All the stuff in the house was different too – the cups, the cutlery, the sheets, the towels; none of it had been taken from Atlantic View. Even though he knew he wouldn't be coming home to Atlantic View, he'd still imagined that their own things would be in the house that Dominique was renting. But she'd reminded him at the weekend that not only had Atlantic View been sold, everything in it had gone too. Her words had been like a blow to his stomach. He'd known they'd have to sell things but he hadn't quite realised the enormity of what had happened. Now, by himself for the first time since he'd come back, he was beginning to understand it.

He'd been so looking forward to finally coming home. It had been hard to be on his own for such a long time. Now he wanted his family around him. The only problem was that his family had other things to do. Not that he should have been surprised. After all, he'd left them to fend for themselves. And that was what they were doing.

He couldn't get over the fact that Dominique had got a job. He hadn't imagined her going out to look for work. He'd supposed that she'd stay on at Atlantic View and that she'd get some support from Lily and Maurice. He'd left what cash he'd been able to lay his hands on in Kelly's book, although he knew that it wouldn't see them far. But he'd hoped that he'd be able to sort his affairs out quickly. It hadn't worked out like that, though. From the time things had started to go wrong, he'd felt like someone caught in a tidal wave, not knowing which way it was taking him. He'd been working furiously and getting nowhere. Doing stupid things simply to try to keep his head above water. When he'd been attacked in Panama, he'd been sure he was finally going to go under. He'd thought he would die there, away from everyone he knew and everyone he cared about.

And then he'd phoned Gabriel, and his brother-in-law had been calm and reasoned and non-judgemental.

Brendan had arranged to meet him in a hotel bar in the Bocas del Toro district of the city on a day when the rain sluiced from the skies and drenched the surrounding area so that it was almost impossible to be outside. When Gabriel – so like Domino in many ways, although she never really saw it – strode across the tiled floor, shaking the rain from his dark hair, Brendan realised that he wasn't as alone as he'd thought after all.

Gabriel had given him a detailed account of what had happened when he himself had turned up at Atlantic View following Brendan's disappearance. He told him how devastated Dominique had been and how shocked the entire family was. He gave him the intimate details behind the newspaper headlines – like Dominique laying all her jewellery on the table and deciding what pieces she could keep (the small diamond on a chain and the locket she'd then given to Kelly for her twenty-first birthday); or like Kelly sitting on the leather chair in Brendan's office, her eyes closed, saying that she was trying to sense where he was; or like Lily making pots of tea for everyone who turned up, trying to lift their spirits even though her own were battered and bruised.

Brendan had cried then and said that he'd made the most God-awful mess of things. Then he'd apologised to Gabriel for saying God-awful, and Gabriel had said that he could say what he liked to him these days, not that it mattered – it *was* a God-awful mess. And then Brendan had said that it was a pity Gabriel wasn't a priest any more because that way he could hear his confession, and Gabriel had told him that confessing didn't matter but being sorry did. Brendan assured him that he was as sorry as a person could be for messing up everyone's lives. Gabriel had said that maybe it was time to come home and face up to things, and that even though it would be hard Brendan would have plenty of support because his family still cared about him. Gabriel said that he knew this because he'd listened to them talking, and although they were angry with him, they were also very, very worried about him. And, he added, Brendan couldn't do anything here, so far away from everyone. He needed to be with the people who loved him.

And so he'd come home.

Even though home didn't mean Atlantic View any more. He'd been horrified when he realised that his beautiful house had been put up for sale, and even more horrified when it had sold much more quickly than he'd expected. He'd been sure that Dominique would get some legal advice that would have allowed her to do a deal with the banks and keep the house. How was it, he wondered, that real criminals managed to hang on to property, while his wife has succeeded in losing theirs? There had been a quote from her in one of the online reports he'd read in which she'd said that she wouldn't be contesting the bank's application for possession of the house because she didn't feel as though she was entitled to stay there any longer. He'd screamed at the computer monitor then and had thought about ringing her mobile to talk to her. But he couldn't. He was still trying to access funds and was afraid that his call would be intercepted and that it would all go even further wrong. Besides, he wasn't ready to talk to anyone and he didn't want them to find out where he was. And he didn't know how he could possibly explain to Dominique the thoughts that had raced through his head the night he'd come home late, bundled up his clothes and disappeared into the night.

But, so far, being at home had all been very different to what he'd expected. Naturally he knew both Dominique and Kelly would be angry, but he'd imagined that once they got over the shock of his return, they'd welcome him back. He knew that Dominique had always dreaded being on her own, and he couldn't get over the independent streak that she seemed to have developed now.

It was almost as though she didn't want him there. As though he wasn't the most important person in her life any more, when she'd always told him that he was. Well, after Kelly, she'd laugh, but then Kelly is still only a kid and she needs me more than you. Sometimes Brendan had been envious of Dominique's relationship with their daughter – it seemed to him a little unfair that they were so close now when in those early weeks he'd been the one to do everything for the baby and the one to keep it all together. Dominique was grateful for that, he knew. She said so regularly. She was thankful that he'd been there for her. So thankful that she'd forgiven him the indiscretion with Miss Valentine, as she'd called Laura Kingston. That affair had been brief and meaningless, and when Dominque had discovered the text message, he'd been horrified at the idea that he might lose everything. So he'd played ball ever since. Hadn't stopped him from losing, of course, but at least he hadn't lost it all to a vengeful wife.

He stopped thinking about the past and began to concentrate on the future. After their meeting in Harcourt Street earlier, Ciara had told him that he would probably end up in the High Court as creditors to whom he'd given personal guarantees pressed for payment, although some had been partly satisfied by the disposal of his assets. She said that it might be possible to work out a settlement, depending on Brendan's resources. She still couldn't rule out the possibility of criminal proceedings and a jail sentence, she'd added. These days there was a lot more anger about so-called white-collar crime. As always, Brendan protested that he wasn't a lawbreaker; he'd just made some terrible mistakes. He hoped that coming home to face the music would show that he regretted them deeply.

Dominique had just sent a quartet of golfers out to the course when the main phone rang.

'Hi, Domino,' said Paddy O'Brien when she answered it. 'I thought I'd check in and see how you were doing.'

It was nice to hear his voice. Nice to hear the genuine warmth and concern in it.

'Not too bad,' she said. 'Though I have a horrible feeling that it's all going to be a bit more public soon and I'm not sure how things will pan out.'

'Have you made any plans?' asked Paddy.

'Not yet,' she replied. 'Brendan was seeing his solicitor today, so I guess we'll know after that.'

'If you need anything at all, just let me know,' said Paddy.

'Thanks,' said Dominique. 'I will.'

'Call me any time.'

'Thanks,' she said again.

She'd only just replaced the receiver when her mobile phone, on a ledge beneath the reception desk, started to vibrate. Staff weren't supposed to use their phones when they were on duty (something Paddy knew, which was why he'd used the switchboard), but Dominique answered hers all the same.

'Hi, Maeve,' she said, having checked who was calling.

'How're things?' demanded her friend. 'Are you all right?'

'I'm fine,' Dominique assured her. 'A bit overcome by the drama of the last couple of days, but OK.'

'Where are you?'

'I'm at work. I'll call you later.'

'At work?' Maeve was astonished. 'Don't you need to take some time off and make plans?'

'I couldn't let them down. I'm the only one on today. Look, I can't talk now, I'll catch you later.'

'All right,' said Maeve. 'But you're mad, you know that? Anyway, I'm rooting for you.'

It was good to know that two people were rooting for her, thought Dominique.

Her phone rang again. She glanced around her before answering.

'Hi,' said a cheerful voice. 'It's Lizzie from the catering company. I hope you had a fantastic night. Is it OK if I drop by later on this afternoon to pick up the glasses?'

Brendan rang her later in the afternoon. He hadn't left the house since his return from Harcourt Street and had spent some time watching the TV, where his return to Ireland had made the news. Nobody had yet figured out where he was staying, which relieved him, but the publicity wasn't good. Once again the reporters gave a litany of the problems associated with his businesses, accompanied by photos of himself and Domino in their Dazzling Delahaye days.

She'd turned into a real beauty, he thought, as he looked at a still of his wife in a black and white dress, her dark hair piled high on her head, glittering diamond earrings in her ears and a matching necklace around her throat. She was still beautiful. The news switched its focus to another story, and the picture of Domino faded.

We were good together, Brendan told himself, and we can make it like that again.

He picked up the phone and called her. But it went to her voicemail. He left a message saying that he hoped she'd be home soon.

She hadn't noticed the phone vibrating because she was very busy. There had been a constant stream of players in and out all day and she'd had her hands full organising them while at the same time taking bookings for the coming week and making sure that everything was on track for the competition scheduled for the weekend. She enjoyed being busy, though. And she liked it when they thanked her afterwards for looking after them so well.

Brendan wasn't sure exactly what time Dominique was due home. She'd told him the previous night that she was working all day, but he didn't know what that actually meant. And she hadn't been very communicative, so he hadn't tried to discuss it any further.

He was startled by a ring at the doorbell. He walked into the front room and looked cautiously out of the window. There was a small green van parked outside the gate, partly obscured by the privet hedge that grew inside the wall. He could make out the word 'Catering' and was debating whether the van was a genuine one or whether it was some ruse by a reporter to get him to open the door when the bell rang again.

He went to the door and opened it. A small, pert girl with a green baseball cap on her head smiled at him.

'Hi,' she said. 'Is Mizz Delahaye in?'

'No,' said Brendan.

'Oh.' Lizzie Horgan looked disappointed. 'I told her that I'd be along to collect the glasses and stuff. I'm a bit early, but I was passing by so I thought it would be worth while dropping in. Do you know where everything is?'

'You catered for the party?'

'Yes,' said Lizzie. 'Were you at it? Did everything go OK?'

'That probably depends on your point of view,' said Brendan.

'The food was all right, was it?' Lizzie looked concerned.

'I'm sure it was. I wasn't actually at the party,' Brendan told her. 'I was a last-minute arrival.'

Suddenly Lizzie's eyes widened. 'You're Brendan, aren't you? How did I not realise it before? You're her husband.'

'Yes,' said Brendan.

'You're back.'

'Yes,' said Brendan again.

'Wow.' Lizzie wasn't quite sure how to deal with this. Ash had always told her to be calm and professional no matter what the situation, but she'd never before been confronted by a possible on-the-run criminal.

'I'd appreciate it if you'd respect my privacy,' said Brendan. 'There's already been plenty of information on the news about my return.'

'Of course,' said Lizzie. 'Well, look, I'm just here to collect the stuff, so . . .'

'I'll help you.'

Brendan brought the boxes of glasses and the small wine chiller to the van and loaded it up.

'Thanks,' she said as she closed the van door. 'I appreciate that very much.'

'You're welcome.' He took his wallet from his trouser pocket and pulled out a fifty-euro note, which he handed to her.

'Everything's paid for,' said Lizzie. 'It's fine, thanks.'

'For your help,' said Brendan. 'It seemed to be a lovely party. And for your discretion.'

'You don't need—'

'Take it,' said Brendan. 'You never know when a bit of cash will come in handy.'

Just before she finished her shift at five o'clock, Paul Rothery came into the clubhouse.

'Hi, Domino,' he said. 'I've just seen the news.'

She smiled nervously at him.

'There are a number of people who know you work here now,' he said. 'If anyone rings to talk to you or tries to harass you, then pass them on to me.'

She looked at him in surprise.

'You're a valued member of our team,' he said. 'We look after our people.'

'Thank you.'

'I hope everything works out,' said Paul.

'I hope so too,' she said.

Sorcha arrived a couple of minutes later to take over. Dominique picked up her bag and walked towards her car. She was startled when another car door opened and someone got out, but then sighed with relief as she realised it was Maeve.

'What are you doing here?' she asked her friend.

'I wanted to check up on you,' said Maeve. 'I wanted to make sure everything was OK, because I didn't think you'd have the opportunity to call me later and I saw the news and I'm worried about you, Domino.'

'Nothing to worry about,' said Dominique. 'Whatever happens happens.'

'Yes, but I'm worried about what you plan to do. With him.'

'Him?'

'Brendan, you clown. He's staying with you, isn't he?'

'Yes.' Dominique frowned suddenly. 'Is that a problem, Maeve? Do you object to him being in your house?'

'Not in the way you think,' said Maeve. 'He's . . . well, he's still your husband and it's not like I'm going to tell you to throw him out, but you've got on fine without him for the last year and done a great job of building a life for yourself, and you don't want to throw it all away, do you?'

'How would I be throwing it all away?'

'Getting caught up with Brendan's stuff.'

'I never did before.'

'You were Dazzling Domino,' Maeve reminded her. 'The country's most famous socialite.'

'Not the most famous.' Dominique grinned. 'Not by a long shot. Anyway, those days are far behind me.'

'It's just . . . well, you're letting him live with you. Are you getting back together with him?'

'I don't know what I'm doing,' said Dominique.

'Is he going to sponge off you?'

'You don't know Brendan,' said Dominique. 'He's resourceful and determined and he'll find a way to make money. It's what he does.'

Maeve looked at her doubtfully.

'He also left you,' she reminded her. 'He walked out without a word. You had to sell everything.'

'He made a mistake. We all make mistakes.'

389

'Not monumental ones like that. What is it about him that keeps you so loyal?'

'I'm not that loyal,' said Dominique. 'But he stood by me when I needed it. And however I feel about what he's done, he needs me to stand by him right now.'

'Just don't lose everything all over again,' begged Maeve.

'I don't have anything to lose,' Dominique told her.

'Yes you do,' said Maeve. 'And you know it.'

Dominique drove back to Fairview more slowly than usual. She was thinking about Maeve's words and her friend's attitude. Maeve hardly knew Brendan, and she was basing everything on his abrupt departure as well as what she had read in the papers. Nothing in the papers gave a true picture of Brendan. Nobody who wrote about him really knew him. Dominique was utterly certain that one day he would make back what he had lost. Not straight away. But eventually. And then they would be back to where they were before.

She couldn't understand what it was that Maeve thought she had now that was worth hanging on to. A life where she worked long hours for a very modest salary and barely scraped by. A house that would fit into the kitchen of Atlantic View. A social life that was dull and boring, even with the occasional night out with Paddy O'Brien. Who she'd certainly have to lose if she and Brendan stayed together. Her husband wouldn't understand her being just good friends with another man. She wasn't entirely sure that he believed she and Greg hadn't once had something between them.

She leaned back in the driver's seat as heavy traffic forced her to a stop. In some ways, having Brendan around made her feel secure. But until the court case was out of the way, she didn't know how to plan for the future. Whatever happened, though, she was sticking with him till then. She'd made a promise to Lily and Maurice and the rest of the Delahayes. None of them would leave Brendan to face things on his own.

Afterwards, though . . .

She had no idea about afterwards.

It was still hard enough to deal with now.

Chapter 33

Brendan's High Court appearance was scheduled for the following month. During that time he worked hard with Ciara to come up with possible settlements so that his time in court would be as brief as possible. Although most of his investments in Panama had tumbled, liquidating others would repay the majority of the money he owed to his investors, and further money had finally been freed up from his overseas bank accounts. Delahaye Developments, having been placed in administration, couldn't be saved, and although Ciara had suggested that the directors (Barry, Matthew and Brendan) might be prosecuted for reckless trading, she thought it was unlikely. She also planned to argue that since the property market had taken a downturn since the investors had given Brendan money, it was unreasonable for them to expect that they would get it all back anyway. She and Brendan were cautiously optimistic that if they got most of it back they would be if not happy, at least a little less angry. And although the money hadn't been in the original account that had been opened in the name of the Barbados scheme, Ciara had successfully argued that Brendan had many overseas projects and that just because specific funds hadn't been paid into this account didn't mean there was a sinister reason for it being empty.

During that time he went through everything in detail with Dominique, explaining the various options with her so that she fully understood what was going on. He was surprised at the depth of the questions she asked him and her grasp of the situation. He found that he was enjoying sitting with her in the evenings, looking at the legal papers and discussing them over a glass of wine. Not since the days before Kelly was born, when Dominique had taken care of the company's accounts, had he spent so much time with her.

'Maybe I should have kept you on as my accountant after all,' he said one night as she queried one of the figures on the spreadsheet in front of her.

'Maybe you should,' she responded. 'After all, none of my charity events ever lost money.'

'It'll be different from now on,' promised Brendan. 'Over this past year I've realised what the most important things in my life are.'

'So have I,' said Dominique.

'I hope I'm part of them.' He put his arm around her. She allowed him to leave it there, but when he pulled her closer and kissed her, she broke away. 'I'm sorry,' she said. 'But I'm not ready for this. Not yet. I need everything to be sorted before I can . . . before . . .'

He nodded. 'I understand. I do, really.' He put his arm around her again, more casually this time, and that was how Kelly (who was now back at college in Cork but had come to Dublin for a few days) found them when she arrived home after a visit to her grandparents.

'Did you have a nice time, sweetheart?' Brendan looked up at her.

'Yes thanks. Gran and Grandad hope you're both OK.'

'Did you tell Gran I'd call over during the week?' asked Dominique.

'Of course.' Kelly nodded.

'Are you coming to stay here next weekend?' Brendan looked at his daughter hopefully, but Kelly shook her head. She was going to a concert with Alicia, she told him. The next time she'd be in Dublin would be for the court case.

'Ciara is very optimistic,' said Brendan on the morning of the hearing. He'd come downstairs dressed in a charcoal-grey suit, deep purple tie and plain blue shirt. 'I hope it all works out as she expects. When it comes to money, people can be very unreasonable.'

'And you blame them for that?' Dominique was wearing black – a simple shift dress with a buckled belt that emphasised the fact that she'd lost even more weight in the last few days. She slipped into her five-year-old black Balenciaga shoes.

'I understand how they feel,' said Brendan penitently. 'But we'll come through this, Domino. As dazzling as ever.'

She looked at her pale face in the mirror. She certainly wasn't Dazzling Domino today. She was Drab Domino. She hadn't intended to be, but her nerves were etched in the worry lines on her face, and no amount of make-up could make her look anything other than wan and terrified. She stared at her reflection and opened her make-up bag again. She might not be dazzling, she muttered under her breath, but she sure as hell wasn't going to be drab.

Kelly followed Brendan down the stairs. Her youth and beauty made up for the fact that she too was pale. She was wearing a Topshop dress in shades of green and gold that complemented her Celtic skin and strawberry-blond hair, and a pair of lime-green high-heeled shoes she'd bought in Marks & Spencer.

'Well,' said Brendan as the three of them stood in the hallway. 'We're ready to take them on. Delahayes United.' He put his arms around them and hugged them close. 'You're the most important people in the world to me,' he said.

Neither Dominique nor Kelly said anything in reply.

Gabriel, who'd decided to stay in Ireland until Brendan's High Court appearance, had offered to drive them to the hearing. Dominique was happy to let him – she couldn't bear the thought of sitting in a taxi in uncomfortable silence. Not that she expected much talk with Gabriel either today, but at least he was family too.

He arrived exactly on time and they got into the car. It was Seamus's car, his ten-year-old silver Ford Focus, which he maintained lovingly. Dominique hoped that some aggrieved investor didn't jump out and hit it with a hurley or a baseball bat.

There was a group of photographers waiting for them outside the big, imposing building by the Liffey. Dominique glanced up at its enormous dome as she hurried up the steps holding Brendan's hand. Kelly was on his other side, also holding his hand.

'Are you sticking by him, Domino?' cried one of the reporters.

'Are you ashamed, Mr Delahaye?' asked another.

'Where did you get your shoes, Kelly?' demanded a third.

There was a flurry of flashbulb lights and then they were inside the round hall of the building, their footsteps echoing on the tiled floor.

The courtroom was smaller than she'd expected, and the judge reminded Dominique of Judge Judy, a programme she'd watched some afternoons in the days after Brendan's disappearance, when she hadn't had the energy to do anything else. But this woman didn't speak in Judge Judy's impatient American voice. She was quiet and determined and she listened courteously to the application that was being made by Brendan's creditors as well as the arguments from his own counsel.

Dominique listened to the arguments but she couldn't entirely follow them. She knew that Brendan's admission of guilt – insofar as he'd disappeared and allowed his company to fail and hadn't given any information to his investors – had earned him a slightly more sympathetic hearing from the judge. But she also knew that just because he was sorry about it, didn't mean that everything was going to be all right.

I never imagined, she thought as she gazed up at the high ceiling and allowed the drone of the legal arguments to pass over her, that this was how things would end up. The first day I saw Brendan Delahaye I thought he was a good-looking, man. And when I went out with him I thought he was decent and hard-working. I didn't think about marrying him then, even though I was probably in love with him. It was the pregnancy that brought it all to a head. But if I hadn't got pregnant, if I hadn't got married . . . where would I be now? Happily married to someone else? A career woman? Divorced? It was all so random, she thought. So unpredictable. You did your best, but sometimes the worst happened and you didn't know why.

She glanced at Brendan, who was looking straight ahead of him. He's not as bad as they're trying to make out, she told herself. He truly isn't. He got caught up in trying to be better than anyone else, in trying to live up to their expectations. And maybe he got caught up in trying to make more money than we ever needed to make.

394

It's all very well for people to say that money doesn't bring happiness, but for a time it probably does. And maybe that always comes at a price.

A shaft of sunlight cut through the courtroom. She thought suddenly of Glenmallon and the fact that today there was a big corporate event on. She'd done a lot of work on the organisation (most of that fell to her these days because she was so good at it) and had been scheduled to be at the club today, but she'd switched with Sorcha. Sorcha had wished her the best of luck in court and said that she was a great woman standing by her man.

Dominique hadn't thought about it like that. She wasn't standing by Brendan for herself. She was doing it for all of the Delahayes, who'd been so good to her. Well, she was doing it for Lily and Maurice, certainly. And in a way for Barry and June too. She still wasn't entirely speaking to June, who, she felt, had been horrible at every available opportunity. But she knew that her sister-in-law wasn't good with stress and she knew that stress could make you act in ways you'd later regret. After the collapse of Delahaye Developments, Barry had been barred from ever being a director of another public company, which had upset June deeply. However, the two of them had somehow managed to get over all their anger and grief and rage and just about everything else and were no longer talking about separating or divorce or even selling their beautiful house. June – as Dominique had always known – had substantial savings of her own, which she'd accumulated over the years that Barry had worked with Brendan. She hadn't really intended this money to be used for anything other than her own special treats, but the financial shock that had hit them after the company folded had meant that eventually she'd come clean to Barry about the size of her slush fund and they'd used it to pay off the accumulating bills. And then, despite all their gloomy predictions, Barry had got a job in the office of a local factory and was doing very well there. So for June and Barry at least, things were looking up.

Dominique was also standing by Brendan to support Greg and Emma. Greg had given one or two interviews to local papers in which he'd come out publicly and stood behind Brendan, saying that his brother might have been foolish and made promises that he hadn't been able to keep, but that he hadn't set out deliberately to defraud people. His comments had been both eloquent and heartfelt and had done Brendan a lot of good.

Emma, despite the newspapers having doorstepped her once or twice, had kept a low profile. But when she eventually had to give a comment she'd said that Brendan Delahaye had always been good to her and so had Dominique, who had been a friend long before they'd both married into the Delahaye family and who, she hoped, would be a friend for a long time to come.

Emma's words had touched Dominique deeply and she'd sent her a text message to thank her. Emma had replied by saying that she hoped she'd see Domino soon, although, being perfectly honest, she didn't care if she never saw Brendan again as long as she lived.

But the main reason Dominique was supporting Brendan was for Kelly. She didn't want her daughter to feel that her father was being deserted by the people who loved him. She didn't want her to think that she didn't care what happened to him or their family. Because it was all very well for the media to poke and pry and to write horrible articles (no matter how true some of the facts might be), but if they were hurtful to Brendan, they were doubly hurtful to the people who loved him. And Kelly, Dominique knew, still loved her father with the same devotion she'd had when he'd brought her to the building sites and given her her own bright yellow hard-topped hat and Timberland boots and told her that one day she'd own the company herself. It couldn't happen now, of course. It probably never would have happened. But that didn't mean that Kelly would want to see her dad hung out to dry by the only people who were still there for him.

The court was adjourned until later that day, and Brendan, Dominique and Kelly hurried past the reporters and across the road to the Legal Eagle, where they had soup and sandwiches (though neither Dominique nor Kelly ate very much). Dominique couldn't help wondering how many times other people had rushed from the court to the pub; how many people guilty and innocent had sat on the seat she was now sitting on, wondering how things would turn out.

396

'I think it's going quite well,' said Brendan. 'Donnelly thinks so too.'

Garvan Donnelly was Brendan's counsel for the court hearing. He had been recommended by Ciara.

'Good,' said Dominique.

'It's great that you're here with me,' said Brendan. 'It means a lot.'

Dominique nodded.

'And you too, honey.' He reached out and squeezed Kelly's hand. 'I love you.'

'I love you too, Dad,' said Kelly. 'I do, really.'

The atmosphere in the court was overwhelming. Dominique supposed that it was meant to be like that, to make you feel nervous and ill at ease. She felt sick as the judge took her place in front of them again, and she realised that she was trembling. She could see, though, that Brendan was holding himself ramrod straight.

The judge started talking.

She reminded Dominique of Evelyn and the way she would lecture her when she was younger. She used the same tone of resigned sorrow that someone could be so stupid and so wrong, as she told Brendan that he had let down the people closest to him but that at least now he was accepting responsibility for his actions. She commented on the strain that had been put upon Brendan's friends and relatives and the stress that had been caused to his employees too. She noted that previous orders had enabled the banks to repossess his home, which, she said, had undoubtedly been very traumatic for his family. She was now making orders freezing the other assets that had come to light and requiring him to make payments to people who had given him money. She realised that not everybody would get back everything, but that Brendan hadn't set out to defraud them intentionally.

'They're probably lucky,' Brendan muttered to himself. 'They're getting cash back from me now, but if they were stuck in the Barbados property deal, they'd be stuffed!'

Eventually the hearing finished. They left the court together and got into the Ford Focus again. Flashbulbs from the photographers' cameras went off in their faces as they drove away.

'This must be what it's like to be Angelina Jolie,' said Kelly with determined cheerfulness as Gabriel drove along the quays.

'She's welcome to it,' said Dominique grimly.

'I guess overall it wasn't as bad as it could have been.' Brendan sighed. 'It all seems so black and white in court, but things are never that simple. Ciara says that it's highly unlikely that the Director of Public Prosecutions will pursue a criminal case now.'

'Thank God,' said Dominique.

He kissed her.

'Thank you for sticking by me,' he said.

'You stuck by me,' she told him simply. 'How could I do anything else?'

Garvan Donnelly had told Brendan that there would be other small issues relating to the case to be dealt with, but that Ciara would look after it all. There would be no need for Brendan to visit the court again, unless he failed to comply with the orders.

'I'll do everything I'm supposed to,' he said. 'I want to rebuild my businesses.'

'How?' asked Dominique.

'Well, I guess there's no such thing as bad publicity,' he told her. 'I'll go back to doing extensions and stuff. I bet people will be keen enough to get a notorious builder like me doing work for them. Give them a feeling of superiority too, to be able to say to their friends, "Hey, had that guy Brendan Delahaye working for me. Remember, he used to be a hotshot. Now he's my brickie."'

'Oh, Brendan . . .'

'Where will you set it up?' asked Kelly.

'I'll start out like I did before,' replied Brendan. 'From home.'

'We don't have a home,' said Dominique tightly. 'It's been sold.'

'Anywhere you are is home for me,' Brendan told her.

Dominique said nothing, because she really didn't know what to say.

It was hard to believe that it was over. Dominique was hoping that the media would forget about them now and move on to the next interesting thing. There were plenty of other people in the news all worthy of attention from the journalists and broadcasters, and now that Brendan was back and had shown himself to be penitent about what had happened, Dominique felt that their lives were no longer the soap opera they had somehow turned into.

After Gabriel had driven them home, Brendan said that he'd make everyone something to eat, but Dominique told him that she wasn't hungry and that actually she wanted to go for a walk. When he asked where, she said that she didn't know, but that she wanted to be by herself for a while.

At first Brendan tried to argue with her, but Dominique told him that, not entirely surprisingly, she had a headache and wasn't in form for talking, and could he just this once understand that she didn't want him with her. Kelly listened to the edgy conversation between her parents with concern and then told her father that she was hungry and he could cook something for her.

Dominique went upstairs and changed into her black skinny jeans and a black jacket. When she came down again, Gabriel, who'd come into the house with them, was standing in the narrow hallway.

'I thought perhaps I could join you on that walk,' he said.

She knew that she and Gabriel had to have a heart-to-heart talk. She hadn't felt able to until Brendan's hearing was out of the way. Now, although she was tired and truly would have preferred to be on her own, she nodded.

They walked in silence as far as Marino Mart, and then Gabriel suggested having a coffee in the café overlooking Fairview Park.

'I know it's been tough for you,' he said as the waitress placed two cappuccinos in front of them. 'You've been incredibly brave, Domino.'

'No I haven't,' she said. 'I've just got on with it, that's all. And I'm still . . .' She closed her eyes for a moment and swallowed hard before continuing. 'I'm still very angry with Brendan. If you want the truth, I'm not sure I can forgive him.'

'You have to move on,' said Gabriel.

'I know that,' she said. 'And the thing is, Gabriel, I've done some monumental moving on while Brendan was away.'

'Moving on from him?' asked her brother.

'Moving on from depending on him,' she replied.

'Will your marriage be all right?' asked Gabriel. He looked quizzically at her. 'What about this man you were seeing?'

'Paddy.' Dominique gazed into her coffee cup. 'I haven't actually seen him since Brendan returned. He's phoned me once or twice to see how things are coming along. He's a nice man.'

'Is there a but?'

'But I'm not sure about men right now. Nice or otherwise. Married to them or not.'

'Well, look, Domino, whatever you do . . . if you need help or advice or anything . . . just call me.'

She sipped her coffee in silence.

'I know I'm not exactly the best person to give advice. I know you're still angry with me too because of Emma. But I'm better with other people's problems than my own.'

'I'm not angry with you,' said Dominique. 'Maybe it's more disappointment. All my life I thought you were the one person who'd always do the right thing no matter what. It was very irritating, actually. Your goodness was a constant in my life, even though I resented thinking that way; then suddenly it was gone.'

Gabriel nodded. 'I thought I was that person too,' he said. 'And even though I kept saying to myself that I couldn't possibly go to bed with her that day, another part of me was thinking why not? I mean, I know why not, but for that mad moment I couldn't help myself.'

'You used to tell me that people can always help themselves,' she reminded him. 'You said it was a pathetic defence to say otherwise.'

'I was arrogant to even think that,' said Gabriel simply. 'All I can say is that when I was in that room with Emma, I couldn't think of anything other than that I wanted to make love to her.'

'But why then?' asked Dominique. 'You'd spurned her before. So what changed?'

'I did,' said Gabriel. 'Oh, Domino, you've no idea what it was like being me. I thought I was so right about everything. I thought I was blessed. I thought I knew it all because God had shown me the way. I thought I was special. I thought I was above petty day-to-day desires.' He smiled shakily. 'It was easy to think that way when I was studying. Even in the seminary, which can be difficult for tons of reasons. But I was fine, I was Gabriel Brady and I knew exactly what I wanted from life. And then I went to the parish and I connected with people for the first time. There was a woman who'd lost her husband. He was only sixty. They'd been married for thirty years. She was heartbroken. Really and truly heartbroken. She told me that it had been perfect with him, that he'd been the only man she'd ever loved. "Oh, Father," she said. "I slept with one or two before. But I only loved him." She looked at me then as though I was supposed to be scandalised that she'd slept with other men, but I wasn't. I was hurting for her and wondering what it would be like to love someone that much and lose them. Because of course you're not meant to lose God. But a person . . . for them to be part of your life . . . I was lonely up there as well, Domino, and I put my arm around that woman and I hugged her and suddenly I wanted someone to hug me and care for me and it wasn't enough to tell myself that God loved me. I got over it, of course. But it niggled at me all the time. And then Emma got in touch and she was worried about her mother and I wanted to help her, and . . . Well, obviously in the end I didn't help her at all, did I? And she was disappointed in me! It was a mind-blowing experience as far as I was concerned, but as soon as it was over I knew that she'd had better. I felt utterly useless. I'd been hopeless at the act that had betrayed everything I ever stood for.'

Dominique hadn't interrupted him. Now she handed him a paper napkin and he blew his nose.

'When I discovered she was pregnant, I nearly died,' he said. 'I thought, at first, that it was my baby. But she told me it wasn't. And I realised I'd been arrogant again in thinking that. And that I'd completely blocked out of my head the fact that she had another life. Not only was I a sinful, useless priest, but I was unwanted by the person I'd sinned with too.'

'Oh, Gabriel . . .'

'She was right, of course. She'd only wanted me to see what I'd be like, and I disappointed her. So she went back home.'

'Would you have left the priesthood for her?' asked Dominique. 'If she'd wanted you to?'

'I knew then that I was going to leave,' Gabriel said. 'I didn't love her, but I wanted to sleep with her again. And at the same time I was supposed to be supporting her while her mother was sick. I was a mess. And then I suppose I came to my senses. When I saw her and she was pregnant . . .' He sighed. 'She didn't love me either, Domino. She just wanted to sleep with me.'

'Emma could never get over the fact that you weren't interested in her,' said Dominique. 'You became a challenge. But she did have feelings for you, I know that. It was what worried me about the two of you all along.'

'Does she love Greg?'

Dominique took a sip of her coffee and then replaced the cup carefully on its saucer. 'Greg is a good man. He's very caring and loving. Maybe she thought that was what she needed. I know that he desperately wanted someone to love him too. Maybe that's what we all want. Will you find someone, Gabe?'

He shrugged. 'Maybe one day. I'm not really equipped yet for emotional attachments. But I'll get there eventually.'

'I hope so,' said Dominique gently. 'You deserve it.'

'At least you have someone,' said Gabriel.

'Huh?'

'Brendan does love you. He said it over and over again in Panama. He meant it.'

'Funny way of showing it.' Dominique sighed.

'He was lost,' said Gabriel. 'He didn't know where to turn.'

'He should've turned to me.'

'He was afraid of letting you down.'

'He did that anyway,' said Dominique.

'Do you forgive him?'

'Do you want me to?'

'It's important,' Gabriel told her.

'Oh, I know.'

'You've been fantastic so far.'

'I know that too.'

'But he worries about the future.'

'So do I.'

'He needs you.'

'Does he?'

'You can work it out,' said Gabriel.

'Maybe,' was all Dominique said in return.

She went for her walk after the coffee. She walked along the seafront and sat on one of the public benches, staring out at the sea, which was being whipped into a froth by the coastal wind. Gabriel wanted everything to be simple, she thought. Right and wrong. Black and white. But there were shades of grey. There always would be.

She just didn't know what her shade of grey actually was.

Chapter 34

The invitation, when it arrived, was a surprise. It was addressed to Brendan and Dominique Delahaye, and because she was home before him, Dominique opened it. It was to a reception in Cork to mark the opening of a new sporting facility in the city. Although Brendan had been involved in the initial planning stages for the centre and she herself had helped with a fund-raising event for it, Dominique nevertheless wondered if the invitation had been sent by mistake. She couldn't imagine that the organisers would really want either of them to attend the opening ceremony, even though the media fuss around the court case had died down. Or maybe, she thought cynically, they'd been invited precisely because of the media fuss, in the hopes that it would create more publicity for the centre. It was so hard to know whether people wanted them for themselves or for what they could bring. The last bit of fuss about them had been Brendan's return to the workforce, which, much to her surprise, had been reported on the news.

She'd been pleased when he got the job so quickly, not starting out again as a brickie as he'd suggested, but working as an adviser to a small construction company on planned future projects. He'd called the managing director, a man he'd met a couple of times previously, and set up a meeting with him, after which he'd come back to the house and told her that they were putting a contract in place. Dominique couldn't believe it had been so easy, and she admired the way he'd simply picked up the phone and made the call, not worrying about what Pat Donnelly thought of him.

There were so many things she could admire him for. And so many things to blame him for. But what was the point in spending your time resenting someone's actions? Brendan had admitted his mistakes, got over his reaction to them, picked himself up and started to move on again. She was proud of him for that. And she was still being as supportive as possible. She knew how important it was to have support when you'd gone through a tough time. She knew how easy it was, even when things seemed to be going your way and you were feeling better about life, to allow despair to creep back into your heart. So she had allowed time to drift by and they were still living together in the house in Fairview and had become, in everyone eyes, Mr and Mrs Delahaye again. Not the Dazzling Delahayes this time. No glitz and glamour and high-profile social occasions. But already there had been murmurings that Brendan Delahaye was doing great work for Keystone Construction, and now they were being invited to a reception along with politicians, councillors, local businessmen and sportspeople. They were being included in the fold once more.

She turned the invitation over in her hand. If they accepted, they would be making a very public statement. About themselves and about their future together. They hadn't yet had a serious conversation about their future, though she knew that it was something they had to do.

In the weeks since Brendan's return, he had lived with her in the house in Fairview but she hadn't allowed him to share the bedroom with her. She hadn't been able to allow him close to her. She didn't know whether it was because she was still, deep down, angry with him for leaving them, or whether it was because she was afraid that if she allowed him into her bed, he'd take back a level of control over her life that, during the months of his disappearance, she'd reclaimed for herself. She didn't say this to Brendan; she simply told him that she wasn't ready to sleep with him, and he'd replied that he understood her feelings and that he would wait until he'd proved himself to her, which made her feel as though she was being harsh and unreasonable, especially as he seemed to have put his foot on the ladder of success again.

Maeve told her that she wasn't being harsh and unreasonable at all, that he'd left her to deal with his pile of shit and that he'd had a damn cheek turning up on her doorstep again in the first place.

406

He'd abandoned her, Maeve pointed out. She shouldn't just take him back. But Dominique had replied that she owed it to him to support him now and that she couldn't tell him to leave. Unless that was what Maeve wanted. Which made Maeve shake her head and say that of course he could stay, even though it was clear to Dominique that she'd prefer it if he went.

Evelyn had also discussed the situation with her. It was on one of Dominique's days off, when she made her fortnightly trip to Drimnagh to see her parents, that Evelyn had, as she put it herself, felt obliged to speak her mind.

'I didn't like him at the start,' she told Dominique. 'After all, he got you pregnant and . . .' She held up her hand as Dominique tried to interrupt her. 'I know that things are different now, but it was how it was back then. All the same, he did the right thing and married you and he stood by you. I know you loved him, Dominique. I could see it every time you spoke about him. And I know it was hard for you after Kelly was born, and I understand how hard it must have been for him too. And for all this I think he was a good man and a good husband. He tried to provide a good home for you too. I always thought he got involved in too many things, and I never liked all of this newspaper stuff and you becoming some kind of Barbie doll, but that's the way things turned out and you seemed to be happy in your life. But when he left you . . . I didn't believe the bad things that people said about him, but he still did some bad things, didn't he? He cheated people.'

'He didn't mean to,' said Dominique. 'Like he said, it all spun out of control.'

'Oh, I know all that,' said Evelyn. 'I talked to Lily about it. She's delighted he's home and has a job, and so am I. But I'm worried about you, because you're looking after him and yourself and you always look so tired.'

Dominique smiled at her. 'I'm tired because I'm working hard, but I truly do like the job. And I'm not supporting Brendan financially either, now that he's working again.'

'But how are you both?' asked Evelyn. 'That's the thing. Are you happy?'

'Even if I wasn't, wouldn't you say that I'd made my bed and I had to lie in it?' asked Dominique, although her tone held a hint of humour.

'Maybe I would've once,' agreed Evelyn. 'But now I think that you should be happy. And I don't know if you are.'

Dominique said nothing.

'When you were first going out with him, I thought that you loved him more than he loved you.'

Dominique looked at her in astonishment.

'You were so taken by him,' said Evelyn. 'You would have done anything for him.'

'I suppose you're right.'

'But now you're a different person. You're an adult. You've done things for yourself.'

'I know.'

'And it's not that I didn't think you deserved all the money or anything, but happiness is more important.'

'Oh, I know that.' Dominique smiled at her. 'It's easier for a camel to get through the eye of a needle than for a rich man to enter the kingdom of heaven, isn't it?'

'If it's right for you, then it's right,' Evelyn told her. 'But if it's not . . . Well, I wouldn't blame you, Domino.'

Dominique looked at her mother in complete amazement. Was she seriously suggesting that she wouldn't flip at the idea of her leaving Brendan now that he was back in Ireland? Did she genuinely think, after so many years of believing the opposite, that happiness was more important than staying together? And had she really just called her Domino for the first time in her life?

'We're going to go,' said Brendan firmly as he looked at the invitation.

'Is it a good idea?' asked Dominique. 'You know the papers will be there, as well as people that perhaps you don't want to see.'

'I can deal with that,' said Brendan. 'Most people haven't lost too much money – a damn sight less than me, anyway! And they know it too, thanks to the report in the *Examiner* last week.'

Brendan had given an interview to one of the newspaper's most experienced journalists. It had been a wide-ranging discussion, in which he'd confessed to having been utterly devastated when the company had run into trouble. He told the journalist that he thought perhaps he'd had a kind of breakdown when it happened. He hadn't been able to function normally.

'Yet you left the country and your family and all the people who depended on you,' the journalist commented.

'And that was the worst mistake of my life,' Brendan admitted. 'I hope I get the chance to make up for it.'

The piece had been sympathetically written and presented, and it was clear that the journalist believed that Brendan had been unfairly treated over the collapse of Delahaye Developments. After all, he noted, the industry had gone into a downturn, and Brendan's wasn't the only company that had run into trouble. It was the manner of his dealing with it and his already public profile that had turned it into such a major news story. The reporter had also commented on the support that had been given to him by Dominique, and how her refusal to say anything bad about him had made people look again at what had happened to the company. He'd called it the Domino Effect Mark 2.

Brendan had been pleased with the article and had already been approached by a number of businessmen asking him about his role in Keystone Construction and the projects they might be getting involved in. He had related all this to Dominique with a smile, telling her that things were coming good and that people were beginning to respect him again. RTÉ had also been in touch, asking him to appear on TV to talk about his experiences. Dominique had begged him not to, saying that she wanted them to keep a low profile for a while, but Brendan was toying with the idea. It would put him back on the map, he said. It would do exactly what Dominique's own confessions years earlier had done. Open doors for them.

Dominique wasn't sure that she wanted any doors opened. Ever since moving to Fairview and working at Glenmallon, her life had been quiet and private, and it suited her. She'd enjoyed making her own way and doing her own thing.

Yet it was good not to feel alone any more.

It was nice to have someone in the house at night.

And it was comforting to think that Brendan still wanted to be with her.

The day before the reception was a busy one at Glenmallon, with every tee time booked and plenty of eager golfers ready to get out on the course. Dominique shouldn't have been working that day, but because she and Brendan had accepted the invitation to the reception, she'd switched her shift with Meganne.

Meganne had asked her if Brendan's return meant the end of her relationship with Paddy O'Brien.

'I don't have a relationship with Paddy. He's just a friend.' Dominique had repeated her mantra to her colleague.

'I'm sure he wants to be more than that,' Meganne told her. 'In all the time I've known him, he's never come to Glenmallon as often as he has since you've started working here.'

'We get on well together.'

'And how will Brendan take to that?' asked Meganne.

Dominique had laughed dismissively, and Meganne had then simply asked if she had something new to wear to the event. Because, she said, if Dominique was going to be in the public eye again, it would be important to look as great as possible.

'I don't need anything new,' Dominique replied. 'I've a nice dress I've hardly ever worn that will do perfectly. Besides, it's not a madly glam do or anything, Meganne. It's just in the new sports centre, that's all.' And a buffet afterwards in one of Cork's most upmarket hotels. Which was why she wasn't simply wearing jeans.

'I suppose if I had gorgeous vintage pieces like you, I wouldn't think of anything new either,' agreed Meganne, and Dominique laughed at the notion that her Chanel shift dress, which had languished in her wardrobe for four years, only having been worn twice, could be considered vintage.

The last time she'd worn it had been to one of her lunchtime charity auctions. The event had taken place at Dromoland Castle, and photographs had appeared in the glossy gossip magazines almost at once. The caption beneath them had been 'Domino Dazzles Dromoland'. The dress had been plain and simple, but it had been perfectly set off by the diamonds she'd worn around her neck and the crystal clips in her glossy hair.

'Hello, Domino.'

She turned around in surprise. Paddy O'Brien hadn't phoned or emailed as he normally did before he came to the golf club. Her heart started to beat faster.

'Hi,' she said calmly. 'How are things?'

'Great, thanks.'

He looked tanned and healthy in a casual white shirt and biscuit-coloured chinos. She knew he'd been in South Africa, where he was advising on a new course there. She'd been glad that he was away, because despite her dismissal of Meganne's question, she hadn't felt able to juggle her friendship with Paddy and her marriage to Brendan.

'When did you get back?'

'Last week.'

He usually phoned when he got back from a trip. She supposed she couldn't blame him for not doing it this time. After all, she was living with her husband again. And the truth was that even though she considered Paddy to be a good friend, men and women were never just friends. Having a man as a friend could complicate a marriage. She'd proved that herself, hadn't she, with Greg?

'Did it go well?'

She'd only spoken to him twice since Brendan's return – the day he'd phoned her at work, and a few days later, when she'd called him and told him that she was a bit caught up with domestic matters, as he might imagine, and that she'd probably be out of touch for a while. He'd been sympathetic and understanding and told her not to worry; he was sure he'd see her again soon. But he hadn't, because shortly after that he'd gone to South Africa again. He hadn't told her about this trip; she'd heard about it at the golf club.

'Pretty well,' he told her. 'I was at the Cape. It's lovely there. Not unlike Cork, actually.' He smiled. 'There's a town called Bantry, too.'

'Really?'

He nodded. 'So a real home from home.'

'I'm glad you had a good time.'

'I was working,' he reminded her. 'It wasn't all about good times.'

And then he laughed. 'Well, it was, to be honest. I like what I do.'
His eyes softened. 'And how about you, Domino? How are things
with you?'

'Oh, you know.' She shrugged. 'Getting on with it.'

He frowned. 'Getting on with what, exactly?'

'Changed circumstances,' she told him. 'Brendan's return.'

'He's living with you?' Paddy raised an eyebrow quizzically.

'Yes,' she said. 'Well, for the moment anyway.'

'For the moment? Has he plans to move out?'

'I don't know.' Dominique looked at Paddy uncertainly. 'We
haven't . . . decided yet.'

'Right.'

'It's been very difficult,' she said.

'I can imagine.'

'You can't.'

'Probably not,' conceded Paddy. 'At least my marriage troubles
followed a well-worn course, both domestically and in the media.
Though from what I can gather, Brendan's old friends seem to be
embracing him again.'

Dominique shrugged. 'It's hard to tell. Those kind of friendships
can be very fickle. So I can't turn my back on him.'

'Are you in love with him still?' asked Paddy.

It was a question she was sometimes asked by the people closest
to her. But, until now, not by Paddy O'Brien.

He waited silently for her reply.

'I can't answer that yet,' she said finally.

'Oh, Domino.' Paddy looked at her sympathetically. 'You still
don't know what you want, do you?'

'No,' said Dominique. 'But I'm fine. I'm managing.'

'There's more to life than just managing,' said Paddy.

The phone rang and she picked it up.

Paddy waited while she talked to a club member, and then, as
the query became more complicated, he shrugged at her and walked
away. He hadn't returned to the desk by the time she left for home.

Brendan wasn't in when she arrived back at Fairview. She changed
out of her navy and white suit and into a pair of sweatpants and a

412

lightweight fleece. Then she sat in the living room with the doors to the yard open and watched the bamboo grasses sway in the breeze.

She remembered doing the exact same thing in their first house in Firhouse. Brendan had planted the grasses along either dividing wall. He liked them. He thought they were restful. So did she. And when she'd been coming through her depression, she'd often sat at the patio doors of the kitchen, listening to the gentle rustle of their slender green leaves in the wind.

She got up from the chair she'd been sitting on and went to the cupboard beneath the bookshelves in the alcove beside the fireplace. She took out a large cardboard box, which had once contained a set of Waterford glass tumblers. Now it was full of photographs.

They were old photos, because in the last few years they'd used their digital camera or video instead of the 35mm Olympus that Brendan had bought on their honeymoon in Majorca. Almost all the shots they'd taken with that camera were in the box. Photos of themselves on honeymoon – she with her newly acquired tan and Brendan with his peeling nose. Photos of Kelly, lots and lots that Brendan had taken when she'd been a baby and Dominique hadn't even noticed him snapping away; she was glad now that he had, because otherwise she wouldn't have any memories of Kelly's first months. Photos of them as a family, too, in Templeogue and in Terenure and shortly after the move to Atlantic View.

She stopped as she looked at one of the two of them, her and Brendan, side by side with the ocean in the background. She was wearing white capri pants and a bright pink top; he was in blue Bermudas and topless. His shoulders, even in the Irish summer, showed the telltale marks of too much sun. They had their arms around each other and they were laughing.

Dominique remembered Kelly taking the photo the summer of their move to Cork. She'd told them to smile and look happy and it had been easy to do, because Dominique remembered that time, when she was still dazzling and before the discovery of Miss Valentine, as being one of the happiest of her life. It had never been quite the same after she'd found the mobile phone with the text message on it.

But we got over it, she reminded herself. Just like we got over all the bumps along the road. We stuck with each other, and it wasn't easy but we kept going together. We can still keep going together, because we understand each other. Perhaps we always will.

Chapter 35

Emma phoned Greg. She'd been thinking about it for quite a while, and now she picked up the phone and dialled his number before she had the chance to change her mind. He sounded surprised to hear her voice.

'I'm sorry for calling you at work,' she said. 'It was just that . . . well, I wondered would you like to come to dinner tonight?'

'Huh?' He sounded startled.

'I have a voucher,' she said. 'I won it in a draw in the supermarket.'

'A raffle?' he asked.

'No, you put your name on the back of your receipt,' she said. 'It doesn't matter how I won it, Greg. I just did. And I have to use it before the end of the month. Lily and Maurice asked Lugh if he'd like to have a sleepover with them tonight and so I thought that maybe you'd like to come out with me.'

Greg hesitated.

'If you don't want to, it's fine,' said Emma. 'I was thinking it would be a good opportunity for us to chat, that's all.'

'OK,' Greg said. 'I suppose there are things we need to discuss.'

So now they were together in the elegant hotel restaurant over-looking the river Lee, with their salmon roulade starters and two glasses of crisp Sauvignon Blanc in front of them.

'How are things with you?' asked Greg as he buttered some brown bread.

'Not bad.' She smiled slightly. 'I've got a job.'

'What sort of job?' he asked.

'Part time,' she said. 'While Lugh is at school. In a café.'

'A café?' He sounded surprised.

'I needed something to do,' said Emma. 'It's a long time since I earned my own money, and I quite like it. Besides, it's lonely in the house when Lugh's at school.'

Greg nodded.

'I probably would've looked for something even if you were still living with us,' Emma continued. 'After all, I'm not really on the ladies-who-lunch circuit any more.'

'Is that a bad thing?'

'Probably not,' admitted Emma. 'I enjoyed myself when I did it with Domino, but it's not as much fun now, and of course I only got invited to half the events because of her anyway.'

'I'm sure that's not true.'

'We're not among the rich and famous,' Emma told him. 'You have to be able to dig deep to go to some of those lunches.'

Greg nodded.

'I don't mind really,' said Emma. 'I like the work and it means I get some adult conversation during the day.'

'Understandable.'

'Anyway, I thought it was important to tell you about the job because you'd hear it anyway and because I suppose it means you should give me less money.'

'You should say all this to your solicitor,' Greg told her.

'I know. But I wanted to talk to you, not him,' said Emma. 'I don't want . . .' Her voice faltered. 'I know we live apart and the divorce will come through eventually, but I don't want it all to be so impersonal.'

'Divorce *is* impersonal,' said Greg.

'No,' she told him. 'It's very, very personal.'

'Depends on your perspective, I guess.'

'I think what I wanted to say was that I'm not trying to get anything out of you, Greg. I'm not looking for anything I don't deserve. I know the solicitors do their thing, but the truth is that I never meant to hurt you and I need you to believe me.'

'You never meant to hurt me?' He cut his bread in half and then in half again.

'I know, I know.' Her voice quavered. 'I have a nerve saying that, haven't I? But I did what I did and I was crazy and stupid and I wasn't thinking of hurting you or not. I wasn't thinking of anything.'

Greg filled her water glass from the jug on the table.

'I should've slept with him at Domino's wedding,' said Emma. 'I'd planned for that, you know. I was wearing my hottest dress and I'd had a fake tan done and everything. But I couldn't get close enough to him.'

'So you got close to me instead.'

'You were more real,' said Emma. 'He was my fantasy.'

As Dominique had, for a time, been his, thought Greg.

'I've been thinking about it a lot,' Emma continued, 'and I want to say that it wasn't that I didn't love you, Greg. It was that . . .' She took a deep breath. 'I always got what I wanted before. When I was a kid, when I was at school . . . I was the girl people wanted to be and I got the boys that the other girls fancied. I know that's pathetic and juvenile, but that's how it was. And I needed Gabriel to want me too.'

Greg nodded silently.

'You were so lovely, and great to me, but the thing was that you wanted me just like all the other guys. Even though you were a million times nicer and more wonderful. Gabriel was a prize. I know that makes me sound even more shallow and selfish than you probably already think I am, but it's the truth. I obsessed about Gabriel, I admit it. But I also thought that maybe I could have the relationship with him that you had with Domino.'

'We agreed no more talk about Domino and Gabriel.' Greg's voice was firm.

'I wanted the closeness,' Emma continued, regardless. 'The kind of understanding that you two seemed to have. I thought I could have that with Gabriel. I don't know why on earth I didn't just realise I could have had it with you.'

Greg was silent.

'I was an idiot,' Emma told him. 'I didn't realise that there was give and take, and maybe I had to change a bit to be like Domino.'

'I didn't marry you for you to be like Domino,' said Greg.

'And I didn't marry you as a second choice to Gabriel,' said Emma. 'To be totally frank with you, I didn't realise how much I needed you . . . how much I loved you . . . until I slept with him. I know that's terrible,' she added as he opened his mouth to speak. 'I know I'm a horrible, horrible person and I understand why you want to divorce me and I understand why you'll probably be glad never to see me again. But I do love you, Greg. I was just too shallow to realise it.'

He stared wordlessly at her.

'Please, please believe me when I tell you I'm not just saying this because I'm lonely by myself. It's not because I need a man, any man. It's you I miss, Greg. I've no right to ask you to think about a life with me in the future, but I have to, because I can't walk away without making the effort. The effort I should've made years ago.'

She took a large gulp of water from her glass.

'I love you. I'm sorry I was so bad at being married to you. But I'm begging you to think again about what we're doing. Think again about the divorce.'

Dominique and Brendan had driven directly to the sports centre. Brendan pulled up in the car park and slotted Domino's Fiesta into a space between two Range Rovers.

'I miss my Lexus,' he said glumly. 'I wonder what kind of price the bank got for it.'

'I'm used to the Fiesta now,' said Dominique. 'It's easy to zip around town in it.'

'Do you see the positive side in everything these days?' he asked as he opened the door.

'Not at all,' she said. 'But I try.'

She stepped out of the car and looked at the new building.

'I would've loved to stay involved with this.' Brendan's eyes followed hers and his voice was wistful. 'I wish it had been different.'

'So do I,' she said briskly. 'But it's the way it is. Nothing we can do.'

He came around the car and took her by the hand. 'We can dazzle them,' he told her. 'We can let them know that the Delahayes are back.'

They walked across the car park and into the foyer of the centre. There was a small knot of people standing there, and Dominique

418

recognised a couple of city councillors as well as a woman from a local sports partnership with whom she'd once had lunch when talking about an initiative to get children in the area more active.

'Brendan Delahaye.' One of the councillors broke from the group and extended his hand. 'Good to see you.'

'Good to see you too, Peter.'

The councillor turned to her. 'And Domino. Glad you could make it.'

'Delighted to be here,' she said.

Everyone else in the group then welcomed them, and as more and more people began to turn up, Dominique found herself being isolated from Brendan, caught up with a different set of people.

'How are things with you now, girl?' Katie Curtin, a governor of the school Kelly had attended, came up to her.

'Not too bad,' said Dominique. 'Getting by.'

'Well I'm delighted that everything's turning around,' said Katie. 'And that you and Brendan are back together. I never believed for a minute half of what people were saying, but you know what it's like, don't you? Once the rumours start, you can't stop them.'

'Indeed I do,' said Dominique.

'That interview with him was great,' said Lena Doyle. 'And fair play to you, Domino, for supporting him the whole time.'

'So listen, are you thinking of coming back to Cork?' asked Nancy Shaw, the owner of the art gallery where Dominique had bought the paintings for Atlantic View. 'We miss you around the place.'

'I don't think so,' Dominique told them. 'Brendan's based in Dublin now, and our house was sold, so . . .'

'He's a fine-looking man, the new owner,' said Siobhan Conners. 'Keeps himself to himself, though. We don't see much of him.'

'But it's not the same as having you there,' said Nancy. 'And of course he doesn't ask people to the house.'

'Do you miss it?' asked Lena.

'Of course,' said Dominique.

'I heard you have a great job in Dublin,' Siobhan said.

'It's just a job,' said Dominique, 'but I enjoy it.'

'You're the kind of person who always bounces back, aren't you?' Lena smiled at her. 'No matter what.'

'You think so?'

'Absolutely,' said Lena. 'I remember hearing you on the radio years ago talking about what a hard time you had after you had Kelly, but you were so positive and cheerful about it all. I remember thinking that you were a great woman, and very inspiring.'

'I'm not really,' said Dominique.

'So listen, Domino.' Siobhan lowered her voice. 'Can we ask you one thing?'

'What?' she asked warily.

'Did you know where Brendan was when he was away? Was he secretly in touch with you? Sending you texts and emails and stuff?'

'No,' replied Dominique shortly.

'He didn't tell you anything?'

'No,' she repeated.

'And you took him back anyway?'

She said nothing.

'It's another lesson to us,' said Lena. 'I keep on throwing poor aul' Paudie out. And he hasn't done anything half as bad.'

Dominique shrugged and then stood to one side as another woman joined them.

'Dominique!' Stephanie Clooney beamed at her.

'Hello, Stephanie.' Dominique could feel a quiver of anger run through her. She might have forgiven Brendan, but she still hadn't forgiven Stephanie for her remarks about the charity money or for cutting her dead in the car park.

'It's so lovely to see you back in town,' said Stephanie. 'We've all missed you so much.'

'Hardly,' said Dominique mildly. 'I haven't heard a word from anyone.'

The women around her looked sheepish.

'Not that I'd have expected to, of course,' she continued, her voice suddenly brittle. 'After all, people were branding me as some kind of gangster's moll.'

'Ah, Domino, that's not true,' said Lena.

'I think it is,' said Dominique.

'Brendan had disappeared with people's money,' said Stephanie. 'You can't blame us for being cautious.'

'No,' said Domino. 'I don't blame you. But I wish you hadn't judged me too.'

'I'm sorry,' said Siobhan. 'I guess I did judge you. And I was wrong.'

'All water under the bridge now,' said Stephanie briskly. 'It's lovely to see you again, Domino, and I do hope that you'll be able to support our functions in the future. I realise times are harder, but you'll be very welcome.'

Dominique said nothing. She was battling with the desire to punch Stephanie Clooney on her big Roman nose.

A slight commotion at the door distracted her and she saw the Lord Mayor arrive, surrounded by more public figures she vaguely knew, as well as some of the players from county teams. Then the manager of the centre got everyone's attention and started the proceedings.

Dominique was on the opposite side of the group to Brendan. She could see him standing beside a local politician and she wondered if he was already starting to build up contacts again. She knew that he wouldn't stay working for Keystone Construction for ever. He was the kind of man who liked to do his own thing. And even though it had all gone so badly wrong for him, he seemed to have the ability to win people back to his side. She'd been worried that coming to this event would give people the opportunity to harangue him over the past, but nobody had. In fact she'd heard one or two remarks about the fact that he'd been badly treated by the media and that he was a local man who'd done his best and who needed their support. She wondered if people felt the same way about her. But then she wasn't a local girl. She never had been.

Her eyes grazed the crowd and then stopped suddenly. Paddy O'Brien was standing among them. She didn't know how she hadn't seen him before, because he was taller than most of the men in the room, even Brendan. It was the first time she'd ever seen him in a suit and tie, and it changed his appearance completely. He'd lost the easy, casual air she associated with him and looked somehow more intense. He was watching the Lord Mayor and seemed to be engrossed in his speech, but then he suddenly looked around, straight at her. She felt herself blush as their eyes met, embarrassed at being caught staring at him. He smiled, and gave her a small nod of acknowledgement. She supposed she shouldn't be surprised that he was here. He was a sportsman after all.

The Lord Mayor finally finished speaking and invited everyone to join him at the hotel across the road, where they'd be able to have some food and drink. Dominique wondered if Paddy would be at the hotel. He'd once told her that he didn't like standing around making polite conversation, even though, as part of his job, he often had to do it.

'Come on, Domino.' Brendan was suddenly beside her. 'Let's go.'

She followed him out of the hall and across the street. Most of the people at the opening came too, and it wasn't long before the function room was buzzing with noise. Dominique stood beside Brendan as he spoke to one of the councillors about his long-gone hopes of being on the county hurling team, and his efforts in the past to support them with sponsorship. He hoped that in the future, when things were better for him, he'd be able to help them again.

It's like he was never away, thought Dominique. He's just brimming with confidence. He's the most amazing man ever.

'And of course, it's lovely to see you again too, Domino,' the councillor said. 'We've missed you at our functions over the last while.'

'I guess it'll be some time before I'm at another,' she said.

'Not at all,' he told her. 'We'd be delighted to see you again. You added glamour to our occasions.'

'Not really,' she said.

'We're hoping that you and Brendan eventually come back to the county,' said the councillor.

'We will,' Brendan assured him. 'It might take a while, because it's a tough time in the business right now, but Cork is our home.'

'Excellent,' said the councillor, and then went off to help himself to canapés.

'Just like old times,' said Brendan to Dominique.

'Yes,' she said.

'Everyone's being supportive,' he told her. 'They realise that I was caught up by circumstances. They're prepared to give me the benefit of the doubt. I wasn't sure that they would.'

'You've known most of them all your life,' she said. 'Maybe you should have given *them* the benefit of the doubt.'

He looked at her in surprise. 'I didn't think of it like that.'

'No,' she said. 'You went off and did your own thing, and you didn't give me or Kelly the benefit of the doubt either.'

'Ah, Domino, don't start a row now,' said Brendan. 'Not when— Micko!' He broke off as one of the county hurlers came over to him. 'How's she cutting, boy?'

Dominique drifted away from the buffet table and out into the main part of the hotel. She headed for the ladies', where she fixed her hair and glossed her lips. She was replacing the gloss in her handbag when the door opened and Emma walked in.

The two of them looked at each other in surprise.

'What are you doing here?' asked Emma. 'You didn't tell me you were coming down.'

Emma and Dominique had begun phoning each other more regularly since Emma's conciliatory comment to the journalist, although they hadn't actually seen each other since the tense night in Briarwood.

'We're just here for the opening of the sports centre,' said Dominique.

Emma's brow creased. 'Why?'

'To be honest, I'm not sure,' replied Dominique. 'We got an invitation and Brendan wanted to come, so . . . we came.'

'I didn't get one,' said Emma.

Dominique shrugged. 'I don't know how or why we were on the list. Maybe someone being curious.'

'How did they get your address?' asked Emma.

'I don't know that either,' said Dominique. 'But they did, and Brendan was keen to come. He's working the crowd just like he always did.'

'And so,' said Emma as she stood in front of the mirror and brushed her hair, 'it's back to the future for the Dazzling Delahayes.'

'Don't call us that,' said Dominique.

Emma took her cosmetics out of her bag.

'So why are you here?' asked Dominique as she watched her sister-in-law freshen her make-up.

'Dinner.' Emma explained about winning the supermarket draw. 'Though I'm sure they were disgusted it was me and not someone far more worthy,' she added.

Dominique laughed, and Emma smiled at her. Quite suddenly, the tension that had existed between the two women for the last few months melted away.

'Who came with you?' asked Dominique. 'Lily?'

'No.' Emma explained that she'd asked Greg, and Dominique's eyes widened. 'You and Greg having dinner together? That's very civilised.'

'So's you coming to an event with Brendan.'

'I guess so.' Dominique smiled without conviction. 'What's the story with the pair of you?'

'I don't know.' Emma capped her lipstick and turned to look at Dominique. 'He's got a lot to deal with as far as I'm concerned. But we both love Lugh and we want to be good parents to him, and we want him to feel part of a family.'

'Which is important when you've split up,' agreed Dominique.

'Yes . . .' Emma hesitated, and Dominique looked at her curiously.

'Are you thinking of getting back together?' she asked.

'I'm not sure I can persuade him of that.'

'But you might?'

'I've asked him to think about it,' said Emma. 'I don't know how likely it is, but I had to try.'

'It would be wonderful,' said Dominique warmly. 'I hope it works out.'

'You mean it?'

'Totally,' she said. 'You're right for each other.'

'I'd better get back,' said Emma. 'He's dropping me home.'

'Well, behave yourself,' said Dominique.

'I feel like it's the first time I ever went out with him.' Emma smiled faintly. She leaned forward and hugged Dominique. 'Who knows how things will turn out? But I'm hoping for the best. And I hope things work out for you and Brendan, too.'

She walked out of the ladies' and back to the foyer, where Greg was standing waiting for her. She told him about Brendan and Dominique and he looked startled for a moment; but then he put his arm firmly around her shoulders and walked with her out of the hotel.

The function room was buzzing with conversation. Dominique hadn't realised that quite so many people had been invited to the event, but Marie Hannay, yet another of her charity circuit acquaintances, had told her that it had been a massive coup for the city to raise the funding for the centre and that lots of people had been involved. It was right, she said, that they should all be thanked.

Dominique nodded in agreement and glanced over at Brendan, who was deep in conversation with the Lord Mayor and the local politician. Dominique was surprised that the politician didn't have somewhere else to go to. In her experience they were always rushing to the next event, always giving the impression that their presence was needed somewhere else. The three men were talking animatedly, and every so often the politician patted Brendan on the back. Dominique was glad to see him in the thick of things where he belonged. Somehow the trauma of the last year was beginning to fade away. It was almost as though it had never happened. Almost as though she was still Dazzling Domino.

Although not quite, because she wasn't in the thick of things herself. There was a hierarchy of women and she wasn't with the main group. Right now she wasn't with any group; she was standing by herself in the doorway. Well, she thought, I'm not here trying to raise money or do anything for anybody. I don't have to work the room. I don't have to be nice to people and persuade them to be nice to me too. I don't really have to be here at all.

She turned away from the reception and back into the hotel foyer. She crossed the cream marble floor and went outside. There was a chill in the late-evening air, and she pulled the light jacket that matched her dress a little closer around her shoulders as she stepped past a cluster of people who'd come outside for a cigarette. She strolled towards the wooden boardwalk that ran along the river at the side of the hotel. There was nobody else around. She rested her elbows on the handrail as she gazed into the swirling dark water beneath her.

She wondered for how long people would remain talking in the function room. She and Brendan had booked into the hotel for the night, but they had to leave early the next morning because she was due to be at the golf club by ten. When she'd said this to Brendan, explaining that she'd changed her shift with Meganne only for the day, he'd frowned and said that she should have taken both days off. And when she'd told him that she hadn't taken a day off, just made a switch, and that she couldn't have done it for two days, he'd looked at her impatiently and told her that it wasn't such a big deal to take a couple of days off, was it? She'd reminded him of all the times he'd ranted about people not turning up to work at Delahaye Developments, and he'd looked abashed and told her that he understood. But earlier tonight, when they'd been standing side by side with glasses of wine in their hands, he'd murmured that it was a right pain that they had to get up at the crack of dawn, because it was nice to be able to do this again.

He was right, of course. It was nice to dress up in her Chanel and feel glamorous for the first time in ages. It was nice to be invited to things. It was nice to feel that they belonged once more, even if things would never be quite the same as they were before. Although she supposed that if Brendan really did manage to turn everything around, it was entirely possible that he could become a successful businessman again.

And then maybe they'd come back to Cork, although she couldn't imagine him wanting to come back and live anywhere other than Atlantic View. And even if he did become a successful businessman for the second time, it wouldn't be easy to reclaim their old house. Particularly as Paddy O'Brien insisted he was very happy living there.

Would it make a difference, she wondered, if she asked Paddy to sell it back to them? Would he shrug his shoulders and say OK because she was a friend? And would Brendan wonder about their relationship if he did?

Not that it was any business of Brendan's what relationships she'd had while he was away. It was more important for her husband to wonder how she felt about him.

She sighed deeply and massaged the back of her neck. She was getting tired of wondering how she felt about Brendan, tired of constantly analysing her feelings. And she was afraid of what it might mean.

Chapter 36

She went back inside. Even though the number of people in the room had thinned out, it was still quite full. Brendan was now talking to a man Dominique recognised as a coach to one of the county football teams. She went over to them, and Brendan smiled at her and introduced her to the county manager.

'Back in a mo,' he then said, leaving her with the coach and turning his attention instead to someone Dominique didn't recognise. This wasn't unfamiliar territory to her. In the past, he would often palm off less important people on her, or people he'd tired of talking to, so that he could move on to someone more interesting or more useful while she launched a charm offensive on the person he'd left behind.

'Not a bad performance by the team this year,' she said to the coach, hoping that they hadn't been utterly trashed but feeling that her remark was sufficiently vague not to leave her open to accusations of total ignorance. And she'd got it right, because the coach beamed at her and launched into a story about their training schedule and the match they'd played against Tipperary being the clincher and a whole heap of other stuff that went completely over her head. But she knew that she was keeping her fixed and interested smile upon him as he explained why they had a great chance of the title the following year and that the facilities at the sports centre were fantastic and that the lads would be delighted to do some indoor training there.

'That's wonderful,' said Dominique warmly. Do I sound sincere? she wondered, and then thought she must do, because the coach was off again, this time describing the kind of training regime he had in mind for the team. Meanwhile, she could see that the politician had joined Brendan and the man she didn't know and their conversation was jovial and friendly.

How long? she wondered. How long before we're back here and part of everything? How long before I become a glittering socialite again? How long before our lives are exactly as they were before?

But they would never be the way they were before. Too much had changed. And although it had been hard at first, there were lots of things about her life now that she liked. And very few about her old life that she missed.

She missed not having to think about money and using her credit cards without worrying, although she was used to it now and so perhaps it didn't really matter much. She missed organising the fund-raising events, but if she was really honest with herself, she didn't miss the events themselves. She missed feeling as though she was doing something useful for the charities, but she'd been involved with a number of Glenmallon's charity golf outings and so she knew she was still doing her bit. And she was working hard too on the day-to-day part of her job. Which she liked very much.

She didn't want to give up her job. Not that it was a prospect while Brendan was based in Dublin. But she knew that he was itching to get back to Cork. Of course she could always get another job if they moved. Brendan hadn't wanted her to work before; not unless she had a little business of her own, he'd said. An antique shop. Or an art gallery. Something stylish and creative and appropriate. She wasn't a stylish and creative person. Not really. She was someone who liked getting things done. Which was surely very appropriate.

'Hi, Domino.' Paddy O'Brien detached himself from a group of people near the buffet and came over to her. 'How are you?'

'I'm fine.' Her eyes scanned the crowd to see where Brendan was now. Still talking to the same person, engrossed in their conversation.

'Enjoying yourself?'

'It's a good event.'

'That's not what I asked you.'

'I can't honestly say I'm enjoying myself,' she admitted. 'It's too difficult.'

'Why? Are people giving you a hard time?'

She shook her head. 'No. Not really. It's just that I feel out of place.'

'Why did you come?'

'Because we were invited. I don't know how that happened. I didn't think anyone knew our address.'

'It's my fault,' said Paddy.

'Yours?' She looked at him in astonishment.

'The organisers asked me. They thought that as I'd bought your house, I might have a forwarding address for you in Dublin.'

'Oh.'

He grinned at her. 'They didn't know that I'd actually been there.'

'No,' she agreed. 'I guess not.'

'They don't know that we have a secret past.'

She laughed. 'We don't have a secret past.'

'We've gone out to dinner together,' he protested. 'And nobody spotted us.'

'It's hardly a secret past, though.'

'Pity. I liked the sound of it.'

'Actually I quite like the sound of it too.'

She saw Brendan look across the room at her and a frown cross his face.

'I've missed seeing you,' said Paddy. 'But I guess you and your husband have patched up your differences, which is probably a good thing.'

'We didn't have any differences,' Dominique told him. 'He walked out on me. That's not a difference. That's a course of action.'

'Right.' Paddy looked surprised. 'But now he's back and you're here with him.'

'The invitation was to both of us,' said Dominique.

Brendan walked over to them.

'Hello again,' he said.

'Hello.' Paddy extended his hand. 'Paddy O'Brien.'

'Yes,' said Brendan. 'I know who you are. You bought my house, didn't you?'

'I did,' said Paddy. 'A lovely house, and I'm sorry about the circumstances.'

431

'But the house wasn't enough. You were seeing my wife too. Trying to move in on all my assets, were you?'

'Brendan!' Dominique sounded annoyed.

'Domino and I became friendly,' said Paddy. 'That's all.'

'She threw a party for you.'

'It's what she's good at. So she said when she offered to organise it.'

The two men looked at each other.

'Well, thanks for taking care of her.' Brendan put his hand on Dominique's back. 'Come on,' he said. 'I want you to meet Timmy Gannon. He's going to captain the team next year and he's great fun.'

'See you, Domino,' said Paddy as Brendan ushered her away.

They moved to the other side of the room and Brendan looked at her.

'Well?' he said.

'Well what?'

'Is he the real reason I've been frozen out of the bedroom?'

'Of course not!' she said, her voice low. 'I told you already. He's a nice guy, that's all.'

'All the time I was away,' Brendan told her, 'I worried about you. I felt terrible about what I'd done. I was working hard to sort things out. But lately I'm beginning to wonder if I needed to worry at all. You seem to have been perfectly all right on your own.'

'Don't start,' she said. 'You know you're talking bullshit.'

He stared at her. 'Am I?'

'Of course you are,' she replied. 'I met Paddy O'Brien at Atlantic View one day and he was nice to me. And then I bumped into him at the golf club where I was working, and yes, we had a couple of drinks together but that's all. I like him, but there's no huge relationship. I was too busy keeping it all together to have huge relationships, Brendan.'

'I just don't like seeing guys who think they can muscle in on my territory.'

'He doesn't think anything of the sort. And I'm not your damn territory!' Dominique's voice rose.

'OK, OK.' Brendan knew he'd overstepped the mark.

432

Dominique said nothing for a moment, and then told him she was going up to the room to fix her make-up.

'All right,' he said. 'But Domino . . .'

'Yes?'

'I want it to be right between us again. Tonight. I'm back and I've paid my dues and I want us to get back to the way we were. I deserve that.'

She nodded slowly.

'There's more,' he said.

'What?'

'Funds I had overseas have been released. It was a sub-account of another account. Difficult to access. But I heard today. Not a huge amount by our previous standards. Around a hundred thousand.'

'Brendan!'

'And because all of the settlements are made, it's our money. So it gives us a bit of comfort now. You don't have to worry quite so much. Plus, I think I've got a deal from tonight too. I'm back, and so are you.'

'You're unsinkable, you know that, don't you?'

She rested her head on his shoulder for a moment. Then she turned away and walked towards the stairs.

She sat on the edge of the bed, staring straight in front of her, remembering the important moments in her life and how she'd dealt with them. Not always well. Not always badly. But never actually realising at the time just how important they really were.

Was tonight important? She thought it must be. Brendan's revelations about the money and the job changed everything once again. She knew how she felt about it, but she didn't know if she could trust her own judgement any more.

She took out her phone and sent a text to Kelly, who phoned her in reply.

'You all right, Mum?'

'Oh, yes,' said Dominique quickly. 'I was just wondering what you were doing later. I wondered if you'd like to have a coffee with me as I'm in Cork?'

'I'm out with Charlie,' said Kelly doubtfully. 'I thought you'd be too busy tonight to meet up. Are you sure everything's OK?'

'Absolutely,' Dominique said. 'I'm just taking a bit of time out. Not used to wearing my high heels so much again.'

Kelly laughed.

'How's Dad?' she asked.

'Back in his element,' said Dominique. 'Meeting everyone, chatting away, not a bother on him.'

'You can't put him down, can you?' asked Kelly.

'No. But that's a good thing.'

'I love both of you,' Kelly said. 'Always. No matter what.'

'And both of us will always love you,' Dominique replied. 'No matter what. Now go on, enjoy the rest of your night. Tell Charlie I said hello.'

'Will do. See you soon. Take care, Mum.'

Dominique slid her phone closed and replaced it in her bag. She was glad that Kelly was happy. She knew that both the time when Brendan had disappeared and the manner of his return had been as difficult for her daughter as it had been for her, and she was proud of how Kelly had handled it. She was a strong girl, thought Dominique. She would be a strong woman.

She glanced at her reflection in the mirror. She'd made a good job of it tonight, she thought. The Chanel dress, even without the diamonds around her neck, had been the perfect thing to wear. She'd looked elegant and unflappable. She'd behaved in an elegant and unflappable way too, even though most of the time her heart had been racing and she'd been shaking with nerves. She'd done what she had to do. She'd supported her husband.

And Brendan had worked the crowd as he'd always done so that it had eventually seemed perfectly natural that they were both there together again. The problems of the past year were history. He'd bounced back and he'd somehow managed to retrieve some of his money too. She wondered when he'd heard about that. And why he'd waited until this evening to tell her. But that was his way. Keeping his cards close to his chest. She might have been involved in helping with the court case, but he was beginning to move on again. Which was a good thing, especially as everyone now seemed willing to forgive him. And embrace her.

She stayed looking in the mirror for a moment, then she slowly pulled the pins from her hair so that it fell softly around her face. The headache that had been threatening for some time began to ease almost at once. She let out a long, slow breath and closed her eyes. She sat in silence, sifting through the memories of the last year, remembering how tough it had been but reminding herself that she'd come through it.

No matter how awful things are, she thought as she opened her eyes again, the world keeps turning and a new day comes around. And somehow we keep going. I keep going. And I do OK.

She stood up. She took off her jacket and her dress and slid out of her high-heeled shoes, wriggling her toes, which had been squashed by the narrow fit. She went to the wardrobe and took out the jeans, jumper and loafers she'd worn for the drive down. She put them on, then went downstairs again. She could hear the buzz and the chatter coming from the function room as she crossed the wide hallway and walked out of the hotel.

She strode purposefully across the car park, opening her bag as she walked. As always, her keys were at the bottom, beneath her purse, her phone and a packet of tissues. She pulled them free and put them in the lock.

'Domino.'

She turned around.

'Paddy.'

'What are you doing out here?'

She stood with the keys in her hand and looked at him.

'It looks like you're leaving,' he said.

'Yes,' she said. 'I am.'

'Why are you going?'

She shrugged.

'There isn't any trouble, is there? Between you and Brendan?'

'No. No trouble at all.'

'Are you sure?' His expression was anxious. 'He wasn't exactly happy to see you talking to me, was he?'

Domino shook her head. 'He can be possessive, that's all,' she said. 'He's always been proprietorial towards Kelly and me.'

'I was afraid that maybe you and he had argued about it.'

'We don't argue very much,' she said.

'No.' He nodded slowly. 'I can see that. I can see how you smooth things over, make it work. I understand now how it was that he could come home to you.'

'Do you?'

'Yes. You'll keep going with him because he's part of your life and he always will be. You feel a sense of duty towards him.'

'You think?'

'Of course. You took him back and you stood by him very publicly, and if it wasn't for you, things might have been a lot harder for him.'

'He's a good man,' she said. 'Despite what happened.'

'You still love him.' Paddy's voice was flat.

'I'll always love him,' she said.

'So where are you going now?'

'Home,' she said.

'To Dublin?' He looked at her in astonishment. 'Now? Why?'

'I love him, but not enough to live with him any more.'

'Why?' he asked again.

'Too many things have happened,' said Dominique. 'Too many things have changed.'

'So . . . have you told him this?'

She shook her head. 'He's having a good time tonight. I don't want to mess it up now. I should stay and talk to him later. But I can't. I can't go through it all with him right now.'

'But you will?' He was watching her carefully.

'Yes.' She opened the car door. 'I will.'

'I'm not sure you should go back to Dublin now,' said Paddy. 'Not by yourself. It's a long drive, it's late and you're tired.'

'Not that tired,' she told him.

'All the same . . .'

'I'm going home, Paddy,' she said.

'You could come to Atlantic View,' he suggested. 'You could chill out and stay there . . . there are lots of guest rooms, as you know. I'm not trying to get you into bed with me or anything.'

436

'I don't know whether I should feel flattered or disappointed by that,' she said, a sudden hint of amusement in her voice.

'Please don't drive to Dublin now,' said Paddy. 'I'll worry about you.'

'There's no need,' she said. 'I'll drive carefully. I'll be fine.'

'Take my car,' said Paddy. 'If you're going to drive to Dublin at this hour, please drive in something comfortable.'

'My Fiesta is comfortable and I'm used to it,' she said. 'I don't want your car, Paddy.'

'Call me,' he said. 'When you get home. Just to let me know you're all right.'

'OK.'

She kissed him lightly on the cheek. He caught her hand for a second and then released it again. She got into the driver's seat and started the engine.

'Domino . . .'

She hesitated, her hand resting on the gear lever as she looked up at him.

'Take care,' said Paddy gently. 'Drive safely. Call me.'

'Of course.'

He waved as she turned out of the car park and on to the Dublin road. When she reached the outskirts of the city, she pulled in and sent Brendan a text message. Then she moved off into the traffic again.

She turned on the car radio. She switched it from the talk radio that Brendan had tuned into on the way down to her favourite easy-listening station, and allowed the mellow music to wash over her. She felt herself relax as the car ate up the miles back to Dublin.

It was nearly an hour later before her phone rang. She was tempted to answer, because it was Brendan's ringtone, but there was no hands-free in the Fiesta, so she left it alone. A couple of minutes later there was a beep to tell her she had a voice message. It had taken him a long time, she thought, to read the text she'd sent him.

It was past two by the time she pulled up outside her house in Fairview. It was strange, she thought, that she felt such a sense of security as she closed the door behind her. But she did. Absolutely.

She sat down on the sofa and checked her voicemail.

'What the hell is all this about?' demanded Brendan. 'What d'you mean, you need to be by yourself? What have I done now? I thought we had an agreement about tonight. About later. And I wanted you to meet someone too. He works in construction. Weathered the downturn pretty well. Some very interesting opportunities. His wife is on the board of governors of a primary school – right down your alley. You need to meet these people, Domino. They could be good for me.'

But not me, she thought, as she deleted the message from her mailbox. Not good for me. Not any more.

There were three more messages from him, each increasingly irate, each asking her what the problem was, why she had left him at the hotel. One of them asked how he was meant to get back to Dublin. She had the bloody car, he said. The bloody Fiesta.

She deleted each of the messages in turn and then sat in the darkness of the living room.

She wasn't sure if she'd told Paddy the truth when she'd said that she still loved Brendan. She would always care about him. He had been there for her when she needed him most in her life. But she'd been there for him too, when he needed her. She'd repaid him. But now they didn't need each other any more. What she felt for Brendan – the affection and the gratitude – wasn't enough to keep them together. Maybe, she told herself, it had never truly been enough. Maybe it was circumstances rather than love that had seen them last so long as a married couple, and the change in those circumstances had changed how she felt for ever.

She wondered how much he loved her. He'd said it many times since he'd come back, but the truth was, she couldn't help feeling that it didn't matter how terrible things had been for him, that if they'd loved each other as equals, he would never have left. Or he would have contacted her after he'd gone away. But he hadn't. He'd left her and Kelly to worry and wonder, and then, when he'd come back, he'd wanted everything to be the same as it was before. Only it couldn't be. Because she'd changed. She hadn't realised just how much until tonight.

She knew that she didn't want to make love to Brendan or kiss

438

him or rest her head on his shoulder in the evenings as she'd once done. She knew she didn't depend on him for comfort or security. She'd forgiven him, but she didn't want to be with him. And so what was the point in staying? Yes, she decided, she had told Paddy the truth. She didn't love Brendan enough any more.

And really she'd known that from the moment he'd first walked through the door on the night of the divorce party. Despite her fury at him, she'd wanted to support him in the way he'd supported her. She'd wanted him to know that she hadn't abandoned him, that she wasn't standing in judgement over him as so many people had done. She'd wanted him to know that he wasn't alone.

But he was OK now. He had his job and his money and he was in Cork working the room like he always had. She knew that he'd be fine. In a couple of years he'd have another woman on his arm, probably a younger, prettier model who'd become a Dazzling Delahaye alongside him. Dominique didn't care. She had her own life now, and it wasn't as glamorous and it wasn't as exciting, but it was hers to do with as she wanted.

Her phone buzzed. Brendan had sent another message.

Stop being so silly, she read.

She wasn't being silly. She knew that. She said so in her reply to him.

Then she phoned Paddy O'Brien.

He answered straight away, despite the lateness of the hour.

'You're home OK?' he said.

'Of course.'

'I was silly to have worried,' said Paddy.

'I'm glad you did,' Dominique told him. 'It's nice to know that you worry about me.'

'Dominique?'

'Yes.'

'That was a brave thing you did tonight.'

'Not really,' she said. 'Brave was getting on with it after he left. Tonight was just about realising what was important to me.'

'And you know what's important now?'

'Absolutely.'

'You're important to me,' said Paddy, after a brief pause.

She smiled in the darkness. 'And you're important to me too,' she said.

She heard him chuckle at the other end of the phone, and she smiled again.

'I'll call you before I come up to Dublin,' he told her. 'Which will be very, very soon.'

'Great,' she said. 'I look forward to that. I really do.'

She powered her phone off and went upstairs. She stood alone in the bedroom, leaning out of the open window as she listened to the sounds of the city.

When she'd first returned to Dublin, she'd hated all the noise. The muted hum of the cars, the sirens of the emergency vehicles and the occasional drone of a distant alarm had kept her awake every night. And as she'd lain in bed, she'd felt desperately alone. She'd cried for everything she'd once had. Cried for the person she used to be.

Now she was used to those sounds. She liked them. They were part of what her new life was. And they never made her feel alone.

She put the window on the catch and got into bed. She'd expected to toss and turn for a while, certain that the jumble of thoughts and hopes and dreams in her head would keep her awake. But she fell asleep almost instantly. Which, she thought as the alarm went off just four hours later, was a good thing.

Because she didn't want to look a total wreck at work on the first day of her new life.

She wanted to be dazzling.

Read on for a sneak preview of Sheila O'Flanagan's
enchanting new collection of interlinked short stories,
A SEASON TO REMEMBER,
coming soon from Headline Review.

Guaranteed to warm your heart
on a cold winter's night . . .

Kilmashogue

I fell in love with Sam in an airport. Which is sort of story-book romantic in some ways but actually – not. Because I wasn't waiting for him to arrive from some distant country and realising how much I cared as I flung my arms around him; nor was I heading off myself and crying uncontrollably at the departure gate because I knew that I couldn't be with him. It was an unexpected thing, waiting to go through security at Dublin airport during the hottest day of the year; a day on which the air-conditioning had broken down and so, as we waited for our hand baggage to be screened, everyone in the queues grew hotter and sweatier and more and more bad-tempered. (So bad-tempered that in one queue a woman actually tried to hit a security guard with a bottle of water he was trying to confiscate from her. The woman was carted off by a posse of uniformed personnel, which probably meant she wasn't getting on a flight any time soon.)

My own irritation quotient was going higher and higher. I'd been directed to the queue with the stupid people. The ones who – despite all of the warnings and notices – had actually packed large bottles of shampoo or matches or penknives or any one of the millions of things that you can't put in carry-on luggage any more. Our queue also contained two guys with an assortment of body piercings who were being sent back through the metal detectors over and over again.

I'd like to think that I can be a perfectly reasonable person. But I wasn't feeling very reasonable that day. Like everyone else I was hot and sweaty and getting more fed up with every passing moment. Besides, I'm not good with too much heat. I'm a crisp, cold morning sort of girl not your lying around the pool type. Suffocating heat does my head in. And suffocating heat was exactly what we had in Dublin airport.

So not actually a very auspicious start for finding love.

In fact, as far as I was concerned, the absolute last place in the world where it might happen. But doesn't everyone say that's how it goes with love? When you're least expecting it and all that sort of thing?

He was standing behind me in the queue. Like me, his reasons for travel were business. His only luggage was a leather computer bag, same as me. He'd already taken the laptop out of the bag, ready to put it through the scanning machine. I'd done the same. And I was ready to put my shiny coral sandals through too because for some reason they always set off the scanners.

So both of us were ready. But both of us were still waiting.

When one of the piercings guys was sent back for the third time, I could hear computer-man (I didn't know his name then, obviously; didn't know he was going to be the man I fell in love with) sighing deeply and loudly. I turned to him and gave him one of those complicit little smiles – you know, the 'are we the only competent people in the universe?' sort of smiles – and he grinned back at me and asked me where I was travelling to. London, I told him. I had a meeting with some bankers there.

He shuddered and then laughed and asked me if I was a banker. Not a question I've liked answering too much ever since bankers were blamed for almost causing the end of civilisation as we know it. I accept that there were very many people who behaved atrociously, but at the time I was just someone who worked in the new business section of a bank and my job actually involved getting in corporate deposits rather than making loans to people who couldn't repay them. So I didn't feel personally responsible for what went on. Nevertheless, you couldn't help but think that somehow you'd thrown in your lot with the devil and it was always embarrassing having to admit to being involved in an industry that had once been respected. (As a result of this I'd dumped my sturdy bank umbrella with its chirpy logo a few months earlier. I was afraid of being attacked on the street if I used it.)

Anyway, I told the man I was going to fall in love with that I did indeed work in a bank, but that I was an honest and trustworthy person, that I'd never lent money to anyone who couldn't pay it back (never lent money at all, I added) and that I hoped that one day the rest of the world would forgive me. I was a sinner, I told him, with a twinkle in my eye, but I had repented.

He laughed again at that and said that he'd once worked in banking himself but had left to set up his own company, something to do with price comparison sites for financial products, and it was going well for him. Though, he added, the whole banking crisis thing had nearly ruined him at one point because he'd been due to get a loan for expansion and it hadn't happened and it had all been very difficult.

During that conversation, the men with the piercings had eventually succeeded in getting through security and the line had begun to move again. I put my stuff on the conveyor belt and walked through without incident. So did ex-banker-computer-man.

'Which flight?' he asked as I stood at the end of the conveyor belt, slipping my sandals back on to my feet. They were very pretty sandals, with kitten heels, which weren't all that fashionable at the time but meant at least that I could walk around in them without being crippled.

'The eleven o'clock to Heathrow,' I told him.

'Me too.' He looked pleased. 'Fancy a coffee?'

We went to the Anna Livia lounge because both of us had passes for that. I like the lounge; at least it gets you away from the milling hordes. I've always struggled with crowds. I don't like lots of people being around me. It makes me feel claustrophobic and I get very tetchy. Which was why I'd been losing it a bit in the security queue.

Computer-man told me his name when we sat down with our coffees. Sam Thornton. It suited him.

'Holly,' I said in reply, as I tipped half a sachet of sugar into my cappuccino.

'Golightly?'

I grinned. 'Gallagher,' I said.

'You could do Golightly,' he told me. 'You have a look of Audrey Hepburn in *Breakfast at Tiffany's*.'

I blushed. He was being nice, because I wasn't Audrey Hepburn material. Actually, I don't think anyone in the whole world will ever be another Audrey Hepburn. She remains for me the most glamorous, elegant woman on the planet. Even as she grew older she never lost her looks. I saw a picture of her once in her seventies. She was still stunning. All to do with bone structure, I guess. Mine isn't Hepburn-fine. Also, my hair is a very light brown, which I sometimes highlight so it's more of a dark blond. Which isn't very Audrey either.

But . . . I did have a kind of impish look about me that under certain conditions might evoke a touch of Audrey in her famous Holly Golightly role. If whoever it was who was looking at me was being generous. Which was clearly the case with Sam Thornton.

'Seriously,' he said as I stopped laughing. 'You've got a lovely face.'

Audrey was in a movie called *Funny Face* once. More appropriate for me, I thought. But still, this guy was good. He was making me feel great about myself even though I was still hot and sweaty and a lock of hair was falling into my eyes.

'Oh bugger,' I said, which made him look at me in surprise. 'Our flight has been delayed.'

And indeed, there it was on the monitor, delayed until 11.45, which was very, very annoying. Obviously, from my point of view, I would've been better off getting a flight to City airport, but it hadn't been possible. So now I was going to be late getting into the hell on earth that was Heathrow and I'd probably be late getting into the City as well. My meeting wasn't until mid-afternoon so I wasn't under any pressure just yet, but the thing that drove me craziest about air travel was all of the time wasted faffing around airports both when you were leaving and when you arrived.

You can see my impatient nature here. Very un-Audrey. But I can't help myself. I'm an impatient kind of girl.

'Never mind,' said Sam. 'Would you like another coffee?'

It's not a good idea for me to drink too much coffee, because I get very jumpy and excitable, but we were here for a while more and there was nothing else to do. So I said yes to the coffee, and when he came back I asked him about his reasons for going to

446

London and all about his company too, although the truth is that I wasn't really listening to him because it had suddenly occurred to me that Sam Thornton was actually the most attractive man I'd met in a very long time.

He was tall – I knew that from our time standing in the queue – and he was dark (almost Mediterranean in his colouring) and he was very handsome (think George Clooney, only sexier). I couldn't understand how I hadn't noticed any of this before, but it was probably because I was too narky with the heat and the delays and everything. So there you are: I was sitting opposite a virtual sex-god in Dublin airport and he was making me laugh and I realised that I liked him a lot and then – bam! – suddenly I was in love with him.

Oh all right, maybe I was in lust with him, but it wasn't just the sexual attraction. Sam was nice. He was a very nice guy. And that was what I fell in love with. Not the Clooney looks. (For a long time, when I was with Sam, I thought about our children. The off-spring of a more-attractive-than-Clooney man and a pale-imitation-of-Hepburn woman. Would they be heartbreakingly gorgeous? Or did genetics do stupid things from time to time and would they be saddled with all of our bad points and none of the good ones? This was the way my mind worked then. Thinking of our children. Me, who'd always professed no interest in having kids whatsoever.)

Of course, as we sat in the Anna Livia lounge, I didn't want him to know that I was having fantasies about him. I kept talking to him about banking and business as though I was a serious person with serious issues to worry about. Which I probably was; after our bank had lost almost half its management staff, I'd been promoted, which was why I was the one heading off to the meeting in the City. I never felt like a real businessperson, though. I can't take it all that seriously: people trying to appear self-important and loading their conversations full of buzzwords and jargon just to make you feel inferior, which a lot of my ex-colleagues used to do. Not so smart now, I thought, a little smugly.

Sam wasn't trying any of that over-the-top stuff, though, he was simply chatting in a perfectly normal way. So was I. But keeping it businesslike too. Just so's he didn't think me a moron.

I was high on caffeine before our flight was called and had another cup of coffee on the plane, which wasn't a particularly good idea because it made me a bit giggly. I told myself that I would have to get back on track by the time I turned up in The Gherkin, that weird and wonderful iconic building where my meeting was to take place.

'Never been there,' said Sam when I told him where I was going. 'I'm afraid my meeting is in an ugly sixties block near Victoria.'

'They say those buildings have architectural merit now,' I told him.

'My arse,' he said, which made me laugh again.

'Are you staying overnight?' he asked when the plane eventually landed (we'd been in a holding pattern for half an hour at that point, which was making me irritated again).

'No,' I said regretfully. 'I'm getting the seven o'clock home.'

He looked disappointed. 'Pity.'

'I don't usually stay over,' I told him. 'Cost-cutting, you see. The bank can't be seen to be lavishing money on unnecessary hotel rooms. Besides,' I added, 'it's Friday; I can't even justify it by having another meeting tomorrow.'

'Why not take the weekend off?' he said.

I stared at him.

'We could go to dinner, have a bit of fun tomorrow . . .'

I continued to stare at him.

'But, you know, if you don't want to, that's absolutely fine.'

'No,' I said slowly. 'No, it would be great actually. It's just that . . . '

'What?'

'I don't have a nightie or anything.'

His navy-blue eyes crinkled. 'What makes you think you need one?' he asked.

Anyway, the truth is I'm not sure whether I fell in love with him in the airport or on the plane or later that night in his room in Claridge's. (Claridge's, I thought. The bank never put me up in Claridge's even when I did stay overnight. The comparison site company must be doing well.) It doesn't matter where I fell in love with him. That's just a detail after all. The key issue is that fall in love I did. With a thud that could have been felt on the other side of the world.

In every relationship there's a point where you start to ask questions, where you don't take everything at face value and where you want to know the bad things as well as the good things about the person you've become attached to. I was having such a wonderful time with Sam that I didn't want to ask any questions at all, but eventually I did. Casually, because I wasn't too concerned; we were taking things a bit slower than you'd expect after me falling in love with him on the day we met, but still, that was then and life isn't like a romantic movie after all. So we didn't meet every single day or even every single week, because as it turned out, Sam lived in Wicklow. In Gorey, which is a little under a hundred kilometres from Dublin, making it just that little bit awkward for a quick drink on a Saturday night or whatever. I'd thought that what might happen was that we'd spend weekends together. In my apartment in town or at his house in the country. I liked the sound of it and the idea of it but it didn't happen that often. He stayed with me a few times (though only Friday nights, never the entire weekend), but I never stayed with him. Which, after a while, began to rankle a little. And so I asked him about it.

Never ask a question when you don't already know the answer. My best friend, Susannah, who's a solicitor, once told me that. I retorted that you ask questions to find out answers, but her view is that you already know the answer you want to hear. And if you're not going to get that, then you're better off leaving the question well enough alone. I should've listened to Susannah. Or perhaps I should've asked the question sooner. But maybe I hadn't wanted to do that. Maybe, somehow, despite myself, I already knew the answer.

We were sitting in St Stephen's Green when I asked it.

'Why don't I ever stay with you?' I pushed my hair out of my eyes and turned to look at him. 'I know Dublin's great fun and all that, but it would be nice to do the more peaceful country thing sometimes, don't you think?'

I saw the shadow cross his face and I felt an icy hand grip my heart.

'Holly,' he said.

'What?'

'We need to talk.'

How I hate that phrase. Cormac Mulcahy, my first boyfriend, used it when he wanted to break it off with me. (We were both twelve at the time. He was a very serious kind of boy.) Dermot Doolin, my second, said the same. And the truth is that I've used it myself too on more than one occasion. So I know what 'we need to talk' means. It means we're having this conversation and it's the last one we're ever going to have and I don't want to have it with you but I'm too soft-hearted to dump you by text.

'Why?' I asked. I couldn't believe how terrible I was feeling inside. Well, I could. I loved Sam. More than anyone I'd ever loved in my life before. I'd had the wedding fantasies about him. Me in a dress that would make me look like Audrey. Him in a tux that would make George envious. I'd designed the dress myself. It was stunning.

'Well . . .' And then he told me.

It wasn't the dumping conversation; it was the other one. The one where the man you've fallen in love with tells you he hasn't been fair on you and he shouldn't have fallen in love with you because as it turns out he's already married.

'What!' Of course you know at that point that you've been utterly, utterly blind and stupid and the fact that he always stays at your place and the times that he hasn't been available and a hundred and one other small things that you've noticed but ignored suddenly make perfect sense.

'I'm sorry,' he said. 'I know you must hate me.'

'Yes,' I told him. 'I do.'

'I didn't mean for this to happen.'

Oh, who bloody does?

'When I met you it was as though the sunshine had come back into my life.'

Yeah, yeah.

'I love you, Holly.'

But you're married to someone else.

'It's not working out between me and Amy.'

Amy. Nice name. Cute and girlie.

'But right now . . . I can't break up our family.'

Family? What family?

'The twins are only two years old.'

OK, one kid is bad enough. But two . . . And twins! That seems even worse somehow.

'It's not that I don't care about her,' he said.

Great. Rub it in, why don't you?

'But I don't love her in the way that I love you.'

And that was what got me. Because he said it like he meant it. Because he sounded so tortured and so unhappy. Because he started to cry.

I have conflicted views about crying men. There's a part of me that thinks it's good for them to get emotional from time to time, to show their sadness in public. There's another part of me that thinks it's fairly pathetic and un-macho.

When our bank nearly went bust, some of the guys cried. They really did. It was the strangest thing seeing them sitting at their desks with tears rolling down their cheeks. They were the hard, macho men who'd often made my life a misery. In front of whom I wouldn't ever have dared to cry, no matter what the reason. And they were blubbing away in front of the Bloomberg screens. Unbelievable!

I didn't cry back then. As far as I was concerned it wasn't something worth crying over. Though I did want to attack the lending manager who'd once made a pass at me in the lift in the full knowledge that nobody would believe me if I tried to make a big deal about it. He was a horrible man and I was glad he was losing his job. I wanted to attack him because other people were losing their jobs thanks to him too, not because of his pathetic pass at me.

All that stuff about the bank and the crying men whizzed around in my head when Sam started to cry. But I didn't feel the way I'd felt then, angry and bitter. I felt sad. For Sam and for me.

'I'm sorry.' He got himself together and gave me a half-smile. 'I'm sorry for not being honest with you, Holly. But the thing is – the moment I first saw you standing in the queue in your bare

451

feet, I felt something I've never felt before. It was like an instant connection. I wasn't thinking then about . . . about what's happened since. I just wanted to keep talking to you and stay with you, and I know that was wrong but I couldn't help myself.'

I told myself that I could look at this objectively. I could decide that he'd made a decision to be nice to me and flirt with me (or whatever was going on in the queue) despite the fact that he was a married man and had no right to be nice to or flirt with girls he didn't know. I could cut him a little slack and decide that the situation in the queue was a bit different, what with the terrible conditions and the way that made people suddenly empathise with each other and comment to each other, just so's you knew you weren't the only one being driven demented with the heat and the crowds. I could decide that having coffee with him in the Anna Livia lounge was simply a friendly thing to do. Perfectly innocent on my part, though obviously not so innocent on his – especially with the Audrey Hepburn comparisons – but harmless enough.

Only it hadn't turned out to be harmless, because here we were now with him crying and me feeling as though my heart had been ripped out.

'Do you love your wife?'

Never ask a question you don't already know the answer to. I knew I shouldn't have asked it before I'd even spoken the words.

'She's a lovely woman,' he said, neatly side-stepping it. 'She's a great wife and a great mother.'

'How long have you been married?' The answer to that question didn't matter too much.

'Five years.'

'Are you going to leave her?' Another one I wasn't sure about. I wondered if I actually liked torturing myself.

'It's all been so sudden,' he said, once again side-stepping an answer. 'I knew Amy and I were unhappy, but I didn't know why. And unhappy is probably the wrong word; it's just . . . I don't think we do love each other any more. I don't know exactly what happened. Whether it's me being away, or whether it's the twins . . .'

I would be breaking up a family with two small kids. I couldn't do that.

'I've got to go.' I stood up and smoothed down the pale skirt of my business suit. And then I walked out of the Green and left him sitting alone on the bench.

I should've left things like that. Of course I should. It's really easy to know the things you should do but not at all easy to actually do them. Sometimes it's like someone else is in your body, operating it, making you do stuff you don't want to do. Or telling you that you have to do it anyway. Which is what some part of me said when, two weeks later, Sam called and said he had to see me.

We met in the Morrison, on the north side of the city. The Morrison is on the quays of the Liffey so is only barely on the other side of town, but there is a cultural divide between north and south in Dublin. I knew why he'd picked it. It distanced him from the south. Being on the north side was, for Sam, like being in another world. (Maybe that was how he felt in the airport, which is also on the north side of the city. Or maybe it's just that airports are self-contained little worlds anyway.)

'I haven't been able to stop thinking about you,' he said. 'Every second of every day all I do is think about you. I think about you the moment I wake up and just before I go to sleep. I think about you when I'm driving in to work and when I'm driving home.'

'Do you think about me when you kiss your wife good night? Or when you're playing with your kids? Or when you're sitting down to Sunday lunch?' My voice was deliberately harsh because my heart was breaking again. I was still in love with him even though he was a traitorous, deceiving swine of a man.

'Don't make me feel worse than I already do,' begged Sam. 'Don't make me say things I don't want to say.'

There was no future in a relationship with Sam. I told myself this over and over again. I would be wasting part of my life, giving him years that could be better spent looking for someone who was available, who could love me the way I wanted to be loved. Who wasn't cheating on someone else. But the thing is – and you have to forgive me for this, because I know it's selfish and awful of me

– there was a part of me that didn't care. I didn't care because I loved him so much, because I could understand the position he found himself in.

I'd nearly got married myself. Four years earlier. With a few months to go I'd got cold feet and called it off. But I'd agonised and agonised about what I should do, and I'd even told myself that I could go along with it for the sake of everyone and get a divorce afterwards. Not rational, I know. But those thoughts had gone through my head. And so I could see how Sam might have married someone he wasn't truly in love with, because when you get on the marriage roller-coaster it's very hard to get off again. (I didn't ask him if he'd had doubts before his wedding. I truly didn't want to know the answer to that one.)

'Look,' I said. 'I like you very much, but there's no point to this.'

'I miss you,' he said. 'I miss talking to you. I know I can't expect to have what we had before, but couldn't we be friends? Maybe meet for coffee every now and then? I need to be able to talk to someone, and you're the only person I can talk to.'

'Oh, Sam . . . I don't know.'

'Give it a try?' He turned his huge dark eyes on me. 'Please?'

And so I agreed. That evening we talked and talked but there was no inappropriate behaviour, and we met for lunch a few days later and all that was perfectly innocent too; and then one evening I met him in town and we went for a few drinks and, sitting beside him in the pub, I couldn't help myself and leaned my head on his shoulder. He kissed me then and I kissed him and he came back to my apartment in Dundrum and made love to me and I knew that I could never let him go.

So that's how it happens. You tell yourself one thing and you do something else, and I wanted to believe everything he told me because, having let him back into my life, I wanted us to be a true love story. And I wanted to believe, too, that one day he'd leave Amy and his children and live with me and it'd all end up happily for everyone. Because in my little fantasy world, Amy was having a torrid affair with one of her Wicklow neighbours anyway.

* * *

454

I was devastated when they went away on holidays, two weeks at the end of September, during which I didn't hear a word from him. I hadn't realised how closely my life had become entwined with his and how many times I texted him during the day with silly comments just to prove that I loved him. I didn't want to text him while he was away in case Amy picked up his phone and asked who Holly was. I realised that I was The Other Woman. It was a bit of a shock to see myself like that.

He phoned when he got home and he came to my apartment, where, as soon as he got through the door, I started to tear the clothes from his back. He did the same to me and we ended up making love in the tiny hallway, where I'm sure we could have been heard by anybody walking past the door.

'I missed you so much,' he said.

'I missed you too.' I held him fiercely. 'I love you.'

He kissed me on the mouth.

He was the best kisser I've ever known. He was the best lover I'd ever known too. I couldn't let him go.

To read the conclusion of Holly's story, and
many more connected fabulous Christmas tales,
don't miss Sheila O'Flanagan's
A SEASON TO REMEMBER,
coming soon from Headline Review.